THE DEVIL'S CURE

Kenneth Oppel

The
DEVIL'S

CURE

HarperCollins*PublishersLtd*

Canadian Cataloguing in Publication Data

Oppel, Kenneth
The devil's cure

ISBN 0-00-225537-5

I. Title.

PS8579.P64D48 2000   C813'.54   C00-930091-0
PR9199.3.O66D48 2000

00 01 02 03 04 HC 6 5 4 3 2 1

Printed and bound in the United States
Set in Monotype Baskerville

For Philippa

The best lack all conviction, while the worst
Are full of passionate intensity.

—"The Second Coming," W. B. Yeats

CHAPTER ONE

Lying wasted in the quarantine room of the prison infirmary, Frank Hayworth had refused all medication, even the pills that would at least numb the pain as his lungs filled with fluid. The room, a cinder block box no bigger than his old cell, was without ornament, and Frank's eyes drifted blearily upwards to the ceiling. He'd spent so many hours mapping the cracked plaster it was like a personal atlas, the country of his own suffering.

He coughed, and the pain was stunning, momentarily knocking the sight from his eyes. Everything hurt now: to breathe, to swallow, to bend a finger. But somehow he'd mastered the pain, made it something outside himself, like the numbing, endless clatter of that goddamn air conditioner. Didn't do a bit of good, either—his bedclothes were always sodden with sweat, clinging to bony joints that had once been covered with muscle and flesh. His arms were like spindly, knotted branches now.

On the table beside his bed was a tall plastic pitcher of water, a paper cup with a straw, and two pain pills—in case he changed his mind. He wouldn't. They'd wanted to do a lot of things to him. It was all the devil's work, trying to invade his body with their needles and pills and IV drips. Tried to put a catheter up his dick because he wasn't pissing anymore, but he'd said no to that too. He didn't need any of it. He would be pure in his death. He'd do that part right at least.

God bless David for that, for showing him the way.

The tiny room had held him for the last two months, ever since the doctors had told him he had tuberculosis, some strain that was especially infectious. "Why not?" Frank had said. "I got pretty much everything else." They'd told him it was his AIDS doing it to him, ravaging his immune system, making him generous host to every bacterium and virus wafting through the cell blocks. No hospital would take him. He was a death row scumbag, and he'd been refusing treatment for AIDS for the last eight months. What was the point of having him in the hospital, spreading germs?

He loved this room. It was quieter than his cell, and he could think here. It contained him, every breath, every thought and prayer. He was glad there was no window to distract him. The ceiling was the only view he needed. He'd traveled its roads and rivers back to his childhood and through all the bad days and bad things he'd done; he'd seen it all, clear as anything, even the heroin syringe he'd given himself AIDS with, in that basement crib in Cabrini Green. Seen the two men he killed in the robbery, revisited his trial and all his years inside.

David came to visit him in quarantine twice a week, giving up his one daily hour of yard time. He was the closest thing to Jesus Frank had ever known his whole life. He'd share his food if you asked for some, and anything he'd bought from the commissary. He didn't expect anything back. Frank had seen him break up fights in the yard, and get punched up for his pains. And all the visits he'd made when Frank was in quarantine—he wasn't even afraid of catching anything. And why should he be? He was an angel. Not one of those ones in kiddie books, with wings and gold hair, all meek and sappy. He was the real thing, fierce and relentless, with eyes that would do a cigarette burn right through your heart and soul.

Frank had already been on the row six years when David moved in three cells down. At first, when David would get on the bars and do his God-talking, Frank would shout him down, like all the others. But his talk wasn't crazy, like some of the other lifers before they got juiced. David talked slow and calm, not trying to raise his voice above the others. He'd just talk it through, and Frank, after a while, started to listen. And it made sense, all of it. It awoke in him a terrible hunger: he wanted to do things right.

The first thing he did was stop taking the medicine, and start praying. That was eight months ago. David was right, his sickness was a punishment from God, for the life he'd led. Why shouldn't he suffer for what he'd done? And he was only making things worse by taking medicine, trying to thwart God's plan for him. Medicine was like all the other sins, just another way to say no to God. If He wanted to heal him, He'd heal him, and all Frank could do was pray for mercy. God might say no—David had told him that from the start—but he mustn't give up.

Frank coughed again, bringing up more blood-stained sputum. He knew this room wouldn't contain him much longer.

They'd propped him up so he could breathe easier. His lips were tinged blue, and his face had the gray, battered look of a bruised pear.

With his left hand, he patted the mattress for the call button and squeezed. A minute later, the duty nurse appeared at the observation window. When she entered, she had a surgical mask across her face.

"You okay?"

His tongue stirred and rasped against the roof of his mouth. It had been a long time since he'd spoken.

"David," he sighed, and pain slashed through his chest. Again he blacked out for a moment, and then he felt a great kicking against his ribs as his heart pounded to catch up.

"David Haines," he wheezed.

"I'll see," said the nurse, and she left.

Frank looked back at the ceiling and started to pray. It wouldn't be long now. He smiled. He'd beat death row to the punch.

*　*　*

In the din of cell block B, David Haines wrote his letter to the distant sound of his own heartbeat, homemade earplugs nestled snugly in place. He'd cut them from the soles of his prison-issue shower slips— a standard trick to block the grinding of motorized gates, the rage of televisions, and the infernal shouting of the condemned. Blocking out the smells was not so easily done, but he had become relatively inured to the stench of dirty laundry, male sweat, unflushed toilets.

Sitting on the edge of his cot, back to the wall, he looked up from his letter. For the past three years this windowless six-by-nine concrete cell had been his home, 23 hours a day, 365 days a year. In winter it was achingly cold, and now, in the height of summer, it felt like a sneak preview of hell, blanketed by the same heatwave which was suffocating Chicago thirty miles to the north. Hulking on the plains outside Joliet, the Illinois Correctional Center didn't even benefit from the winds that blew off Lake Michigan.

Joliet, Chicago, Lake Michigan—all these places seemed so long ago to him, so irrelevant. Even the geography of the prison itself was a cipher, he saw so little of it. He knew it was huge, a modern citadel of punishment, thirty-three-foot-high walls enclosing sixty-four acres and over two thousand convicts, most of whom enjoyed a luxury of freedom compared to him. For David, there was only the scruffy chain-link-fenced yard an hour a day—and the cell. It was his bedroom, living room, dining room, and bathroom all in one, the room in which he would end his days.

The heat seemed to make the cell contract further. It was not enough space for most men to occupy sanely, and for someone like David, who was six feet tall, with a body that had once thrived on physical exertion, it seemed an even crueler confinement. For him, keeping an ordered cell was the same as keeping an ordered mind: there was no escaping either. In the far left-hand corner was a combination sink and toilet, steel and lidless. To the right was his bed, always neatly made. Every third day he painstakingly washed his clothing and hung it to dry on a line fastened from the ventilation grille above his bed to the bars at the opposite end of the cell. The television that jutted from a shelf over the head of his cot was usually silent; he rarely resorted to watching it. He preferred to combat his boredom, that cancer of prison life, by reading.

There were times when he felt positively blessed, rejoicing in his monk-like luxury. He had time to read his Bible, over and over, and to keep up with the journals to which he subscribed—*Nature*, *Science*, and *The New England Journal of Medicine*—which he kept stacked in order against the left wall, beneath his towel rack. In some ways he was glad he was spared the endless medley of entertainments offered the general population: ceramics, drama, music, softball, movies—like some perverse holiday cruise, the grinning deck staff replaced by over two hundred cantankerous correctional officers, eager to use their truncheons. He would rather read.

He had done his work in the world, as long and as well as he could, and now he could devote himself to prayer and reflection.

And his letters.

From the very start, he'd been deluged, and over the months he'd quickly pared down his list of correspondents. It was not difficult to determine which were insincere and unworthy—teenage pranksters, lonely thrill-seekers, the clearly deranged, who took indiscriminate pleasure in any sort of violence. These people he sloughed off instantly. They saddened and sometimes disgusted him. But there were also those in whom he sensed an embryonic fervor, a holy hunger.

4

Some had even tasted divine truth, and they wanted instruction. He felt that he must give it to them, in the same way he'd offered God's teachings to his cell mates, to anyone who would listen.

Frank Hayworth had listened. And so had five others, scattered across the continent, connected to him through letters. For the past month, he had written to them almost daily. They had convinced him of their devotion, but now it was time for them to enact their beliefs, to take up his holy work. He knew what he was asking them was difficult; he tried, in his letters, to guide them, to be as reassuring and explicit as possible. They needed constant coaxing and sterner exhortation. And he prayed that it would not be long before he saw the fruits of their labors. He had great hopes for one of his brethren in Detroit.

He signed and folded his letter, then stroked his tongue carefully across the strip of glue and pressed the envelope shut. He savored the taste: it had become, for him, a hopeful taste, a wish for righteousness. Prison regulation forbade sealing envelopes—letters had to be read by censors before they were mailed—but these particular letters would never pass through the prison system.

From memory he addressed the last envelope, then placed it with the other four inside his Bible.

"Thy will be done," he breathed to himself.

"Haines."

The voice reached him as a whisper, and David turned, wondering how long Bob Jarvis had been standing outside the bars. He pulled the plugs from his ears. Jarvis was tall and wiry, and his guard's uniform seemed to hang from his shoulders, the trousers cinched and bagging slightly around the waist. His weedy appearance was deceptive; his body had a whip-like strength and quickness. On B block, Jarvis had a reputation as one of the most ill-tempered guards. He was quick to anger, and he seemed to like using his stick or cattle-prod. In the early days he'd beaten David once for taking too long in the shower.

"Frank's going. He asked for you. Finlay said it was okay for you to see him."

David nodded and stood.

"May I bring my Bible?"

"Fine."

David picked it up and passed it through a horizontal slot in the bars. It was through this slot that all his meal trays were delivered.

Now he stood with his back to it, and slid his wrists through so that Jarvis could shackle them. The door was buzzed open and David stepped out.

"Here." Jarvis handed him back his Bible.

With satisfaction, David noticed that the four envelopes were gone, slipped into one of the voluminous pockets in Jarvis's tunic.

He'd been surprised when, many months ago, Jarvis had started pausing to talk outside his cell during his rounds. At first he'd been taciturn, but David was patient, and he'd let him take his time. It came out that he hated doctors; they'd killed his mother. She'd gone from one to another, each one saying she had something different. After they'd treated her she got even worse, and she died in terrible pain.

"And now I'm sick," he had told David, "and damned if I'm going to those doctors."

David said he would pray for him. He suggested Jarvis pray too. Jarvis grunted, said nothing, but his visits became more frequent, and God heard their cries and answered with His healing. The chest pains and nausea did not return. Since then, Jarvis had been one of his faithful. He'd agreed to mail out his letters so that David could speak his heart more truly, without fear of being censored. And Jarvis opened a post office box in Joliet, so David's flock could write back to him with equal candor. Without Jarvis, his ministry outside the prison would have been nothing but a longing.

"They'll go out tonight," Jarvis whispered to him, and then they started down the broad corridor, past the neighboring cells: Harper reading his endless supply of comics, Winslow masturbating shamelessly while watching "Brady Bunch" reruns, Tucker weeping, always weeping. David had tried to help them, but their hearts were hard.

"They want to take your blood." Jarvis's voice was tight. "I heard one of the nurses talking. They think you might've caught something from Frank."

David's step almost faltered. In the past he had submitted to the prison doctor's fumbling physical examinations, but he had never allowed his blood to be taken. His blood was his life, the matrix of his immortal soul, and removing it from his body was terribly wrong. It was a desecration to treat the blood like some common fluid and subject it to the myopic scrutiny of their machinery.

David continued walking and tried to calm his mind. Returning to

6

his cell would only delay the doctors. And he would not abandon Frank now. But he could not allow them to take his blood.

When he arrived outside the quarantine room, Frank was fighting for breath, his body panicking as it began to drown. His face was bloated and gray, his cheek stained with his own coughed-up blood. Through the observation window, David could see the fear in his eyes as Dr. Finlay and the nurse tried to keep him still, taking his blood pressure, shining a penlight in his eyes.

Finlay glanced at the doorway. "You'd better get in here," he snapped. "But get masks on first."

David took the surgical mask Jarvis handed him and obediently slipped it over his face. He didn't need it, but he wanted to get to Frank as quickly as possible. Jarvis, his own mask in place, opened the door and escorted David inside.

"Frank."

The dying man stared back at David for a few moments, uncomprehending in his fear. But after a second he gave a quick nod, and his body sagged back slightly against the mattress. His lips twitched in a pained smile.

David felt his eyes sting: the suffering Frank had endured was a true sign of his devotion and repentance. God had chosen not to heal him, and David could only accept that this was as it should be, given Frank's sinful past. But he marveled at Frank's courage. Healthy, he might have achieved so much on the outside, so much good.

"You will die if we don't treat you," Finlay told Frank loudly. "Do you understand? Do you want us to treat you?"

David looked at Finlay with contempt. To tempt him now in his greatest anguish. *Get thee behind me, Satan.*

A small grunt emanated from Frank's throat as his head twitched to one side: No. Gulping breath now, his eyes were beginning to roll as he dipped in and out of consciousness.

David took Frank's hand. It felt heavy and damp, something not fully connected to his body. He was already leaving it behind.

"You've done the right thing, Frank. The holy thing."

Frank didn't seem to hear, but a few seconds later he mumbled thickly, "Okay."

His eyes were half closed now, and his breath came only in infrequent gasps, like startled afterthoughts. David sat on the bedside, opened his Bible and began to read, and when he next looked up, Frank was looking straight at him. David knew he was gone.

Dr. Finlay put his stethoscope against Frank's chest.

"His heart's stopped."

David closed the Bible. "'Verily I say unto you, today will you sit with me in paradise.'"

He could feel Dr. Finlay's animosity emanating from him like heat. David reached over and drew his hand gently over Frank's face, closing his eyes.

"I'll need to check you," Finlay told him.

"I'm not sick."

"You've spent a lot of time with Hayworth. I don't want you spreading anything through the prison population." Finlay walked to the door. He nodded to Jarvis, who brought David out of the quarantine room and into the infirmary.

David saw, waiting across the room, three more guards, and his heart kicked up.

"I don't get sick anymore."

"That so?"

David smiled at the doctor's thinly veiled condescension. He knew Finlay hated him and everything he believed. But in David's eyes, he was beneath notice, a third-rate doctor practising bad medicine in prison because it was the only place that would take him. Finlay was irrelevant.

"Up there, please," Finlay said.

Jarvis at his side, David sat up on the edge of the examination table. Finlay washed his hands, and David watched the three guards by the door. If they all held him down, there'd be no way he could resist.

Finlay shone an ophthalmoscope into his eyes.

"Headache or muscle pain?"

David shook his head patiently.

"Fever? Night sweats?"

"No. And no coughing or any other sign of respiratory distress. No abdominal indications either. No weight loss or diarrhea. And no swelling of the lymph nodes."

Finlay ignored him and lifted the front of his orange prison uniform. He put the stethoscope against his bare chest and listened.

"Deep breath, hold it. Let it out. Another deep breath, hold. Okay."

He went round behind Haines and pressed the stethoscope to his tunic.

8

"Fabric causes distortion, doctor. That's first-year med school."

Again, Finlay ignored him, listening, then let the stethoscope drop. "Lie down please."

David closed his eyes and allowed Finlay's cold hands to probe his belly and check the lymph glands in his groin, under his arms.

"You seem healthy, but I'm going to need some blood."

Calmly David replied, "I've submitted to your physical, but you're not taking my blood. 'The soul of the flesh is in the blood.' Leviticus 17:11."

"I'm screening for infection and TB and I want a baseline liver function. That's first-year med school too, Haines."

"You can do chest X-rays, and a skin test."

"Oh, don't worry, I'll do those too."

He saw in Finlay's face the coward's pleasure in victimizing a helpless man. The doctor cracked a syringe from its sterile package. "Put out your arm, please."

"I'll remind you of my religious beliefs, and ask that you respect them."

"I'll say the Lord's Prayer as I take the blood."

"I want to speak to the warden."

Finlay looked up from the disinfectant swab he was peeling from its package. "He's okay with it. I checked."

"You can't take blood without my permission."

"We don't need your permission on this one, Haines. This is a matter of public health. The greater good comes before God, I'm afraid."

David had his manacled hands around Finlay's neck and his thumbs gouging into his trachea before the guards were upon him. They slammed him back against the examination table, pinning him flat against its surface. As he struggled, he could hear Finlay coughing and cursing.

Jarvis had him by the shoulders, pushing hard, and even in his outrage, David understood it was what he had to do. He felt his arm get snapped out straight, past one of the guards' waists. It was Finlay.

"You crazy son of a bitch," the doctor hissed. He cinched a tourniquet around David's bicep and jabbed the needle into a vein. As the blood left his body, David could only close his eyes in silent rage against this blasphemy.

CHAPTER TWO

Entering the operating room, Laura Donaldson felt her fatigue and anxiety evaporate, her mind and senses tuning themselves to a purer frequency. The procedure itself was routine, one she'd performed hundreds of times. But this particular operation marked the culmination of two years of research and preparation—months of in vitro trials, mouse and monkey trials, then the long battle with the FDA for permission to test her new therapy on just one person.

"Good morning. We all ready?"

Emily Wiltshire finished double-checking the instrument trays with the scrub nurse and nodded. Like Laura, Emily had specialized as a surgeon before becoming a research oncologist. She was the senior member of Laura's team, and in the lab or operating room they achieved a wordless symbiosis, anticipating the other's next thought or move effortlessly. Laura had always preferred working with women in a testosterone-free environment, free from the spasms of Paleolithic egos.

"They're bringing Gillian up now," Emily told her. "Should be here in a couple minutes."

"All right. Sam, you've got everything you need?"

Samantha was another member of her team, and this morning she was acting as pathologist. They'd set up a portable workstation to one side so that she could instantly run tests on any tissue Laura might resect from Gillian Shamas.

"I won't keep you waiting," Sam said.

"I know you won't. Hi, Melanie." She smiled at her anaesthetist, whom she'd worked with many times before and trusted completely.

"Big day for you," said Melanie.

"Let's hope so."

"And now a few words from our corporate sponsor," said Emily quietly, as the doors swung open and Adrian Crawford entered with Tom Powell, both men, like the surgical team, gowned, gloved, and masked.

"Adrian, Tom, we're going to be starting in just a few minutes. Why don't you come over here where you can get a good view."

She wasn't happy about having an audience, but Adrian had been insistent, and she didn't see how she could deny him. His biotech company, MetaSYS, had funded her research at the University of Chicago for almost three years. In fact, it was they who'd built the new research center that housed her state-of-the-art lab and hired her to run it, in a joint appointment with the university. Laura knew her position triggered envy in most of the scientific community, and rightly so; she couldn't imagine a better setup. Connected by overhead walkway to the university's own hospital complex in Hyde Park, her lab was unrivaled in terms of wet bench space and top-of-the-line hardware. She'd been allowed to hire the people she wanted, and they were the best. Most important of all, the private operating budget liberated her from spending a third of her time applying for research grants. Even at the National Cancer Institute, world-renowned doctors had to scrabble for funding.

But MetaSYS's corporate largesse was hardly without strings: they had exclusive rights to any patentable discovery she made. She knew Adrian had sunk millions into her and her research, and now he was anxious to reap the rewards.

"You must be tremendously, tremendously excited," Powell said to her.

Laura had seen Tom Powell on television only a few times and had never been a fan. His easy superlatives, deeply resonant voice, and earnest, unflinching gaze all seemed a bit cynically engineered.

"I'm very hopeful," she said cautiously, refusing to grant soundbites.

Despite Laura's strong reservations, Adrian had leaked the news of her clinical protocol to "Headline," the ABC newsmagazine that Powell hosted, and they'd leaped at the chance for an exclusive feature. Laura thought it bad form. She'd wanted to publish her final results in an accredited journal first. But Adrian needed the publicity to bolster his sagging stock price. So, six weeks ago, both Adrian and Tom Powell had been present when Laura had given Gillian Shamas her first gene therapy transfusion. At Adrian's urging, Laura had also granted Powell a filmed interview. A few weeks later, Gillian, back at home and feeling surprisingly well, had also let Powell interview her.

Laura glanced up to the gallery and saw Powell's camera crew getting ready to film. She was used to cameras in her operating theaters—she used them all the time to document surgical procedures—but these images she knew would be broadcast across the continent, and she couldn't quite shake the feeling that they were tempting fate. She banished the thought from her head: superstitious crap. Her clinical protocol would succeed or fail on its own merits.

"I understand the scans show Gillian's tumors have shrunk," Powell said. "Significantly."

"What we've seen so far is promising. And this morning we're going to verify that."

"What do you hope to see when you look inside?"

"Nothing."

Powell chuckled. "No tumors at all, you mean."

"That's right. But I'd also be happy if I saw radically diminished tumors, or dead tumor tissue that I can resect."

"And that would mean you've cured her?"

"We'd continue to monitor her."

"So it could come back?"

"Sure, a recurrence is always possible."

"Let's remember," said Adrian, "this is a woman whose tumors didn't even blink at radiation or chemo. Three months they gave her. Laura's the only doctor in the world who could've helped her."

She met his gaze, hardly needing to see his mouth to know he was smiling at her. His eyes had a way of narrowing to crescents, exuding such warmth and affection that she felt uncomfortable now—angry, too—at this reminder of all the private smiles he'd once bestowed on her.

Sure, he was happy to be her corporate champion right now, but MetaSYS needed another product soon and Adrian, she knew, was getting anxious for results. And if this was a failure?

Why the doubts, always? she chastised herself. *Look at the pretrial results, look at the scans, all the indications so far.* But she knew the risks, too. If Gillian's tumors weren't significantly reduced, the FDA might stall further trials. And if Adrian didn't get results from her, maybe he'd go elsewhere. She closed that door. Time to focus now.

She turned to Powell. "Have you watched surgery before, Tom?"

"On TV or live?" She noticed his words were clicking from a dry mouth; his forehead was already greasy with sweat. She hoped she didn't have a swooner on her hands.

"The real deal."

"Um, no, no, I have not."

"There's a chair over there." She pointed. "If you feel faint, I'd suggest you take a seat. The floor's hard. And it can get quite hot in here."

Adrian, she knew, was solid. He'd been to medical school and had done clinical research before turning entrepreneur. Fifteen years ago, he'd taken MetaSYS public on the strength of his own time-release hypertension drug. Since then, the company had struck home with several other big hitters, including a type of beta-blocker for coronary artery disease.

"She's here," said Emily.

Laura turned as the theater doors opened and an orderly wheeled in Gillian Shamas on a gurney. To Laura's eye, her lack of hair—the legacy of chemotherapy—only made her more beautiful, emphasizing her exquisite green eyes and the fullness of her mouth. In her green surgical smock, her slender feet clad in white cotton socks, Gillian looked as vulnerable as a child.

You could be next, Sandra.

The thought slithered into Laura's head, and she clamped down on it, hard. She didn't want anything distracting her.

"Good morning," Laura said. "How are you feeling?"

"Great," Gillian answered.

Laura smiled. Gillian's unflagging optimism throughout the protocol had impressed her; she was determined she would get better, and Laura hoped to God she wouldn't be disappointing her today.

"Well, you're doing great."

Less than a year ago, Gillian had noticed a lump in her thigh. It was excised and found to be a grade 3 synovial cell sarcoma, one of the most aggressive cancers known. A few months later, they found subcutaneous metastatic lesions on her back, and three large, inoperable sarcomas on her liver. Chemotherapy and radiation both failed her. Her doctors gave her a prognosis of three months. That made her far gone enough to qualify for Laura's clinical protocol.

Laura checked through the instruments on her tray. Gillian was only thirty—thirty, for God's sake, married only two years, wanting a family, and now faced with this. And so cheerful through everything, never complaining, even when, after receiving her first treatment, her temperature had soared to 105, and she'd gone into respiratory failure.

"We're ready to go if you are," she told Gillian.

Gillian nodded. "Good luck." Their eyes met and held for a second, and Laura felt their shared pulse of anxiety and hope.

"You too, Gillian."

She turned and nodded at Melanie to begin the intravenous. Everyone in the room watched silently as Gillian took a few breaths through the mask and then plunged into a deep sleep. In a few moments, Melanie had her intubated and hooked up to the ventilator that would do all her breathing for her.

"She's down," said Melanie.

The scalpel, poised between thumb and forefinger, was a cool extension of Laura's hand as she made her primary incision, a midline vertical cut from the bottom of Gillian's ribs to her navel. After that, Laura's entire universe contracted to the swath of tissue and muscle opening beneath her. The ambient whisper of the air conditioning and the rhythmic sigh of Gillian's ventilator melded with the mantra echoing softly through her head: *Let this work. Make this happen.*

In principle, her experimental therapy was simple. A human's immune system alone was inadequate to fight cancer. White cells, so efficient at combating other diseases, often didn't recognize cancer cells as harmful, or if they did, they were still insufficient in strength and number to halt a tumor's growth. Laura wanted to give the immune system extra ammunition.

In the late 1970s researchers had identified something called Tumor Necrosis Factor, a protein produced by human white cells, which killed cancer cells. Over the next two decades, numerous variations had been found, and just three years ago, Laura, heading a team at Sunnybrook Hospital in Toronto, had discovered the most potent one of all, which she'd dubbed TNF-12. The problem was, she couldn't grow enough TNF-12 in vitro to inject into cancer patients with any beneficial effect. And even if she could, TNF-12 was highly toxic—it had to be delivered to the site of the tumor itself to do any good.

Laura's plan was to inject the gene for TNF-12 directly into the cancer cells, using a modified retrovirus as the vehicle. Once inside the cancer cell's nucleus, the TNF-12 gene would splice with the native DNA and start producing its deadly proteins on site, killing the tumor from the inside out. The poetic justice pleased Laura: cancer reprogrammed to commit suicide.

Six weeks ago, Gillian had received an intra-arterial liver infusion of over a billion engineered retroviruses. Before the protocol began, Laura had outlined the risks to her. There were many; this was uncharted territory. But without treatment, Gillian would surely die.

"Here we are," Laura said. "The liver."

Adrian had asked her to do some basic narration for Powell's benefit. Emily quickly pulled back the skin and hooked away the other internal organs to give Laura a clear view of the liver. Immediately, Laura's focus was pulled to the three sarcomas. Just by looking at them, she could tell their outer surface was dying, and that they were being replaced by healthy tissue. Relief washed through her, and there was a slight tremor in her voice as she spoke.

"We have definite shrinkage in number one, number two, number three," she said. "I'm going to resect ..."

Her voice trailed off as her eyes strayed from the tumors. Jesus Christ. Studded across the surface of the liver were hundreds of tiny gray nodules, so small and so numerous that she hadn't noticed them at first. She felt as if she'd been suddenly wrenched from her own body and was hovering overhead, staring down dispassionately, like Powell's cameras. *It's not happening; it's just something on television.*

"What the hell are those?" she heard Emily say softly.

A horrible leaden silence descended on the theater. Laura came back to herself, her heart breaking into a gallop. She was aware of everyone's eyes on her. The quiet wheeze of the ventilator was suddenly thunderous.

"Why didn't we see them on the scan?" Emily said.

"Too small," said Laura, her mouth parched. They were less than a tenth of an inch in diameter, and could easily have escaped detection on the CT or MRI scans. She felt her stomach give a quick, sickening clench.

"What are they?" It was Adrian, all the confidence and joviality stripped from his voice.

"I don't know yet." Without hesitation she carefully resected one of the nodules, making sure not to puncture it. "Sam, tell me what this is, please."

Sam took the specimen back to her workstation and quickly started breaking it down. It would take only minutes. Laura looked at Gillian's face, asleep, oblivious. *Please don't let this be what I think it is.*

"Laura?" It was Adrian again.

"We may have some new malignancies."

"I don't understand," Adrian said. "You said they were shrinking."

She ignored him. "Let's take a look at the pancreas, please."

Emily met her eyes and understood. If there were further metastases they'd missed, the pancreas was a good place to start looking.

Despite the air conditioning, Laura felt feverishly hot. The scrub nurse dabbed the perspiration from her brow as Laura maneuvered her way through the abdominal opening. Gently she began exploring the tucks and folds of the pancreas, her fingertips sensitive as antennae. She swallowed and looked up at Emily. With horrifying frequency, the pads of her fingers were grazing what felt like minuscule hard pellets.

"We've got more on the pancreas." She turned quickly to her pathologist. "Sam, have you got an answer for me?"

Laura heard the horrible verdict echoing in her head even before her pathologist uttered it.

"It's a hepatoma."

"Oh my God," said Emily.

"What's happened?" Adrian asked.

I've killed her, Laura thought. *That's what's happened.*

"You gentlemen should leave now," she said tightly.

Powell, his face green, at least had the decency to turn and make for the door; he had his story, and maybe, as far as he was concerned, a sad ending was as good as a happy one. But Adrian hesitated, looking at her, his eyes above the surgical mask beseeching.

"Please," she said.

She stared at the surface of Gillian's liver, the hundreds of tiny gray hepatomas. *You little bastards.* How could she have known? Yes, her liver function tests had been abnormal before the operation, but she'd attributed that to the three sarcomas she'd already known to be present, albeit shrinking.

"It's our retrovirus," said Emily softly. "It must be."

Laura nodded. It was always one of the risks, the thing she'd most dreaded.

"Must've mutated," she said. The retrovirus she herself had designed had mutated inside Gillian, and it had started creating cancer faster than it killed it. It had peppered Gillian's liver and pancreas and God only knows what else. Her miracle cure.

"What do you want to do, Laura?" Emily asked.

With cold fury Laura took a clean scalpel from the tray. She would not let Gillian die like this, would not let those things remain inside her. She excised another nodule, then another, her heart thundering in her ears. She would not stop cutting. She would save her, must save her. Save Gillian.

Save Sandra.

"Laura!"

She turned to Emily, whose eyes were sorrowful as she shook her head. Laura looked around at the other staff, Melanie, Sam, all watching her in communal mourning. She knew Emily was right. There was no way she could remove every nodule without destroying the liver, and the pancreas.

She looked at the young woman's face, still at peace, oblivious.

I'm sorry, she thought.

Softly she said, "Let's close."

CHAPTER THREE

"What can I tell you, Kevin, we're treating this as a routine homicide. Banji was the victim of a mugging that went bad. He also happened to be a doctor. I see nothing to connect the two."

Kevin Sheldrake nodded—patiently, he hoped. Outside, it was topping a hundred, and inside Captain Paul Miceli's office, it wasn't much better, a single desk fan periodically blowing a humid insult across his face. Apparently the air conditioning in the whole west wing of the precinct was down in honor of his visit. Behind his desk, Miceli was sweating enthusiastically, his armpits already ringed, the air of his office soured by cologne and deodorant.

"If Banji had been a GP," Kevin said, "even a run-of-the-mill specialist, I'd be inclined to agree with you. But he was doing cutting-edge AIDS research. *Newsweek* did a story on him a couple months ago. He's been working on a new vaccine. Very high-profile stuff."

"Last time I checked," Miceli said, "doctors weren't immune to violent crime." He smiled gravely, his animosity hidden behind the facade of a wise and sternly benevolent patriarch. He was a big man, with a big voice and an overbearing physique he had obviously worked hard to preserve into his fifties. His burly wrists, festooned with hair, terminated with butcher block fists, whose knuckles tapped almost inaudibly against his cluttered blotter.

Kevin smiled back amicably. He'd always been wary of big men, had noted since childhood their easy propensity to become bullies. Kevin himself was tall but slim, and to this day, he still felt diminished in the presence of slabs of meat like Miceli. Look at him, hunched over his desk, being huge, as if it were a divine right to rule instead of genetic fluke. Kevin felt his smile begin to decompose.

He'd hardly expected a jovial greeting from Detroit Homicide. After all, a Special Agent at the doorstep was about as welcome as a

Jehovah's Witness, only less so. It meant headaches, wounded egos, possibly a turf war. Normally, he was careful to avoid stamping on anybody's toes. But right now, he had a razor-line headache, it was hot as a kiln in here, and he wanted, desperately, to get onto this case.

Pleasantly, he said, "I wouldn't be sitting in this little indoor inferno of yours if I wasn't very concerned about this."

Miceli chuckled. "Look, you could've saved yourself the trip from Chicago. I know you're worried this is some kind of David Haines copycat. But as I recall, Haines was a sniper, right? He used a high-powered rifle, and he was a good shot. One, two bullets most, from a distance. Left the bodies as they fell. Didn't dip in for cash. Banji was shot at close range with a semi, four shots in his chest—messy, street stuff. And his wallet's missing. Not much of a copycat."

"I'm not particularly worried about a copycat."

Miceli's eyes widened. "Then why are you here?"

"I'm worried this might be the real thing."

"Meaning?"

"A copycat models himself after an acclaimed predecessor, like some gruesome homage. It's an aesthetic decision, nothing more. But you may have a person who genuinely shares Haines's beliefs. If it were me, if I didn't want to attract undue attention, I'd change my MO too."

"Well, that's very imaginative. But most perps, fortunately, aren't. After twenty-five years working the streets, you learn that."

Kevin didn't miss the subtext. Cops thought the Feds were wet-behind-the-ears college boys with no field experience. They might be skilled looking at computer screens and tax ledgers, they might have an impeccable telephone manner, but when it came to flat-on-your-ass detective work, they were Feebs—a favorite nickname.

"The timing troubles me too," Kevin said, ignoring Miceli's slight.

"Why's that?"

"Haines's execution is in three weeks. I need to be sure this isn't some kind of protest. Or the beginning of one."

With the big date approaching, Haines was enjoying a modest revival in the media—a mere dribble compared to the tidal wave of ink and air time he'd commanded four years ago, when he was still an anonymous killer on the loose.

In his day-planner, Kevin had marked the execution date. He'd kept track of it with the vigilance of a child opening windows on an advent calendar. Unlike Christmas day, however, the date, over the years, kept getting pushed back. There were maybe ten appellate steps between the death sentence and actual execution; Haines had taken them all now. A former medical student, he had killed seven doctors in four states, and maimed three others. He'd targeted only leading researchers in oncology, immunology, hematology. He'd planned his murders carefully, and executed his victims with the precision of a CIA assassin. It had taken Kevin and his task force three years to track him down. The Illinois state attorneys had insisted unflinchingly on the death penalty.

Haines had helped them. He'd confessed to all his murders and insisted on a guilty plea. When his lawyers had tried to plead not guilty by reason of insanity, he'd fired them and submitted to testing by psychiatrists. He was found sane.

Kevin could have saved them the time. Haines's murders had not been committed in fits of insanity or passion; he knew well the difference between right and wrong, and he would pay the ultimate price at the hands of the people.

Miceli was shaking his head regretfully, as if forced to reprimand a promising but overexcited student. Kevin had to look away, feeling his face begin to flinch with irritation.

"Listen, I followed the Haines case too, like most people. Damn impressive work on the Bureau's part, even if you did have a small army of people working with you. I lift my hat to you for taking him down. But trust me, Haines is the kind of case that comes along once in a career. You've had your David Haines. I'm sorry, but what we've got here is plain boring. A guy shot in an underground parking lot. What happened to Banji is tragic, but nothing special. A reasonable man would assume it was a sad coincidence."

"What makes you think I'm a reasonable man?" Kevin said soberly, and when he refused to return Miceli's smile, he saw the captain's eyes lose their composure for the first time. Only then did he allow a conciliatory grin to cross his face.

"I'm *not* a reasonable man, and I didn't catch David Haines by being one. What he believes, the things he did, are not reasonable by most people's standards. Twenty years working cults and religious fanatics, I can tell you all about unreasonable, and you know what? It's *stopped* seeming unreasonable to me. What happened to Banji doesn't surprise me. What surprises me is that it didn't happen sooner."

Since the day they'd locked Haines up, Kevin had never been free of the persistent anxiety that something like this might happen. And as David's execution drew nearer, his fear had intensified—to such an extent that for the past two weeks he'd been having nightmares again, shouting himself awake from the reruns of the Haines case his unconscious had been broadcasting. Like Charles Manson and Ted Bundy, David Haines had seared himself into the nation's consciousness. After hunting him for three years, Kevin felt personally branded, and he didn't expect the scar tissue on his own soul to heal. As far as he was concerned, the terrible power David had defined would never go away; it just lay dormant, waiting for another able host.

But Miceli, he saw, was looking dubious. "With respect, maybe this is just a case of reading too much into things."

"Oh," said Kevin, "you think maybe I'm obsessing—"

"Look, I didn't say that—"

"Maybe too much time on my hands over at the Bureau. Well, I sincerely hope you're right. And I'll be more than happy to assist in any way. Prove myself wrong."

He watched Miceli's face. This was a local matter, and the FBI had no jurisdiction. Kevin needed to be invited onto this case.

"I appreciate your generosity, Agent Sheldrake, really. And I'll certainly keep you up to date, but I've got a feeling we'll wrap this one pretty soon."

"Is that right?"

"Yeah, we've got a witness. The parking attendant. He heard shots, got a good look at the shooter as he ran for the east exit. He's the one who called it in. From his description we've got a pretty good guess who it is. My boys tracked him down just before you showed up. Lots of cash on him. They're bringing him in now." Miceli grinned, obviously feeling generous. "You're welcome to stick around for the lineup, if you like."

*　　*　　*

In the darkened viewing room, Kevin waited with Miceli and his two homicide detectives, Lowen and Valgardson. Judging from the looks they gave Kevin, they seemed to share their boss's less than kindly view of the Bureau. Behind the glass, the six suspects filed in.

"Okay, Will, take your time with this," said Miceli.

Kevin turned his attention to Will Andrews, the parking attendant who'd called in the shooting. He was a mild, weedy-looking man who seemed faintly repelled by his surroundings. Kevin didn't blame him. There was no fan here, and a pall of stale coffee and nicotine seemed permanently suspended in the air. Andrews stood, slightly stooped, his arms folded across his chest, as if trying to minimize his body's contact with the malodorous room.

Andrews pointed. "That's him."

"Number four?"

"Yes."

Kevin would have been hard pressed to conjure up a more volatile-looking specimen. He had long, stringy hair, a ratty mustache, and small close-set eyes that radiated ignorance and rage. Above his waist he wore nothing but a sleeveless jean jacket revealing wiry arms, twined with tattoos. Almost all his knuckles were scabbed over. A text-book offender.

"You want a few more minutes with this, Will?"

"No, I'm sure. That's definitely him."

As if on cue, the man exploded. Even through the glass his voice was alarmingly loud.

"Fuck you!" he shouted, jabbing with his finger. "You fuckin' cunts! You want to see me, get on in here. I'll fuck with you myself!"

"Deal with him," Miceli snapped into the intercom. As Kevin watched, two officers hurried over and tried to take hold of the man, who was still shouting furiously. He lashed out, holding the cops at bay for a moment before they slammed him face-first against the wall, cuffed him, and marched him off.

Kevin sighed inwardly. Imagining this man committing murder wasn't difficult. Maybe he did kill Banji—just another senseless act of violence for a few bucks. It was depressingly common. A sudden weariness drifted through him. Maybe Miceli was right. Maybe it was just a coincidence.

Instinct had brought him here to Detroit, but was his instinct any good anymore? Maybe, as he sometimes feared, it had been blunted and deformed by his three years on the Haines case. Maybe. But no way was he ready to give up yet. If Banji was the work of a doctor-killer, he wanted onto the case. He could do this. And he needed it. He needed to prove to Hugh back in Chicago that he could handle more than the chickenshit cases he'd been given over the past couple of years. And he needed to prove it to himself, too.

He caught Miceli sending him a smarmy grin and raising his eyebrows. Obviously Andrews had selected the right man, their prime suspect. But Kevin still didn't buy it—the whole thing was way too easy.

"Quite a show for you, Mr. Andrews," Miceli said to the parking attendant.

"Yeah, well. Do you need me for anything else?"

"Just to sign a few papers for Detective Lowen." Miceli offered his hand. "Thank you very much for coming in."

Andrews, Kevin noted, was less than eager to shake Miceli's hand. He did it quickly, afterwards discreetly wiping his hand on his pants. Interesting little compulsive disorder, Kevin thought. Shaking off the dust of the world?

"Do you need a lift anywhere?" Detective Lowen asked Andrews.

"No. I'm fine. Thank you."

Detective Lowen opened the door and Miceli walked out ahead. Kevin was bringing up the rear when Andrews stopped short, as if he'd forgotten something. Before Andrews could raise his fingers to pinch his nose, three fat drops of his blood splattered quietly on the linoleum.

"Ah, geez, it's this damn heat," said Lowen. "You want an ice pack? We've got an ice pack somewhere I think."

Kevin watched as Andrews faltered at the doorway, looking down at his blood on the floor. The expression on his face was one of great concern, bordering on horror. Kevin's heart shifted into high gear, waiting to see what would happen.

"Come on out and sit down," Lowen was saying. "I'll go grab that ice pack."

"Yeah, okay," muttered Andrews. But still he did not move forward. Kevin saw his Adam's apple bob anxiously, once, twice. Then with his free hand Andrews hurriedly extracted a tissue from his pocket and bent down to wipe his blood carefully from the tile.

"Don't worry about it," said Lowen, beginning to sound impatient.

Finally Andrews straightened up, his eyes lingering for another moment on the floor before leaving the room.

Kevin looked down to the tile. Every last drop of blood was gone. Andrews hadn't left a trace.

"I think you're about to arrest the wrong man," Kevin told Miceli back in his office.

"We just got a perfect ID. His name's Chris Washington. He's well known to us, believe me. He spends a lot of time in the area of that parking lot. He's working on page two of his rap sheet—assault, mugging, illegal possession of a handgun. He's just crossed into the big time. When Andrews gave his description, we had a pretty good idea who he was talking about."

"All the same, you should put Andrews under surveillance."

He looked with loathing at the fan on Miceli's desk, still performing its futile little rotations and managing to blast sour air into his face at every turn. He shifted his chair.

"Come on," said Miceli, "you think we didn't check him first thing? He's clean. He's not even in the system. Not so much as a speeding ticket."

"I'm not surprised."

"Then what makes you think he's the killer?"

"His nosebleed."

All during the lineup, he'd felt that something was wrong—Washington wasn't their man. But it wasn't until Andrews's blood hit the floor that he'd understood. Thank God for that nosebleed. Now he knew his instincts hadn't been wrong about the Banji killing, and he felt a swell of pleasure and relief—not a total burnout after all. Still, he knew how hard it was going to be to explain this to Miceli.

The captain looked at him, then laughed. "His nosebleed? What about it?"

"The way he wiped it up, as if his blood was something precious, and he couldn't bear to—"

But Miceli cut him off with a snort, his patience beginning to splinter. "So he's considerate. My wife would've done the same. Doesn't like messing up someone's floor."

"Look," he said, "are you Catholic?"

"Used to be, why?"

"A priest drops a Communion wafer by accident. Does he just sweep it into the garbage, or wait for mice to eat it? He blesses it and takes it himself."

"Oh, for fuck's sake. That's different."

"Not for someone like Haines," Kevin pressed on. "His blood carries his soul, and he doesn't leave it on the floor to be stepped on. A doctor like Banji would've been a prime target for Haines. AIDS research. First, you've got the associations with homosexuality, which he views as a sinful plague. More important, you've got a doctor trying to find a cure for a God-sent scourge."

"Okay, I think I've heard enough of this."

"What, doesn't sound *reasonable* to you? Doesn't it seem odd that Andrews has only been on the job five weeks?"

"No. It's the night shift. The pay sucks. The hours suck. There's a fast turnover."

"How do you know he didn't take the job to watch Banji? Maybe it was the only way to get close enough to kill him. He knows his car, knows his hours. Plus he gave himself a decent alibi. It worked on you, didn't it?"

Miceli's voice had the leaden calm of someone trying hard to control his temper. "I admire the Bureau, and the work you've done for it. But I'm telling you, this is a good old boring murder. And we've got our man."

A blast from Miceli's desk fan hit Kevin in the face again, and without hesitation he leaned forward and slammed his hand down on the power button. The fan swirled to a standstill.

"You arrest Washington, and a few weeks down the road, maybe a few months, there's going to be another dead doctor. And another. Think about how that's going to look for you and your squad. Washington's not your man. He's too obvious. Andrews set him up."

"Too obvious? I'm sorry it's not imaginative enough for you, my friend, but usually the most obvious answer is the right one. I don't have the luxury of formulating lavish motivations and plots. I see what I see and I make decisions."

"And this is the wrong one."

"Look at our stats. Violent crime in this city has dropped 15 percent over the last two years. What've *you* got to show for yourself?"

"Captain, will you or won't you put this man under surveillance?"

"No. I don't have the manpower, and more important, I don't have the slightest inclination. This one's over."

"No," said Kevin, "it's not."

25

CHAPTER FOUR

Laura's hand trembled as she tilted the watering can. The houseplants, neglected for so long, sucked the water hungrily, the soil whispering as it released its loamy fragrance. She breathed it in gratefully, waiting for the water to bleed through the bottom of the pot before moving on.

She could feel the Valium starting to work, weaving its gossamer veil between herself and the world, helping to impose a soothing architecture on her chaotic thoughts. She lifted her eyes to the living-room window. From her apartment's high vantage point she could see the lake, and off to the right a small curve of the skyline, bleached chrome white by the August sun. It had been a long time since she'd been home in the middle of the day.

You killed her.

It was a few moments before she realized her jug was empty. She hurried to the kitchen and blasted the tap, as if hoping to drown out her unbidden thoughts.

Gillian's husband had been there in the recovery room, and her parents, who'd flown up from Miami. She'd had to tell patients of imminent death before, but never like this, never in circumstances where, just hours before, there had been so much hope. Gillian's fingers had traced her husband's wedding band as she held his hand, listening. At the end, Gillian had thanked her, told her not to give up. Laura shuddered now as she remembered her awkward, cowardly retreat, past the stunned faces of her patient's parents, the bowed head of her husband.

The jug was overflowing. She turned off the tap, closed her eyes, tried to focus. *The umbrella trees. Do them now.* She crossed her spartan living room, an arrangement of modern Scandinavian furniture she'd bought virtually complete from the Art Shoppe showroom, and turned down the corridor toward her bedroom.

Two years of work, gone.

She exhaled, her abdomen taut. After seeing Gillian, she'd navigated the hospital corridors in a stupor. Someone had smiled at her, and she'd looked away, startled and amazed that someone could not know about the tragedy that had just happened. When she arrived at her lab, she realized she'd been counting her every footstep, as if in some attempt to stay tethered to the world. Emily had forewarned the rest of the team, sparing Laura the task of breaking the news. She didn't know if she could have borne watching their expressions shift from expectant joy to dismay.

Alone in her small, cluttered office, she stood rooted behind the closed door. She looked at the sheafs of computer data on her desk, the abundant handwritten marginalia, and it looked like hieroglyphics to her, impossible to understand. She saw her message light blinking angrily, and at that same moment the phone rang. She knew intuitively that it would be Adrian, wanting to know what had happened, what had gone wrong, what there was to be done. She didn't pick up. She walked out—out of her office, the lab, past Emily, and Sam, and her anxious technicians. She scarcely remembered the drive home.

In her bedroom, she watered the two plants. Her limbs were beginning to feel pleasantly heavy, adrenaline spent, her body finally surrendering to exhaustion. She set down the jug, pulled the blinds on the midday sun and lay down.

On her night table, the phone. Propping herself up on one elbow she reached for it, fingers lifting the receiver slightly before letting it drop back. Part of her wanted to call—how she wanted to talk—but she couldn't face telling Sandra right now. But she'd be expecting her call, wouldn't she? Maybe not. She was off in Maine on vacation with Mike and the kids, and Dad was there too. At first, Laura had been hurt when she'd heard they'd all be away for the culmination of her trial—but that was when she'd expected triumph. Now she was almost glad they were out of town. Maybe Sandra had forgotten about Gillian Shamas's biopsy date—it wasn't as if her little sister expressed that much interest in her work at the best of times. Good, then. She'd tell them all a little later, after she'd pulled herself together. She was just so tired, so unbelievably tired.

The pillow was cool against her feverish cheek, and inevitably her mind started wandering, back three months to the spring, to that dinner at Sandra's ...

* * *

As always, Sandra's dinner table was festive, bright with candles and wine glasses, polished silverware and napkin rings. Laura set down the serving dish with the asparagus and went back to the kitchen to help her sister bring out the rest.

The air was humid and succulent with the smells of cooking. Through the French doors, Laura could see Sandra's garden beginning to flourish in Chicago's ten-day spring.

"This looks fantastic," Laura said, surveying the pork tenderloin, sliced into medallions and garnished with apricots and raisins and herbs. Sandra smiled as she filled a casserole dish with wild rice. She was flushed, her green eyes bright. On the cluttered counter, cooling, were two homemade pies—an apple, and a pumpkin, their father's favorite. Laura couldn't suppress a twinge of irritation. Their Sunday meals here had been a tradition since Laura had moved back to Chicago three years ago, and she knew how important they were to Sandra. But honestly, with the news she'd had six days ago, couldn't she have given herself a break? Discreetly, she kept an eye on her sister. Was Sandra just flushed from the warm oven, or was she feverish? She didn't look unwell, but Laura wondered if maybe she'd lost some weight.

"It's strange," Sandra said, "but I feel really good."

"That's great." Laura forced a smile and nodded, wanting to be encouraging. But she was used to the cruel ironies of cancer, how sometimes a patient could be fatally riddled with tumors, yet still feel tremendously vigorous, even close to the very end. She wondered if maybe Sandra didn't realize, or hadn't yet accepted, how serious her prognosis was.

As Sandra finished filling the casserole, a wisp of chestnut hair fell across her face, and with a sister's reflex, Laura reached over and brushed it gently back behind her ear. Good: Sandra didn't feel feverish.

"Thanks," said Sandra.

Laura looked at her sister's beautifully sculpted face, and then her eyes dropped, as they so often did now, to her chest. A little over a year ago, they'd found cancer in both breasts. It was aggressive. They'd performed a double mastectomy and Sandra had spent the next six months in and out of hospital for a radical course of radiation and chemotherapy. Laura couldn't believe how brave Sandra had been about the whole thing, upbeat, uncomplaining. She'd been filled with admiration. If it had been her ... And now, less than half a year later, the cancer had come back, making major incursions into Sandra's lymph nodes and, even more damaging, her liver.

"I wish you'd let me do dinner tonight," Laura said.

Sandra just shook her head. "I enjoy it. Really. I'm one of those deviant homemakers who like making dinner for people." They were side by side at the counter, and Laura smiled as Sandra slid an arm around her waist, their bodies fitting snugly together. Laura tipped her cheek against Sandra's. Her sister's skin, her hair, smelled exactly the way it had when she was a kid, and for just a moment, Laura wanted nothing more than to be ten years old, cross-legged on her bed behind Sandra, combing out her sister's hair. She stiffened. Too painful to think about.

"Here, let me take that," Laura said, reaching for the huge dish of rice.

"You'll need mitts." Sandra nodded to a pair on the counter. Laura put them on and carried the heavy casserole out to the dining room, Sandra following with the pork. Dad and Mike were making their way in from the living room, talking about mutual funds, still finishing off their glasses of the Australian Chardonnay Sandra had served earlier with the smoked salmon.

When they were all seated, Mike said grace. Laura bowed her head politely, but felt the familiar involuntary clenching of awkwardness and embarrassment in her jaw. She lifted her eyes to look at her sister's husband, his brow furrowed slightly as he offered his thanks. He was handsome in a nondescript way, but she'd never quite been able to restrain herself from thinking *plodding* whenever she looked at him. Not that he was overweight in the least; he had a trim body, and he kept in shape jogging. If you'd asked her to describe his face, she'd have said pleasant, even features. Brown hair that wasn't thinning too badly. He was a good husband to Sandra. Mostly.

It was no big deal, she knew that, but Laura noticed the furtive way he looked at her sometimes. Before Sandra's illness, it might've given her a pulse of guilty pleasure, but now, it simply made her despise him. If his eyes had to rove, she wished they would do it outside their own house. She could only hope Sandra hadn't noticed.

"I meant to tell you," Dad said to Sandra, as they set about serving themselves, "the Spiegels *and* the O'Connells both called me yesterday, to say they'd seen you on television."

"You were on TV?" Laura asked. "When?"

Sandra was shaking her head modestly. "It was nothing, just—"

"They thought you conveyed great warmth and intelligence."

"It was a little thing on channel nine," Sandra explained. "They were doing a piece on soup kitchens, and they'd heard about the new one we set up in Edgemont. I was on for all of twenty-five seconds."

"Sounds great," said Laura.

"Well, it's great if it makes more people aware of the problems in the city."

Sandra worked part-time for the church that she and her father both attended, organizing their network of soup kitchens and shelters across the city. And because she was articulate and beautiful, it seemed to Laura she was always being asked to appear on local television panels and talk about child poverty and homelessness. After every appearance, Dad's sizeable circle of fellow retirees would inevitably call in a state of great excitement to congratulate him on his celebrity daughter.

"Gretchen Spiegel said you looked beautiful, as always," Dad told Sandra.

"That's sweet of her. I've still got to write her a thank-you for Alex's birthday present."

Laura listened politely as Dad brought Sandra up to date on the doings of his various friends, and felt the usual boredom tinged with guilt: she was so removed from it all.

She took another bite of her pork. It was delicious, and the first proper meal she'd had in days, but she felt a tightening of her throat that made it hard to swallow. She glanced across at her father, wondering if he felt it too, the strain of talking about everything but what was uppermost in all their minds.

She glanced over at Sandra, laughing at something Mike said, her face glowing in the candlelight. Was she in denial? She appeared strangely jubilant.

"Alexander," said Dad suddenly, unable to hide his amusement, "what are you doing up, young man?"

Laura smiled. Peeping around the archway was Sandra's five-year-old son, his body soft in plaid cotton pyjamas, face bright with mischievous delight.

"You guys are *loud*," Alex said.

He hurried into the dining room, holding out the dinosaur toy that Laura had brought him tonight as his belated birthday present.

"Look at this, Aunt Laura, I did all the pieces."

While climbing unself-consciously onto her lap, Alex launched into a highly detailed account of how he'd assembled all the pieces of the Stegosaurus skeleton in bed. Laura bent her head to listen, relishing the soothing warmth of his small body. She always thought of Alex as some kind of miraculous gift. She loved his sister Rachel, too, but Alex was her favorite. She'd never been particularly good with kids, but from the very start, Alex had simply *chosen* her. He seemed to like the grown-up way she talked to him. And they had things in common. The way things worked fascinated him. The Science and Technology Museum was his idea of heaven. And he was probably the best companion she'd ever had at the Field Museum, so surprised and delighted by everything it was as if she herself were discovering these things all over again. She only wished she had more time with him.

"Back to bed, Alex," said Mike. "Go on now."

Alex popped out the Stegosaurus's spines once more, and then Laura reluctantly released him.

"Night, Aunt Laura," he said, giving her a kiss on the cheek.

"We'll try to be quieter," she promised solemnly.

With Alex gone, she felt anxiety filling her up again. She caught herself playing with her napkin ring and forced her hand back into her lap. She tried to be still, but her foot pumped up and down, seemingly unstoppable. She took a tiny sip of wine.

"Very abstemious," Mike said, grinning at her glass, her plate of mostly uneaten food. She smiled politely, thinking, *If you only knew what I put into my body.* He probably just thought she was on a diet. That's what she'd been telling people when they commented that she looked slimmer. Diet and too much work.

"How're those poor lab mice making out?" her father said, by way of asking about her work. Her day-to-day activities were so minute, her attention so absorbed in a microcosm of cells and molecules, Laura was often at a loss to explain what she'd been doing in anything but bewildering scientific terms. Laura glanced at Sandra. Tonight especially, she didn't want to talk about the project.

"Oh, it's never been very much fun being a lab mouse," she replied humorously, hoping Dad would just drop it. Sensitivity had never been one of his strong points.

"You said last time you were making progress."

"Well," she said, irritated, "it's a very slow process."

"How soon before you can test it on people?"

Laura took a moment before replying. She knew her father's interest now was far from conversational.

"Well, we'll probably have to put that off a bit."

"Why the delay?" There was a certain sharpness in his voice, tinged with dismay, and Laura felt flustered.

"The last animal trials were ... the retroviruses got contaminated somehow ... anyway, we'll probably, we'll have to push the human trials back."

"Oh," said her father, "that's unfortunate."

"Happens all the time, Dad." She felt prickly. "We have to get approval from the FDA and we can't get that until we do enough animal trials that work."

"I see," said her father understandingly, but Laura knew he thought she was a slowpoke; he didn't understand the time horizon for a project of this magnitude. And she knew that right now he was deeply disappointed in her. He'd hoped somehow she'd just whip off a miracle cure for his beloved youngest daughter, and she'd failed him. As if she didn't have enough doubts of her own, every single day in the lab, wondering if she was smart enough to make this thing work. She took another mouthful of rice and managed to wash it down with some wine. Appetite vanquished, she set her fork down.

She looked out the window at the garden, wanting to be out. Wanting to be back in the lab, working. When was the last time she'd actually *felt* she'd earned a night off?

She helped Mike clear away the dishes, then Sandra brought out the pies and ice cream. Laura picked at hers, watching her sister. She could see a strangely giddy, expectant look in her eyes, as if she were about to announce an engagement, a pregnancy.

"I've decided to try an alternative therapy," she said.

"What do you mean, alternative therapy?" Laura asked cautiously, holding out a frail hope that Sandra had been accepted in a clinical protocol.

"There's a clinic in Tijuana I've heard about."

It was impossible to rein in her dismay. "Oh, Sandra. Those guys are all quacks."

"They specialize in metabolic therapies," her sister went on evenly, "and they've had a lot of success."

"What about the chemo? I thought you were going to—"

"No more chemo."

She'd always known that her sister entertained wobbly notions of medicine, but she hadn't thought she'd ever take it this far. This had to be Mike's fault. He bought into all that crap about self-visualization and self-healing, served up in book after best-selling book by self-anointed gurus and shamans from around the world.

"Sandra, you should really think about this a little more."

"I have. I've talked to some of the patients who've gone there, some of them were sicker than me. They cure people."

"*Cure* people. Look ..." She scarcely knew where to begin. "Who says these people weren't cured by the chemo or radiation they were on before? Maybe they didn't even have cancer. And if they did, maybe it wasn't even really gone at all, just in remission. And how do you know they're not lying?"

"Why would they lie?" The innocent shock on Sandra's face both shamed and angered her. How could she be this naive?

"Laura, this is not some hole-in-the-wall operation," said Mike. "They sent us a lot of material. They've got facilities like the best clinics up here, all the latest equipment, CT scans and ultrasounds, magnetic resonance imaging, and all the rest of it."

Sandra was nodding, no doubt hoping to appease her with this mention of scientific hardware.

"They may have all that equipment there," Laura said, "and maybe even technicians who know how to use it. But the so-called doctors ... I wouldn't trust their interpretations of the results. And I certainly don't trust their treatments."

"The woman who runs the clinic, Dr. Frieda Wendt, she's published a book about her therapies," Sandra said. "It's filled with testimonials from her patients."

"Okay, but just let me ask you this, has she done any proper studies? I mean, has she published her findings in scientific journals, peer-adjudicated journals?"

"I don't think the establishment would be terribly interested in what Dr. Wendt's got to say," Mike said with an infuriating smugness.

Laura tried to swallow her outrage. Disgruntled patients were forever referring to doctors as the *establishment*, uttering the word as if it were akin to some sinister underworld syndicate. Didn't Mike know how insulting this was to her? But she just nodded patiently, not trusting herself to look him in the eye for fear he'd be incinerated by her fury. "And why do you think that is, Mike?"

"I just don't see a lot of openness among doctors to explore other possibilities. They've got their little club, and only *they* can know the answers to the universe."

You big plodding idiot, she thought. "Well, I've heard all this before. Wicked doctors closing themselves off within the walls of their own arrogance and training, disregarding the true wisdom of the world. If we ignore this stuff, it's because there's nothing to go on. No decent sample groups, no double-blind tests, no published studies. It's all anecdotes from people who, I'm sorry, aren't very bright."

Sandra looked impatient for the first time. "Laura, the doctors you sent me too were all really nice and everything, and I'm sure they're the best at what they do, but ... they didn't help ..."

"The mastectomies and chemo saved your life."

"It came back."

"There are lots of other things you can try. More aggressive chemos. Look, I can put you in touch with—"

"Laura, no thank you."

No thank you? She looked over at her father in panic. Why wasn't he saying anything? This was his daughter! When Sandra's cancer was first diagnosed, Laura had felt useful. This was her domain, after all. She'd given advice, counseled, obtained expert referrals, fast. Her father had called her with all his worries, and she'd been able to reassure him, offer comfort and hope. For the first time, she'd felt that he really valued what she did—and Sandra too. In the six months after the chemo, everyone had been buoyed up with optimism. But now that the cancer had come back, worse than ever, Laura felt somehow responsible.

"Sandra ..."

"We've talked about it," said Sandra. "I just think it's time to take another option. And pray." Across the table, Mike took her hand.

Laura swallowed. This was just getting worse and worse. "Pray?" she asked dully.

"Some doctors also believe in God, Laura. Dr. Wendt thinks that prayer and imaging techniques can be useful adjuncts to her therapies."

"Sandra, please don't do this."

"Maybe we should all calm down here," said their father, looking pointedly at her. Laura felt rigid with anger. Calm down? Like a disobedient child?

"I'm sorry you think it's a bad idea," said Sandra. "I want to live, and I just think my chances are better with Dr. Wendt."

"She's probably not even a doctor."

"You *study* cancer, you don't know what it's like to *have* it, have it killing you."

It silenced her for a moment, Sandra's bluntness. Killing you. Killing your little sister. Oh God, there had to be something she could do. But mixed with this terrible feeling of impotence was an acid resentment. No, *of course* she didn't know firsthand what it was like to have cancer. But she might know how to fight it better than anyone else, and why couldn't Sandra acknowledge that, give her that at least?

Calmly, Laura said, "You don't have to take my word on it. Give me a couple of days and I can send you a ton of articles about this stuff. Then at least you'll have a more balanced view."

"I know how bad the prognosis is, I'm not kidding myself." Sandra looked at her beseechingly. "You can't say for sure this won't work. This gives me something to hope for."

Their father looked at Laura. "Can it hurt?"

"I don't know what the therapy is. Some of them can hurt, yes. What are we talking about here, Sandra, what's her cocktail? Some urea, a little shark cartilage, maybe a pinch of cesium chloride or laetrile for good measure? Some of these nice herbal remedies are seriously toxic."

"More toxic than chemo?" Mike asked. "*World Report* just ran a cover story about people in clinical cancer trials who ended up dead, just so real doctors could try out some fancy new techniques."

"At least those doctors are properly trained, and the patients know the risks. These people down in Tijuana, they probably don't know what they're doing. They can't really know the effect of the things they hand out, on any serious biochemical level. Plenty of people die from these alternative therapies, too, Mike. And even if it's harmless, it's taking you away from something that might help. Sandra, I think you should take the next course of chemo," Laura said, feeling her voice start to shake. "Dad, come on, agree with me on this."

"I'm not doing the chemo again, I've told you."

"You sure, Sandra?" asked her father, grieved.

"Just tell her to take it," Laura snapped impatiently, then instantly wished she'd held her tongue.

"Daddy, I'm sure," Sandra said. "Two people I talked to said their doctors gave them six months to live, and after Dr. Wendt's treatment they've lived three and five years and are still healthy."

"With your mother's cancer," said Dad, "well, you were there, Sandra, day by day, you know what it was like for her. I never felt very confident she was being helped. And I've always been inclined to think there are more things in heaven and earth—"

"This isn't one of them," Laura said.

"But you don't even know what it is," Sandra told her, "and already you're ruling it out, just like that!"

"If she doesn't take the chemo, what other options does she have?" her father asked Laura.

Since I failed, you mean, Laura thought. *Since I didn't come through.* She was working as hard as she could: didn't her father think she was rushing, with the hope, always at the back of her mind, that she could develop a therapy Sandra could benefit from? What her father didn't seem to understand was that even if her protocol were ready to go ahead, right this minute, Sandra might not even qualify. And if she did, she might be used as a control and never receive the therapy. She said nothing.

"You have my blessing, if it's what you've decided," her father told Sandra.

"I'm sorry you don't approve, Laura," Sandra said, "but I have thought about it."

Laura nodded, staring miserably at the table, not knowing what more to say.

*   *   *

For a few blissful moments as Laura woke, sleep still cradled her in its warm, aquatic embrace, as though all her burdensome belongings, her very identity, had sunk to the bottom of the ocean. Within seconds, though, a wave of memory crashed over her, and she was terrifyingly awake.

Gillian Shamas, tracing her husband's wedding band, weeks to live ... And how long before the FDA would approve another human trial—*if* she still had a lab to call her own after this. And Sandra ... what chance did she have of curing Sandra now?

It all pinned her down like a hundred-pound anvil, squeezing the air from her lungs. *You've failed.* With a huge effort she sat up and swung her legs over the edge of the bed, riding out a swell of nausea, trying to calm her blasting heart. It was still daylight beyond the blinds. She glanced at her bedside clock—6:57—and blinked in surprise when she saw the AM sign. She'd slept through the whole day and night, eighteen hours. She shivered in the room's air-conditioned chill.

She stumbled to the bathroom but couldn't face switching on the light. In the pale illumination from the open door, she braced herself against the counter and confronted her reflection in the mirror.

Oh my God, it looked as though her face were falling off her skull, her skin slack with exhaustion, purple smudges beneath her eyes. She couldn't remember the last time she'd looked so tired, *felt* so tired, so old. She thought of her lab, the immensity of the job ahead of her— an endless corridor of one closed door after another, each ingeniously locked. *Go back to bed. Can't face it, can't do it anymore, fucked it all up.*

Automatically, her hand slid open the medicine cabinet and took out the vial of phenmetrizine. *Just one more.* But unscrewing the top, she faltered. She brushed the tears from her eyes. *You promised: after the protocol, no more. Down the toilet they'd go.* But that was assuming the protocol was successful, and it wasn't. Now there was more work to do, lots.

It's logical, she told herself firmly. She had work to do and she could not work like this, wasn't that obvious? So, if she wanted to work, today, she had to take the speed. Phenmetrizine, she quickly corrected herself. It was a drug, not something she bought on the street in a Ziploc bag. It was a drug, and she was a doctor, and she knew exactly how addictive it was, and how easily it could be abused. She knew the difference between master and servant, and the phenmetrizine was definitely a servant, one she'd needed over the last four months to push ahead to the human trial.

The vial was open. It would be easy to dump it into the toilet and flush, and then it would be gone. But she knew she'd just write herself another prescription.

Okay. Take it now, but you're going to start phasing it out. She'd like nothing better than to stop cold turkey, but she knew what would happen. The crash would last three days, not just eighteen hours, like last night. Then there'd be the depression, fear, the shakes, and nausea for two, maybe three weeks. She couldn't afford the time. She'd phase it out slowly. All she needed was the discipline, and she knew she had that.

She washed the pink tablet down with a glass of tap water.

* * *

Still damp from her shower, she stood before the mirror, hands placed lightly on her head. She stared critically at her breasts, following their full outer curves against the hard tapered lines of her ribs. She'd always been pleased with them, even though she thought them slightly too big for her slender frame—something which, she knew, seemed to bother only women. She might not have Sandra's sculpted neckline, or her green eyes, her perfectly flat stomach, but men noticed her breasts. That was her consolation prize. After that, it was all downhill as far as she was concerned, even on days when she didn't look so dire. Her aquiline nose was too strong for her triangular face, and her eyes too narrow, giving her, she thought, a somewhat slatternly look. Her brown shoulder-length hair was boring, her ankles and upper thighs were slightly too thick. Her mouth was okay, reasonably full, but unlike Sandra's inviting lips, there was something dismissive about hers.

She stretched her arms above her head and, with a practised eye, checked for any changes in her breasts, any puckers or unusually prominent veins. It was a monthly ritual she kept religiously, especially since Sandra's illness. Back in the bedroom, she lay down on the duvet, dragging a pillow beneath her head. With the pads of her middle three fingers, she circled her areolas, dark against the fairness of her skin. Her nipples stiffened and she closed her eyes to concentrate. Her fingers spiraled slowly over her breast. What was that? She retraced, and exhaled. Nothing. *Thank you,* she thought raggedly. Everything was fine.

She stared up at the ceiling, thinking of Sandra. In May she'd flown down to Dr. Wendt's International Metabolic Clinic in Tijuana. The name itself pissed Laura off, the attempt to bestow an aura of global knowledge and scientific legitimacy on what was, in her mind, a real quack shack. Three weeks at six thousand dollars a week—uninsured, naturally, since not even Mike's super-duper health plan at the bank would cover alternative therapies in Mexico. Early in June, Sandra had come back home with a suitcase full of supplementary medications, jubilant, feeling better than ever, she said, with Dr. Wendt's assurances that her cancer was disappearing. That, in fact, it had never even spread to her liver in the first place—contrary to what she'd been told in the medieval hamlet of Chicago. Laura didn't buy it for a second. But despite her urging, Sandra had refused to return to her oncologist for another checkup and biopsy.

Over the summer, Laura had watched her fearfully, sure she was losing weight, but Sandra's confidence was unassailable. The weight loss was to be expected, according to Dr. Wendt, she replied. She said she could feel the tumors shrinking. She was focused—taking the medicine, doing her exercises, praying the cancer away—and she knew she was getting better.

Laura never knew how to respond. Was she supposed to fake it and say, "How wonderful, I'm so glad"? She supposed there was a chance the cancer *had* gone into remission, but she doubted it. All her experience, all the statistics, told her that Sandra's cancer was not going away, that it would be back, with all its terrible rapacity increased.

All through the summer at the lab, Laura was having one breakthrough after another. After the rhesus monkey trials, she got FDA approval in late June and started treating Gillian Shamas.

And now what have you got to show for yourself?

Nothing.

Don't think about it now.

The phenmetrizine was kicking in, and she felt clear and focused—the real her. It didn't change her, just cleared away all the noise and distractions so she could be herself. As she dressed she ordered her thoughts. She'd go back to the lab, hold a team meeting before noon, and get started, working through her protocol backwards until she found out what had gone wrong. Probably the retrovirus had spliced at the wrong location, or accidentally enabled an oncogene. Luckily they had the tumors she'd resected from Gillian. They'd start with those, try to determine their genesis ...

When the phone rang she felt a stab of anxiety. She hesitated only a moment before picking up, fearing it was Adrian, or her father, or Sandra, all asking about yesterday. She exhaled and reached for the phone. She couldn't put it off forever.

"Seven-thirty and Wonder Woman's not in the lab?"

It took her a second to place the voice, and when she did she felt a rush of relief.

"Howard," she said.

"You're not going to tell me I woke you."

As students at Johns Hopkins, they'd been close friends, and years later, after a boozy dinner, he'd let slip that he'd been in love with her but had never had the guts to do anything about it. Fear, he'd muttered, fear she'd never go out with a guy like him in a million years. She was glad he'd never asked, because he was right in a way; she could never have imagined herself as his lover, but she wanted very much to have him always as a friend. They'd stayed in touch ever since.

"I was trying to get hold of you all last night," he said, his cell phone crackling. "I've got something I really want you to look at. Some blood work that came into my Joliet lab last night."

After med school, Howard had discovered his real love was diagnostic machinery and turned entrepreneur, starting a chain of state-of-the-art lab services all across the Midwest. His equipment was better than the stuff in a lot of small hospitals. Just last year Laura had asked him to advise her on some incubators and a scanning electron microscope for her own lab.

"What kind of blood work?" she asked him.

"I don't want to bias your reaction. I just want you to see it for yourself."

She sighed. "Howard, this is going to be a crazy bad day for me." She couldn't quite bring herself to tell him what had happened. She'd always thought of Howard as one of her staunch admirers, a person she could always count on to think she was wonderful and brilliant. Everyone should have a Howard. But if he knew about yesterday ...

"Look, you're really going to want to see this, Laura." He sounded so excited that she was genuinely curious now. "Hey, you've got a VCR, right? I'm literally five minutes away from your building. You want me to bring it on up? It doesn't take long to watch."

"You *taped* it?"

"Yep."

Laura looked at her watch. It wasn't even eight yet. She could see Howard's blood, and still be in the lab before everyone else. And she thought it might cheer her up to see Howard, someone who was free from association with yesterday's disaster. She said yes.

While waiting, she made herself a coffee and toasted a bagel, and ten minutes later she buzzed him up. Even in his twenties, there had been something faintly middle-aged about Howard, but now it suited him. He seemed comfortable with his slightly portly body, his beard—a benevolent father figure. Which of course he was—the proud father of three children. He smiled at her, and she immediately felt guilty that she'd skipped his housewarming in March.

"Nice to see you, Howard. How're Karen and the kids?"

"They're all great."

She kissed him on the cheek. He looked decidedly more rumpled than usual.

"You seem pretty excited," she said.

"Yeah, well, I was up half the night getting snapshots for you." He was already rooting through his voluminous briefcase, and he brought out a videocassette.

"Come on in."

In the living room he spotted her VCR and slid in the tape, the remote already wagging in his hand. Laura smiled. It had been a while since she'd seen her remote in a man's grip.

Howard sat back beside her on the cream sofa, breathing loudly through his nostrils. "I don't know how the hell to interpret this, so I thought, 'Just show it to the genius!'"

She smiled at his compliment, touched, and only wished she could believe it. Right about now she felt as though she'd probably flunk first-year biochemistry.

"So what is this, Howard? Come on!"

"I got a specimen in late yesterday from Illinois Correctional. We do all their lab work."

"A convict?"

"Yeah, I don't know who. They just give us their DOC numbers. Anyway, I don't know what they were screening him for, but we did a baseline liver function, and that was fine, but when we tried to do a CBC, the machine kept saying his white count was sixty-five."

"Those new toys of yours, huh," said Laura. A normal white count was between three and eleven: a sixty-five was almost unheard of.

Howard grinned self-deprecatingly. "Well, that's what I thought at first. But I ran it through our old GE, same thing. Then I did a manual count and ... well, you'll see for yourself."

Laura prepared herself for the usual pale aquatic wash which, over the years, had become intimately familiar to her—the ringed red cells, the shell-like platelets, and the myriad white cells, slithering like sea worms, splitting, rejoining. As a cancer doctor, especially when she was doing clinical work, normal blood was always a relief. But she had made her career looking at abnormal cells.

Still, she'd never seen anything like what flared up on the television now.

She inhaled sharply. The microscopic image was teeming. Never had she seen so much cellular activity in a blood smear. There was so much movement it was, at first, difficult to identify the various cells. It took only a second, though, to realize that Howard and his machines weren't wrong. She was looking at an aggressive broth of white cells.

"He should be dead."

"Yeah." Howard nodded. "That's what I said. At first I thought leukemia ..."

"But there are no blast cells," muttered Laura. She got up from the sofa and sat cross-legged on the parquet floor, hunched forward intently for a better view. "Something's triggered this. You don't get an immune response like this without ... a catastrophic infection, maybe."

"I checked that too, but there's no sign of bacterial activity. Now here's where it really gets good. I did some vital staining to beef up the resolution ..."

There were a few seconds of black on the screen before the next image snapped up. Howard was right, the image was hugely improved, crystalline, and Laura found herself looking at a teeming mass of white cells. But there was something else now, spinning into the image from the right. It didn't even take a second for her to recognize the dense, rapidly dividing cluster of cancer cells. It had always struck her as fitting that cancer cells actually *looked* malevolent— misshapen, their membranes jagged, and fast. In tissue, tumors were gray, sometimes an even more ominous flat, light-eating black. They looked alien in a human body.

These cells before her were dividing with freakish speed, adding clones of themselves to the outer layer of the cluster, which grew even as it rolled slowly across the screen like some dark planet.

"These aren't leukemia cells," she said. And it was rare, extremely rare, to see any other type of cancer cells in the blood. They had to be metastatic, though it was impossible to tell from what source, from what organ. But it seemed clear the cancer cells had dispersed through the patient's bloodstream, looking for new homes.

"This is a very sick man, Howard."

"But watch this," he said.

As a scientist she was always skeptical when she read of some unprecedented phenomenon in journals. She was open-minded; she knew that human biology was endlessly surprising, and that many things were possible; but far more possible was that someone had screwed up an experiment, or grossly misinterpreted results. A dirty petri dish could ruin a trial. The first thing she did when she read about a new procedure was try it herself. If she couldn't replicate the results, it was wrong.

If anyone had told her about what she now saw on the screen, she would have smiled and been politely disbelieving.

It was a slaughter. That was the word that immediately leapt into her head. From among the swirling mass of white cells, there was a selective and lightning-quick attack. T-cells shot toward the tumor and locked onto it like a pack of hyenas worrying a rhino. Laura could see more of the same white cells coming from offscreen, binding with the cancer cluster until its entire surface was carpeted with the killer T-cells.

She'd spent years watching immune responses, and she'd never seen such a fast and absolute one for cancer. Despite the air conditioning, she felt feverish. Incredible. The protein receptors on these T-cells must be so precise, so sensitive, they had locked instantly.

There was more.

The tumor was now encircled, and destruction followed just as quickly. She'd seen lymphokine-activated killer cells revved up on Interleukin-2, and even they took minutes to wipe out malignant cells, and much less dramatically: all you saw there was a gradual withering and slow dispersal of the cancer cells. A grunt of amazement escaped her lips. These cancer cells were rupturing, visible gashes opening in their membranes, deflating like punctured balloons. The wounded cells spiraled away from the tumor, disintegrating. Faster now, the remaining layers of cancer cells began to explode as more T-cells moved in on them.

In less than a minute, the tumor was decimated to its core.

"Oh my God," she breathed. Without realizing it, she'd worked her way across the floor to within inches of the television screen. She stared at the image, mute, but her mind was sprinting, trying to explain what she'd just seen. The T-cells, after locking on, were obviously releasing some potent cytokine that was violently toxic to the cancer cells. She'd studied a lot of tumor-killing agents in vitro, but nothing like this.

"Have you ever seen stuff like that?" Howard was asking her. His voice sounded a long way away. "I mean, that's not normal, right? You've got to tell me, because I really don't know."

She shook her head. "No, it's not normal. Whoever this blood belongs to, he has the most highly adapted immune system I've ever seen."

"But he's got cancer?"

"Definitely. Or he *did*." She exhaled and shook her head. "If this is typical of his immune response, he may already be cured."

"You're kidding."

"I'm guessing. I mean, there are probably less than a dozen medical accounts of spontaneous cures in the last forty years. I don't mean long remissions. Cures. And some of those cases were pretty long ago—they might've been mistaken remissions, or maybe the subject died of other causes first. But whatever this guy has inside his T-cells, I've never encountered it."

"So this is interesting to you, right?"

She looked over at him and nodded. Her mouth was dry. "Oh yeah, this is pretty damn interesting."

Howard chuckled, pleased. "Good. I thought you might like it. You're also the only person I could think of smart enough to understand what the hell was going on. Do you?"

"No. But I'm going to find out. How much blood do you have?"

Howard let out a big breath and winced apologetically. "Well, none. Between all the tests we ran, and what I used for the vital staining, I used it all."

"I'm going to need more, lots more. I mean, if this is what I think it is, if I can isolate those T-cells, whatever they're producing, figure out what their receptor sites are like ... maybe we can synthesize it, or maybe ..." She knew she was verging on incoherence and forced herself to stop, take a deep breath. "You don't know who this is?"

Howard shook his head. "Look, this is a little dicey for me. Probably I shouldn't be showing specimens around, even to specialists. But I'm making an exception. I'm formally referring this to you."

"Who should I talk to?"

"The chief physician at Illinois is John Finlay." He opened his Filofax and scribbled a phone number down for Laura. "I've only ever talked to him a couple times."

"Thanks, Howard."

"Hey, if this is useful, do I get a footnote?"

"You get a big footnote."

*   *   *

"Hello."

The one word, bitten off with an irritated sigh, told her all she needed to know about John Finlay. Howard had left only ten minutes ago, and Laura had wasted no time calling the prison.

"Dr. Finlay, I hope I'm not calling you at an inconvenient time. My name's Laura Donaldson, and I'm an oncologist with the MetaSYS research center at the University of Chicago. Dr. Howard Morgan asked me to consult on some tests done in his lab last night. They were for one of your patients, ID number 12-790062."

There was a short pause on the other end.

"I'm sorry, I don't understand why this was referred to you."

"Well, his white count was highly abnormal, and—"

"You're saying he has leukemia?"

"I don't think it's leukemia, but I certainly think he may have some rare type of cancer."

"Uh-huh." She heard Finlay sigh. "Look, did you runs the tests I asked?"

"Dr. Morgan did. They were all negative."

"So there's no indication of TB or hepatitis, because that's what I was screening him for."

"No. Do you mind if I ask why you were testing him?"

"He's been in close contact with another inmate who was infected. But his skin test was negative, the chest X-rays too. In fact, I'm surprised you found anything abnormal. I gave him a full physical and he was perfectly healthy."

"No fever?" Laura was skeptical.

"No. No swollen lymph nodes, no signs of anemia or bruising. He's been in good health throughout his incarceration, as far as I can tell. Maybe your machine's broken."

"No, we verified the results manually. Look, we saw something in his blood, some type of highly adapted T-cell, and—"

"Forgive me for being blunt here, Dr. Donaldson, but in your opinion, does he pose any risk to the prison population?"

"None. Whatever he has isn't infectious."

"That's really all I wanted to know, Doctor. Thank you."

His comment had a condescending air of closure.

"Look, Dr. Finlay, I'm heading up the cancer research center over here, and I think your patient might be producing a cytokine that could be very important to us."

"Well, I wish I could help."

His words conveyed disappointment, but there was almost a perverse pleasure in his voice. Was he bitter enough with his dismal posting, his lot in life, to actively hamper cancer research?

"All I'm asking for is permission to examine your patient myself, and conduct some further tests."

Finlay laughed. "You can forget about that, I'm afraid."

Laura tried to keep the anger out of her voice. "What do you mean?"

"He won't consent."

"I don't understand."

"Listen, Dr. Donaldson. His name's David Haines, and he's slated for execution in ten days.

CHAPTER FIVE

The tinted windows of the boardroom overlooked a swath of Forest Preserve and a slow curve of the Chicago River as it passed through Morton Grove. Laura had admired the view on previous visits to the MetaSYS headquarters, but not now. Today, all her attention was focused on Adrian Crawford as he watched the video footage for the second time, his patrician features giving nothing away.

Tanned, he exuded good health, and, unlike most of his heftier contemporaries, he was still trim enough to look dashing in his double-breasted suit. At fifty-one, Adrian's curly, close-cropped hair was shot through with white, and though his wrinkles were few, they seemed to enhance rather than diminish his considerable appeal. Lifting her gaze back to the screen, she wished she didn't still feel attracted to him.

You've got to be impressed by this, Adrian. You need this. And so do I. It was the tenth time she'd watched the tape, and every time she saw those T-cells annihilating the malignancy, she thought: *Sandra.*

After her conversation with Finlay at the prison, she'd called Adrian and told him everything about the blood sample—everything except the identity of the donor. She didn't want that getting in the way up front. She wanted to hook him on the idea of the blood before she let it slip.

She glanced over at Paul Rapke, sitting across from Adrian at the head of the long black table. Paul was chief legal counsel for MetaSYS, and Adrian had asked him to sit in on the meeting. Laura had met him a few times before and never taken to him. She wasn't sure if it was his vague Ivy League smarminess and pontificating Boston drawl, or his hair. It was unseemly, a forty-five-year-old with a luxurious blond thatch that he tended to brush absently off his forehead, as if to say, "Oh, by the way, look at all my hair." Right now his eyes, too, were fixed on the monitor.

The videotape ended, and static briefly rattled the television before she switched it off. Silence engulfed the boardroom. She glanced out the window, at the treeline, the hazy sky, and remembered to breathe. She wasn't about to let Haines's blood slip away, and she needed Adrian to flex his corporate muscle to get it for her. But after her recent catastrophe, why should he listen to her? She'd be lucky if he didn't fire her here and now. She also knew that this videotape might be her lifeline to her position at the lab. Still, she had one hell of a sales job ahead of her.

"What do you think, Adrian?" she asked.

"Impressive," he said, "very impressive." But his brow was furrowed, and she could tell he was distracted. "Look, any clue yet about what happened with Gillian Shamas?"

A weary sigh escaped her lips. "We're working on it. All I know is my TNF-12 gene must have triggered an oncogene, maybe spliced at the wrong locus, and set off accelerated tumor growth. We'll know more after we start breaking down those hepatomas and checking out their RNA."

"I know how hard you worked on this, Laura, what it meant to you personally. I'm sorry."

She almost wished his eyes weren't so sympathetic. She didn't want his sympathy, didn't want to be reminded of tenderness and deeper intimacies she could no longer have. It was hard enough sleeping with your boss, harder still once you'd *stopped* sleeping with him. Fortunately, she didn't often have reason to meet with him, except in boardroom settings like this. Right now she wanted to keep things purely corporate. But maybe his kindness *was* corporate, she thought, with a jolt of alarm. She didn't want Adrian feeling *too* concerned about her, thinking she was somehow unable to carry on after such a defeat. Or, oh Jesus, was this sympathy in *advance?* Preparing her for more bad news?

"I take it you've already spoken with Gillian," Adrian said.

"I offered her a new chemo treatment; it's had fair success slowing tumor growth. She said no. She's had enough."

"She'll die, then."

Laura took a breath. "With or without treatment, yes. I'd be surprised if she lived through the fall. We're taking care of her. She won't be in pain. I think she'd like to get home as soon as possible."

Adrian scratched an eyebrow and took a deep breath. "Tom Powell called me this morning. ABC's airing the story in two weeks. I'm trying to anticipate the effect on our stock price. Somewhere between severe and disastrous, I'd say."

Laura said nothing for a moment, unable to repress a twinge of irritation. She knew Adrian's company would suffer, but all along she'd cautioned him about leaking the protocol to the media, and he'd charged ahead anyway. Certainly if he hadn't ignored her, they could have avoided such a public airing of their failure. *Her* failure.

"I know, and I'm sorry. I wish I could've delivered for you yesterday." She nodded at the television. "But this might help."

Adrian glanced back to the blank screen. "Yes, that was quite a show."

She could hear the reticence in his voice. "Have you ever seen anything like that?"

"Look, Laura, I know what you're thinking, but we both know magic bullets are few and far between, and usually very expensive—"

"If I can get more blood, I can take those T-cells apart. The receptor sites are more sensitive than anything I've seen, even the ones we just engineered. And then I need to know what kind of cytokines the T-cells are producing. It might be a more powerful variation of TNF-12, I don't know. But judging from this, it's very, very potent."

Adrian was nodding politely, but she knew he was far from won over. "Laura, I hired you because I thought you were the best, and I still do—"

She felt her stomach plunge. "Jesus, Adrian, this sounds like a very depressing preamble."

"Listen to me. The work you've done is incredible. But I've got to be honest with you: we haven't introduced a new product in eighteen months, and our R&D money is stretched. To the limit. If it were up to me, I'd write you checks from now till doomsday, but I've got restless shareholders and two thousand employees, and I don't enjoy laying people off."

"If this *is* a magic bullet," she said insistently, "you won't have to worry about that ever again."

Adrian sighed. "James Hagen's had a breakthrough."

Laura felt the air rush from her lungs. For the past year, Hagen had been working at the MetaSYS research center in Stanford on an

Alzheimer's vaccine. She took a ragged breath, feeling queasy. "Well, that's great," she said.

"I'm in a bind, Laura. I can't back everybody at once. Hagen's gotten FDA for animal trials, and I'm wondering if we need to make a big push on this one."

He met her gaze evenly, unapologetically. This was business, it had nothing to do with their past. Never had she expected preferential treatment from him, and she'd have been disappointed if she'd got it. During their affair he'd been, if anything, *more* critical of her work, her progress. She didn't want a favor from him, especially not now, but she *did* want him to see how important this was—and she was delivering it to him on a platter. She couldn't lose this; she needed it for herself, for Sandra.

"Of course you should back Hagen," she said carefully. "But we'd be crazy if we passed on this one. You saw what happened to those tumor cells, Adrian. They were *devoured*. If I can isolate the agent that did that, and decode it, we might be able to genetically engineer it."

Adrian shook his head in frustration. "Even if you could, that hardly solves your problem. Okay, let's say this special cytokine does turn out to be a potent killer. Great. But how do we deliver it without a repeat of yesterday?"

"There are other options," she said. "Maybe we don't even need to synthesize the cytokine. Maybe this guy's T-cells are the ideal machinery. They home in on cancer cells, lock, and produce the cytokines naturally."

"You think you can grow enough of them to treat someone?"

Laura hesitated. T-cells were notoriously difficult to grow, even in culture. And you needed millions just to treat a single patient.

"Maybe," she said quickly. "But we may not even need any of that. There's a chance that his T-cells might be producing some variation of PML ..." She was postulating even as she spoke, riding on adrenaline. PML was a protein that some researchers thought enabled the body to recognize and attack cancers by attaching a peptide molecule to the surface of the actual cancer cells. Once that marker was in place, the body's immune system could mobilize effectively. The problem was, cancer seemed to be able to shut down the production of PML. If you could figure out how to switch it back on, that might be all you needed to affect a cure.

"Maybe this guy carries the master switch," she told Adrian. "And that's why he can massacre tumors like we just saw. Either way, I need more blood to even get to first base with this." She could feel her need gnawing at her like an early-morning ulcer. "Come on, Adrian, you've done clinical research. You know there's no easy path. For every success there are a hundred failures."

"Shareholders aren't as patient. In this industry we've got long-term R&D and short-term stockholder patience. It's a bad marriage. They see a failure, they start looking at Glaxo Wellcome and thinking, 'Hmmm, maybe they're a safer bet.'"

She could see him silently weighing his corporate options. Just as, six months ago, he'd weighed his personal options, and decided on Helen and the kids over her. Didn't want to wreck his family, he'd told her sorrowfully; didn't want to repeat the sins of his own father. They'd have to end it; he couldn't marry her. But it was Adrian who had brought up the idea of marriage in the first place, not her.

"You're right," she told him now, "I can't promise anything, but I just don't think we should let this one slip by. And if you won't back me on this, I won't give up until I find someone who will."

She saw Adrian's eyes widen at this, and as he held her gaze, felt her bravado start to disintegrate. Shouldn't have phrased it that way, a not-so-subtle ultimatum. Leave MetaSYS, and after yesterday, was there any guarantee she'd land another good position? Not as good as this one. Stupid, Laura, very stupid. She watched Adrian's eyes, waiting for them to harden, but instead they turned to Paul.

"Paul, is this something we could own?" he asked.

Laura watched Paul as he released a measured sigh, tips of his fingers grazing his lips, head cocked to one side, making the most of his performance. *Give me a break*, she hissed inwardly, wanting to take a pair of clippers to his head.

"I think ..." Paul began to say, eyes fixed on the blank screen, and then trailed off, looking at her for a moment. "I think yes. Especially if we're dealing with mutant genes and cell lines arising from it. I'd say we could make a pretty airtight patent application. That way we have ownership of the T-cells, the cytokines they produce, and the source genes themselves. We can lock it up."

Laura found herself smiling at Paul. Not such a bad guy after all, if he'd just lose the hair. She turned back to Adrian, grudgingly admiring his shoulders as he stood up, hands jammed into his pockets.

51

She hadn't set out to have an affair with a married man. At first she'd even turned down his dinner invitations, tried (sure, half-heartedly) to avoid him at various corporate functions. But he'd been insistent, and was she really expected to pass up a man she found so attractive? She was almost forty, and men like Adrian came along more rarely with every year. She hadn't liked doing it; she'd known it was selfish. And she'd paid for it in the end, the same way women always seemed to pay for it.

She watched Adrian now as he walked to the window, waiting impatiently for his latest verdict.

"Well," he said, "I don't suppose it would hurt to ask this gentleman for more of his blood."

Relief crashed through her. "And a bone marrow sample, too. If I can get a good batch of stem cells, I can try to generate more T-cells for research."

"So, who's the billion-dollar man?"

Adrian turned to look at her, eyes compressed into the smile she'd once loved so much, but she felt her stomach give an unpleasant turn. Oh God, maybe it had been a mistake holding back on this one. Should've been honest up front. But it had worked, she *had* them, and now she just had to *keep* them.

"It's David Haines."

It was a common enough name, and for a moment, Adrian waited expectantly for more details. Then a look of disbelief jolted across his face.

"No," he muttered, "not the religious nut?"

Laura nodded. "And he's got less than two weeks."

During Haines's three-year killing spree, she had luckily been out of the country, working at Sunnybrook Hospital in Toronto. But there, like everywhere else on the planet, it had been impossible to miss the coverage. Normally she made a point of ignoring such sensational stories—there seemed to be a new one every month—but Haines's choice of targets had been horrifically close to home. She'd known several of his victims, not well, but had met them at symposiums, shared information via e-mail. They were her colleagues, and they'd been ruthlessly slaughtered.

"The irony's pretty hard to miss," Laura said. "A man who hates medical science, and he might be a walking cure for cancer."

"Oh, Jesus," said Adrian. "You might have told me this earlier, Laura."

Yeah, surprises suck, don't they? Her eyes flicked to Paul, expecting to see his mouth turned down in sour disapproval. *Get ready for a lecture on medical ethics.* Instead, she saw something approaching excitement in his eyes. Maybe this was a challenge that appealed to him.

"How did they get this sample?" he asked her.

"The prison doctor was screening for tuberculosis and hepatitis B. Apparently, it took four guards to hold him down."

"Why can't we do the same?" Adrian said.

"That would've been a public health matter," Paul answered. "Theoretically, the prison was within its rights to do that. But for the kind of tests we're wanting, we'll need his consent."

"Finlay says he won't give it," Laura said.

"It's grotesque," said Adrian disdainfully. "The man's a serial killer. If they can take his life, surely we can take some of his blood beforehand."

"I know, but it doesn't work that way," said Paul. "He's deprived of his freedom, yes, and in this case, ultimately, his life. Other than that, he has the same rights as you or me, so long as he poses no security or public health risk to the prison. It's an interesting scenario, very interesting ...."

Laura knew Paul was right. It was something every med student learned in first-year ethics. You cannot force someone to give blood or submit to medical tests against his will, even if he is at risk of death— even if he carries a potential cancer cure in his veins. It would be a violation of his constitutionally safeguarded rights.

"Can't we just wait until he's dead?" Adrian asked.

Laura shook her head. "Technically we'd still need his approval. Anyway, it'd be far from ideal. By the time he's declared dead, his blood's starved of oxygen and shot up with curare and potassium cyanide. Best case scenario, we get a little usable blood, but not enough. And we certainly can't go back for seconds if we need to. We need him alive."

"Any chance it's hereditary?" Adrian wanted to know.

"A small one. I've already thought of that. I'll get someone to run his genealogy."

"He has a brother for sure," said Paul. "What was his name?... Rick. He gave evidence to the FBI, remember?"

"But I think we need to work both ends," Laura insisted. "Tracing a relative might take weeks, and by then we've lost Haines, and he's the only sure thing we've got. We need *his* blood."

"Laura, I just don't see how you're going to get his signature on the dotted line," Adrian said. "He murdered doctors; he's not about to give them his own blood for research." He exhaled impatiently. "I'm sorry, but I don't see how we can pursue this."

"Well, I had an idea," she said hurriedly. She could see Adrian's determination was already flagging and didn't want to risk losing it altogether. "We make Haines an offer."

"What are you going to offer him? Money? He's got a few days left on earth. And as I recall, he wasn't an acquisitive type."

"I know, I know," she said. It was an idea she'd developed in desperation, and it was still half formed, maybe even laughable. But it was all she had to convince Adrian.

"Life," she said. "We can offer him more life."

"A little beyond our power, don't you think?" said Adrian, amused.

"If Haines agrees to give blood," she said, "why can't we petition Governor Klein for a temporary stay of execution?" She didn't risk looking at Adrian or Paul, fearful that any expression of incredulity would throw her off. "Now, even if he agrees, that only gives us thirty days, but it's enough time to go back to the board, whatever that board is ..."

"State board of pardon and paroles," Paul said, and she saw he was nodding almost imperceptibly, as though thinking through a very intriguing problem.

"Right, we go to them, and can't we apply for clemency so Haines can be made available for further testing? As long as Governor Klein's onside, I think we've got a shot. We sell Haines as an invaluable natural resource. A potential cancer cure. Giving something back to society. Repaying debts, blah blah blah. All that stuff."

In the ensuing quiet, Adrian stared at her a moment, mute, then turned to Paul, forehead creased. "Paul, is this real?"

"I think ... I think it's not a route we should rule out."

"You mean it's worth a try," Laura prompted him.

"It hinges, of course, on getting Haines's approval beforehand."

"This is Haines's last chance, though," Laura said. "It was on the news a couple of nights ago."

"True." Paul ran a hand through his ample hair. "He just lost his final appeal to get his sentence commuted. His lawyer's Vic Greene, I went to school with him. Big civil rights advocate, been fighting the death penalty most of his career." At this, Paul smiled. "Now, he doesn't want Haines to die any more than we do. I bet he'll work with us on this one."

"Will he share costs though?" Adrian said. "Jesus, Paul, this sounds like it could turn into a lawyer's orgy."

"Governor Klein's a big supporter of medical research." Laura had met him just last month at a fundraiser for the University of Chicago Medical Center. "He'll back us, I know it. What a coup for him if a breakthrough cancer treatment were found in Illinois."

Adrian sighed. "But will Haines go for it? What about his religious beliefs?"

"If we're talking about saving your own life," Laura said, "I'm willing to bet even fanatics can be a little flexible."

"I must be out of my mind," said Adrian. "All right, let's do it. But I want this thing capped, Paul. We're hemorrhaging money as it is."

Paul nodded. "I'll make a proposal to his lawyer first thing tomorrow."

*   *   *

"No."

Through the scarred plexiglass shield, David could see the dismay on Vic Greene's face.

"Did you really expect any different?" he asked his lawyer. David was disappointed in him. He knew Vic was a practising Catholic, and even though his church was a miserably failed shadow of God's true design, it had given him an illusion of solidarity with his lawyer. Now he could see he'd simply been indulging himself.

"Why would I whore my blood to them?" he said, trying to keep the anger from his voice. "The very people who have contempt for God's sovereignty on earth?"

"They're offering you a chance at more life." Vic's voice was tinny through the telephone, something remote and unimportant. "They'll make a joint application, with us, to the Governor for a temporary stay, and then apply to have your sentence commuted to life without parole."

David tried to marshal his thoughts. He took a deep breath to slow his racing heart.

"They said it was an enzyme?"

"Yes, or ... something about T-cells, too. I'm sorry. I didn't take down the specifics."

David could see Vic was struggling with the terminology. "A cytokine produced by my T-cells?" he suggested quietly.

"Yes, I think that's what he said."

"And they saw it destroying a tumor in my bloodstream."

Vic nodded.

"I see."

At first, when Vic had told him about the blood, he'd thought it was some horrible joke engineered by Dr. Finlay to mock him. The very idea was ludicrous—that *his* blood was riddled with cancer. But as Vic had continued, he could see it was in earnest. How could this be?

He had never viewed science and religion as mutually exclusive; he knew that science was merely God's handmaiden, just another tool at His disposal. All his training in science had not been lost or forgotten once he'd found God, only turned to a greater purpose. In his prison cell he'd honed his knowledge of the human body further. He knew that every single molecular action was the work of God; every time a strand of DNA was incorrectly translated, giving rise to a tumorous cell, or a rogue enzyme, that was God. Scientists had tried to explain it away, foil it, but God always found a way around their feeble attempts. He was not willing to be disobeyed.

He smiled ruefully at Vic.

"It's to tempt me," he said.

"What is, David?"

"My blood."

He'd felt it even as Vic outlined the MetaSYS offer. A chance at life. Over the past two months, he'd sometimes woken suddenly in the night, thrashing himself clear of his nightmares—needles in his veins, a suffocating fist closing around his heart. Sometimes, in the morning, his bowels would liquefy without warning and he'd hunch, shivering, on the toilet, waiting for the wave of panic to pass. His body, he knew, was crying out in despair at its impending demise. Spirit willing, flesh weak.

"I've been proud," he confessed to Vic through the shield. "I thought I could easily forsake life. But now that it's offered back to me ... how sinfully I cling to it."

"It's natural, David."

"Natural does not mean right."

"No, it doesn't."

"The soul is in the blood, and it is not what goes into a man but what comes out of him that condemns him. And if I let them take the blood from my body, then I condemn myself. Because if what's inside me truly is a cure, then it's an unholy one."

He saw Vic look away awkwardly, embarrassed, no doubt. He'd grown so used to these looks that he was almost disquieted when his teachings and beliefs were greeted with anything less than contempt. It had almost become, for him, a testament to their veracity. They flew in the face of all the world's assumed wisdom and knowledge. But only those who hate the world will gain everlasting life.

And he knew instantly what he must do.

If his body contained a cure, he must deny it to the world, at all costs. He felt himself regain control over his heart, his breathing. Serenity returned to his mind. He would defy them all. That would be his last and triumphant good work for God.

"Time's up," said the guard at the door.

"David, listen to me. If you don't sign, they might try to force you anyway. And you'll die in nine days all the same. I know what they can do. They'll try to get your blood whether you sign or not. Give yourself a shot at life. Sign, please."

"Because of what's in my blood, or because you want me to live?"

"Both."

He felt so sorry for Vic. He saw in him the seeds of a truly God-fearing man, but so deluded by sin.

"If they try to force me, will you fight for me?"

Vic hesitated for a moment. "I'm your attorney, David. My job is to protect your rights. Certainly I'd fight."

"Thank you. For all you've done for me."

David hung up the phone, stood, and walked to the waiting guard. He hoped he would never have to see Vic again, sitting there on the other side of the glass, imprisoned by the world.

CHAPTER SIX

J udge Homer Lillard reached for the huge plastic cup beside him and took another long drink. "If I don't pass these little bastards by tonight, they say they'll do surgery. And I'd really rather skip that."

Kevin had appeared before judges countless times, but never one who was being treated for kidney stones. In his private room at Detroit's Henry Ford Hospital, Lillard was robed in a terrycloth dressing gown, feet slippered, his ample body slumped in an armchair near the window. Peering through his bifocals at Kevin's application, his fleshy face suddenly contracted, eyes clamped into pained slits. After a second he carefully let out his breath and relaxed.

"All right?" Kevin asked.

"You know, I had a heart attack a few years back, and it was nothing on this."

Kevin winced in sympathy. "They've got you on something, don't they?"

"Hell yes. It makes it bearable, just. So let's recap. You want a surreptitious entry and search, and all you're showing me is a man who had a nosebleed and wiped it up."

Kevin sighed inwardly. He'd spent his last two days in Detroit fighting. He'd fought Miceli to get on the case, and lost. Over the phone he'd fought Hugh Carter back in Chicago to okay a parallel investigation into Banji's murder—and won, just. He could guess what his boss thought of him. Obsessed. Trying to claw his way back to the glory days. Deluding himself. But in the end Hugh had agreed to liaise with the Detroit field office and try to get him some help. He was giving him three days. If he hadn't turned up anything on Will Andrews by then, Kevin would have to come home to the small mountain of uninspiring files on his desk. Probably Hugh had agreed just to shut him up, sensing that he wasn't about to get off the phone, or return to Chicago, until he'd got what he wanted. *Humoring me,* Kevin thought. *With a touch of pity thrown in?*

And now he was trying to convince a federal judge to give him a warrant to search Andrews's apartment. Charles Richter, the Special Agent in Charge of the Detroit office, had told him to go to Lillard. It seemed that Richter was in line for a favor, and he was willing to use it up on Kevin. As far as Kevin was concerned, a favor was about the only way he was going to get this warrant. But, of course, as luck would have it, Lillard was in hospital with miniature stalactites lodged in his urinary tract. Kevin didn't want to risk taking his application to another, less accommodating, judge. But he was beginning to worry that Lillard's pain would push him into an impatient denial rather than consent.

"You know," said Lillard, with a smile that wasn't altogether kindly, "I'm getting the feeling the boys in the Detroit office have me marked as an easy lay. Now look, Agent Sheldrake, I appreciate what you're saying about the blood and how Andrews wiped it up, but you're extrapolating his religious views from that, and that's not hard evidence."

"No, but it gives me reasonable suspicion, given the nature of the crime. And Andrews's close connection with it."

Kevin watched the judge for a reaction. He should have just broken into Andrews's apartment himself. It couldn't be harder than this. Yesterday he'd followed Andrews as he'd left his shift at the parking garage, home to a dumpy apartment block on the east side. He'd seen his name on the directory, noted the inadequate security. Wouldn't have been difficult to break in, but he didn't have much experience with that, and he'd surely leave traces. Worst of all, he knew that if he did find anything, it would be inadmissible in court without a warrant.

"You haven't even questioned Mr. Andrews yet?"

Kevin tried to control his impatience. "Because if he is guilty, he'll start hiding things. Things I might find in his apartment."

"Such as?"

"The murder weapon—which, I might add, Captain Miceli has yet to produce. Correspondence, diaries, books with words blacked out, human body parts in numbered jars—I really don't know, Your Honor, until I look, and that's all I want to do. Look. I don't want wiretaps or bugs or cameras, and if I find nothing, case closed, I go back to Chicago."

"You know you're talking about a gross infringement of privacy. And you're giving me precious little to go on here—other than your reputation, which, I'm aware, is considerable in these matters."

"I know it looks weak on paper, I know that. But to me, all the evidence was in Andrews's face when he saw his blood on the floor. I knew that look. I knew what it meant. Andrews could very well be the killer, and I don't want to see another headline in the papers a month from now."

Lillard winced again, exhaled. "Okay, look, give me a half hour to think about this." He rose to his feet tentatively. "Now, if you'll excuse me, I'm going to have a good long piss and hope something comes out."

"Thank you, Judge."

He took the elevator down to the main floor, eager to escape the hospital's smell and sterility, but the heat that hit him on the other side of the revolving door changed his mind. He found his way back to a lounge where a few dressing-gowned patients listlessly watched daytime television, a sight he found extremely depressing.

He went to the bathroom and took a leak, trying not to think of Lillard doing the same upstairs. He didn't hold out much hope for the warrant. He hadn't told the judge that he'd already put Will Andrews through every Justice Department database he could think of, including CultWatch, a system he'd helped set up ten years ago. No matches in any of them. Andrews came away clean. Still, he would not ignore his instincts.

Washing his hands, he made the mistake of glancing up into the mirror. Under the fluorsescents, his face was an interesting shade of yellow. He looked like he should be checking himself in. Why the hell would you do that to people in a hospital? They didn't feel lousy enough without making their flesh look like it was in a state of early mummification? With a grimace, he drew a hand through his hair, testing the two receding scoops at his temples. His hair was about the only thing he liked about his hangdog face, and he wanted to keep it glued to his scalp. It was good hair, dark and thick and wavy where it was still stubbornly holding on. He'd started avoiding going to the hairdresser, fearful that with every visit his hairline would be shown to have retreated even more. He would not make a good bald man: his face was too long, too narrow; and he was too thin.

Back in the television lounge, he tried to shrug away the tension in his shoulders. Dragging out his cellular he called his machine for messages. There was just one, from Rebecca, asking him what time he'd be picking her up Friday. Shit. He dialed his old home number from memory.

"Hello?" It was Diane.

"Hi. It's me. Kevin," he remembered to add. Even after two years it was automatic. *It's me.* As if there were still some part of himself unwilling to let go of this little privilege, this intimacy. "I just got Becky's message. Look, I'm in Detroit."

"Can't make it?"

"Probably not."

"I can't say I'm sorry, after that place you took her last weekend. All she talked about for three days was Vishnu."

"We visited a Hindu temple."

"You both meditated, she said."

"Yes."

"Jesus, Kevin, do you really think this is appropriate?"

"She liked it. Did she tell you she didn't?"

"That's not what I mean."

"Would you be happier if I took her to Sunday school and she did papier-mâché Noah's Arks?"

"I don't like you forcing ideas on her."

"I'm not *forcing* anything on her. I tell her about what different people believe and sometimes we visit different places." Over the past year he'd taken her to a synagogue, a Buddhist monastery, a mosque, a Taoist shrine, the Baha'i House of Worship, and various Christian churches. "I get her weekends, and this is sometimes part of what I do on weekends."

"Look," she said, "I know you're seeking, or whatever you call it, but leave our daughter out of it."

"Just tell the truth, Diane. You don't like her getting any exposure to religion, period."

"That's right, I don't. And when she was born, we agreed we wouldn't give her any religious instruction. Remember?"

"This isn't formal religious instruction. I'm showing her the choices."

"She's twelve, Kevin. She's not old enough to make choices."

"When she's ready."

"You're biasing her.

"Oh, and you're not? Never talking about religion isn't a bias? Please. She knows you think it's all garbage. Let's just say we even each other out, how's that?"

"Why would you want to encourage her to indulge in fantasy?"

"Just because I can't believe doesn't mean it's not true. And why would I want to deny Becky that?" He was surprised at the sudden passion in his voice, his heart racing. One of the patients in the lounge turned to stare at him. He lowered his voice. "Look, I really ... I can't have this conversation right now, all right?"

He stood up and started down the noisy corridor, where at least he wasn't disturbing anyone, and no one was listening in.

When Diane next spoke her voice seemed genuinely pained. "I still can't believe this is really you. Why didn't ... you should've kept going to Dr. Bale. We both know what happened to you after Haines."

He'd tried, so many times, to explain it to her, but she didn't understand, didn't want to. Depression at case end was common in the Bureau. And after a person like David Haines had inhabited your mind for three years, become as intimate as a schizophrenic's second voice, it was difficult to dislodge him. Kevin would have liked nothing better than to have sunk the memory of him like a weighted coffin in the ocean. But he couldn't escape the fact that Haines had unlocked something in him—the horrible truth of his own faithlessness.

Diane's voice was gentle. "You think you lost something. But what you had back in God's Children wasn't faith, Kevin."

For twenty years he'd written it off as a mistake. A communal farm on the San Juan Islands, emaciated on a diet of potatoes and rice, broken down by group coercion and lack of sleep, and love, and the glory of God. He was eighteen. He'd been brainwashed, duped, robbed of sixteen months of his life. And after returning to school, and joining the FBI, he'd taken special pleasure in discrediting cults that engaged in illegal activities. He was a proud atheist, and there was only the world, and he filled himself up with the world, his work, his family. But with every day he'd pursued Haines, his life had seemed more thin and insubstantial, a crippled replacement for what he truly craved.

"You're not going to find it," Diane said. "Because it isn't there."

"I'm not ready to call it a day yet."

He didn't blame her for leaving. She must have felt betrayed. He was no longer the man she had met and married. She'd stuck by him three years while he chased Haines, drifting away, and then when he'd finally finished, he'd come back a wraith who found no meaning or solace in her love. He'd broken her heart. But he felt powerless to heal her. And she could not help him, either. When she'd asked him for a divorce, he'd felt as though he was listening in on someone else's conversation.

"You know," Diane was saying now, "Becky goes along to these places because she wants to be with you."

For a moment, Kevin didn't trust himself to speak, so stung was he by the image of his pale, anxious daughter carefully humoring him, hungry for any time with him at all. He'd told her so many times they didn't have to go on these visits, but she'd always seemed genuinely interested. Maybe he was deluding himself. But he wasn't in any hurry to trust Diane's judgment. She was hardly disinterested.

"When she tells me herself, I'll stop."

"I'll tell you one thing, Kevin. I don't want her exposed to anything weird—"

"Diane, come on, of course I'm not going to—"

"—any kind of *cult* thing. Hare Krishnas, whatever. If I find out about it, I swear, I'll apply for a court order."

Anger flared through him, and before he could rein it in, words were rushing from his mouth. "You try to keep me from my daughter, Diane, I swear to God you'll regret it. You can't take her away from me, and no fucking judge in this country would let you. Don't ever threaten me like that again."

She hung up on him.

Still throbbing with anger, he went back to the lounge and got an orange juice from a machine, waiting for his heart to calm. Time to go hear Lillard's verdict. May as well get some more bad news since it was coming thick and fast.

Upstairs, he was greeted by a pale but beaming Lillard.

"Damn near killed me, but I think I just pissed myself out of surgery."

He handed Kevin back his search warrant. It was signed.

CHAPTER SEVEN

The lounge on the fourteenth floor of the U.S. District Court looked west over South Dearborn. Waiting for Paul Rapke, Laura stared out across the plaza, trying to distract herself: to the left, the black latticework of the twin federal building; on the right, the splendid colonnaded roofline of the Marquette Block; and straight ahead, above an almost unbroken edifice of imposing honeyed-stone office blocks, rose the gaunt head of the Sears Tower, scraping the underside of Chicago's leaden sky. From the air-conditioning grille at her feet came the urgent hiss of frigid air. She touched the warm glass with her fingertips.

She was going to court.

After Haines had refused their offer, she'd felt almost unhinged with despair. But Adrian had suggested applying for a court order to compel Haines to give blood. Paul was dubious, but it turned out one of Adrian's golfing partners was Superior Court Judge Sam Garrity, and Adrian was sure that if they could get Garrity—and Paul had timed their application to coincide with his chambers duty this morning—the court order was in the bag.

Thank God for men playing golf, she thought. She could see little appealing about such a ridiculous game. Doubtless it was highly symbolic in Freudian terms, a metaphor for domineering male sexual aggression, popping all those little white testicles around the green. But men seemed to enjoy it, and when they played golf together, they were more likely to do business together. Hell, she wouldn't scoff if it got her the blood.

She checked her watch. Paul was late, and their chambers hearing was in just fifteen minutes. She willed her stomach to unclench. She hadn't had much sleep—hardly unusual with the phenmetrizine coursing through her. But in the early hours of the morning, she'd been unable to stop thinking about Sandra, and the conversation she'd had with her father the night before.

He'd called her from Maine. Should have been the other way around, but she'd been so busy, and she'd been waiting, hoping she could tell them she got David Haines's blood. And there was another reason she hadn't called: her habitual fear that she'd find her sister suddenly much, much worse.

"How's Maine?" she asked her father.

"Oh, they've got a wonderful place here, right near the water, you can see it from the deck. Five minutes and you're down on the beach. The weather's been good, and the kids really are loving it."

But she detected an uncharacteristic lack of enthusiasm in her father's voice, which set her on edge.

"Everything all right?" she asked. *Sandra.*

"Well, your sister's going back to Tijuana."

"What's wrong?"

"She was due to go back for follow-up in October, you remember, but she hasn't been feeling altogether well—"

"What does that mean, not well?"

Her father cleared his throat and his voice softened, as if worried someone might hear him. "I think she's lost a fair amount of weight, and she's been vomiting at night. She's tired out."

"Dad, you've got to tell her not to go back to that clinic. She won't hear it from me, but she might listen to you if you're insistent. That place is not helping her. Isn't this proof enough?"

"She says Dr. Wendt told her to expect another phase like this, and that she'd need to come back for follow-up treatment anyway."

"Yeah, at six grand a week, why not?" Laura said angrily. "You'll talk to her, won't you?"

There was an awkward pause. "I was wondering about that woman you used in your last tests, Gillian Shamas?"

Laura flinched, wishing somehow that this moment would never come, when she'd have to admit her failure to him, to Sandra. Now she listened to the expectant silence on the other end of the phone. She knew what he was hoping.

"Dad," she sighed, "it didn't work. It made her worse."

"Worse? But she was getting better, wasn't she?"

"That's what I thought. I was wrong." She didn't want to get into the details; he wouldn't understand them anyway, and she felt suddenly extremely weary. "I'm sorry, Dad, but ... who knows, Sandra might've said no to it anyway. Mike's got her hypnotized with this alternative crap."

"I'm sorry." Laura wondered whether her father was sorry at all for her professional failure, or just for Sandra. "It seems like Dr. Wendt's her best bet, then."

"No, Dad, she's not."

"She won't do anymore chemo, Laura. She says it made her too ill and wasted too much time, and she can't face it again. You weren't down there, but she started looking and feeling so much better when we were in Mexico last time."

"Do you think if I talk to her—?" Laura wanted to know.

"Best to leave it, probably. She seems in good spirits about going back to the clinic. I'm going to be going down with them."

"When?"

"Tomorrow, we're leaving direct from here."

"Let me talk to her, Dad."

"She's still down at the beach. I didn't tell her I was calling. I just ... wanted to know about that therapy of yours."

"Look, there's a chance that—" She was about to tell him about David Haines's blood, but stopped herself in time. No more raised hopes and disappointments. *Wait until you know, one way or another.* She drew a slow, small breath into her lungs. "I've got the number of the clinic. I'll call Sandra in a few days when she's settled in."

"Good. Thank you," said her father. "I'll talk to you later, then."

"Bye, Dad."

After hanging up, she'd stood with her fingers still resting numbly on the handset, feeling sick to her stomach, and hoping that Adrian was right about the court order.

* * *

Paul Rapke's reflection shimmered in the lounge window as he approached from behind.

"We're in trouble," he said quietly, one hand sliding through his bangs.

"What's wrong?"

66

"Garrity's mother died late yesterday and he's flown out to Ohio for the funeral."

"What does this mean for us?" she asked warily.

"It means Judge Augustine Helms is filling in. And we're probably going to walk out of here with nothing but a kick in the ass. She's African-American, big on convicts' rights. We're fucked."

Laura couldn't believe it, the Ivy League smarminess was sloughing off him like snakeskin. His mouth looked distinctly queasy. She wondered how much courtroom work he'd done.

"We'll convince her. We've got to."

They only had seven days, Laura knew, before Haines was slated for lethal injection. They couldn't afford to screw up now. Late yesterday the genealogist she'd hired to trace Haines had faxed in her report. Bad news: Haines's parents had died five years ago in a car accident, and they were both only children. No aunts or uncles for David, no cousins who might have the same genetic make-up. David and his brother Rick were the end of the line.

But no one even knew where the hell Rick was. After the trial, he'd disappeared to avoid the media frenzy, and rumor was he'd moved out west, maybe even changed his name. The genealogist had suggested an Internet research service, which, for seven hundred dollars, would find him. Laura had filled in the form and sent it off but knew she might have to wait up to three days to get results. Even if they did track Rick down, chances were he wouldn't have the same immune system. Too rare. And by then, David might already be dead. They had to get his blood, now.

Paul's face was taut. He met her eyes briefly, then glanced away. "Look, you know what we're up against. Our argument's weak. There's really no good legal precedent for what we're asking. Garrity was probably our only chance at getting this thing."

"Don't tell me this, Paul." She needed him strong. She needed him to go into the judge's chambers and give the oration of his career. "You'll do it," she said with a confident nod. But her heart was pounding down the seconds to their hearing.

* * *

"Mr. Rapke," said Judge Helms, glancing up from the documents to fix Paul with an imperious stare, "I see that you gave Mr. Greene only twenty-four hours notice for this motion."

"Yes, Your Honor. I apologize for the inconvenience, but given the circumstances, I felt the application concerned an emergency in the public interest."

Augustine Helms raised her eyebrows dubiously. "I look forward to being convinced."

Laura had seldom seen a more ferociously elegant woman. She was dressed in a dark silk blouse, her graying hair pulled back and fastened with a simple silver clip. Her eyes gave the impression of having seen it all; she'd dealt with every manner of legal bullshit under the sun and bludgeoned a generation of lawyers into submission with those daunting eyes.

Laura had logged hundreds of hours in sterile operating theaters performing life-saving surgery, but sitting in a wing-backed chair in Judge Helms's gracious chambers made her acutely nervous. At least in the OR she had her instruments, she could go to work, make things happen. Here she was a helpless voyeur. The office was warmly furnished like a home study, one entire wall lined with bookcases, armchairs arranged around a large oak desk. Curtains, not blinds, were drawn back from her window, allowing a pleasing view of art deco stone across the street. Playing softly over hidden speakers came Handel's *Water Music*. On the walls hung a collection of African tribal masks, as well as a number of impressionistic vignettes of African-American street life. The mood seemed intended to invite calm and friendly discussion, but Laura knew what awaited them would be anything but soothing.

Judging from her unblinking gaze, Helms was not terribly impressed by Laura's presence, but she had grunted consent earlier when Paul insisted she was a crucial component of his application. For his part, Vic Greene had looked comprehensively pissed off from the moment he'd entered chambers—no doubt, Laura knew, because he'd had less than a day to prepare his position. She felt a flicker of sympathy for him, but quickly suffocated it. All's fair in love and war, and this was a war she'd been waging all her professional life. She wasn't about to give up. She looked at Paul now, desperately hoping he'd pulled himself together.

"Your Honor," he began, "as you know, David Haines is a ward of the state, and slated for execution in seven days. We've discovered that his blood contains an agent that might be instrumental in developing a cure for cancer. Dr. Donaldson has prepared an affidavit outlining the importance of this find, which you have before you, and I wanted her present to be able to answer any of your medical questions first-hand. Now, we've already tried to gain the subject's permission to give us blood samples voluntarily, and he's refused, despite an extremely generous offer we've conveyed via Mr. Greene. We believe the necessity to extract his blood constitutes a public health emergency, and is for the greater good and safety of all the state, and the nation."

Good, Laura thought, *that was pretty good*. She winced as her foot suddenly cramped, and realized how tightly she'd been holding her body. She exhaled slowly, bending her toes up, waiting for her muscles to unclench.

Greene was already replying. "Needless to say, I think this entire application is an outrage, Your Honor. These tests would grossly infringe my client's first amendment rights, and his religious beliefs. If David Haines were anything other than a death row felon, I don't believe MetaSYS would have the temerity to pursue such an order. My client has exercised his constitutional right to make a choice. It's unethical and illegal to take blood against a person's wishes. This is simply a case of oppressing the weak and marginalized."

Laura's eyes drifted anxiously across the artwork on Helms's wall, fixing on an historical etching of slaves being lead off a ship in shackles. *Oh God*, she thought miserably, *are we ever in trouble*. Greene was pushing all the right buttons. She looked back at the judge, who was nodding almost imperceptibly as the lawyer continued.

"In my opinion, Your Honor," he was saying, "this shouldn't even be a chambers hearing. If there's any legal question it should be raised in a full hearing, not settled in some snap decision today."

Judge Helms gave a smile that could only be called icy. "Mr. Greene, I can assure you, my decisions may be quick, but they are certainly not irresponsible."

"What I meant is, this question is a large one that requires extraordinary consideration."

Helms grunted. "Mr. Rapke, you know the onus is on you to provide a relevant point of law to back your application."

Paul cleared his throat; he looked decidedly pasty, Laura thought with alarm. "Of course. And I cite the federal Emergency Health Measures statute of 1964, which was invoked two years ago during *Hurricane Debra*. You might recall there was fear of a cholera epidemic and the Centres for Disease Control used the statute to undertake mandatory blood and stool screening in individuals they considered at risk."

Laura watched Helms's face, trying to gauge her reaction to this. Adrian had told her that Paul had worked through the night in the law library, frantically trying to find some precedent for what they wanted to do to Haines. So this was as close as he'd come. It seemed reasonable enough, but all she got now from Helms was an inscrutable widening of her eyes.

And Greene could barely conceal his disdain.

"Please, that is not a precedent. The Emergency Health statute was intended to control an epidemic. My client has no infectious disease. He poses no risk to the public health whatsoever."

Laura could feel her heart pulsing hard through her body. *We're losing.* Trying to clamp down on the panic stirring within her, she looked at Paul. *Come on, Ivy League, get to work.*

"I disagree," Paul said. "Your Honor, Haines poses a public health risk by denying his blood for testing. If Haines does carry a cure, then I would argue he exposes all of us to the very substantial risk of cancer by withholding his blood."

Good, Laura thought. She could hear some of that confident Boston drawl coming back into his voice. But Greene barked laughter. "That's ridiculous. Cancer is not an epidemic."

"It's worse," said Laura, before she could stop herself. "It's an epidemic with no end in sight."

Greene sighed wearily. "I'm sorry, Your Honor, are we allowing Dr. Donaldson's unsolicited contributions here?"

"I apologize, Your Honor," she said. Stupid. Paul had told her ahead of time to keep her mouth shut unless addressed. Paul's face looked pained. But honestly, if he were kicking ass like he was supposed to here, she wouldn't have to do the talking ...

Helms looked at her, but she thought she caught a hint of indulgence in her eyes this time. "Well, since we have the unusual privilege of her presence, I'm willing to allow her opinion. Dr. Donaldson."

"What I wanted to ... make clear ... is that a classic epidemic runs its course. It's confined to a period of time. Cancer is a 24-hour, 365-day-a-year plague that hasn't shown any sign of abatement in the decades since we've monitored it. In fact, many types are on the increase. It kills millions every year. If this doesn't constitute an epidemic, what does?"

Judge Helms leaned back in her chair. "Dr. Donaldson, I must say, I'm somewhat surprised to see you backing this motion, when surely you know it violates medical ethics."

"Your Honor, I'm committed to finding a cure to this disease. And the only thing I consider unethical is cancer itself. It attacks anyone at any time. It doesn't respect civil rights, or gender, age, or race. It takes our parents, our siblings, our spouses; it takes our children."

"Well, that's very pretty grandstanding," said Greene, "but it doesn't have much bearing on the legality of the matter at hand."

"Granted," said Helms.

Laura fell silent, regretting her little performance. She'd gone too far, pandering to the audience like some bad TV lawyer. She glanced at Greene, saw a smile barely visible at the corners of his mouth. He knew she'd blown it.

Helms said, "You needn't worry, Dr. Donaldson, I'm well aware of what a destructive disease we're talking about. My father is currently fighting it."

Her heart skipped. "I'm very sorry to hear that."

"And I must say what worries me most is whether he's getting the best treatment. There seems no end of different opinions, different regimens. It's hard enough to find even one doctor to talk to, much less the best."

She met the judge's eyes and saw that she'd just been asked a favor. "I can understand your concern, Your Honor. What hospital is your father at?"

Vic Greene cut in hurriedly. "I believe this is a simple civil rights issue, Your Honor. But the other thing we haven't addressed is the highly conjectural nature of their medical evidence. They don't even know if my client carries a cure. Yet they're willing to infringe his rights just to satisfy their curiosity."

"Very true," said Helms. "How would you reply to that, Dr. Donaldson?"

"He's right. We don't know. But we'll never know if we don't take his blood. And from what I've already seen, I would consider that a very great tragedy. I've been in this field over fifteen years and this is the most promising evidence I've ever come across."

Helms turned her attention solemnly to the application before her. Laura glanced at Paul, but his stony face gave no clue as to his appraisal of their situation. Greene, she noted, was looking a little flustered.

"Two units of blood," remarked Helms, looking back at her. "Is that a lot?"

"That's a medically acceptable amount for one sitting."

"And a bone marrow harvest?"

"That's to secure what are called stem cells, Your Honor. So we can try to culture an eternal supply of his white cells for study."

"And these would be obtained under humane and safe conditions?"

A surge of hope went thought her like a shot of adrenalin. "Absolutely. I'd perform the procedure myself under hospital conditions."

She allowed her eyes to stray to Greene for a split second and could see the alarm spreading across his face.

"Your Honor," he said, "I would stress again that there is no powerful controlling authority for this application."

"I agree," said Helms. "However, given the circumstances, and the testimony I've heard, I'm not inclined to oppose it today. In this instance, I'm willing to weigh the interests of the community as more important than the interests of a condemned man. Dr. Donaldson, you'll have your blood."

CHAPTER EIGHT

The room was monastic.

Kevin hadn't really expected some gothic interior, mired in shadow and grime, walls papered with giant photos of Dr. Amit Banji with his eyes razored out. But he wasn't exactly prepared for the minimalism of Will Andrews's bachelor apartment either. From where he stood, just inside the doorway, he could see pretty much everything. A single bed, a chrome-sided table, and two vinyl-covered chairs. Along one wall was a kitchenette, the counter clean, no dirty dishes in the sink. Everything in order.

Just like the bunkhouses back on the farm, he thought, those long, converted chicken coops where he'd slept when he was with God's Children. Spare and scrupulously clean. No need for possessions. Keep your mind similarly uncluttered, and devote it to the contemplation of God.

As he pulled on his cotton gloves, Kevin filled his lungs, feeling feverish with the heat. The building wasn't air-conditioned, and the two windows, though partially opened, didn't help. Beside him stood Rafe Marquez, a young surveillance expert on loan from the Detroit office. Rafe had gotten them inside, flicking the door open like a bored locksmith. Around his waist hung a toolbelt bristling with equipment. Kevin could see his eyes already sweeping the room methodically, making an inventory for the search. It was 1:45 a.m.

On the way to the apartment, Kevin had swung past the parking garage to make sure Andrews was on duty. He didn't want any surprises. Now he looked over at Rafe and nodded: *Let's get to work.* Words weren't necessary. Kevin had gone over the procedure in the car and it was simple. Rafe's job was to check for hiding places, every inch of floor, wall, and ceiling, every piece of furniture. Not one goddamn inch unchecked.

On the surface of the kitchen table, in plain view, was a pad of writing paper. Kevin walked over to take a look. The pad was about half finished. So Andrews was a letter-writer. The top piece of paper was blank but bore a few faint indentations. With his gloved fingers, Kevin carefully peeled off the sheet and slid it into a Ziploc bag. He doubted the lab could do anything with it, but it was worth a try.

A letter-writer, but to whom? And did anyone ever write back? No family photos in sight. There was no desk, no filing cabinet. The closest thing to a bookshelf was an upended milk crate that served as a night table. Kevin stooped down. *What's our bedtime reading been lately?* One by one he pulled out three library books, all on the birds of North America. He flipped through them, checking for letters, scribbled notes in the margins. Nothing.

No books on religion or spirituality, no street pamphlets, nothing on natural medicine or prayer.

No Bible.

That troubled him most. Why wasn't there a Bible, at least? He looked over at Rafe, who was now on his hands and knees, checking the floor.

Kevin started on the small, beat-up chest of drawers. In his career he'd rarely had to perform searches like this, and he'd never much liked it. Once, searching a cult compound in New Mexico, he'd found a collection of jarred testicles, which the male members had had voluntarily removed, in preparation for their celestial journey to another star.

Andrews kept his drawers neat, socks balled, underwear folded. It fit with what Kevin had seen of his character, that compulsiveness, that fear of being soiled.

Kevin's whole body was filmed with sweat now. He finished with the drawers and moved on to the closet, the grooved doors buckling open. Andrews had few clothes, and only one other pair of shoes. Kevin patted everything down, then left the doors ajar for Rafe, who would check inside for false walls.

He paused for a moment, looking around the room. From the next apartment he heard the distant sound of a toilet flushing. At first he'd been encouraged by the pristine character of the apartment, but maybe he was wrong. No TV, no radio, no phone—it was unusual, but not unheard of. Few belongings, but so what? He had a low-paying job and didn't waste what little extra money he had. Hardly cause for indictment. He liked birds. He liked things tidy.

Shit. Maybe they were right, Miceli, Carter, Lillard. Maybe Andrews was just a parking attendant who got a nosebleed and wiped it up. Maybe he *was* obsessed—and he was just being indulged by the Bureau, on his way out to pasture in a desk job. The Haines case had blunted him.

He tried to shut out the nagging voice of self-doubt. His earlier conversation with Diane wasn't helping either, segments replaying unbidden in his head. He didn't actually think she'd try to bar him from Rebecca, but he hated the idea that she might try subtly to poison his daughter against him. Becky's solemn face floated into his thoughts.

He watched Rafe, finishing up with the linoleum floor tiles. Another shake of the head.

Angrily, Kevin walked to the kitchenette and opened the cupboards under the sink. Not a roach to be seen—probably a first in this building. A few pots and pans, scoured clean, cleaner than his ever were, goddamnit.

There was a loud thud against the door, and his heart leaped. His Glock was in his hand instantly. A key skittered around the lock. *Fuck, he's back.* He caught a glimpse of Rafe, his gun aimed at the door too, waiting.

A slurred voice carried through the wall, saying something unintelligible, but then it was moving away, and there were more thuds on other doors. Kevin heard a few shouted "Fuck offs" from angry tenants as the drunk continued down the corridor in search of his own apartment.

Kevin's hand was trembling. He holstered his gun. Maybe he should have requested a cover team, but he hadn't thought it would be necessary—and he didn't want to strain his welcome with the Detroit office. Stupid. He remembered the pictures of Banji's body, punctured with bullet holes. He looked at Rafe, who grinned back weakly.

Together, they finished off the kitchen, going through the dishes and the containers of food in the cupboards, pulling back the small range and fridge. Inside the freezer, Kevin probed a bag of peas and a carton of ice cream to make sure nothing was frozen within.

Nothing. Mattress and pillows. Light fixtures. Brickwork around the outside of the windows. Nothing.

Only the small bathroom was left.

The mirrored cabinet above the sink contained a toothbrush, a tube of toothpaste, a safety razor, but no medicine. No expired bottles of prescription drugs, not so much as a bottle of Tylenol or Tums. Kevin felt his pulse quicken. Interesting, but still nothing he could make a case on. So he didn't like painkillers or antacids. Maybe he never got sick. Just like Haines. Power of prayer was all you needed.

You're not crazy, he told himself. But he needed something. His mind focused in. He pointed to the ceiling vent, and Rafe immediately drew a fibre-optic scope from his toolbelt and stepped up on the rim of the toilet. Kevin checked around the bathtub, but the plumbing fed directly into the wall, with no other access portals. He looked back at Rafe as he withdrew the scope from the slits of the vent. Nothing hidden up there, either.

Kevin looked at the toilet, an old one without a back cistern, the wide base bolted to the floor. He knelt. The bolts were skinned with rust, but around the sides, there were striations of silver—scratch marks from another tool, maybe a crescent or socket wrench.

He made eye contact with Rafe and nodded.

Seconds later, they had the bolts loosened. Brownish water and a septic pong leaked out from underneath as they tipped it up a few inches, the plumbing preventing them from raising it any higher. Kevin knelt and peered underneath.

Two Ziploc bags were wedged against the pipes.

He reached in and dragged them out.

One contained a gun.

The other, a Bible.

Rafe's face was split with a wide smile.

Kevin unsealed the bag containing the Bible. He had little doubt that the gun was the murder weapon, but some instinct urged him toward the Bible. It had been a long time since he'd handled such a lovely edition, quite large, with a black tooled leather cover. He opened it.

From Leviticus to St. Matthew, the pages had been excised, and in their place, sewn with painstaking care into the spine, was a thick sheaf of handwritten correspondence on onionskin paper.

Hurriedly flipping, Kevin's eyes danced down several pages until he came to a signature at the end of a letter.

His heart beat so quickly he thought he would black out.

The Gospel According to David Haines.

"They're coming at seven this morning. Driving some kind of mobile lab right into the east loading bay. They're bringing their own security people for the inside."

David stood with his head against the bars, Bob Jarvis whispering into his ear. It was 1:00 a.m., and the cell block was blissfully quiet. Even Tucker had finally sobbed himself asleep, his TV still gabbling softly to sour whatever dreams he might have.

Late yesterday, Vic Greene had visited him again, to tell him what had happened. Well, he'd expected nothing less from these people; he'd only hoped his execution would beat them to it. He closed his eyes to concentrate on Bob's words.

"She'll be there, David. Waiting for you on the other side. Here."

He took the slip of paper that Bob offered him through the bars. It was a hand-drawn map, careful and precise. He found the east loading bay and followed the network of roads leading away from it, etching them into his memory. His eyes gravitated to the X Bob had marked.

"That's where she'll be," said Jarvis. "It's an old dirt farm road between cornfields. About five miles from here."

If you can get there.

Unspoken, the words seemed to linger ominously in the humid air. David took another slow, careful look at the map and handed it back to Jarvis.

The guard hurriedly crumpled it into a pocket. "Now don't eat your breakfast tomorrow. I heard they're going to lace it with sedatives, your drink too. So flush it down the toilet or pass it on over to Winslow, or something, but make like you're real dopey anyway."

Haines nodded silently.

"I've volunteered for a double shift. I'm going to be one of the ones taking you down to the mobile lab, all right? I'm going to try to leave your handcuffs unlatched. They'll look closed but they won't be all the way. It'll just be me and that new boy Tim Hibbins outside—Tim's got himself a new Walkman, I'll make sure he's listening to it. Gerry's on gate duty. I'll do what I can to get you through and buy you some time."

"God bless you, Bob."

"You take care of things inside that lab, and I'll try to clear you a path out of here. And that's about all I can do. Do more if I could."

"You've done plenty."

"You think you can ...?" He looked at his boots.

"Do I think I can escape?"

Jarvis nodded.

"I'll die trying."

"You just give me the word, and I will too."

"Your time may come, but not now. You've got work I need you to do here. If I should die."

Jarvis nodded. "Well. Get some sleep, then, I guess. I'll see you first thing." He hesitated, awkward. "All this time I always felt like I needed your blessing, but it never occurred to me you might be in need sometimes too. So. God bless you, David. If that's not disrespectful."

"Not at all, Bob. I'm very grateful."

Stretched on his cot, hands laced beneath his head, he listened to Bob's boots against the concrete as he continued on his rounds, then the slam of the inner cell block gate. The corridor fluorescents lent a dirty wash of light to his cell. It was never truly dark here. Hell would be like this, never properly day or night, just a horrible, eternal limbo. He looked around at the walls that had boxed him for three years.

He would leave no traces.

All the letters he'd received from his faithful he had destroyed immediately after reading them, their contents easily sealed in a capacious memory already embracing virtually every line of Scripture. Indeed, he'd instructed his faithful to destroy his own correspondence to them. They shouldn't need to rely on physical artifacts, and nothing should be left behind that might endanger the others. Especially the post office box in Joliet.

No, when he walked out of this cell tomorrow morning for the last time, there would be nothing within its walls he would take with him. He turned and eased himself onto the floor. Spread-eagled, he pressed his cheekbones against the concrete and tried to clear his mind. He smiled self-mockingly. Sin of pride. He'd become complacent in prison, thinking his work was done, his place in paradise secured. He'd allowed himself to take comfort in that. And God had seen his weakness. What were his former good works, really, compared to the ones that awaited him?

To deny the world his blood.

That was what God expected of him.

He'd considered suicide. It would not be difficult. But he knew this was just a siren's song designed to lure him off course. No, self-murder would be the path of error. He still had more work to carry out before he'd be allowed to leave the world behind.

God was not finished with him yet.

To deny the world his blood was only the first step.

God willing, he would escape this place and, with the help of his faithful, he would continue his ministry, enlarge his ministry, and once more blaze the narrow path of God's righteousness across the nation.

*   *   *

"Haines told him to kill Banji. The letters are explicit. When, where, how to do the killing. The whole plan's in there."

It was 5:15 a.m. and Kevin had reached Hugh Carter at home. Hours earlier, after arresting Will Andrews at the garage, he'd retreated to his hotel room and carefully read every single one of Haines's letters sewn into the Bible.

"I don't get it," said Carter, his voice still hoarse with sleep. "How the hell did letters like that get past the prison censors?"

"They didn't. They never went through prison mail."

"How?"

"Must be someone on the inside, mailing them for Haines. And whoever it is also opened a post office box in Joliet for his incoming mail."

"For the whole three years?"

"No. The earliest letters went through the prison system. They're very careful. Jesus, he's smart. He talks about the power of prayer, spiritual purity, I mean, there's nothing here the censors would've flagged. It's all just freedom of speech. No risk to prison security, nothing illegal. But starting about eighteen months ago, the letters don't bear the prison stamp, and in the very first one he tells Andrews not to send his letters to Illinois Correctional anymore. He gives a P.O. box in Joliet. And then the letters really change."

Page after page about the evils of modern medicine, the holy necessity of killing doctors, argued with a hypnotic logic. Kevin was familiar with Haines's skewed theology, but even so, he felt the delirious lure his words created on paper. Standing after he'd finished the last letter, his stomach had knotted without warning and he'd made it to the toilet just in time, hunched, body racked by a succession of dry heaves.

He should have known, should have known Haines would write epistles, reach out like a demented St. Paul to the faithful. He was a preacher, and the walls of a prison wouldn't stop him, just help him by lending him the mantle of a martyr. Years earlier, before he'd started killing, when he'd still been a member of a cult called the New Apostles, Haines had written several letters to his brother Rick, expressing his views on prayer and science and medicine. Later, when David had started assassinating doctors, Rick had reluctantly passed these letters on to the FBI, worried his own brother might be the killer. It had turned the case.

A letter-writer. *You knew that,* Kevin thought, sick with guilt. As soon as David was incarcerated, he should have got a subpoena to have all his outgoing prison mail logged and copied.

"You've got Andrews taken care of?" Carter asked.

"He's in the lockup at the field office."

"Good work, Kevin. I'll admit, I thought you were off base with this one. Miceli's going to look like shit. We'll make sure to send him a gift basket. It's been a while since I've seen you sink your teeth into something like this."

Meaning I've been coasting for three years? Kevin thought with a wry smile.

"You bagged another doctor-killer. I can't believe it."

He was alarmed by the jovial tone of closure in Carter's voice. "Hugh, this isn't finished."

Carter chuckled. "You want to slap Haines with counseling murder? He gets juiced in a couple days. His letter-writing days are over."

"I'm not talking about that."

"I know, I know. You want his prison helper."

"I'll need a subpoena to find out who opened that post office box. My guess is it's a prison guard."

"We'll get him on aiding and abetting a known felon. No sweat."

"And I want to sit on that post office box and see if anything else comes in."

There was a brief, sickly silence on the other end.

"Jesus," said Carter, "you're not serious."

"Haines might've written to others."

"Might, Kevin. Might. Is there anything in the letters?"

"Nothing explicit, but ... it's the tone. Hugh, for all we know he's been breeding a cult from prison, right under our noses. We might have more doctor-killers out there. I'm coming back on the first flight out."

CHAPTER NINE

On the outskirts of Joliet, Laura caught her first glimpse of the prison, its high outer walls bathed in a red wash of early-morning light, shimmering in the distance like some malignant Camelot.

She'd had a lousy night, the little sleep she got perforated by bizarre dreams of domestic breakdown: a toaster that kept incinerating the bread, no hot water for the shower, the elevator taking forever to reach the ground floor. At five, she'd finally dragged herself from her damp, tangled sheets, exhausted and unable to face breakfast. Twenty-five milligrams of phenmetrizine washed down with coffee. She'd been phasing it out, just as she'd promised herself, and had already cut her doses down by five milligrams, but this morning she'd lapsed, just to give herself the edge.

As the mobile lab pulled off the interstate, she felt the first icy punch of fear in her guts. During the excitement and urgency of the past several days, she'd had no time to contemplate the actual event she was fighting for—coming face to face with a serial killer, and taking his blood. Worse, she was exactly the type of person he might once have targeted. Probably it was only a geographical fluke that he hadn't. Hell, maybe he *had*. She could feel gooseflesh erupt across the nape of her neck. Maybe she'd been one of his intended victims, and only his capture had saved her. The thought that he might know anything about her at all was chilling enough.

For reassurance she glanced at Joseph and Allan, the two armed guards Paul had insisted accompany her to the prison. Allan, at the wheel, was the head of security for MetaSYS, and a fifteen-year veteran of the ATF. She liked his confident and careful driving, and his soft-spoken manner. In his early forties, his face was weathered and kind, and she imagined him with a large family, a backyard filled with an inflatable pool and lopsided swing-set.

She preferred him to Joseph, who was fifteen years younger, with a kind of bulky, insincere charm that she didn't doubt was popular in the kind of places he hung out. She could see him with a cowboy hat, a big shiny belt buckle, line dancing.

"These guys'll take care of you," Paul had told her before they'd set out.

Of course it wouldn't be necessary. She'd asked the warden to put a powerful sedative in Haines's breakfast. She didn't want a repeat of what had happened to Finlay when he'd tried to take blood. Anyway, even if the psycho did have any fight left in him, he'd be strapped the whole time to a table with enough restraining belts to defy Houdini on speed.

But none of this could still the queasy ebb and flow of her stomach. *It's simple. You take two units of blood, you take the bone marrow harvest, and you're out of there.* She just hoped it would be enough. Once he was executed, that would be the end of the samples: no second chances.

They were on a service road now, parallel to the prison's thirty-three-foot-high walls, topped with coils of barbed wire. She looked up at a guard tower and saw a vigilant shadow beyond the smoked glass. She let out a long breath.

"Here we go," Allan said, making a turn and pulling up outside a chain-link gate. He rolled down his window to talk to the solitary guard in the booth.

"We're Dr. Donaldson's team."

"Just let me put a call through to the warden." It didn't take long; they were expected. "Go on in. Loading bay two there, straight ahead. They're bringing him down now." He flipped a switch and with a jerk, the gate rolled slowly back.

The mobile lab eased into the loading compound. Four bays projected from the wing, metal doors down. Theirs was the only vehicle in the compound right now. Deliveries, Laura had been told, started at eight, by which time she was supposed to be finishing up. The asphalt pavement was already shimmering with heat. On the radio she'd heard a high of 101 was expected. She was glad they had air-conditioning.

Allan pulled alongside the loading bay and killed the engine, placing the keys on the dash. Laura hastily unclasped her seatbelt and walked to the back.

The mobile lab was a remodeled Gulfstream motorhome, everything behind the cab converted into a state-of-the-art medical clinic. The kitchen cupboards, bench seats, and bunks had been replaced with stainless-steel cabinets, refrigeration units, anesthesiology console, and racks of electronic diagnostic and monitoring equipment. The low-pile carpet had been ripped up and replaced with ceramic tile. To help ensure sterile conditions, the windows had been removed, and the whole inside chassis had been ventilated and soundproofed up to hospital standards. In the centre was a fully adjustable operating table, with an umbrella of lights overhead. She knew that surgeons could perform anything from simple suturing to a splenectomy here. But her needs today wouldn't be anywhere near as involved. As requested, the table had been fitted with thick leather security straps.

"All right?" Allan asked her.

"Fine," she said.

"I'm going to wait for them out by the bay."

He opened the side door, admitting a sluggish wave of heat, and stepped down onto the shimmering asphalt. He closed the door.

Joseph stayed inside, looking around the lab. He stretched, displaying the muscles in his upper arms. Laura wondered if it was for her benefit.

"Don't suppose we can smoke in here, huh?"

She compressed her lips into a smile and wondered if he was nervous, too. She hoped he wasn't a talker. She didn't want any distractions, any static. To discourage him, she began methodically preparing her blood extraction apparatus. Swabs, a catheter, tubing, two blood bags, a bone marrow needle, and a selection of sterile vials to receive the samples she would take. From the cabinets she took an ampoule of 1 percent xylocaine—all she would need by way of anesthetic. She rolled the IV stand to the head of the operating table and slung the first blood bag onto the hook, after labeling it carefully.

"Yeah, I remember this guy," Joseph said. "Made the cover of *Time*, remember that? I kept the article. I kind of have an interest in those things."

"Is that right?"

She supposed it didn't matter if she disliked him, as long as he did his job. Which was, after all, very simple. Paul had assured her that both men were experienced, capable, and dead aims. She caught a glimpse of his holster and wondered how many times he'd reached for his gun in his career. Probably more often than he'd needed to, she guessed.

As he prattled on about other serial killers whose careers he'd followed, Laura crouched down to check the cooler. In the gleaming steel cabinet she caught her distorted reflection and looked hastily away, knowing that the purple smudges under her eyes were darker than usual, her skin sallow with exhaustion.

She opened the lid of the cooler, releasing a current of pleasantly icy air. There would be plenty of room inside for her samples. She closed it and stood. For just a moment she felt light-headed, and she touched the cool steel cabinet for reassurance. Despite the air-conditioning, her armpits prickled, and she wished for fresh air, a childhood breeze from the sea. She took a slow, silent breath, and jolted as the side door swung open. Allan looked up at her.

"They're coming," he said.

The loading bay door rose with almost unbearable slowness, revealing legs, torsos, heads. Flanked by two prison guards, David Haines shambled down the steps to the asphalt. He was shackled at his wrists and ankles, his head bowed. Allan backed up the steps, guiding him into the lab, while the two prison guards followed close behind, hands clamped around the convict's elbows.

She was not prepared for how handsome he was. She'd seen the news photos, but they were generally distant and grainy, his face half turned from the camera. Now she saw that his features were finely etched, with large, alert brown eyes that she might have called compassionate, had she not known who he was. His hands she noticed as well, a surgeon's hands, the fingers long and supple, intelligent. Even in his short-sleeved Department of Corrections tunic, it wouldn't have been difficult to superimpose another life and identity upon him. She wished he were ugly.

"You're aware," said one of the prison guards, "that this man is now your responsibility until he leaves the vehicle."

Allan nodded. "That's right."

The prison guard handed Allan a set of keys, which he promptly put in his pocket.

"Those are for his manacles. We suggest you leave them locked at all times."

"Very good. Let's secure him," said Allan.

Working together, the four guards moved Haines onto the operating table and proceeded to strap him in, pulling the belts tight, one across his chest, upper thighs, his calves. Separate straps encircled his biceps and forearms. Through it all, Haines was silent and impassive, allowing his limbs to be shunted around as if he denied ownership of them.

"For God's sake," Allan said irritably. "What kind of half-assed job is this?"

Laura looked over in alarm to see Allan holding the open loops of Haines's wrist manacles.

"Good thing I tested this. You boys asleep on the job?"

One of the prison guards, a wiry, hatchet-faced man in his mid-forties, shook his head in disbelief. He looked pale. "Geez, I can't ... look, I'm sorry, I was sure they were tight. He's so dopey he kept staggering away on me."

Laura watched as Allan locked the wrist manacles, tested them, then quickly checked Haines's ankle manacles, too. They were fast.

"We'll be waiting outside the loading gate," the prison guard said. "If he's any trouble, give us a shout."

"Yeah," grunted Allan. "Thanks."

The prison guards walked out through the side door, and Allan closed it after them, slamming the bolt home. For a moment, the only sound was the low drone of the air-conditioning.

"Don't worry," Allan told her. "He's snug as a bug."

"Thanks." She walked to the head of the table and forced herself to meet David Haines's gaze.

"I'm Dr. Donaldson." She was startled at how parched her mouth was.

"Yes. They told me about you."

She did a quick analysis of his voice: the tone was neutral, without any trace of antagonism. She felt encouraged.

"Then you know what I'll be doing this morning."

"Yes."

On the way down from Chicago, she'd tried to predict what his behavior might be during the procedure. For all she knew, she was in for an unceasing fire-and-brimstone rant. She'd also deliberated on what manner she herself should adopt. In the end, she'd come down on tried-and-true professional detachment. She would not speak to him any more than was absolutely necessary. She would not engage with him in any way, and she would certainly not argue with him. She'd promised herself that several times. She was not here to win a debating match. All she wanted was the fluid in his veins, and a bountiful bone marrow harvest. Then she could find out whether this would be just another heartbreaking footnote in the annals of cancer research, or a triumphant headline.

She made her voice brisk. "We'll start with the routine blood work, and save the bone marrow till last. Is that all right with you?"

She was already reaching for the sterile swab, grateful for the small tasks that would keep her from looking at his eyes.

"You think you're helping people."

His tone was less accusatory than simply incredulous. She swiped the alcohol pad over his inner elbow, the muscles of his forearm rippling involuntarily. She knotted the tourniquet around his bicep, tight.

"Make a fist, please."

"But it's you people who are spreading disease."

She felt curiously reassured by his inflated rhetoric. If he was beyond the realm of measured, rational discussion, it would be easier to write him off as a freak, a specimen.

She slid the catheter into his vein and taped it against his skin. Notching the tubing onto the back of the catheter, she released the tourniquet and watched as the blood began to leave his vein, drawn slowly up toward the vacuum bag. With a sense of wonder, she thought of all that might be in it—some magical elixir from a fairy tale. How strange it should be carried in such a vessel.

He was watching her. She'd always found brown eyes in men softer, vulnerable even, but David Haines's eyes had intent. They were not a predator's eyes exactly; she knew she was not an object of desire to him, but something more chillingly abstract. She wasn't a woman at all, just a metaphor, a handmaiden of Satan. She looked away.

"I'm going to draw two units. It'll take about half an hour for each." She wished she could take more, but 500 ccs was a maximum at one sitting, an ethical limit.

She checked on Allan and Joseph. They stood with practised poise at either end of the lab, hands clasped at their waists, weight evenly distributed on both legs, alert. Their eyes never left Haines. Laura walked to a small fridge and took out a can of fruit juice. She cracked the tab and dropped in a straw.

"I'd recommend it," she told Haines. "Keep you from getting dehydrated."

She tilted the straw towards his mouth, and he accepted it. She took this as a good sign, perhaps even a symbol of surrender, or at least acquiescence. But he took only a small sip before he pulled his head back.

"You're afraid to talk to me, aren't you? A man strapped to a table, slated for execution. Afraid of what you might hear?"

"I'm not afraid to talk to you."

She looked at the blood bag above his head, wishing it would fill faster. Maybe she shouldn't have said anything. She knew she should be avoiding conversation with him, and it was obvious he was trying to goad her. Her eyes flickered to Allan, but his expression offered her no reproof; no guidance, either.

"Ignorance is only a sin if it's willful," Haines said.

His self-righteousness rankled her, the implication that she was a thoughtless drone, pathetically misguided.

Before she could check herself she said, "People have a responsibility to educate themselves, I agree."

Shit. Why couldn't she just ignore him? She'd been worried about this: at the best of times she was hard pressed to maintain a noncommittal silence. It ran against her grain. She was aware of her heart racing. She placed the fruit juice on the instrument tray; he didn't seem to want any more.

"You're exactly right," said Haines. He sounded solicitous. "So you should know that prayer is the only real cure."

"Lots of atheists getting over the flu, last time I checked."

It came out more flippantly than she'd intended, but sudden anger flushed away her regret. Why should she be afraid of him? Why should she hold back? He was strapped to the table, watched by two armed guards, at least one of whom would like nothing better than to shoot his very own serial killer. And in an hour he'd be escorted back into that godforsaken pile of stone that would become his morgue.

Her entire life was devoted to curing cancer, and she would not be cowed by this man. She would not pretend to politely consider his views; and she could not endure the idea of him misconstruing her silence for agreement, or worse, defeat. If he flew into a psychotic rage, so be it. His blood would still flow from his veins into her specimen flasks.

But far from exploding into a passion, Haines seemed unperturbed. He gave a small, friendly smile.

"I was like you once. I used to believe in modern medicine. But maybe you haven't been keeping up. Tuberculosis, pneumonia, and meningitis are on the comeback. Bacterial strains so powerful antibiotics are useless. Ebola and necrotizing fasciitis. Scramble all you want for new cures, but the bacteria have the numbers, and you're losing the battle. Find a new antibiotic, too late, they're already resistant in India, and all it takes is one sick man on an airplane to spread it across oceans. All God's way of telling us we've been defying his will too long."

She'd heard variations on this spiel before, of course. The failure of modern medicine. It was splashed across papers, a favourite topic of TV newsmagazines. She'd had dozens of conversations on the subject herself, and it was one about which she had fierce opinions.

"You're saying modern medicine has failed?"

"Not failed. Was never meant to be."

She knew that he'd studied for two years at medical school, and the very idea was almost inconceivable to her. How could someone with such a background convert to some dime-store belief system?

"Well, there've actually been studies about prayer," Laura said. "I've read them, with interest. But they are all seriously flawed. There's not a scrap of real scientific proof it works."

"I'm proof. I never get sick anymore."

"I've seen malignant tumors in your bloodstream. You've just got a good immune system."

"God rewards the worthy. The others were meant to die for their sins."

"A two-year-old girl with retinoblastoma? What's her sin?"

Haines looked at her impassively. "Your sentimentality is so common now. We're all of us sinners, but our age has tried so hard to deny it. You all fear death so much, but death is not the worst thing that can happen to you."

Her hearted pounded with anger as she turned away, knees weak. She didn't want to talk anymore. It had all been a mistake, a folly of her own egotism, and she regretted it. She couldn't believe she'd actually been readying journal citations, statistics for his edification. Pathetic.

She began to label the second blood bag, trying to still her shaking hand.

"You think you've found some miracle cure inside me? God's not the only one who works miracles on this earth. It's a devil's cure. And God have mercy on you if you unleash it."

She looked up at him.

"That's exactly what I'm going to do."

His eyes were mournful.

"Then better you had not been born."

*　*　*

She removed the second bag of Haines's blood from the stand and placed it beside the first in the cooler. That done, she removed the catheter from his arm. Then, from a sterile package she took the bone marrow needle and showed it to Haines.

"You know what this is, right?"

It was hollow, about four inches long and as thick as a pen refill. At the top was a removable knob that enabled you to put the force of both hands behind the needle.

Haines said nothing.

"I'm going to drive it into your hip bone until it hits marrow. I'll take an aspirate in two locations. It'll hurt. Are you allergic to any drugs?"

Haines just sniffed contemptuously.

In her years as a resident she'd gained plenty of experience taking stem cell samples from the marrow. Like most neophytes, she'd been too delicate at first, afraid of inflicting pain, afraid of the needle skittering off the bone into unanesthetized flesh. But she'd learned you needed to put your full weight behind the needle, gouging into the bone until you felt the give and knew you'd entered marrow. She'd learned to close her eyes when she pushed: it helped her to concentrate, to feel her way through the bone by touch; and it meant she didn't have to look at the patient's suffering.

In her experience it was often the children who were bravest, the ones who had become so accustomed, so early, to pain and indignities that this was simply another excruciating procedure to be endured. In her early days, she had provided the tears for them, turning her face so they wouldn't see her eyes as she ratcheted the needle into their hips.

"I'll give you a local anesthetic—unless you don't believe in those either."

Again, Haines said nothing. She preferred it this way.

"We're going to roll you onto your side first."

She nodded to Allan and Joseph and they smartly approached the table and methodically began to loosen some of Haines's straps. She'd told them ahead of time this would be necessary. The two straps across his right arm had to be removed altogether, the chest and hip belts slackened.

Haines rolled over onto his left side easily, even cooperatively. Laura thought she detected a certain resignation to his body gestures. Blood loss. She was right to take the blood first, he'd have less fight in him for the harvest. His eyes had a glassy sheen, and his lips were forming inaudible prayers. Good. Let him keep himself busy. The two guards re-tightened the straps around Haines's new position and stood back to watch.

With a sterile syringe Laura pulled back five ccs of xylocaine. She swabbed his hip.

"I'll pray for you, Doctor."

Her forearms erupted in gooseflesh. The words, spoken so calmly, sounded like a benediction, but one perverted with menace.

She pricked the flesh below the crown of his hip, slowly pushing deeper as she dispensed the anesthetic, and drawing back on the needle periodically to make sure she hadn't hit a vein. If she did, there'd be a telltale seep of blood back into the needle; too much xylocaine into the bloodstream and you could have a cardiac arrest on your hands. The plunger hit bottom and she slid the needle out.

"We'll give it about a minute to take effect."

She turned away from him to put the spent needle back on the tray. She registered the look of shock on Allan's face before she heard the noise—a horrible gurgling emanating from Haines's throat. She whirled, found him writhing against the restraints, his face already red and misted with sweat.

All at once she was back in the emergency room, an anxious intern, mind narrowed to imperatives. Assess. Allergic reaction. To the xylocaine itself? No, almost unheard of. The carrying agent was the only real possibility, the chemical preservative mixed with the anesthetic. So rare, but it had been known to happen.

From Haines's grinding jaws, saliva and sputum seeped into the pillow and paper sheets. Her throat constricted sympathetically.

"I need him on his back!" she shouted.

She saw Allan and Joseph both hesitate.

"He's choking!"

They came forward then, their faces pale masks of shock, and started loosening belts.

Laura ran to the cabinets and snapped open three cupboards before she found the crash cart. Shit. Why hadn't she imagined this as a possibility, at least had things standing by? She dragged the crash cart across the room, eyes darting over the contents of the pre-assembled emergency kit: de-fib paddles, syringes, ampoules of adrenaline and epinephrine, surgical tape, a penlight—and the intubation equipment. She'd have to get a line down his throat before it closed completely.

Haines was on his back now, eyes bulging, jaws working desperately to force air down his throat. Laura yanked the eight-inch plastic hose from the crash cart, inserted the guide wire.

"Help me hold him still!"

Allan put one large hand across Haines's forehead and pressed down. Haines's teeth were clenched tight and Laura had to pry them apart with her hands, getting bitten twice in the process. She put the penlight in her mouth and clamped hard, keeping the beam focused on his throat. He was coughing and gagging so much it was difficult to see the extent of the swelling, but the mucous membranes did look dangerously inflamed. Without hesitation she shoved the tube through the gnashing teeth and down his throat—no time for delicacy. He fought it, bucking, but she got it down to his vocal cords in time. She pulled back the guide wire and checked for air flow. Good.

But when she looked at his eyes she saw he wasn't blinking. He was going into shock. Quickly she taped the tube to the side of his mouth and reached for the crash cart again, fingers dancing over ampoules until they hit the pre-loaded syringe of epinephrine. She wished she'd kept the catheter in his arm—it would've been quicker access for the drugs. Intramuscular was her only option now. She checked the dosage, half a millilitre and—

The syringe, suddenly, was in his hand.

"Hey!"

Haines closed his fist around it, and his right arm described a small, perfect arc, slamming the needle up to its hilt in Allan's eye socket. Screaming, the guard plucked frantically at the syringe. But he couldn't move, because Haines had hooked his fingers around his chest holster, snapping the catch. The flap sprung open and Allan finally lurched back. His gun slipped free into Haines's hand. Haines's index finger was already crooking itself around the trigger.

Laura saw his eyes then, and they were not the eyes of a man in anaphylactic shock. In that sliver of a second she knew he'd faked everything, and done it infallibly, down to the last detail. His breath came in harsh, rapid bursts, amplified grotesquely through the plastic tubing still in his throat. His eyes locked on hers as the gun swung towards her.

"Move!"

She felt Joseph's hand on her arm, wrenching her to one side so that he'd have a clear shot. A volley of gunfire reverberated through the lab before she even hit the floor. Crouched beneath the operating table she saw Joseph sit down suddenly, like a surprised toddler. The left side of his face was missing. Another shot hit him in the chest, knocking him flat.

All her senses had become strangely sluggish: her vision had contracted to a tunnel; she was aware of no sound except the bizarre whistling gasp of Haines's breathing directly overhead. She stared dully at the blood pooling around Joseph's body—an impossible amount, it seemed, until she realized it wasn't all coming from Joseph. Her eyes swung slowly to the wall cabinets. Bullets had blasted apart the cooler, and in numb horror she understood that it was Haines's blood that was seeping across the floor, mingling with the guard's. She blinked, feeling an overwhelming sorrow.

"Goddamnit!" The word, shrieked in agony through clenched teeth, snapped her from her reverie. It was Allan, one hand clamped over his eye socket, trying to stand. She didn't want to watch, but before he'd even straightened up, a bullet hit him in the abdomen, and he folded over onto himself, collapsing in a heap. He gave a long, defeated wheeze and was still.

Laura looked at the door, wondering how long it would take to get there, slam the bolt open, turn the handle. How many shots had he fired, how many bullets left? She didn't even have time to tense her muscles for flight. Haines's hand swung down beneath the operating table, the gun steady, aimed squarely at her face.

His voice rasped, hollow, through the tube.

"Unlock me," he said.

CHAPTER TEN

She was already outside herself, ready for flight: she'd be miles away when the bullet hit. Calmly she moved out from beneath the table, and turned to face Haines.

"My arm," he wheezed through the intubation line. The gun was trained at the center of her chest.

Haines's left arm was still fastened by leather straps at his biceps and forearm. She needed both hands to pull the straps hard enough to loosen the pin and buckle.

Both arms now free, Haines used his left hand to tear off the tape fixing the tube to his cheek. In one swift motion he drew it out. He coughed, but didn't retch, his eyes, and his aim, never wavering from Laura.

"Get the keys," he told her, nodding at Allan's body.

Distantly she wondered where the prison guards were? Hadn't they heard the gunshots? The soundproofing wasn't that good, surely. Why weren't they breaking down the door?

She bent down over Allan and put her hand into his pants pocket, still warm against his leg. Off to her left, she saw Joseph's gun lying near his shoulder, only a few feet away. Even if she got to it in time, she'd never fired a gun before. There was no point even trying: Haines would shoot her before she'd reached it. Her fingertips closed around a key ring and she drew it out.

Haines had managed to undo the remaining leather straps and now swung his legs over the table.

"Do the manacles," he said.

She bent down to his ankles and inserted the key in the lock. The manacles snapped open, and Haines shook his feet free. They hit the floor with a dull metallic thud.

Laura stood back. He had no further use for her now. If he did it right, at least she'd hardly feel a thing, just a big, numbing concussion in the center of her chest, and then eternal blackness.

"Up front," he said. "You're driving."

No sign of hesitation, as if he'd already thought it all through. Passing through the portal into the cab, she slid into the driver's seat. Habit made her strap the seatbelt across her chest. The keys were on the dash. The engine turned over smoothly.

Only now did Haines slip into the passenger seat, the gun trained on her head.

"To the gate."

She'd never driven such a large vehicle. She put it in gear and aimed it slowly towards the gate. Inside the booth she could see the guard look at her with confusion, then alarm. In her side mirror, she saw the two prison guards come running alongside, shouting.

Haines reached over suddenly and jerked the wheel to the right, nearly crashing the Gulfstream into the guard booth. Laura braked, grazing up against it, then winced in shock as Haines jumped up and pressed the gun muzzle hard against her temple.

"Open the gate!" he shouted at the bewildered guard. "Or I kill her!"

Laura let her eyes slide to the guard in the booth. He was young, and he looked panicked, not knowing what to do. *Open the goddamn gate,* she caught herself thinking. *Do it, just do it!* But she knew it was probably not what they'd been taught. He met her gaze, and she saw terror in his face, and for the first time she felt her own terror, reflected in his eyes. She looked away, her heart kicking up. A small whimper clawed at her throat.

"Open it!" screamed Haines.

Laura could see one of the other prison guards, the hatchet-faced one, burst into the booth, whispering urgently to the young gatekeeper. The gatekeeper nodded gratefully and pressed a button. Slowly the chain-link began to slide open.

"Go," Haines told her, "now!"

She eased the Gulfstream through the gate.

"Faster!" Haines stamped his foot on top of hers and floored the gas. "Like that."

The Gulfstream lurched ahead down the deserted service road, simmering in the heat. The speedometer crept up: thirty, forty, fifty.

Haines pulled back his foot and sat down, sideways in his seat, facing her, gun still on her. He glanced through his side mirror, and so did she, hoping to see a column of screeching police cars in pursuit. Nothing.

They'll come, they'll come, she chanted inwardly, and felt no reassurance from it. She doubted Haines would spare her life in any case.

"Where are we going?" she asked. She felt an almost overpowering urge to talk. Talk, talk, talk. Anything to short-circuit the terror starting to course through her body now. Why was he keeping her alive? He could drive just as well. Unless he didn't want to lose even the precious few seconds it would take to shoot her and drag her body out of the driver's seat. Unless he'd need her later.

She glanced over at Haines, his eyes fixed to the road as if trying to remember something. He wasn't buckled in. The speedometer crested fifty-five. She took a deep breath, clenched her teeth, her arms braced against the steering wheel.

She slammed her foot down on the brake pedal.

The seatbelt bit searingly into her neck and across the top of her left breast, snapping her head back just half an inch from the steering wheel. All the breath was punched out of her, her vision a purple smear ...

She was back, choking in air, shooting a look at Haines. Slumped forward, his head against the dash, he was motionless. And the gun ... she spotted it on the mat beneath the glove compartment. Groggily she jabbed at the seatbelt release and heaved herself up. She lumbered back through the portal to the main door, only six feet away, hand outstretched for the handle. And then she was flat on her face, Haines's fist clamped around her ankle.

She thrashed to free herself, screaming hoarsely, a string of obscenities, trying to claw forward. He held tight. Did he have the gun? He was scrambling towards her now, up along her body.

Against the cabinets she caught sight of the bone marrow needle, rocking to and fro. Lunging, she caught it in her fist. She wrenched herself round, swinging the needle until it hit flesh. She saw it gouge into Haines's arm, and his grip weakened in time with his howl of pain. She kicked free.

At the door, slapping at the bolt, a whimper rising in her throat as every second stretched out and she was sure she'd feel the dull thud of a bullet's impact. The door swung open and she lunged, tripping and rolling on the hot asphalt.

Scrambling to her feet, she cast a look back over her shoulder as she ran down the road. What she expected was Haines hurtling through the door after her. But the engine roared, the motorhome straightened out and pulled away from her.

She watched as it picked up speed and disappeared over a gentle rise, and she felt a bizarre sense of disappointment. It was amazingly quiet on the road, the sun a ball of growing fury in the eastern sky, the heat already pounding down on her, raising heat mirages on the distant road. She turned both ways, not knowing which direction to go. The cornstalks whispered in a breeze too gentle for her to feel against the heat. She removed her white lab coat and folded it neatly over her arm.

She touched the raw diagonal abrasion on her neck where the seatbelt had cut in, then looked at the hail of lacerations on her right forearm. She put her wrist to her mouth, licking it clean, tasting dust and blood intermingled. A crow circled above the cornstalks, cawing monotonously. It had been a hell of a week.

She started to walk back towards the prison, and then she felt her knees go watery, and she sat down at the side of the road, panting. In the distance she heard sirens.

*   *   *

At the wheel, the motor's powerful vibration passed through his hands up his arms, and for a moment he felt exultant. Three years in a concrete box and here he was, outside, the landscape surging past him: the cornfields, the big horizon, the bleached sky. Almost instantly, though, his mind sobered. *Forgive me, Father, for the two lives I had to take. And thank you for Jarvis at the gates.* If Bob hadn't talked to the guard on duty, he might still be locked in the loading bay, forced to take his own life.

Sirens in the distance now. He knew it was only a matter of minutes before they'd reach him. He took the turning that would lead him across the tracks. His plan, he knew, was seriously flawed, but he'd had precious little time and few resources to do better. It was nothing short of miraculous that he'd made it out of the compound.

In his side mirror he now saw the flare of swirling lights. Up ahead he could see the railway crossing, and the arm starting to drop, the red warning beacon flashing. Far off to the left, riding slightly above the cornstalks, came the dark shadow of a train.

He checked his mirror again. If he smashed through the arm, he could make it across the tracks—but so could the cruisers if they gunned it. And then he'd never make it to Gail in time. He had to destroy the blood in the cooler. And, if necessary, himself.

His decision was made. He accelerated, snapping the arm apart like a twig with the front of the Gulfstream. He braked, cranked the wheel hard to the left, and brought the motorhome in line with the tracks. He touched the gas and felt the steering wheel twist as the tires caught, locked on course. He floored it. When he got it up to sixty he switched on the cruise control. The train hurtled towards him, horn blaring, brakes shrieking in his ears.

*   *   *

The cornfields grew to a height of seven feet, making a golden canyon of the deserted dirt road. Inside her red Honda Civic, Gail Newton sat anxiously, her hands cold in the air-conditioned chill of the car. She checked her watch again: still 8:37.

She'd called in sick. That's what the man had told her to do over the phone late last night. He hadn't told her his name, but she knew he had to be one of David's faithful. The instructions were precise: she'd filled up a whole sheet of paper with the directions. She was to wait here from seven in the morning till noon.

Waiting for David.

Her heart trembled, tripping for a moment before stumbling back into normal rhythm. He might not make it; she'd felt sick when the man had told her that. And if David didn't come, she'd know he'd been caught, or worse. At the back of her mind, she didn't know what she feared more: seeing him, or not seeing him.

Never had she met him, although she knew every detail of his face from magazines and newspaper clippings, and news shows, which she videotaped whenever she could. His face had become as familiar to her as her own mother's, and more precious.

Still, the first time she'd written to him, she'd felt so guilty. Imagine, sending a letter to a murderer in a state penitentiary! She hadn't told anyone, not her mother, not even Sue at work, who gushed all her secrets. How could she expect them to understand? But her conscience told her she had nothing to be ashamed of. The very first time she'd seen his picture in the paper—that one they always show of him now, staring out solemnly—it was as if he'd been looking right at her, and she'd felt her heart opening to him.

Of course it hadn't happened all at once. But she'd sought him out, in the newspaper, on the TV. She'd clipped all the articles she could find and read them over and over—about what he'd done and why. It wasn't long before, when she looked at his picture, she saw not a murderer but a man who had the courage of his convictions and who did the right thing, even if the whole world thought he was crazy. Standing up for what he believed—who did that anymore? Not the church ministers and not the politicians, God help us. But David Haines did, and now they'd caught him and put him on death row.

She wrote to him. She opened herself to him in a way she'd never done for anyone—because who'd ever been interested in the contents of her soul anyway? But she was 100 percent sure that David was. It was in those eyes of his. She heard people say he had scary eyes, dark eyes without any spark of remorse or humanity in them. They were wrong. It was all there, all mixed in, just like when she mixed her acrylics. All colors went into black, you just had to look deeper.

He wrote back. To say it changed her life would be an understatement. It was the *beginning* of her life—that's how she looked at it. He made it all so clear, all the things he believed. It was all there in the Bible, really, if only you read it right. It was wrong to take and traffic in blood; it was wrong to try to thwart God's wishes for us, to ignore him, and to put our faith in false idols. People were so blind! Couldn't they see where it was all leading? Plagues and holocausts, right out of the Book of Revelation.

In that first letter, she felt as though he was trying to explain himself to her. He had to be so terribly alone, in that little cell, surrounded by child molesters and rapists. To be treated like that, a man like him. She cried when she thought about it. He needed her. She would have to write back to him.

Those first six months were the happiest of her life. The elation she felt when she'd come home from work to find one of his letters waiting for her! She would spend several days writing her replies, and when each evening she put her pen down, her face would be flushed with the sheer intimacy of telling this man about herself. She didn't care that prison censors would skim her letters—there was nothing she was ashamed of anymore. Still, she told no one about her correspondence with David.

8:39.

She looked anxiously through the windows. Which direction would he come from? She couldn't remember which way the prison was. *Please Lord look over him and deliver him safely into my care.*

Then, about eighteen months ago, his letters had changed. Right away he told her not to write to him at the prison anymore; he had a new address, a post office box in Joliet. And his own letters no longer bore the stamp of the prison censors. Before, he'd talked about the evils of modern medicine; now he began writing about the holy need to kill doctors. And with every letter, his tone became sterner, saying it wasn't enough simply to believe, you had to bring your beliefs to life, to testify and let the world see them.

Three months ago he'd asked her to kill a doctor. She'd wept, not because she was shocked, but because she was afraid she wouldn't be able to do it. He'd given her a name. Dr. Laura Donaldson. And he'd told her how to do it. She knew it was the right thing to do, but she was weak. It wasn't even that she was afraid of getting caught—though she was—she just knew she wouldn't be able do it. She told David her worries, and he was so understanding. He would reassure her, tell her he understood her misgivings. After all, to take a human life was a serious matter, and normally a grave sin. But this was different. And she knew he was right, he was always right. It was her, her weakness getting in the way.

She tried her best. She found out where Dr. Donaldson worked, and lived, and she even followed her home one day, trailing behind in her car as she drove to her swanky apartment building on the Gold Coast. There was no underground parking; she had to park on the street and walk to the entrance. "Make that your opportunity," David had written her.

The first time she'd tried to buy the gun, she'd entered the store and asked for the one David described. But her stomach felt like it was getting squeezed so tight she couldn't breathe, and she'd almost thrown up, right there at the counter. She'd had to leave, half doubled over.

She'd wanted to do it for David, but there was this part of her, this weak, cowardly part holding her back. She'd read his letters over and over again—even though she was supposed to destroy them—and felt horribly unworthy.

But now he was giving her another chance. When the call came last night, she knew she couldn't say no. David always said you mustn't refuse the Lord's call when it comes, and she'd failed enough already. Here was her chance to do something remarkable, something worthy.

She'd never gone to visit him, though she'd wanted to desperately. Every night she thought of him, alone in his hard cell, no one to look after him. That terrible prison food slipped into his cell three times a day, guards who shoved him around, not even a window to see the sky, or the birds he loved so much. He talked about birds sometimes in his letters, and it made her love him even more. How she wanted to look after him! But she'd never made the trip to the prison, even though it was only an hour away.

It wasn't so much that she was afraid of seeing him; she was afraid of *him* seeing *her*. She glanced furtively in the rearview mirror, hating her stupid frizzy hair and her marshmallow face. She'd tried, this morning especially, to make something of her fat features with make-up. She checked her lipstick, her eyeliner—she'd got up extra early so she'd have time to get ready for him. Was that sinful, to be so vain?

Please God don't let him think I'm ugly.

She wrenched her hands together, trying to warm them up. How could she be cold when she was so fat? She was so used to people looking away from her, or even worse, seeming to look right through her—just another plain, fat woman who'd be better off invisible. No one except her mother had come close enough to her to ever kiss her. Maybe if she'd been special in some other way ... smart, or funny ... but she wasn't. And it would be too much to bear if David could never meet her eyes. In the pictures he always met her eyes.

In a plastic bag on the passenger seat she'd brought some clothes for him, just an oversized T-shirt she liked to sleep in (she'd laundered it at five this morning) and an old pair of sweat pants. "Just find something to put over his prison clothes," the man on the phone had told her. If she hadn't had to leave so early, she'd have gone out to buy some new things for him. In the glove compartment was a box of apple juice, and a tuna fish sandwich, cut diagonally and wrapped in wax paper. She wondered if maybe she should have made another sandwich, just in case he didn't like tuna.

The muted blare of a train whistle reached her through the windows of the car; she'd been only vaguely aware of the low, rhythmic churning of the train as it drew closer. Again the whistle sounded, louder now, and for a long time. Then came a terrible shrieking of steel on steel, and a series of dull, crumpling thuds that left a sickening memory in the air, even as silence fell.

Gail hesitated for a moment, then got out of her car, softly closing the door so the coolness wouldn't seep out. She stood in the aquatic wash of heat, light-headed. Even on her tiptoes, she couldn't see over the tall stalks of corn. She peered in the direction of the noise. A dark smudge seemed to hover on the horizon, but that might just be a heat mirage.

A dry rustling wafted through the air, and she thought she saw a shimmer of movement at the tips of the corn stalks. The sound built until it was like footfalls on dry autumn leaves, and then the stalks were swaying, she could see them. She touched the car for support, her heart whirling. A figure was bursting through the field, the stalks whipping back away from thrashing arms. It was Moses parting the Red Sea.

David Haines vaulted out from the edge of the field, racing towards her.

CHAPTER ELEVEN

As the helicopter swung down, Kevin Sheldrake could see the wreckage of the freight train cutting a dark scar through the cornfields. Boxcars were wrenched from their couplings and scattered, their contents spilling out into the fields: stacks of lumber, a colorful selection of Volvo sedans, and a slick of some fluid, which was being hosed down by a yellow-robed emergency crew. He was glad there'd been no passenger cars, otherwise God knows how many casualties there might have been. Kevin winced as the harsh vibration of the helicopter chiseled pain across his eyes; he'd been up more than twenty-four hours and his mouth tasted like cheap carpeting.

At the head of the derailment, he saw that wide swaths of the cornfields had been flattened by a small battalion of vehicles and personnel. Ambulances, fire and rescue trucks, and over a dozen cruisers were angled haphazardly over the crushed cornstalks, lights flashing. In the distance he could see several lines of men searching, with tracker dogs, through the cornfields, moving towards the bordering woods to the northwest. Kevin's fingers traced the stubble on his chin as he looked on in astonishment—it seemed incredible that one man could create such elaborate havoc, and all within minutes of escaping from a super-max prison. At first glance the scene looked like some punitive act of God. The thought resonated hypnotically in his mind, and he quickly suffocated it.

He'd heard the news just as he was ready to board his flight back to Chicago. Hugh Carter hadn't known much, and the few facts he'd related had struck Kevin as almost surreal—that Haines had some-how managed to escape while undergoing medical tests in a goddamn Gulfstream motorhome. He'd taken two guards and a doctor hostage. The doctor had escaped. Less than fifteen minutes later Haines had slammed himself headlong into an eastbound freight.

The flight from Detroit had been almost unbearable. At least Hugh had arranged a helicopter for him at O'Hare. He checked his watch. Eleven fifty-six, and the escape had been reported at around eight-thirty. If David had survived the crash, he'd had over three hours to clear off. And Kevin didn't believe for a second he was dead—even though that seemed to be Hugh's assumption. No way David would have escaped just to kill himself. He could have done that in his cell. Besides, suicide ran counter to his religious beliefs.

Kevin lifted his gaze over the shimmering landscape—David, out there somewhere—and his incredulity finally gave way to outrage. He'd spent three years of his life getting Haines into that damn cell. All that work, evaporated. Who the hell let this happen? Who'd put Haines in a Gulfstream in a loading bay five days before his execution? He should have been nice and cozy in the isolation wing.

The chopper touched down. Kevin threw open the door and ducked out, wincing against the sun's blistering heat. With the swirling lights, the noise, and the crowds, the scene was like some grim carnival midway. Kevin started walking towards the train wreck, around state police, paramedics, highway patrolmen, forensic photographers.

He wasn't happy to see Seth Michener, but he was hardly surprised: "Mitch" worked the fugitive squad.

"Shit, nice entrance," said Michener, walking towards him and tilting his head at Kevin's helicopter without breaking stride. "What's that cost the taxpayer, a ride like that? Half a grand maybe?"

"Spare me." Kevin fell into step beside him.

"Me and the other fellas, we just drove. But Hugh always did have a soft spot for you. Watch your step there, wouldn't want to get your brogues muddy."

Dressed in his characteristic khaki jeans, sneakers, and FBI sweatshirt, Michener was short, with pouchy, hyperthyroid eyes, coarse skin, and a scrawny body. Physically unimpressive, he nevertheless had a feral intensity that could be surprising, and sometimes frightening. He reminded Kevin of a small yappy dog you try to brush off, only to find it's fastened its teeth around your leg and is trying to drag you down. He was a bundle of muscle and will, with a severe Napoleon complex.

"Where's the Gulfstream?" Kevin wanted to know.

Michener snorted, took another slug of his Coke, and jerked his head.

"Jesus." About twenty yards in front of them, a Union Pacific boxcar lay atop the mangled motorhome, completely crushing the cab and about a third of the body. Anyone in the driver's seat would've been fused with the twisted metal. A rescue vehicle with a crane and winch was stationed alongside the boxcar, and a crew was fixing the hook.

"He won't be inside," Kevin said, but after seeing the motorhome he somehow felt less certain.

"Well, we'll see about that," Michener replied. "I've had a team sweeping for the last hour, and he sure isn't anywhere else."

"Have you seen Hugh?" Kevin asked. He really didn't want to talk to Michener anymore.

"He's around here somewhere, maybe filling out some forms or something, I don't know." He winked at Kevin, as though sharing a conspiratorial joke about the arthritic pace of management in the field.

Kevin sighed. It pissed him off that Michener was on the scene first. "How long have you been here?"

"A little over an hour. You want me to bring you up to speed?" Without waiting for an answer, he started in on a breakneck account of Haines's escape.

"What kind of medical tests?" Kevin interrupted.

"I don't know, what's it matter? Medical tests. Anyway, he fakes some kind of seizure and the dopes loosen his belts and he somehow gets a gun and takes out the guards. Makes the doctor drive. Asshole prison guard let him through the gate."

"Is he still around, the doctor?"

"She. Got to watch that, Kevin. Laura Donaldson."

The name was familiar to him, and he quickly knew why. A cancer doctor, prominent. He'd come across her name during the Haines case, and more recently, he seemed to recall reading about her somewhere. *Newsweek* maybe. What was she doing with David Haines? Clearly Michener hadn't had either the time or inclination to find out.

"So I told her to stick around," Michener went on. "I think one of the medics is looking at her. She got a bit scuffed up. I'll need her to ID the bodies inside."

Kevin bridled at the proprietorial tone with which Michener was already discussing the case.

The winch was slowly hauling the boxcar off the Gulfstream,

crushed like a smashed milk carton. Kevin could make out the jagged, punched-in outline of the main door.

"Anyone see him drive into the train?"

"A couple highway patrolmen. They were stationed at the prison and hauled after him as soon as they heard. They said he pulled up on the tracks and gunned it."

"He jumped."

"We'll see."

"What about the train driver," he asked. "Alive?"

"Barely. Unconscious, him and the chief engineer. They've already taken them into Joliet."

The boxcar was dragged clear of the Gulfstream and settled with a resounding clank on the field. Almost instantly, a rescue team moved in with their gear, ladders, crowbars, saws.

"All right," said Michener, moving closer, "here we go."

The air was shot through with gasoline. A rescue worker was cutting open the mangled door with a power saw.

"How many?" Michener called out.

"Two. I think," said one of the crew.

"You think?"

"There's a lot of body parts. From the impact," came the rescue worker's voice. "Definitely only two back here."

"Up front?" Michener asked.

"Doesn't look like it. Just the two."

"Fuck," said Michener.

"They'll be the guards," said Kevin. He felt like a know-it-all in the schoolyard, but somebody had to say it.

Michener ignored him.

It took some time for the crews to extract the bodies and their attendant limbs from the wreckage. They were lain out on the ground on stretchers. Turning back the sheets to look at them, Kevin felt an intense spasm of indignation on behalf of the two men, their bodies battered like this. Their faces were terribly damaged, but even so, he could tell right away neither belonged to David Haines.

Kevin looked at Michener and lifted his eyebrows. The wreck was all a colossal diversion, and it had worked. Almost three hours now since Haines's jump from the doomed vehicle, and Kevin was tortured by the notion that he was getting farther and farther away, a steadily advancing line across the map superimposed against his mind's eye. Which direction? Any point of the compass. He had to get to that post office box. He was wasting time here. He looked around for Hugh Carter. Where the hell was he?

"He won't get far on foot," muttered Michener.

"He had someone helping him from the inside. My bet's he got picked up. He's long gone."

Michener's eyes flashed up at him dangerously. "There's a lot of ground to cover here, Kevin, and I intend to do it." He yanked out his cell phone, punched buttons, and started yelling into it without preamble.

Kevin had crouched over the bodies to pull back the sheets when, behind him, he heard someone say: "I need to get inside."

He turned and saw a slender woman dressed in a sleeveless crew-neck top and pleated olive trousers. In the sunlight, her face, framed by wavy, dark hair, seemed shockingly pale. She had a high forehead, almond eyes, with twin smudges of darkness beneath them. A bruise was already coloring the skin around her left eye. Her nose seemed slightly too big for her narrow, tapered face, and her wide mouth was sensuous without being generous or welcoming. A striking face, certainly, but he couldn't decide if it was attractive or not. Right now, it seemed disconcertingly immobile.

"Dr. Donaldson?" he said.

She nodded. "I need to see if any of my samples made it."

There was an almost preternatural calm to her speech. She turned her eyes on the two bodies. The spectacle didn't seem to disturb her much, and Kevin felt a twinge of dislike for her. Then again, he supposed she was used to seeing dead bodies. He'd expected to be angrier with her: if not exactly the catalyst, she was at least a pawn in Haines's escape. But she looked so decidedly numb; he held his temper in check.

"Haines got away then," she said.

"God knows he had lots of help," said Michener, walking over and looking at her with open antagonism. "These your two guards?"

"Yes. Allan and Joseph. I'm sorry, I don't remember their last names. The people at MetaSYS would know."

"Uh-huh."

"Dr. Donaldson, I'm Special Agent Kevin Sheldrake."

"I really need to get into that lab," she said.

He had to remind himself to stay patient. Was that all she cared about, her fucking samples? Didn't she see what had happened around them? Train wreck, two men dead, and a mass murderer on the run? He was starting to share some of Michener's distaste for her.

"No one's going in right now except our team," Michener told her.

"I see," said the doctor. She turned away from them and started walking purposefully towards the wrecked Gulfstream.

"Hey!" shouted Michener. Angrily, he started towards her, but Kevin touched his arm.

"I'll deal with her."

She'd broken into a jog now and he hurried after her, but she was inside before he could reach her.

Doubled over, Laura squeezed into the mobile lab. The interior was so mangled it was almost unrecognizable to her. It was stifling inside, the air thick with the smell of blood: she could see it stickily coating almost every surface. She heard the FBI agent clambering in after her, calling for her to come out, but his voice seemed a long way away, muffled by the pounding of her own heart.

It took her a second to orient herself, and then she saw the cabinet where she'd stored the cooler. It was against a buckled-in wall, the doors bent out of shape. *Please, please, please*, running through her head like a crazy mantra. She could do without the bone marrow harvest maybe, but not the blood. If she just had the blood. She gripped the handle and pulled, but it was stuck.

"Dr. Donaldson!"

She saw him in her peripheral vision and felt his hand on her arm. She wrenched herself free and pulled again at the cabinet once more: the door snapped open, and she tumbled back onto her tailbone. She stared.

The cooler was a nest of shards, glued together by Haines's congealed blood.

"Oh God," she said quietly. The words to her own ears carried no dismay, only a weary finality. The samples were ruined, tainted, all the cells killed in the intense heat.

"I need you out of here, Doctor," Kevin said.

She turned to him, and was surprised by the look in his eyes. She'd expected bald anger, but instead she saw something approaching compassion, tinged with alarmed incomprehension.

She allowed herself to be ushered out of the Gulfstream. She noted dully that her pants and shirt were smeared with blood. The hazy shell of unreality that had encased her for the past couple of hours started to crack. It seemed suddenly too hot, the choking smell of diesel fuel, two corpses on the ground, gleaming blindingly in their shrouds—and what had she done? All screwed up, messed up, lost. Lost. Her heart was beating too fast, and she felt her stomach clench. She closed her eyes, took a deep breath, trying to ward off the familiar inward shrill of panic.

"Here."

She opened her eyes. Kevin Sheldrake was offering her a misty bottle of mineral water. She saw her hand reach out to take it.

"Thank you."

"All right?"

Nodding, she took several sips. Kevin Sheldrake had thick wavy hair combed back from his forehead, only a few streaks of silver at his temples. His large, round eyes were heavy-lidded but utterly attentive, and in combination with his long face they gave him a somewhat mournful, lupine appearance. He was handsome, in a lean, hungry sort of way. Quite a contrast anyway to that little rodent Michener. Earlier he'd treated her with barely concealed disdain, as if she were an accessory to murder. *And maybe you are*, she thought, *maybe you are.*

"You were taking blood samples from David Haines?"

She nodded.

"And he gave his permission?" He sounded incredulous.

"We had a court order," she said tightly.

"I see. And what were they for, the tests?"

The last of her panic decomposed into pure exhaustion. She'd intended to tell him as little as possible—that's what Paul had advised her when she'd called from a cell phone half an hour ago. He was on his way down, but he hadn't wanted her telling anyone about the nature of the tests. Didn't want any competition from other companies, she guessed. But what was the point of trying to hide it? It had to come out.

"Cancer research," she said, and saw Sheldrake frown.

"Haines has cancer?"

"Possibly."

"I don't understand."

"I've seen some of his blood already. We think he might have some kind of enzyme that breaks down tumors. We wanted samples."

"We?"

"MetaSYS Pharmaceuticals."

"And does Haines ... did he know this, about his blood?"

"His lawyer told him."

She saw Sheldrake's eyes stray from her and flick distractedly across the horizon.

"Okay," he said, "look, I'm going to need to talk more about this, but not right now. I'd like you to come down to our Chicago office tomorrow morning." His tone was brusque; he seemed to want to get away. He pulled out his wallet and handed her a card.

"Are you in a house or apartment?"

She just looked at him for a moment before understanding his question. Her knees were buckling; she wanted to sit down.

"You think he'll—" Her words snagged in her dry throat and she coughed.

"I'm just inquiring for your own safety," Sheldrake told her.

"Apartment."

"Unlisted?"

"Yes."

"That's good. Any reason why he might know where you live?"

"No, I don't think so ..." She stopped. "Oh God." She hadn't even thought of it before now. Sickened, she remembered that she'd left her purse in the glove compartment when they'd arrived at the prison. Inside: her wallet, her Filofax. Her whole goddamn life.

"My purse," she told him.

"You left it in the Gulfstream?" He eased a slow breath through parted lips. She followed his gaze to the mobile lab, the cab mashed into a weave of twisted metal.

"Bottom line," Sheldrake said, "it's probably still there. He wouldn't have had time to root around for things. I'll get them to check as soon as they can. But you and your family are going to need to stay somewhere else tonight."

"I live alone."

"We're going to put you up in a hotel, okay?"

"Is this really necessary?" she asked weakly.

"You're familiar with his religious beliefs?"

She nodded.

"Well, you took his blood, Dr. Donaldson, you committed blasphemy against his body. And I hate to tell you, but you're his idea of the perfect target. Let us take care of you, tonight at least."

"All right," she mumbled. "Thanks."

From across the field, she heard an excited shout: "We've got footprints!"

"I've got to go," said Kevin.

Before she could stop herself, she blurted out: "You'll take him alive, won't you?"

But he was already gone, running with the other officers.

Kevin could see a small knot of people up ahead, Michener among them. He followed them to the other side of the tracks, climbing between two toppled boxcars, and came out into unflattened cornfields. Here, in a slight depression, the ground was still boggy after last night's rain. The tracker dog was whining excitedly, pulling at its leash.

He drew closer and looked. In the mud he saw two prints, far apart: a man running. He followed the line of the stride and could see a vague corridor of battered cornstalks. One thing was certain: Haines wasn't suffering from a sprain or a broken leg. No one could take strides like that injured.

He heard a click and saw Michener cocking his revolver. Then they were all moving, crouching through the stalks. On the drier ground, the prints all but disappeared, but the trampled stalks became their guide.

Kevin pulled his Glock. He still didn't expect to find Haines anywhere in the vicinity, but he wasn't taking any chances. There was a good chance he'd taken a gun from the guards, and it might still have some bullets left.

Abruptly the trail brought them out onto a dirt service road. Not even a road really, just a lane wide enough to move farm equipment down. He scoured the soft ground, but it seemed too grassy to offer clear footprints.

"Look at this," said a marshal. He was pointing to a fresh-looking set of tire marks in the earth, and a few yards down, twin gouges, like someone spinning tires to get away fast.

"These aren't tractor tires," said Michener. "Looks like a hatchback maybe, something small anyway."

Kevin had expected as much: the getaway car.

Michener didn't even look at him. "All right, people," he shouted. "Looks like our boy had wheels. Now somebody must've seen this car. This is a farmer's field, right, so I want someone to find me a farmer. Big straw hat, overalls, piece of grass hanging from his mouth, the real goddamn thing, okay? You go get me one of those."

Michener turned to him with a smile. "Well, looks like you *were* right, Kevin."

He wondered how much Hugh had told Michener about Detroit, the letter-writing, the post office box. He wasn't ready to tell Michener yet, not until he'd talked to Hugh. He had breaking information, and he wanted onto the task force—not just *onto* it, he wanted to *supervise* it. Haines was his, and he didn't want Michener heading up the manhunt.

"Hugh said you nailed a pen pal in Detroit," Michener remarked.

Kevin nodded. Shit, so he already knew.

"Had someone inside mailing the letters?"

"That's right. He must've opened a post office box."

"Well, that's our lead," said Michener. "You've got the number and address?"

"Yeah, I've got it," Kevin said.

"Good, you're both here."

Kevin turned to see Hugh Carter walking out from the trampled corn with Stephen Matic, another agent from the fugitive squad. Even in the melting heat, pushing through cornfields, Hugh managed to look robust and undaunted while emanating an air of imperturbable authority. In Kevin's mind, Hugh looked exactly the way most people imagined a senior FBI agent should look. At six-foot three he was physically impressive, with a large, weathered face and a thick Marlborough Man mustache. He was fifty-seven but he still had that big-cocked walk—that slightly stiff, almost bowlegged gait which suggested there was something unbelievably big and heavy jutting out between his thighs. What Kevin found most maddening about Hugh was his utter refusal to see himself as a walking cliché.

"He had a car waiting," Michener told him. "He's probably long gone."

Hugh nodded, then put a hand on Kevin's back and took a few steps away from Michener so they could talk in private. Kevin took this as a good sign, but his hope was short-lived.

"I need you to work with Mitch on this one."

"Define *with*."

"I want you as assistant supervisor for the task force."

Assistant. Which would make Mitch supervisor. He looked across the fields of corn, anger pulsing at his temples, not trusting himself to speak. He wiped a knuckle across his damp, itching eyebrows.

Slowly he said, "Hugh, I should be heading this one up. It's mine. I know Haines."

"That's why Mitch is going to need your help. He's the best bloodhound we've got, but he's not as smart as you."

Far from placating him, the disingenuous flattery only stoked his fury. He'd worked damn hard in Detroit, refused to back down, and he'd nailed Will Andrews. Who'd thought he was going to come back to Chicago with a doctor-killer? What's more, the letters he'd found gave him the post office box through which Haines funneled all his nefarious correspondence—and to Kevin's way of thinking, this was the best lead they had right now. And to see it all gift-wrapped and handed over to Michener ...

Even through his outrage he could see the machinery behind Hugh's decision. Michener was on an amazing winning streak. Last year he'd brought in a record number of fugitives. It was the kind of statistic that got people re-elected, and placated Republicans all over the country. *Your tax dollars, keeping the scum off the streets.* That some of Michener's fugitives were returned dead rather than alive in no way compromised his status as a hero. Next year he'd probably make supervisor of the whole Violent Crimes squad. People clamored to work with him. After all, he made law enforcement seem like such a ferociously good time, if you were the right kind of man, with big enough balls. Michener certainly had a big mouth, and a funny one, if you favored the kind of movies that have audacious, quasi-suicidal cops who won't take no for an answer. But Kevin had never liked him, and he certainly didn't like his style. Several years ago, one of Kevin's key witnesses in a case had skipped bail, crossed the border, and Michener had tracked him down. A high-speed chase had ended with Kevin's witness crumpled dead in his car against a concrete divider.

He dragged a hand down his face. No way someone like Michener could catch Haines—Haines was too smart, too unusual. Michener might understand greed and malice and lust, but he couldn't understand what drove Haines. All his instincts would take him nowhere.

"Hugh," he began, and then, with a cough of incredulous laughter, shook his head, knowing it would be futile to argue further.

"Work with him, Kevin. Together you'll make a hell of team."

"Yeah."

He walked over to Michener and waited for him to finish yelling into the phone. "The box is in Joliet."

"All right," said Michener, giving Kevin a friendly slap on the back. "Let's go get it."

CHAPTER TWELVE

The living room was infested with angels.

David stepped inside, eyes passing over the china cabinet crowded with figurines fashioned from porcelain, crystal, wood, wire, dried beans. More angels perched on doilies on side tables. In each corner of the room, a doll-sized angel coyly peeped out from behind folded wings.

Large paintings in pastel colors hung from the walls. Gail had written about her paintings, but he was unprepared for how hideous they were. Some were poorly realistic, benevolent robed figures with wings spread; others were more abstract, bright plumes of pink and gold and mauve against vague celestial backdrops. As a depiction of divine power, he found them lacking: he was wary of all sloppy, sentimental depictions of God's love. He knew that it was not so easily won, and was not as indiscriminately accommodating as many liked to think.

After the calming austerity of his cell, he found the room oppressive, but he was acutely relieved to be inside, to be safely housed once again by walls and ceiling. He'd spent the hour-long drive into Chicago in fervent prayer, not speaking, as if the very sky and air were antagonistic to him, crushing down.

A white cat padded across the room and rubbed itself against his leg. Almost involuntarily he reached down and stroked its back. It was the softest thing he'd touched in three years. When he straightened up, Gail was beaming.

"I knew it," she said. "I knew she'd like you. She knows about people."

David smiled tolerantly, hoping he'd not made a mistake in choosing Gail. Always he'd found something repellent about people who lavished love on animals—so misguided. There was only one thing worth loving.

"Where's your bathroom?"

"Down this way. I'm sorry if it's a bit messy, I didn't have much time." She laughed awkwardly, as if suddenly realizing that he was far from a normal houseguest.

"Thank you," he said, closing the door behind him.

The bathroom was carpeted in mild pink, with a matching toilet seat cover of excessive fluffiness and an abundance of plush towels. Around the sink were two shallow bowls filled with crushed flower petals, and an angel toothbrush holder. On a tall set of wicker shelves was a clutter of baskets filled with an incomprehensible selection of soaps and oils and cosmetics. He sat down on the toilet. The wallpaper was patterned with a million roses. Despite this alien decor he felt strangely at home, and then he realized that the bathroom was about the same size as his cell. He closed his eyes: unbelievable quiet. He heard only the small hum of the air-conditioning, the whisper of a car passing outside.

He washed his hands and studied himself in the mirror. When he returned to the living room he found Gail still standing, awkward, an abandoned stranger in someone else's home.

"Do you have a pair of electric clippers?" he asked her.

"For your hair?" she asked, unable to hide her dismay at the idea of him disfiguring himself.

"It's better that way."

"I don't have any, but I can get some. You'll need clothes, too. I'll just need your size."

His size. It had been a long time since he'd had to think about things like clothes. Gail went down the hall and returned with a tape measure.

"I'm sorry for the expense," he said.

"I'd spend my last penny on you," she told him as she measured his feet, then his waist. When she came to his neck, he could feel her hands trembling.

He sensed that she was only now realizing what she'd done, the risk she'd taken. Helping a death row felon escape. Harboring him. The fear was natural, but he needed her to be strong. He touched her shoulder.

"It's all right, Gail. Don't be afraid."

She tilted her face up to him, tears streaming silently down her cheeks.

"I'm not crying because I'm scared," she managed to choke out, "it's because I'm so happy you're here. This is the best thing I've ever done."

* * *

Gail drew the clippers gently across his scalp, and David watched with satisfaction as his sandy hair fell away to stubble in neat rows. Seated before the bathroom mirror, a towel around his shoulders, he felt strangely liberated, as if being pared down to a truer, elemental self, the spare exoskeleton that housed his soul: bone, sinew, skin. He was Samson in reverse, gaining strength as the weight of all things unnecessary fell away.

He'd spent the better part of two hours alone in the house while Gail was out buying him clothes and electric clippers. He'd prayed for half an hour, kneeling on the living-room floor, and then walked from room to room, the bungalow seeming to him as massive as a cathedral.

And just as full of vain ornament. The furniture, the angels, the rugs and towels, the doilies: the clutter. Was Gail too attached to her worldly things? *Where you heap your treasures, there will your heart be also.*

He was even more disturbed when he saw his portrait.

Pacing the hallways he'd glanced into her bedroom. There, above her bed, hung a large watercolor rendering of himself. He flipped on the light. It was painted in the same overwrought style as her angels, his face radiating light, his body swathed in misty pastel energy. His painted feet seemed scarcely to be touching the ground, levitating. He could only assume she removed this picture when she had visitors, though he knew this would be rare. And he doubted she had ever shared her bed with anyone, certainly not in the time he'd been corresponding with her.

That Gail was lonely and unattractive he had easily gleaned from her letters. And he'd never been entirely blind to the possibility of her mistakenly, sinfully, forming some kind of romantic dependence on him—but her letters had seemed too devout, too disciplined. He didn't doubt her devotion to him, but now he questioned its nature. Was it his teachings she loved, or him as a man? He'd always known it was a risk, choosing a woman as one of his faithful. He hoped he hadn't erred with her.

Not for the first time, he wondered if he should have let Bob Jarvis shelter him. But it was too difficult to arrange. He'd needed someone to pick him up outside the prison, and Bob had been on duty that morning. Anyway, Bob lived in an apartment block, whereas Gail had her own house. And Bob might fall under scrutiny now.

And there was Gail's job: an international directory assistance operator with Ameritech. While he was still in prison, he'd used her twice to find the addresses of doctors—one in Canada, one in Georgia—which he'd passed along to his faithful. If he was to continue his work now, she would prove invaluable.

She met his eyes in the mirror.

"How did you do it?" she asked awkwardly. "Escape."

"They wanted my blood." He told her quickly about what they'd found there. She looked aghast when he related their blasphemous attempts to steal it. "The doctor they sent was Laura Donaldson."

He saw Gail's face crumple. She drew back the clippers, as if afraid of nicking him. "I'm sorry," she said brokenly, eyes wet. "I should've ... if I'd done what you asked me, this wouldn't have happened ..."

"It worked out for the best, Gail," he told her gently. "It gave me the chance to escape, to continue my work. And you the chance to help me."

Gail sniffed and nodded. "I know I've disappointed you."

"It's a heavy cross to bear," he told her.

"Now that you're here, I know I can be stronger."

He smiled, wondering. So far, Will Andrews was the only one who had fulfilled his duties to the utmost. David had seen the story in the newspaper just two days before his escape, and was filled with pride. Here was a man who had been given so little by life, and had made much of it. More than pride, it filled him with a sense of relief—the certainty that his work would live on, that all he had preached through his acts would not simply dissolve into thin air.

"You can stay here as long as you like," Gail told him. "No one'll ever find you here."

He saw the need in her eyes. "Thank you, Gail."

With the clippers she made a last pass over his scalp. "I'll shave the rest off. I got some shaving cream, and a razor."

"Gail," he said quietly. "I'm just a mortal servant, like you. I'm not an angel."

He saw her flush. "You saw the portrait? You didn't like it?"

"I was very flattered. But we mustn't forget who we're serving. I don't matter. What I *do* matters. Same with you." He turned and reached up and put his hand right on her cheek. He felt her flinch, take a step back, then go very still, her eyes locked on his.

"The outside things don't matter. Real beauty is not a question of the flesh."

She stepped away from his hand and busied herself with the can of shaving cream. "That's pretty much the nicest thing anyone's said to me in a long time," she said quietly. She spread the foam over his skull and filled the sink with hot water. Then she began to shave off the stubble.

"What will you do now?" she asked.

At first he'd thought his chief task would be to evade the authorities, to escape. He'd even thought of making his way across the border. But he knew instinctively that wasn't right. He'd already spent many hours questioning why his blood contained what it did. He understood that God was jolting him out of his complacency, reminding him that his work was not done yet. But was he merely to continue his earlier work, or was there a new direction?

He felt her nick his scalp.

"Sorry!" said Gail.

In the mirror he could see a small red stain blooming through the white foam. As Gail hurried to get a tissue, he stared at the bead of his own blood. Was he a solitary freak? Was he the only one in the world who carried this enzyme? He let his mind work back along the still-familiar pathways of his science training.

Possible, yes, that it was a chromosomal mutation particular only to him. Or maybe it was something he'd inherited from his parents. And maybe ...

He could understand why he'd been chosen to carry this devil's substance in his blood, but would God also have given it to his younger brother? What if Rick carried the same blood in his veins? What would the purpose of it be?

The answer came to him like a premonition of nausea: *I come not to unite but to divide, to set brother against brother ...*

He felt humbled again. He'd indulged himself, in the quiet cell of his own mind, imagined making for the border, escaping from his pursuers. But there was a lot for him to do here. There would be no running.

As always, the path was clear, though he'd tried to obscure it with his own desires, his own selfishness and vanity.

Several weeks ago, in prison, he'd received a letter from his brother, a farewell letter of sorts, a self-serving attempt to make amends and assuage the guilt he felt because of what he'd done. Rick hadn't given a return address, but the envelope's cancellation stamp told him he was in Chicago. He knew Rick would be unlisted, but Gail could do the rest.

Gail finished shaving his head and, with the towel, wiped off the remaining foam. David stared. His face was startlingly elongated. Cheekbones jutting, he looked almost gaunt. He nodded at this stranger in the mirror, satisfied.

"I'll need your help now, Gail, more than ever."

She nodded eagerly, though he wondered if that was a shadow of reluctance in her eyes.

"I need my brother's address. Richard Haines. He's here in town, unlisted. Can you do that for me?"

She seemed almost relieved. "I'll do it first thing tomorrow," she promised.

*   *   *

They put her up in the Swissôtel on East Wacker under an assumed name. Her room looked out over the Columbus Drive bridge, and she could see north along the mountain peaks of the Magnificent Mile, all the way up to the tapered summit of the Hancock Tower. Directly opposite her was an office building, each floor a diorama of workstations and offices and heads in front of computer monitors. The familiar landscape, the sight of people so near at hand, should have comforted her, but somehow, trapped behind the hotel's sealed windows, it just enhanced her sense of isolation.

It wasn't much past five o'clock, and it seemed almost impossible that life could be going on normally elsewhere. People getting ready to go home, make dinner, talk to their lovers and husbands and wives. She felt as if her own personal clock had been arrested at the moment she'd escaped from the mobile lab, and now she existed in some horrible airport lounge limbo. She wished she had a balcony, some way of getting fresh air.

She remembered Haines and involuntarily took a step back from the window. He might not even be in the city—that's what Kevin Sheldrake had said—but that was little comfort. He *might* be there, and that was all that really mattered. He was like some nightmare stalker who'd been jarred from her subconscious into the real world, enfleshed, hideously autonomous, and now maybe doing his damnedest to reunite himself with her. For the first time in her life she wished she owned a gun. She drew the curtains, but that only made her feel more alone, more cut off. She opened them again.

She paced, hating this. She had nothing: no credit cards, no driver's license, her car was still parked in the MetaSYS lot in Morton Grove. She felt powerless, immobilized. But she knew she was too scared to go anywhere right now—and she hated that even more.

She sat down in one of the tasteful green-and-white-striped armchairs, her can of pepper spray beside her—one of the few things she'd grabbed from her apartment when her Bureau escort had taken her by earlier to pack an overnight bag.

She wished she had some phenmetrizine. She could feel the last of her adrenaline leeching out of her, leaving a familiar headachy smear of weariness, self-disgust, and looming anxiety. And she didn't want to get dopey; she didn't want to sleep here. Stupidly she'd put her last bottle in her purse this morning, and her purse was either mashed into oblivion in the Gulfstream or in the hands of a psychopath.

All day, surrounded by people, she'd felt little but a crushing sense of failure. Now, in the silence of the hotel room, her fear broke into a gallop. In her mind's eye she saw Haines with the contents of her purse spread before him—every piece of ID, her credit cards, the photos of her family—thank God at least they were out of town. Her whole life was laid bare to him, down to where she got her hair cut, for God's sake. She'd have to move, everyone would have to move, how could she go to work again without feeling afraid ...?

Be rational. What were the chances Haines had her purse? It was in the glove compartment. Why would it occur to Haines to look there? There had been only minutes between her escape and his collision. He'd been at the wheel. He wouldn't have been able to reach over and drag through the glove compartment. Kevin Sheldrake had said as much. She summoned up his tired, lupine face and felt strangely comforted. It didn't last long.

You're his ideal target.

He'd said that, too. That was not comforting.

Somehow she hadn't expected she'd be left all alone. She'd imagined an FBI agent in an adjoining room, the door open. But after seeing her into the room, her female escort had left her a list of emergency numbers and told her she'd be back in the morning to drive her to the field office. Watching the door close behind her, a childlike voice had keened through her head: *Don't leave me.* She'd stared mutely at the door for a second, and then hurriedly shot the deadbolt into place.

Now she picked up the phone, her finger poised over the buttons. Who could she call? Her father had already left for Mexico, and the number of the clinic was in her Filofax. She dialed Emily at the lab, and got voice-mail. Halfway through Adrian's number, she hung up, realizing that what she really wanted was comfort. Wouldn't do it. What did she expect him to do, rush straight over and hold her hand? She tried Paul instead—he could at least give her the facts—and got voice-mail there, too. Probably everyone had already left for the day. She turned on the television.

Surfing, it wasn't long before she came across some coverage of Haines's escape. The aerial footage of the train wreck seemed unreal, shimmering in the heat. Then a squat man with excessively blow-dried hair and a dusting of dandruff on his navy-blue shoulders appeared on screen. A caption identified him as the warden of the Illinois Correctional Institute. He looked harried before the bristling phalanx of microphones.

"—they had a valid court order; it was taken out of my hands. The guards responsible for Haines were not my officers. They were private security personnel from MetaSYS. Now that's all I can say at this time."

She felt a jolt of surprise at the mention of MetaSYS, but what had she expected? She just hadn't thought the news would spread this fast. Even in her numbed state she knew this was shaping up to be a public relations crucifixion for the company. Impulsively she dialed Adrian's office number and, at the sound of his voice, felt a quick rush of gratitude and relief.

"Laura, thank God. They've got you in a safehouse?"

"I don't feel very safe, but yeah, I guess that's what they call it."

"You're okay?"

She was ashamed of herself for taking pleasure in his seeming concern for her. "Just a bit scraped up, but I'm fine."

"Paul told me what happened in the lab—"

"My mess. I should've known he was faking," she said miserably.

"You did what any good doctor would've done. Are you going to be okay where you are?"

Footsteps sounded outside her room and she stopped breathing, listening as they faded away and ended with the slam of a door. Insane: how could Haines possibly know where she was?

"Laura?"

"Yeah, I'm here." Her words came out as a breathless wheeze.

"It's really, really bad here," Adrian said. "Have you seen it on TV?"

"Just now."

"We're probably going to take part of the fall. Paul says we're looking at criminal liability, possible lawsuits with the security guards' families, the rail company—even the Department of Corrections may want a piece of us for this. Goddamn mess."

"I'm sorry, Adrian," she said.

"Anyway, look, you're going to be fine. There's a huge manhunt for Haines, and they're saying they'll have him in twenty-four hours. They might already have him."

"Then we can take more samples, right?"

She heard him exhale. "Not so simple. The court order was good for the day. We'd have to reapply."

"So we reapply." But she felt her mind clouding with disappointment: as if it had been easy the first time.

Her eyes roved restlessly across the buildings outside her window, settling on the letters across the summit of the Equitable Building. Her view cut off the first letter of its name: Quitable. She wished she could open a window.

"Look, Laura, Paul just got a call from Vic Greene. He's already filed an emergency appeal with a higher court to overturn our court order. Greene says he's got the ACLU onside. It's going to be ugly. Apparently he's holding a press conference tomorrow. And I think I know his strategy: powerful corporate bully violates religious rights of vulnerable individual. The media'll love it."

"But we *are* reapplying, right?"

"I want to, but Paul's not too confident about our chances."

Figures, Laura thought angrily. *All of you, a bunch of quitters.* "We won the first time."

"It'll be different now. Full hearing, three appeal court judges. And according to Paul they tend to rule on the letter of the law. It'll come down to constitutional issues."

"It's cancer, for God's sake!" Laura said. "We can get medical experts to testify."

"So can Greene. Look, I'm calling our own press conference tomorrow at noon, see if we can preempt Greene's. It'll look better if we have a world-renowned cancer specialist up there, saying this guy might hold the key to a cancer cure."

"I'll be there."

"And I think we should show the footage."

For a moment she didn't know what to say. Show the footage for the whole world to see? It was like revealing the coordinates of her own secret treasure trove. Would every cancer researcher in the country be lining up for a shot at it? She sighed; perhaps it was unavoidable. The important thing was to get the blood.

"Yes," she agreed.

"I'm doing my best here, Laura, but the board's called an emergency meeting tomorrow afternoon. If we fight this case and lose, we'll take a public relations beating. I mean, Haines may not even get taken alive."

Laura thought of Michener, his buggy, hunter's eyes, and winced, knowing this was a real possibility.

"I know."

"Try and get some rest, Laura. I wish I could be there with you, but ..."

Come, she wanted to say, but wouldn't. "I'm fine, Adrian. Thanks."

When she hung up the phone, the silence of the hotel room closed oppressively around her. She stared mindlessly at the curtains, tracing the floral pattern until it made no sense, just a tangle of lines, going nowhere, nowhere. Her protocol, now Haines: she'd fucked both up. Why the hell didn't they have windows you could open here?

Somehow she made it to the bathroom, her head a sandstorm of panic. Hunched over the toilet, she looked desperately around the room, trying to focus on one thing at a time, name things, keep herself from flying off the face of the earth. Hair dryer, marble countertop, flex mirror, Neutrogena dispenser, telephone, count the buttons, one, two ... I can't ... three, four, no good, no good ... There was virtually nothing in her stomach to bring up, but she retched in vain again and again, as if trying to expel her corrosive sense of failure and helplessness. Shivering, she sank down on the marbled floor. *Get up. Can't. Turn on the lights. Can't. Turn on the tap. Can't. Sorry, Sandra, sorry.*

She leaned against the tub, trying to focus on the cool porcelain against her cheek, only this, only this. The panic slowly leeched out of her body, and with it all her energy. There was nothing she could do to get Haines back—it was out of her hands. And even if she did get the blood, what made her think she could wrest a therapy from it? Look at her recent track record. Suddenly the urge to flee surged through her. To get away from all this, away from her lab and MetaSYS and David Haines, go somewhere he couldn't find her. Once she got her credit cards back she could go to the airport, book a flight, anywhere, anywhere she liked, spend a week in Paris. Go to Tijuana and see her sister ...

But even as she imagined herself in various postcard settings, she knew she wasn't going anywhere.

David Haines might be lost to her. But maybe his blood wasn't. She knew what she had to do.

Find the brother. Find Rick Haines.

* * *

"This isn't a good idea."

Seth Michener made no reply; he only eyed Kevin impassively as he lifted the Coke to his lips and finished it off. Putting his can down on the table beside two other empties, he picked up his raspberry danish.

Kevin pressed on, quietly. "We should keep Jarvis under surveillance. We can get a wiretap by midday, maybe some parabolic equipment moved in across the street. We need to hold tight for a bit, Mitch."

"I've gotta take a piss."

Michener slipped out of the sticky booth and headed back to the washrooms. In his sloppy sneakers, fraying jeans, and windbreaker, he fit right in with the rest of the early-morning crowd at Donut Time. Joliet was a dismal little town, whose only distinction was being home to three penal institutions. Kevin looked out the window at the wasteland of empty parking lots, strip plazas, and car dealerships on the outskirts of town. He wanted a shower; he wanted sleep. It was 4:07, and they were waiting for their tactical team to arrive.

Yesterday—though it hardly felt like yesterday to Kevin; it was all one big continuous smear of time—he'd left the crash site with Michener and driven into Joliet to track down the post box company. As it turned out, they didn't even need to promise a court order to follow. The manager, after seeing their FBI badges, became almost frighteningly accommodating. Information spilled out of him. In seconds they had the name and address of the man who had opened the box.

Bob Jarvis.

Kevin asked if there was any mail in the box right now, but it was empty. He'd left his card with the manager and asked him to call if any other letters came in: his help would be of great importance to the Bureau's investigation, Kevin made sure to point out. Kevin had rarely seen a man look happier.

The next stop was Illinois Correctional. Warden Humphries hadn't been pleased by Kevin's suggestion that one of his guards had been colluding with Haines. But when Kevin gave Jarvis's name, the warden's face turned even grayer than it had been when they'd arrived amidst the media feeding frenzy. Jarvis had been a guard at the prison for fifteen years. They pulled his file, got everything they could on him, including his photo ID. Jarvis was still on duty, but Kevin decided not to interview him right then—he didn't want to risk tipping him off. They had his address and that was enough.

By four o'clock he and Mitch were back in Chicago, setting up their command post in the main conference room of the field office. They pulled everyone they could from the fugitive squad and the violent crimes squad and had eighty-seven special agents working leads on the street by dinnertime, plus a dozen deputy marshals and officers from the Chicago police force.

Kevin sent someone to watch Laura Donaldson's apartment building, just in case Haines was sloppy enough to try to get to her. It was a long-shot—Haines would know they'd be watching, and he had his own survival to think of now—but he didn't want to miss the possibility.

By eight o'clock, after putting together a surveillance team around Jarvis's apartment, he'd managed to steal a minute to call Diane.

"Hi. Look, David Haines has escaped."

"I heard." The anger in her voice was barely concealed, as if he'd personally opened his cell door and shown him the exit. "You're saying we're in danger?"

"No. You're unlisted, and it's not in his nature to do anything out of revenge. I'd just ... just maybe take Becky over to your Dad's place for a while, just until things settle down."

He wondered if he was being egotistical even to entertain the idea that Haines might harbor a hatred of him so intense he'd take it out on his family. Realistically, he doubted he figured anywhere in David's thoughts right now.

"Is he around the city?"

"We don't know yet," he told her.

"Jesus," she said. "Well, I'm sure you're delighted to have him back in your life. But he was never very far off anyway."

"Just please take Becky somewhere, okay."

"All right." There was brief pause, and he wondered if she were going to tell him to be careful. "Thanks for telling us," she said and hung up.

Michener slid back into the booth.

"Haven't done too many of these, have you, Kevin?"

Kevin looked at him evenly, fully expecting to be called a scaredy-cat, or maybe some other second-grade insult.

"Raids, no," he said, "but that's not why I think it's a mistake. Remember Waco, Texas, back in '93?"

"Prehistoric. But yeah, quite a light show."

"We fucked it up," Kevin said. "And we're going to fuck up right now if we raid Jarvis."

Michener shrugged. "It's easy. We go in, they'll be asleep, we take them both down, we'll all be back in the office by nine filling out forms. Nine-thirty, latest."

Michener, Kevin knew, was used to picking up his fugitives in the most appallingly obvious places—at the homes of their wives, girl-friends, parents, siblings, grandmothers. It almost made you throw up your hands at the paucity of human imagination.

"Haines won't be there."

"Says who?"

"There's at least one more accomplice. Who do you think drove the car? Mitch, give it twelve hours. Jarvis can lead us to Haines, and maybe his other devotees."

"If you can't stomach this, you can go home and I'll call you."

Kevin could tell he wasn't going to change Michener's mind, and there was no way he was letting him go in there alone. He knew too well about Michener's tendencies to downsize his fugitives' first amendment rights. Cop, judge, and executioner all in one little mangy package.

"We all come out alive, Mitch. All of us."

"Of course we do," said Michener, making his eyes all big, as if this was insultingly obvious. "Although," he added, "I don't know why you give a shit. This guy's killed how many people? Nine now, counting the security guards. I don't think any tears will be shed for him." His grin went from amicable to icy. "Let me tell you something. If there's any risk to me or our men, and I mean *any* risk, we'll be shooting, and if you're smart you will too."

Kevin could imagine Michener's blood pumping with caffeine and sugar, like a shaken pop bottle ready to explode. This was going to be really bad. He didn't want to go in: Jarvis would certainly be armed. He was a career prison guard, and he was probably pretty damn good with his gun. And on the off chance Haines was there, he'd probably be armed too, either with a gun he took from the Gulfstream, or one Jarvis provided for him. They might even be expecting them.

He was afraid of going in, yes, of course he was. Anyone who wasn't afraid was an idiot. But with a start he also realized that he was even more afraid of Haines getting killed—and not just because of what Donaldson had told him about his blood.

He didn't want Haines to die. It was personal. For a long time he'd guiltily yearned for his execution, but now he realized it had always been mixed with at least equal parts dread. He didn't want Haines to go—and what the hell did that mean? With a knuckle he rubbed his burning eyes. What did it matter? If they got him alive, he'd get his lethal injection in days anyway. He couldn't save Haines from that. *Save?* Where did *that* come from?

Michener looked at him, amused. "I know you think I'm some kind of cartoon character, Kevin. Just some gung ho cowboy, no brain, whatever. But listen to this: I know what I'm doing. It's what I've done for sixteen years, and I'm good at it. I might surprise you."

He looked past him, out the front windows. Kevin turned to see a black van pull up in the parking lot. Two men in flak jackets stepped out of the cab.

"All right," said Michener, "our boys are here."

*　　*　　*

Bob Jarvis's apartment was on the third floor. In Michener's hand was the master key he'd got from the super. Kevin watched as he slipped it into the lock, turned, eased the door open a fraction of an inch, enough to see the chain on the inside. Michener backed up and pulled his Colt .45. It was a big bastard of a gun, unwieldy, and totally illegal for law enforcement. Kevin could guess why Michener used it. You saw a gun like that pointed at you, you thought twice. It scared the shit out of him just to look at the thing.

Kevin's 9 mm. was already in his hand. The other eight members of the entry team had pump-action shotguns. He hated guns. At Quantico, the first time he'd peered through the telescopic sights of a shotgun and seen someone's head in the crosshairs, he'd felt, coupled with the sense of appalling power, a ferocious pang of nausea. It was so catastrophically easy: one simple squeeze of the trigger and, like a witch crooking her finger, he could spirit away someone's life. And this too: he'd never been a great shot. He felt his heart hammering against the weight of his flak jacket. Michener made eye contact with him and smirked.

"I *love* going first," he whispered, then lunged with all his weight, heel slamming against wood. The door exploded, and suddenly Kevin was inside, deafened by the hollering from Michener and his men.

"FBI—"

"—armed and in pursuit of David Haines—"

"—hands on your fucking head!"

The super had given them a floor plan. The door brought them right into the cramped living room, the early-morning light filtered sourly through cream roller blinds. Kevin's eyes skittered round the furniture, searching for anything human.

"Clear!" he shouted, and already knew they'd screwed up. No pull-out bed, no blankets. It was a one-bedroom apartment. No one sleeping in the living room. No Haines.

There was only one short corridor and all the rooms led off it on the right. Michener and his men were already whirling down, flanking the doorways one by one, making their way to the bedroom at the far end.

"Kitchen, clear!"

"Bathroom, clear!"

That left the bedroom. Gray light came from the open doorway, but before Michener had even reached it, two shots rang out in quick succession, smacking into the corridor wall.

"Put your gun down!" Michener shouted, hanging back.

No answer. Kevin waited in the narrow hallway, sweating. Jarvis was holed up in there, probably behind his bed, gun leveled at the doorway. It was just as he'd feared.

"Put your fucking gun down!" Michener shouted again. "We've got a man outside, and you're in his crosshairs. Don't make me give that order!"

It was bullshit, and Jarvis probably knew it. There was no sniper on a roof. All the windows faced out onto a narrow alley. And they didn't have a marksman in the apartment directly opposite.

Still no answer.

"Bob," said Michener, actually chuckling, "give me a break here, all right? I come into that room, one of us is gonna get shot. Now I want to see that gun of yours come sliding out into the hall, okay?

Nothing.

Jarvis was calling his bluff, knowing perfectly well that no sane person would volunteer to throw himself into a gunman's line of fire.

"Bring up the smoke," Michener said into his lapel mike.

In less than a minute an agent came through the door carrying the metal canisters and a string of gas masks. Kevin hurriedly pulled his over his head, breathing the stifling, rubbery air.

"Bob!" Mitch shouted. "I'm gonna count to five and if I don't see that gun, we're pumping smoke in there. One ... two ... three ... four ... five!"

Michener inched forward, pulled the metal tab on the canister and lobbed it in an arc into the room. Then he cracked open a second canister and let fly. He peeled on his own mask just as the dense pall of yellowish smoke hissed out into the hallway.

Kevin pulled back with the others, taking up position with a clear view down, waiting. The single shot sounded like a thunderclap, and Kevin's finger instinctively tightened around the trigger. But there was no sign of Jarvis in the hallway, even as the smoke began to dissipate. Anyone in there would have been forced out by now. Anyone alive.

"Bob!" Michener called out.

"Shit," Kevin muttered. He'd been afraid this would happen. Stupid, stupid to launch a raid. He stood and started walking down the hallway, past the tactical shooters, still crouched in position.

Michener grabbed his arm. "What the fuck're you doing?"

Kevin pulled his arm free. He walked into the doorway and looked. It took a moment for the smoke to clear. There, slumped on the bed, was Bob Jarvis, his head half blasted away by his own bullet.

CHAPTER THIRTEEN

"I have some concerns about Mitch heading the task force."

Concerns. That was putting it mildly, Kevin thought. You were concerned about a misplaced file, a holdup at forensics. Concern didn't even come close to what he was feeling. After what he'd seen in the last few hours, he was comprehensively disgusted—and very afraid that with Michener heading up the task force, Haines would have ample opportunity to target and execute more doctors.

"Sorry, Kevin, just give me a ... come on, Luna, take it now, take it down."

In the center of his office, Hugh Carter was trying to cajole his enormous husky into swallowing a pill concealed within a gooey ball of peanut butter.

"First couple times, no problem," Hugh told him over his shoulder, "but then he must've started tasting the damn pills through it, and now he's not going ... come *on*, Luna!"

Hugh now seemed to be trying to part Luna's sizable jaws forcibly with his bare hands, and the dog was growling with what sounded to Kevin like genuine annoyance, though Hugh showed no sign of backing off. Apparently, Luna was on a course of antibiotics, and now that Hugh was divorced, there was no one at home to give the dog his pills during the day. So here it was, in Hugh's office, eight forty-five in the morning.

Hugh's devotion to the dog was obvious, judging by the not one but three framed photos he had on his desk. Even when Hugh was still married, Kevin couldn't remember more than one picture of his wife, Linda. Now it was just Hugh and Luna, and apparently, things had never been better. For the past year, Hugh had even been trying to convince Kevin to get a dog.

Impatiently, Kevin's eyes roved round Hugh's corner office. The blinds were already lowered against the morning glare along South

Dearborn, and the fluorescents were giving off a low buzz that mixed with the hiss of the air conditioner beneath the windows. As far as executive offices went, it was nothing special, but offices period were a rarity in the field office. As Special Agent in Charge, Hugh got one, and so did the Associate Agent in Charge. There were a couple of other shitty ones for squad supervisors, and that was it.

"All right, you swallow now!" said Hugh, clamping the dog's jaws shut with both hands, using his considerable weight as a lever as Luna fought him. "Take it!"

With a snort, Luna swallowed, and Hugh let go and gave him a good rub on the head. Now liberated, the dog turned its attention to Kevin, fixing him with hungry eyes, tongue lolling.

"Sorry about that, Kevin. You're worried about Mitch?"

He said it in such an easy, conversational manner, Kevin knew instantly that Hugh wasn't going to take this very seriously.

"I don't think he really understands the kind of person Haines is, and what his accomplices might do for him."

"You wanted surveillance for Jarvis?" Hugh said.

"Yeah. Jarvis would be alive right now, and we might have a solid lead on where Haines is being harbored."

Hugh leaned back against his desk, the centerpiece of his office, a quite hideous black laminated affair. Hugh himself looked as though he'd just come off the ironing board, all crisp angles. He exuded good health, and it made Kevin feel sick with exhaustion just looking at him. Then again, Hugh hadn't been up all night having donuts and Cokes and coffees with Seth Michener, then storming an apartment in a flak jacket. Kevin hadn't even had time to change before coming here; he'd wanted to talk to Hugh as soon as possible. He didn't like doing it, but he didn't see any other way to get this thing back under his control.

"Well, I haven't been right since the Flood," said Hugh, one of his favorite expressions when he was about to follow up with a powerful assertion. "But I think Mitch did the right thing. We needed to get in and see if Haines was there."

"We could've done that with surveillance. I told Mitch that Haines wouldn't be there, and that Jarvis would rather die than betray him."

"For all we know, Jarvis would've killed himself under any circumstances."

"Not if we'd left him alone."

"Maybe, but Haines might've killed again while you were dogging Jarvis, hoping for a break."

"Jarvis was our one solid lead. I could've made him talk. Now ..." he left it unfinished.

"Anything in his apartment?"

"The Evidence Response Team's still going through it." Jarvis was Haines's mailman: he must have known all the names and addresses of Haines's acolytes. Whether he wrote them down anywhere was another matter. If he was diligent, he would have stored that information only in his head, which was now unfortunately, thanks to Michener, shattered into pulp.

"Letting Michener run this thing is like letting a nine-year-old drive a tank."

"What else are you working?" Carter asked, clearly wanting to change the subject.

"We'll get Jarvis's phone records. See who he's been calling. We're talking to neighbors, and I'll be going back to Illinois Correctional to talk to the other death row inmates, and the correspondence officers, about Haines's mail."

Before Haines had Jarvis acting as mailman, he must have sent and received letters through the prison system, and some of the recipients might have become his acolytes. The fact was, ingoing and outgoing mail was rarely read, and even then, censored only if it contained information that might compromise the security of the prison, or in some way violated the law. And plenty of times, even those got through, often in legal mail, which was strictly confidential: chain mail schemes, fraud, hate mail, murderous threats. All outgoing phone calls by the inmates were monitored and recorded, all visitors were recorded in a computer log at the front gate—but no record of ingoing and outgoing mail was kept. There was simply too much of it, and it wasn't deemed necessary.

Still, Kevin kicked himself for not getting a court order and having Haines's correspondence surveilled all along. But when they'd caught Haines, three years ago, it had been so obvious that he was working alone, without accomplices, just like the Unabomber back in the early '90s. Haines had confessed to each shooting, and there'd been nothing until now to suggest that he was part of a larger network. He'd made his own network from prison, and now Kevin would have to scramble to find out how big it was. His only hope was that one of the mail duty officers might remember an unusual address or name from several years back.

"What about the brother?" Hugh wanted to know.

"Michener tracked him down and called to tell him about the breakout."

Rick Haines, it turned out, had moved back to Chicago last month, after almost three years of exile in San Francisco to escape the scene of his brother's carnage. He was married now, and he'd quietly bought a house in Evanston, but his number was unlisted.

"Haines won't go to him," Kevin said. "Everything David needs he already has. Car, money, food."

Kevin was certain of it: David wouldn't risk trying to find Rick, not after his role in turning him in three years ago. David had nothing to gain, and everything to lose, since Rick would doubtless report any attempted contact. More to the point, he'd have no idea where Rick lived.

He looked over at Luna, who was still eyeing him with malevolent intent. Kevin wondered if the dog somehow saw him as a threat to his master, if he might just regress to his wolfen ancestry and take a leap at his jugular. Luna yawned innocently, revealing twin mountain ranges of teeth, and put his head down on his front paws.

"What's it going to take to change your mind, Hugh?"

"Kevin, you already brought Haines in, three years ago. That's all yours, and no one's going to take that away. Michener's on cleanup duty. Like I said, fugitive manhunts aren't your thing. They're for coarser talents."

"Very flattering. But I don't think this is a job for a coarse talent. Four years ago, Mitch was wasting time trying to find pissed-off patients who might want to kill doctors." Kevin didn't think he needed to spell out the rest. He'd been the one, not Michener, who'd intuited that the killings were all religiously motivated, and committed by the same shooter. It was his knowledge of cults that had narrowed their search and taken them to the New Apostles.

He looked away from Hugh, who was nodding, more from politeness it seemed than in agreement. Pathetic, having to dredge up details from his glory days. Shit. It should be him heading up the manhunt, not Michener. Why couldn't Hugh just look past the last few years?

After the Haines case, sure, he'd come back from his leave feeling dulled, unexcited by his work, he'd be the first to admit that. But look at the files he'd had to deal with! Anyone's talents would atrophy on a steady diet of those. Most of them were losers. They rarely led to prosecutions, except one involving a serial multi-state parking violator, who'd racked up eight thousand dollars in fines. Yep, he'd nailed the parking guy real good. Banji's murder marked the first time in a long time he'd felt a flare of passion for his work.

At the field office he'd always been considered somewhat of an oddity—and not just because he didn't give a shit about the Cubs. It was his interest in cults, and his own onetime membership in one. Now, after his sick leave—his breakdown, as he knew a lot of people, including Hugh, thought of it—it was as if everyone's suspicions had been confirmed. What else could you expect from someone weak enough, gullible enough to get sucked into a cult? As if he'd always had some tragic flaw running through him, and the Haines case had split him open like a sharp crack from a chisel. He was damaged goods.

And this, he suspected, was the real reason Hugh wouldn't go to bat for him. He didn't believe he had the juice anymore to bring Haines in. And he didn't want Kevin dragging him down by association.

"We leave Michener in charge, this thing stretches on, and we'll be giving David Haines a second act and an encore. More dead doctors— and that's not going to make anyone look good. Even if Mitch does get Haines, there's a good chance he'll get him dead. And then we lose his personal Rolodex, the names of all his acolytes. We need him alive. I can get him alive."

"Come on, Kevin, you don't believe for a second Haines would talk anyway."

"He might." Even though he suspected Hugh was right, he refused to admit it. He'd done his fair share of deprogramming when he was younger ("exit counseling" was the more polite term), but he seriously doubted he could ever make much of a dent in David's belief system— and he wasn't even sure he'd want to try.

But to Hugh he said, "We need him alive, Hugh, or we'll have more guys like Will Andrews out there."

"Bad news about him, actually," said Hugh, wincing slightly.

Kevin felt his mood worsen.

"We might lose him."

"What?"

"No prints on the gun. No witnesses. The lawyer says his guy never saw that gun or Bible before, blah blah blah."

"What about all those letters addressed to Will?"

"Another Will, they're saying. There might be reasonable doubt, who knows. I'm not saying he'll walk, but the U.S. Attorney's not exactly thrilled with the case."

"Oh, Jesus," muttered Kevin.

"It's not your fault, and not your problem anymore," said Hugh encouragingly. "It's like I said, though, I'd try to start letting this one go. At the end of the day, it doesn't matter how we bring Haines in, as long as we bring him in."

Another of Hugh's favorite expressions: *At the end of the day*. Usually it was used when he was wrapping up, a sign he really didn't want to talk about it anymore. But Kevin could never help finding it intensely irritating. At the end of *what* day, for Christ's sake? At the end of *whose* day?

Part of him just wanted to nod and agree. Sure, move on, just follow Michener's orders and let him do his job—except that he wouldn't be doing the job, he'd be screwing up, and he couldn't stand the idea of him botching the case. His case. And he had every intention of keeping it that way, officially or not.

"Thanks, Hugh," he said.

Hugh beamed at him, as if they'd just come to a hugely satisfactory agreement, then sat down behind his desk and picked up the phone.

Outside in the hall, D'Onofrio was walking towards him. "Hey, Kevin, that doctor's here."

"Donaldson?"

"Yeah."

The woman who'd let the genie out of the bottle. He didn't particularly feel like interviewing anyone right now: he looked terrible, and felt worse. He'd been up forever and was owed a shift break, but he needed to talk to her first. She was the last person to see Haines, and in the absence of any other leads, he was hoping she might be able to tell him something that would spin the case for him. He needed to know whether Donaldson's tests had simply given David an opportunity to escape, or provided him with a deeper and much more ominous motivation to reenter the world.

He walked to reception to meet her.

*   *   *

His smell, as he ushered her into the room, was of a man who'd been up working too long, and had put on deodorant in lieu of a shower and change of clothes. And she was surprised by an unexpected pang of arousal—some kind of involuntary pheromonal reaction, no doubt. She sighed, finding his animal pungency unwelcome. She glanced at his face critically, as if hoping to find grounds for dismissing him. His skin was pale, taut around his eyes and the bridge of his nose, stubble hollowing out his cheeks—of course, he'd probably had less sleep than her, if any at all. A sort of gloomy grandeur there around the eyes and forehead and mouth, a slightly coarse face, but interesting. Involuntarily she glanced at his left hand and saw no wedding band. Never married, or divorced? She looked away, wanting to be clear and focused, not responding to a man's body odor like some feral cat. She wanted only two things from him: Rick Haines's address, and his assurance that the FBI was doing everything it could to take David Haines alive.

She'd dozed fitfully in the hours after dawn, as if the rising sun were somehow protection from predators: a child's logic. She'd been woken by the sound of the FBI agent banging on her door, to ferry her to the field office. Even now she felt sluggish with fatigue, a sense of unreality clinging to her. She hoped they had her purse, because she could really use her phenmetrizine for a little pick-me-up right now.

Late last night she'd gotten through to Emily at her home and asked if that Internet research company had faxed through any information on Rick Haines. Nothing yet. She was starting to worry that they wouldn't be able to track him down at all. After all, she hadn't been able to provide them with any tips—no SSN, no previous address—and Rick Haines was hardly an unusual name. But Agent Sheldrake must certainly know. Whether he would tell her was another question. But surely, once she made clear how important the blood was, he'd help her.

The room was ugly, a twelve-by-twelve white box with a brown wood laminate desk and a chair on either side, a garbage can by the door, clock mounted on one wall, and a Department of Justice crest on another. This couldn't be his office; this couldn't be *anyone's* office. Must be some kind of interview room. She'd just taken a seat in front of the desk when there was a knock on the door, and a man handed Kevin a large Ziploc bag.

"Thanks, Vince."

She recognized her purse, and felt a cool balm of relief.

"Yeah, good news," Sheldrake said. "They found it in the glove compartment. They dusted for prints and it's clean; Haines didn't even touch it." He held it out to her. "You should have a check anyway, just to make sure everything's there."

It was a functional purse, more like a camera case, with a good strong strap. From the outside, it looked remarkably unblemished for something that had been pincered in a snarl of metal. But as she took it in her hands, she could tell the contents were mangled. She slipped it from the plastic wrap and snapped open the clasp, and she felt a pang of self-consciousness. Had Sheldrake examined the contents? Of course he had. Everyone had. Probably everything inside was now itemized on a document somewhere. How much could you tell from a woman's purse? Plenty, in her case. Beside the mangled Filofax were two sharply splintered plastic vials, green and yellow pills mostly ground into powder at the bottom. Uppers and downers. She glanced at Agent Sheldrake, but he was seated behind the desk, riffling through the contents of a folder. Jesus, was that all about her? She tried to make out the label along the side but couldn't.

She hurriedly checked through her wallet. All her ID seemed to be there, credit cards, driver's license, Social Security, bank stuff. Her keys, too.

"I can go back home then?"

She made it sound more like a question than she'd intended, like some uncertain schoolgirl.

"I'd like to keep you in the hotel."

So they hadn't caught him yet. "He's in Chicago?"

"We don't know. But we'd prefer it if we knew you were taken care of. That means staying away from your lab for the time being, too."

"Is that really necessary?"

"We can't force you. But David Haines isn't the only one out there who might want to kill you. He has at least one accomplice. And we don't know who. Did you read about Dr. Banji in Detroit? Four days ago?"

She frowned. "Amit Banji?"

"The killer was corresponding with Haines from prison."

"He was *murdered?*" She felt a prickling of horror across her skin. She hadn't even looked at a newspaper in the last few weeks, she'd been so busy. She hadn't known Banji personally, but she'd heard him speak at a couple of conferences, and she'd always read his journal articles.

"It was staged like a mugging, in the underground parking lot of his hospital. I'm telling you this because you should know what these people can do."

She knew her dislike of the hotel was irrational. It was just that she felt so alone there, so cut off from her own things, her own world. She could imagine dying there.

"I'll think about it, thank you."

Agent Sheldrake was still looking at her, and she felt impelled to glance away: those eyes of his, something almost indecent about their patient, penetrating gaze, as if waiting for her to account for herself. As if he knew something about her: it was some stupid FBI interview technique probably. Well, it worked, it made her distinctly uncomfortable. What *did* he know? Maybe for starters about the amphetamines in her purse, and what would he think of a doctor who dabbled in speed? *Who cares what he thinks about you,* she told herself irritably.

Kevin saw her break eye contact once again, and thought: *This is a woman who is not at ease with herself.* She shifted in her chair, recrossing her legs, one foot pumping. And her eyes were never still. He wondered if it was the speed. He hadn't looked inside her purse; he hadn't needed to. He'd skimmed the list forensics had made of its contents when they'd dusted for prints. He'd recognized the prescription. Her little secret, probably. During the Haines case he'd spent a fair amount of time with high-powered research doctors, and he knew what workaholics they were—and how arrogant they could be. He'd found many of them unpleasant and condescending. Then again, he'd never liked doctors much—certainly not any of the ones he'd seen during his long bout of depression. They didn't listen, they thought they knew it all, and they thought they could control everything with pills. They wanted to medicate, to eradicate, to reduce all human suffering to a chemical equation. Like Dr. Donaldson, apparently. It must be so easy just to dash off a little prescription, and they were naturally too smart to let it get an edge on them. He wondered if she was addicted. Still, he'd felt a strange pulse of intimacy with her when he'd seen the pills—a symptom of some deep unhappiness.

"I know you've already made a statement to Agent Michener, but I was hoping you might go through what happened yesterday for me, in as much detail as possible." He caught the scent of her hair and couldn't remember the last time he'd smelled anything so nice in one of these wretched little rooms—or anywhere else for that matter.

"Sure," she said, but she glanced at her watch and added, a bit apologetically, "Someone's coming to the hotel to take me up to the MetaSYS building at eleven. There's a press conference. Will we be done by then?"

"Of course," he said.

As she began to talk, he pulled over a notepad. He wasn't particularly interested in the mechanics of Haines's escape, but he was hoping she'd offer up some detail of his behavior, something he'd said, that might give away his motivation or plans. Her account was succinct, but so far, nothing new.

She wasn't beautiful, but he wanted to keep looking at her: all that ... *fury* was the word that came to him. As if he could actually see all that ambition and intelligence and passion compressed into the slender frame of her body, like some volatile substance. A bottle of nitroglycerine teetering in the palm of your hand. And she had those eyes, something about the long slant of them. Saucy. He almost smiled at the antiquated expression: he'd read too many Victorian novels. Not defiant but saucy. He found the very word arousing somehow. Tired, he was too tired to be doing this interview right now. He forced his eyes down to his pad, tried to focus.

"Can you tell me what it was you actually discovered in his blood?"

He saw her draw a quick breath through her mouth: no doubt she expected this to be painful, explaining her work to a lowly civil servant. She began haltingly, simplifying and downgrading her terminology for his benefit. He listened carefully, and with increasing alarm.

It virtually defied credibility.

Here was a man who thought all medicine was sin, and now he'd been told he had a potential cure for cancer inside him. Kevin's empty stomach gave a queasy growl. How would Haines possibly rationalize such a thing? But Kevin already knew, oh, he knew. He'd never lost the ability to travel the conduits of his lost fervor, though now it was little more than the sterile circuitry of a microchip, with only the occasional flare of passion to animate it. If he were David, he knew instantly how he would weave this earth-shattering information into his world-view.

It was a test from God, wasn't it?

Yes, of course it was.

It was God asking David for proof of his fidelity, and what a glorious request it was. It would involve him risking his own life. It demanded renewed vigor and a new paroxysm of holy violence.

Because you must never let the world have the blood in your veins. In denying your blood you must show the world once again its own sick and sinful reliance on medicine and science, its own spiritual poverty.

Kevin put down his pen, feeling the interview room slide back into focus. He wished he'd brought a glass of water.

It was much worse than he thought. He could understand how Haines might have used the opportunity of the medical tests to try to escape. But his motivation, he could now see, was altogether more powerful. Not just to escape execution, but to stop at nothing to avoid getting caught.

It would make catching him all the harder.

He cleared his throat, tried to form his next questions. "Will he feel sick right now?" he asked Dr. Donaldson. If he did, it would affect his actions, how far he'd go, how much he could do. If he was sick, he would be impatient, sloppy, make mistakes.

"He seemed totally healthy. There's even a chance he might have cured himself."

To Kevin it sounded nothing short of miraculous, a man who could cure his own cancer. But not to David. To him, it would be only what he'd expected in light of his unflagging devotion. He had served God, and God was blessing him.

"Power of prayer," he said aloud.

The doctor grunted scornfully.

"That's what he'll think it is, though." And Kevin, even in his perpetual state of faithlessness, couldn't quite rule it out. But if God were answering David Haines's prayers, keeping him healthy, what did that say about Haines? Or God?

Laura Donaldson was shifting impatiently in her chair, and her eyes briefly made contact with his. "What I never could understand was, he was a science student, wasn't he?"

"A very good one, apparently. He started med school."

"So how do you go from that to someone who thinks doctors are the scourge of the earth?"

By now he was used to the question, and he understood its underlying assumption, but it still irked him.

"It's not a simple question of intelligence or stupidity. People are capable of believing anything," he told her. "And it's not just a matter of brainwashing and indoctrination. They want to believe. And if they want it badly enough, they'll cling to those beliefs—doesn't matter how transparently irrational or contradictory or vile they are. They'll cling to them till death sometimes. Look at Jonestown. Waco, Texas. Solar Temple. Heaven's Gate."

"But it just seemed ... from what I read about him, his background, he was too smart for all that crap."

All that crap. No doubt in her opinion an awful lot of beliefs fell into that category. Science was the only thing worth worshipping in her mind, and what a fall for David, from the lofty heights of med school. It must have seemed incomprehensible to her, that an embryonic doctor, one of the chosen people, had turned out this way. He wondered if his annoyance showed on his face, because her eyes slid away from his once again. He doubted she knew about his own past.

"You're right about Haines being smart. But it's got little to do with smart," he said coolly. "At Solar Temple they were all successful business executives and civil servants. The Heaven's Gate cult was mostly computer experts who also happened to believe if they castrated themselves and jettisoned their human canisters they'd get picked up by a spaceship trailing the Hale-Bopp comet. I'm not even convinced the people who join cults are any more gullible than average. Have you heard of the Raelian church?"

She shook her head.

"Well, they've got over forty thousand members worldwide, and they've managed to raise seven million to build an embassy for space aliens in Jerusalem by 2035." He smiled. "Now, I personally think these people are freaks, but they're freaks with jobs and families and college diplomas. Matters of faith have always existed outside the reach of so-called rational intelligence."

Laura sensed she'd annoyed him somehow. She'd merely been trying to get him to talk—she knew how men loved to talk, and she'd wanted to soften him up for her own questions. He was smarter than she'd expected. She tried to guess at his education—maybe accounting, or law, she knew the FBI liked that. But maybe it was nothing more than psychology, which was pretty much her idea of useless when it came to understanding real science, or anything else for that matter. But it was his face that gave her the most reassurance. She had a theory that you could tell a person's intelligence by his eyes, and Sheldrake's told her he was smart.

"You'll take Haines alive, won't you?" she asked. It came out sounding more peremptory than she'd planned.

"That's always our aim, but he's a fugitive, and he's killed two people since escaping. And he may not allow us to take him alive."

"Aren't there stun guns, or tranquilizers ...?"

"Impractical. You can't expect every officer on the street to have that gear ready if they spot him. Look, Dr. Donaldson, if we're in a situation where our lives are in danger, we're trained to shoot with deadly force."

She looked at her hands, knowing she'd overstepped. "I understand that, but I thought, given what might be inside him—"

"With respect, our first priority is not to help you do your job."

She could see the antagonism sparking in his eyes. "A cancer therapy," she said pointedly.

"Even so, our first priority is getting Haines back in custody. Afterwards, you're free to try to get more samples from him, through whatever channels are legally available to you."

She could hear the distaste in his voice. What was he, a Jehovah's Witness or something? A Christian Scientist?

"We had a court order," she couldn't help saying.

"I'm aware of that."

She looked at his impassive face. Unbelievable: she'd been kidnapped by a psychopath, nearly killed, and this man had the temerity to chastise her. Her voice trembled with suppressed anger as she spoke. "I'm sorry, are you suggesting what we did was unethical?"

"You had a court order, as you said."

"But you're saying we violated his religious beliefs?"

"Yes, but legally."

"Well, that's touching. You have my vote for civil libertarian of the year. I'll put a possible cancer cure above the rights of a psychopath any day."

144

"He didn't want his blood taken, Dr. Donaldson. I suspect that's why he fought so hard to escape. And now he's on the loose and might kill more doctors."

His hostility was naked now; she'd been wrong about him. Yesterday, how was it she'd thought he was sympathetic? Her eyes roved restlessly around the room. It irritated her intensely, the smallness of it, the ugliness of it. Wasn't this where they interviewed criminals? It was an insult. What the hell was she doing here? Should have asked Adrian or Paul to come with her; they wouldn't have treated her this way in front of a goddamn lawyer.

No way was Agent Sheldrake going to help her. He wouldn't tell her where she could find Rick Haines. With acute mortification she realized she'd harbored the notion of sweet-talking him. Now it seemed absurd and childish. Obviously, whatever feminine wiles she had were useless on Special Agent Sheldrake. She'd never seen a man so completely indifferent to her. Not that she thought she was beautiful, irresistible, like Sandra, but she was hardly ugly.

She wasn't even going to ask; couldn't bear the idea of this man saying no to her, and giving her another little lecture about FBI policy and confidentiality. She could get Rick's address somewhere else—if not from the Internet service, then from another private investigator.

"Is there anything else you wanted to ask me?" she inquired coldly. "Or are we finished?"

"We're finished for now. But we need to know where you'll be. I may need to talk to you again."

"My father's," she said, deciding instantly. She always kept a spare key to his place, and she'd rather stay there than a hotel; she wanted no more connection with the FBI, or with Agent Sheldrake. "I'll give you the number."

Kevin escorted her out to reception, said a polite goodbye.

When he returned to the bustling command post, he was still irritated, not just by her arrogant disdain, but by his own poor performance in the interview. He'd talked too much, way too much—was he trying to impress her?—and he'd goaded her, he'd cared too much about what she thought of him. He'd been conscious of his crumpled shirt and his stubble, his red-rimmed eyes and his stale breath. He'd let himself feel insulted.

Probably she'd expected him to call headquarters then and there, get the Director on the line, and deploy every special agent in the country to apprehend (daintily), gift-wrap, and deliver David Haines to her lab.

A cure for cancer. Hadn't he heard all this before? Seemed at least once a year the cover of *Time* or *Newsweek* blared some kind of break-through and then ... nothing. You never heard any more about it. And people just kept on dying. He was sure he'd read somewhere that just as many people were dying of cancer now as thirty years ago, slightly more, even.

He remembered the smell of her hair and felt a stirring of regret. He'd just got his ass kicked by Hugh, he was dog tired, he'd sat across from a smart, good-looking woman and felt belittled, and what he wanted now was to go home and get some sleep.

*   *   *

"How soon can we reapply for another court order?" Laura asked, walking with Paul and Adrian away from the reporters and camera-men assembled in the MetaSYS atrium.

Adrenaline was still singing through her. The press conference had gone well, she felt. Very well. At first, she'd wondered if she was crazy coming here, with Haines on the loose. Despite Adrian's assurances that security had marked a perimeter around the whole building, and there were plainclothes guards everywhere, she'd still felt queasy, wish-ing, as she'd looked out at the mosaic of reporters' faces haloed in the camera lights, that she'd taken a bigger hit of phenmetrizine. But once the press conference had begun, flanked by Adrian and Paul at the table, she'd felt strangely insulated—and somehow vindicated, too, after her outrageous grilling at the FBI.

Adrian had been right about showing the video footage. They'd projected it onto a huge screen, with a dubbed narration that sounded as though it had been performed by a professional actor. It was clear and scientific, but the whole thing played with the portentous drama of a movie trailer, and the reporters loved it. Judging by the flood of questions she fielded, Laura could tell they were onside. They saw the importance of Haines's blood, and with favorable stories transmitted across the country, maybe even the FBI would pay attention now, see how essential it was that they take him alive. Only one thing had both-ered her. In the final question, a reporter had brought up Vic

Greene's promise to fight any move to take more blood: was there going to be a big legal battle? Paul had taken the question, replying that it was being discussed internally within the company. Probably it was just cautious corporate rhetoric, but it had an ominously indecisive ring to it. Now she wanted reassurance.

She looked over at Paul, saw with exasperation his face assuming pontification mode, lips pursed, nostrils flaring with an intake of studious breath. It was Adrian who answered.

"We're trying to be very careful here," he said. "Get a sense of what Vic Greene and the ACLU are planning. It may be that a fight's futile. We might have to accept that, all of us. We've got the board meeting later, too. I'm doing my best, Laura."

She felt her glimmering of unease harden into something more substantial. Was Adrian leveling with her? But if he wasn't behind her, why the press conference? Why bother to go to all the trouble of laying out their case for the media? Or was she merely being used, a valiant female figurehead for the corporate vessel. She just nodded at Adrian, knowing she was overtired, probably getting paranoid.

"We'll get another court order if it's at all feasible," Adrian told her reassuringly.

"That was a hell of light show, by the way, what you did with the video."

"I think they liked it."

"I'm looking for the brother," she said. "I've got someone searching for him."

She purposely hadn't mentioned it at the press conference. Pulsing at the back of her head was the fear that she would somehow be scooped. Some other researcher would get the blood first. She felt the need for secrecy, even though she knew it was probably futile. Everyone would come to the same conclusion she had about Haines's blood relations—but she still had a head start finding Rick.

Adrian nodded his approval. "What are the chances?"

"Small, but with Haines up in the air, it's worth a shot."

"Let us know if you need anything. You find the brother, and he has the same blood, we'll all save ourselves a lot of heartache over David Haines."

* * *

She was glad to have her Volvo back. It was a C70 convertible, and she loved the look of it: one of the few European cars on the road that hadn't been transmogrified into an oversized jelly bean. As she raced down Lakeshore towards the campus, she felt a reassuring sense of command, and liberation. To her right the lake flashed between the trees; she could see swimmers on the beaches, triangles of sails against the sky, and felt a buzz of optimism. She'd find Rick Haines.

She pulled off Lakeshore onto 56th and turned past the Doctor's Hospital at the north end of the campus. Twin banners hung from the building's facade proclaiming a new fundraising slogan: *Caring is the best cure.* Laura wondered what genius thought that one up. Caring? It was something Sandra or Mike might say. Caring and prayer had about the same effect on disease, she figured, which was pretty much zilch. Good science was the best cure.

Down East 59th, towards the gothic spires and crenellations of the Chicago Hospitals complex, she was glad to see plenty of white campus police cars pulled up on the sidewalks of the grassy Midway Plaisance. The wide swath of park wasn't heavily treed and didn't offer much cover for snipers, but the police obviously weren't taking any chances. She turned down Maryland and found a spot not too far from the entrance of the MetaSYS research pavilion. She took a breath and stepped out of her car, locking the door with a beep from her keychain.

She could see two campus policemen strolling watchfully along the walkways between the various wings, but still felt a sudden pang of panic. She shouldn't have come, but she'd told the Internet research service to fax Rick's information through to her lab, and she needed to see if it had come. If it wasn't there, she'd have to think about hiring a real private investigator.

She caught herself tracking people in her peripheral vision. How was it Haines killed people—rifle, right? From a distance, usually in their homes. He wouldn't have much luck in a hotel or apartment building. But here ... For a moment the back of her head felt hot as she imagined a red dot on her skull, the kind they always showed in movies, that fatal end point of the gun's discharge. She stumbled in her urgency to reach the door. Swiping her card through the security lock, she hurried into the cool interior, heart pounding.

She took the elevator to the third floor and walked down the deserted hallway. The main door to her lab was locked and she punched in her code.

"Hey, excuse me!"

She jerked round with a start and saw a young campus policeman striding towards her.

"Can I see some ID please, ma'am?" he said.

"I'm Dr. Donaldson." She fumbled in her purse.

"You're Dr. Donaldson?" he said, recognizing her with some awe. "You sure you want to come in here, ma'am?"

"It seems like you're keeping an eye on things. How long are you on duty?"

"Just till six, and then we cut off till eight a.m."

Laura nodded. "I won't be working late then."

The familiar astringent tang of chemicals greeted her nostrils as she entered. Despite its generous size, the lab still seemed cluttered, the main walkway lined with humming freezers, filing cabinets, torpedoes of liquid nitrogen. Narrow aisles contained workbenches with computers, microscopes, sinks, and laminar flow hoods, which provided a controled environment for procedures. High shelves were crammed with books, vials, and a dizzying supply of glassware.

She couldn't remember the last time her lab had been empty like this, and so eerily quiet. She turned on the lights. Obviously Emily had succeeded in getting her team to take some time off, and she was glad. She didn't want them taking any risks. Still, just being here made her feel guilty. Should be working, working, working, doing something. Taking apart the botched TNF-12 protocol instead of chasing after pipe dreams ...

Not a pipe dream, she told herself.

She walked quickly back to her office and checked the fax machine. There was about half an inch of paper in the basket and she rifled through it hurriedly.

The letterhead was so nondescript she almost passed over it. Total Research. There was no covering note, just a small block of information in the center of the page. Her eyes skittered over it hungrily:

SUBJECT'S NAME: Richard F. Haines.

CURRENT HOME ADDRESS: 473 Wright Close, Chicago, IL

PHONE NUMBER: 312 758-1658

Chicago? Laura's surprise was instantly tainted with incredulity. He was supposed to have fled the city, gone someplace to shake off the media hounds. She couldn't believe it. It was too lucky. They must've given her the wrong Rick Haines.

She sat down and took a few deep breaths, trying to calm her thoughts, practice her speech. She dialed. An electronic voice-mail system picked up almost immediately. There was no greeting, just a machine bleep, and she hung up without quite knowing why. It was a hell of a message to leave on an answering machine—especially since she wasn't entirely convinced this was the right Rick Haines. For all she knew, this poor guy had already had a hundred calls today from reporters desperate to talk to the brother of a serial killer.

She waited twenty minutes and called again, and again got the machine. This time she left a message.

"This is Dr. Laura Donaldson calling. I'd like to talk to you about your brother."

Then she programmed her office phone line to automatically forward all calls to her father's, and left the lab.

*   *   *

As she entered the empty apartment, its familiar smell, wedded forever in her mind with childhood, filled her with melancholy. Even after Mom had died, and Dad had sold the house in Evanston and moved into the one-bedroom condo, that smell had traveled with him as a constant: some sort of combination, she supposed, of freshly ironed clothing (her father was compulsive about ironing everything), the faint mustiness of aging upholstery and books, and the pleasant tincture of Dad's pipe tobacco.

She dropped her overnight bag on the floor, beside his pair of house slippers, locked and chained the door behind her, and sat down in an armchair. Every trip to this place was like revisiting a condensed version of her childhood home: all the furniture was still the same (though much of it, of necessity, had been given away to Sandra and herself); the spines of the books in the bookshelves, their color and height and arrangement, were all instantly recognizable; the drapes, the dining-room table and chairs. The stereo and television and the odd lamp and side table were really the only new acquisitions.

She was always amazed by how neat her father was. When he was out of town, she often stopped in to water his plants and sift through his copious mail, and the place was always spotless, the kitchen counters and sink gleaming, the last few dishes he'd used just before his departure neatly stacked in the drainer. Some of this was due to his weekly housecleaner, but my God, you should have seen his chest of drawers, his clothes folded with military precision, socks bundled. Everything else was snug in little boxes and wrapped in elastic bands: pencils, stationery, combs, nail clippers, bank receipts from twenty years ago. She'd often thought she'd inherited her exacting nature from him, but it still hadn't stopped him from preferring Sandra. Not that it surprised her really: Sandra was easy to like, and people liked people who were nice to them. Laura was too prickly.

From silver-plated picture frames set on cabinets and side tables, Sandra watched her, smiling beatifically. Usually she was accompanied by Mike and Rachel and Alex. On her last visit, Laura had actually counted the photos, mortified that she was doing such a thing, but that hadn't stopped her. There were sixteen of Sandra and her family in this room alone (more in her father's bedroom), the picture frames proliferating with Sandra's family vacations and portraits. Laura was not as dutiful a supplier of memorabilia (Oh, and here's a picture of me and my adulterous lover, Adrian). There were three of her on display, one as a child, then a high school graduation picture, then one with her and Sandra, about two years ago. She had to hand it to her father, he had a knack for selecting the least flattering photographs of her. There she was in Vermont, seven years old, squinting at the sun, her cheek bruised from falling off a log. In her graduation shot, she looked decidedly fat in her dress. And in the one with her and Sandra, her sister looked predictably fabulous, but Laura's mouth was moronically half open, as though either about to speak or drool.

She doubted there would be any shots from Sandra's latest trip, lying in a hospital bed in Tijuana, taking her laetrile and herbs and urine extracts and who knows what else and praying, putting her life in God's hands.

With a sigh, she got out her Filofax and looked at the two numbers her father had given her. One was the hotel where he and Mike and the kids were all staying; the other was the clinic, which she dialed first. The receptionist put her through, and Sandra picked up after only one ring.

"Laura, thank God," Sandra said, "we've been calling you all morning since we saw it in the newspaper!"

"I'm really sorry," she said, squeezing her eyes shut, "I haven't even been checking my home messages—"

"Daddy's going to be so relieved, they should be here any minute. So you're okay, you're safe and everything?"

"I'm really sorry," she said again, all she could think to say. "But yeah, I'm okay."

Sandra made her recite the whole story, and already it felt like something from another person's life.

"So where are you staying now?" Sandra wanted to know.

"Dad's, actually."

"That's safe?"

"I think so. Even if he was going to waste his time tracking me down, I doubt he'd know this place." She tried to say it with more conviction than she felt.

"I think you should go back to the hotel, Laura, really. It sounds a whole lot safer."

"Well, maybe I will. Look, I called to find out how *you* are."

"A lot better than a few days ago."

Laura didn't doubt it. They probably had her unwittingly dosed up on major painkillers and anti-nausea meds.

"They did some tests, and they're saying there's no sign it's enlarged or spread, so that's pretty encouraging."

"Good," said Laura, trying to inject some enthusiasm into her voice, "that's good."

"I was probably just overdoing it in Maine."

"How're Rachel and Alex?" Laura asked.

"I feel bad, they were having such a good time, and I think they needed it. I mean, they're okay here, they like the pool at the hotel and everything, but they know I'm in hospital and you can tell they're feeling anxious about things. That's the worst part, really, worrying them."

"It's great Dad could come down," said Laura.

"He's been a godsend."

"How long do you think you'll be down there?"

"I don't know," she replied vaguely, "I guess about the same as last time, a couple more weeks. We'll see what Frieda thinks."

"Frieda?"

"Dr. Wendt.

Great, thought Laura. She was on first-name terms with her quack.

"Come down to see me, Laura," Sandra said, and there was such plaintiveness in her voice that Laura felt her throat thicken. *She's dying.* The words unveiled themselves in her head.

"Sandra, you're being honest with me, right. You're feeling okay?"

"Look," her sister said, more robustly, "you could stay down here until they catch Haines. Wouldn't you feel better, away from it all?"

"I would, believe me," Laura said. "And I want to see you, I really do, but my work's ..." she somehow felt selfish even bringing it up. "It's just there's something I have to do up here first. The brother, Haines's brother, he might have the same blood. I'm trying to track him down."

"Is that safe for you?"

"Yeah, it's safe. It's fine. Just promise me something, okay? Promise me that if I get the blood, and make something happen with it, you'll let me treat you."

"Oh God, I don't want you doing this for me," Sandra said abruptly. "Taking risks. I'd rather you just came to see me, all right?"

"Sandra, I can't until I get the blood," Laura said, frustration starting to saturate her voice. "I want the blood so I can help you. They don't know what they're doing down there. If the cancer's spreading—"

"But it's not. Look, Frieda's just come in to see me. We'll talk later, okay?"

"You'll think about my offer, right?"

"I will. Promise. I'm so glad you're safe. Please come down."

"As soon as I can," Laura said numbly. "I love you."

"Love you, too."

*   *   *

She called Rick Haines's number regularly throughout the afternoon and evening, and it was eight-thirty when she finally got through.

"Hello?" A man's voice, brusque.

"Hello, may I speak to Rick Haines, please?"

There was a short silence. "Who's calling?"

"My name's Dr. Donaldson and—"

"You were with him when he escaped."

"Yes."

She heard him exhale deeply. "A lot of people've been trying to get hold of me. Reporters mostly. I just heard the word doctor, and thought, 'Oh God, it's another shrink who wants to write a book and find out if David wet his bed as a kid, or frizzled ants with his magnifying glass.' I just erased the message on reflex. Took me a few seconds to remember your name from the news."

"You are his brother, then," she said.

"Yeah." The single word, carried along on a sigh, conveyed intense weariness. "I'm really sorry for what happened to you, Dr. Donaldson. I'm glad he didn't hurt you badly." There was a short, awkward pause. "Why did you want to get in touch with me?"

Relief crashed through her, and with it, an unpleasant flush of shame. Until this moment, she'd seen Rick Haines as nothing more than an acquisition, a vessel from which she could extract something useful. Now, talking to him, hearing the fatigue and pain in his voice, she felt callous. But she knew she had to ask.

"I'm sorry to be intruding," she said quickly, as if afraid at any moment he might change his mind, hang up, and never answer the phone again. "I know this must be a terrible time for you. But I wanted to reach you because there's a chance you have the same kind of immune system as David."

"Meaning what?"

"That whatever David has that kills cancer cells, you might have too."

"And you want me to give blood?"

"If you have no objection, yes."

"How involved is all this?"

"It's not, not up front anyway. All I need is about 20 ccs. If I get a negative from that, that's the end of it. If you're positive, then we'll need to talk again about more samples, and your proprietary rights."

There was a pause and she waited anxiously, foot pumping, her hand drawing spirals on the notepad.

"Look," he said, "I'm out of here first thing tomorrow morning. I'm going back out west until this thing's over and they've got him back and ..."

She waited, struggling with herself not to cajole him.

"... so if you want your sample, you better come and take it tonight."

She closed her eyes in relief. "I can do that. If you're sure it's all right."

"Yeah. I'll give you my address."

She wrote it down again, even though she already had it, her hand shaking with excitement.

"I can be there in half an hour," she said.

CHAPTER FOURTEEN

He turned the rice down to simmer, slid the frozen lamb chops under the grill, and set the table for himself. Nothing fancy: a cotton placemat flanked by knife and fork and a napkin. It was something Kevin tried to do the few nights he made himself a meal at home, a practice he clung to partially out of nostalgia (Diane had always insisted on sit-down dinners) but also because of a vague fear of turning into something slouched and drooling in front of the TV. He could see the television just fine from the table anyway. CNN flickered from the screen, the volume turned down low. Back in the kitchen he filled a small pot with water, ready for the frozen peas he'd boil later to round out his idiot-proof meal. He took another slow mouthful of wine, a decent one for a change, and felt it sharpening his hunger.

In his book-filled bedroom, he got out the ironing board and started to press his last clean cotton shirt. After interviewing Laura Donaldson this morning he'd come back home and slept a dreamless eight hours. He'd needed it; even now his body felt heavy and sluggish, greedy for more. Then he'd had a good long shower. There was just time for dinner, and then it was back to the command post for his next shift.

The phone rang as he was finishing up his shirt, and, as he'd hoped, it was his daughter. They had most weekends together, but during the week, she would call him, maybe once or twice, just to talk, and he'd come to prize these brief night-time conversations as much as the wine and books that were, after his daughter, his main solace and companionship.

"Sorry about last weekend," he said.

"Oh, that's okay."

He tried to gauge her voice, whether she was lying or not. Above all else, he feared hurting her.

"What'd you end up doing?"

"Kira's mom took us to a matinee of that new Leonardo DiCaprio movie."

"Any good?"

"So-so."

He smiled; he'd always liked his daughter's relative imperviousness to mass culture. While her friends swooned over celebrities, she would rather read a good book.

"Then on Sunday we all went down for Venetian Night."

"Sounds great," he said, feeling a pang of jealousy. He'd planned on taking her to see the carnival himself. From Monroe Harbor to the Planetarium, boats gloriously lit up the lakefront, with a fireworks display to cap it all off. Rebecca was tactful enough not to mention his name, but Kevin knew that "we all" meant Ted had been with them. Diane had been seeing him for about six months now, another counselor at her clinic. Kevin had met him briefly a couple of times, and he seemed like a decent enough guy, although Kevin had clandestinely run him through the NCIC database just to make sure he didn't trigger any matches. He'd been clean, of course. It was healthy that Diane was dating—though really she'd moved beyond dating with Ted. He didn't doubt that she would end up remarrying—if not Ted, someone else. He couldn't bear the idea of being downgraded from Dad to Kevin, a friend Becky occasionally had lunch with. Helplessly watching her drift away from him.

As he listened to her describe the boats she'd seen at the carnival, he looked around his room and wondered if he'd ever share his bed with anyone again. He was used to his solitary homecomings, the day's spent adrenaline, frustration, and impotent lust—that bank teller he would have liked to have acrobatic sex with—clinging to him like dust. He knew he was lazy, knew he should make more of an effort. With whom? An image of Laura Donaldson played across his mind. She'd said she lived alone. No wedding or engagement ring. Probably had a boyfriend. Absurd, anyway, the idea she'd be interested in him. Especially after their friendly interview this morning; she'd probably walked out thinking he was a religious fanatic.

"How's your Mom?" he asked Rebecca.

"Okay. She's pretty upset about David Haines."

He felt a stab of guilt, as though he'd personally resurrected this trauma for his family. For Becky it had to be bringing back unpleasant memories: her house, depleted and poisoned by her father's work. His pursuit of Haines had effectively gobbled up three years of her life, years when he'd often been away from home. And maybe his absence had been the easiest part for Becky, easier than seeing her father so distracted and testy, hearing him waking up in the night shouting incoherently, hacking up Bible verses before Diane could calm him down. And now he was having nightmares all over again, Haines climbing through the windows of his dreams and robbing his sleep. He hoped it wasn't the same for Becky.

"Are you safe, Dad?"

"Sure," he said, touched and concerned by the worry in her voice. "That's something you don't need to waste time thinking about."

Hypocrite. She must have known it was his idea that she and Diane move out of the house for a bit—and what was the reason for that if everything was perfectly all right?

"So tell me what you did today," he asked her.

Listening, he remembered his dinner and migrated down the hallway with the cordless, glancing into Becky's bedroom as he passed. He'd been financially imprudent and rented a two-bedroom, so that Rebecca had her very own room when she came for weekends. It was the room Kevin had taken most care over. It had a futon sofa that doubled as a bed, shelves lined with books and games he'd bought for her. On the walls were the posters he'd encouraged her to put up, some of which he'd bought for her on outings to musicals or museums. He wanted to make a home for her, a distinct home, in which he could feel again as though he had a family, broken though it now was.

In the kitchen, the smell of the lamb chops under the grill made him almost light-headed. The last time he'd had a proper meal was back in his Detroit hotel, if you could call that polystyrene cuisine a proper meal.

"What're you making?" she asked him, when she heard him clattering pots. He told her and heard her chuckle.

"What, you don't approve?" he asked.

"You always have that."

"It's easy."

"Kira's dad does all the cooking, he's pretty amazing. Once when

I was over he made Beef Wellington, all the pastry and everything from scratch."

"Uh-huh," said Kevin, pouring his frozen peas into the water.

"You're pretty good though, Dad, really," she said placatingly. "Most fathers can't even do omelets."

"I do the best with what little talents I have," he said, with mock despair. He had no intention of telling her he wouldn't actually be eating the meal. Even if he explained himself—and she was good at understanding—she'd think it was too weird, and he couldn't bear that. He'd been weird enough in the past. He checked the lamb and rice, and turned off the elements.

"Hey, listen," he said. "Last time I talked to your mom she didn't sound too thrilled about our visit to the Hindu temple."

"She's not thrilled about any of our religious field trips."

"Right," he said, taken aback slightly by her directness. "Now, you tell me, Rebecca, I'm not going to be hurt if you want to stop them. Last thing I want is to drag you along to something that bores you silly. I just want to spend time with you, okay?"

There was a worrying pause. Maybe Diane was right, maybe it was irresponsible to take Becky to these places, grafting onto her his own cravings.

"But I love those visits," Becky said, and she sounded hurt.

He smiled at the floor. "Great, that's all I need to hear. We'll keep it up, but to be honest, I think we're going to run out of religions soon."

Even he couldn't believe it sometimes, the seriousness with which she wanted to know about these faiths. She was just twelve; could a twelve-year-old really be interested in religion? When he was twelve, God had been a painting on some church roof. And the first time he'd got a taste of it, he was unprepared, like some kid whose parents never let him drink until he was nineteen and then he binges and gets pig drunk and does something he regrets later. He didn't want that for Becky. He wanted her to see all the choices, all those ambrosial bottles lined up behind the bar, to select or reject as she wanted.

"I can hardly wait for our trip," she said.

"Me too," he said, wincing. They'd planned a week-long summer holiday to Prince Edward Island later in August. It was a place she'd always clamored to go, since reading and falling in love with the *Anne of Green Gables* books. But if he worked the Haines case, he might have to cancel that, too.

"It's still on, right?" And he detected the cheery cautiousness of a girl who's been disappointed too often in the past.

"Shouldn't be a problem," he said, disliking himself. It would only be worse later if he did indeed have to cancel.

"You'll have him caught by then, won't you?"

He couldn't help smiling: the way she put it, he was out there single-handedly tracking Haines down with a magnifying glass, pipe in mouth, barking commands. How far from the truth.

"I think so."

"Some of the kids at day camp are talking about him like he's some kind of evil superhero, you know, with all these powers. That stuff about his blood and being able to cure cancer."

Kevin managed a laugh, a lighthearted one, he hoped.

"No, he's just a very misguided man."

They said their goodbyes, and he arranged his meal on a plate: three perfectly cooked lamb chops—he checked: they were nice and bloody in the middle—a big helping of rice, a ladle of buttered peas, which filled up the rest of the plate. He stood for a few moments, savoring the sight and smell of it, feeling the indignant, empty swirl of his stomach.

Then, he carried the plate to the garbage bin and, with a fork, swept his meal into it. His stomach bubbled and knotted so sharply he winced. Good. *Accept this as a penance, knowing that through suffering and self-mortification comes enlightenment.*

In the living room he turned off the television and knelt on the parquet floor, not allowing himself to sink back against his heels. Eyes closed, his chin dropped slightly towards his chest.

He knew David would be doing the same.

Fasting, praying. Asking for guidance.

So Kevin asked too. He began with his usual cheating little disclaimer: *Dear God, if there is a God, if You're there, let me know what he's going to do. Bring me in close to him* ... It was what he'd done four years ago when he was chasing David for the first time. Knowing that the best way to find him was to emulate the rites and observances that were his, and once Kevin's, too.

He tried to pull all the shutters of his mind, make it black. In a few hours he'd be back in the command post, and there he'd have no time for any kind of meditation, or communion with David.

Help me. Show me. Please.

Bony knees stinging against the floor, a tremble already working through the backs of his thighs. *Use it all to take you someplace else.*

His thoughts were already becoming untethered from words, but that was all right, it was all right to wander ... In his mind's eye he saw the wreckage of that freight train across the cornfields, and felt the tectonic plates of his reason slip open. Act of God. A sign. Of what? That David was favored by God? Escaping super-max prisons, smiting his enemies, miraculously curing himself ...

"Then he called his twelve disciples together and gave them power and authority over all devils, and to cure diseases ...."

Divine power or genetic fluke?

To cure yourself, to be given a sign like that ...

I've never had any sign, he thought. *Give me something unassailable, and I could shed my atheism. Butterfly liberated from its cocoon. Show me something. "Blessed are those who have not seen, yet believe." Yes, but what about "Ask and ye shall receive?"*

"Thou shalt not put the Lord thy God to the test."

Why couldn't he have a sign? The apostles had them in abundance. Jesus walking on water, raising the dead, the loaves and fishes. He'd settle for any one of those. Sorry if it was inconvenient and he was breaking the rules ...

His calves were shaking now too, stomach twisting. *Thank you for this gift of penance, thank you for this chance of drawing closer to you.* Even as he knew how crippled his doubter's prayers were.

David had no doubts. Maybe he was the servant God had been longing for, and God was altogether fiercer and more vindictive than Kevin liked to imagine.

Remember that: David has no doubts.

The room seemed to lurch suddenly, and his eyes snapped open on instinct. One hand shot out to brace his fall. His heart hammered. He checked his watch. Only twenty-five minutes he'd managed. A pittance compared to his days with God's Children, or even a few years ago. Diane would find him, pale and wasted on his knees after two hours, and think he was crazy. And maybe he was.

Grunting, he stood, knees singing with pain, and none the wiser. But he was just beginning. He'd keep fasting. No more wine. He would cut back his sleep, read the Bible, read the letters David had sent to Will Andrews. If that's what it was going to take to bring him back to David, that's what he'd do.

He flicked the television on again and caught sight of Laura Donaldson. He got the volume up in time to hear her tell a reporter how important it was that Haines be taken alive. He snorted, admiring her chutzpa. Tell it to Michener. The screen then filled with a shot of writhing microscopic cells. With a start he realized that this was Haines's blood, and, listening to the voice-over, watched mesmerized as the cells devoured a tumor within seconds.

After the footage they cut back to the studio, where three expectant people were assembled around a table. Liz Braun was heading the panel.

"Hilary, was this worth it for MetaSYS?"

"Well, the science of it's weak, that's my problem," said Hilary, who, according to her supertitle, was an oncologist. "Those pictures we saw today are impressive, but I think Dr. Donaldson's sorely mistaken if she thinks it marks the easy road to a cure."

"But it is a possibility, yes?" asked Braun. "Michael?"

"A possibility, yes," conceded Michael O'Hare, another doctor, but Kevin wasn't paying much attention to his title. "The stumbling block will inevitably be that what works in one system might not work in another. There have been other cases of self-healers documented, but trying to replicate the exact conditions under which the healing occurred is very difficult."

"How many people would have blood like this?" Braun asked.

O'Hare just shrugged.

"What I think we have to keep in mind," said the third guest, a medical ethicist called Jack Gromaldy, "is the conditions under which this blood was taken. If we allow this man's blood to be used against his will, we're opening the doors to some very invasive practices in the future."

"But Dr. Donaldson," said Braun, looking at her notes, "seems to think it's essential that she get more of Haines's blood for research. What if his is the only blood of its kind? This is, after all, a cure for cancer."

"A *potential* cure for cancer," Hilary emphasized.

"Well, the agent in his blood might be familial," said Gromaldy. "Haines might share it with someone else in his family who's willing to give it. As I recall he has a brother, doesn't he?"

Kill him.

Kevin was sickened by how effortlessly the words slid into his mind, the brutal, necessary logic of it. For a moment he sat, not hearing the TV, trying to calm himself.

Kill him.

He hadn't put anyone on Rick Haines's house—a waste of time, he'd thought. But now ... if there was a chance Rick had the same blood as his brother, David would try to kill him. He would stop at nothing to deny the world his blood.

He grabbed his jacket off the back of the chair and yanked out his notebook, flipping through it for Rick's number. He'd just moved back to Chicago. There was virtually no chance David would know where he lived. The number was, he knew, unlisted. But David would make finding him his first priority.

He'd need to get Rick out of there fast—Jesus, was his wife with him? They could put someone inside and put the place under total surveillance. If Haines came, they'd get him.

He found Rick's number and dialed, willing him to pick up. After just one ring, electronic voice-mail cut in and gave him a beep prompt. Shit.

"Rick, it's Special Agent Kevin Sheldrake from the Chicago office. We're going to need you out of the house right away. I'm worried your brother may—" He was about to use "make an attempt on your life" but it seemed stupidly euphemistic—"may try to kill you. I'm leaving for your place right now." He looked at his watch. "It's nine-forty, Tuesday night. If you get this message before I'm there, leave and call me on my mobile." He gave the number and hung up, then called once again just in case Rick had been on the other line. Again, just a beep prompt. He hung up, grabbed his keys, and ran for the elevator.

* * *

The night smelled like a wet dog.

Laura swung her car door shut and walked up the driveway, already perspiring in the cloying heat. It was a generous brick house with a deep yard backing onto a park. Beyond the high wrought-iron fence, she caught glimpses of a jogging path and a children's playground through the trees.

There was a car in the driveway, a sporty Lexus coupe, and lights on in the house. She carried a case with the blood-extraction gear.

She rang the doorbell and watched through the small diamond-paned window as a man came down the hallway towards her, a half-full tumbler in his hand. He didn't really look much like David Haines, and she was relieved. She wouldn't have said he was more than thirty, a good-looking man, a little heavier than she liked, with a neatly trimmed goatee. His face had the slack look of exhaustion, the eyes red-rimmed. She wondered if he'd been drinking.

"Dr. Donaldson?" he said as he opened the door to her.

"Yes. Thank you for being so cooperative."

"Well, I don't share my brother's views on modern medicine, let's put it that way."

She could smell a faint tang of alcohol on his breath. He led her down the hall and into the living room, which was filled with boxes, taped shut most of them, and an odd assortment of furniture. For just a moment her mind surrendered to paranoia: did the brother of a psychopath share anything of his sibling's emotional chemistry? In another room, the phone rang, and Rick just shook his head.

"Been like that pretty much all day. How'd *you* get my number?" he asked.

"A research service."

He smiled tiredly. "You and everyone else. I didn't know it was so easy to get unlisted numbers. I barely got the phone hooked up here."

The phone rang a second time and again he let it ring.

The house seemed too big for a single man, and too expensive, until she remembered that he was, or had been, a stockbroker. The floor was gleaming oak, inlaid with a darker walnut border. He sat down in a slingback Swedish armchair and indicated a sofa. It was a handsome room, with a fireplace at one end with a pillared mantelpiece, and on either side built-in bookshelves with pilasters and templed peaks, giving the room a neoclassical look. There were no curtains on the window yet; she saw a car pass down the street, its taillights disappearing around a bend.

"You're moving out?"

"In, actually. We took possession a couple of months ago and had some work done on the place. My wife's still out west, finishing off a contract. I came out ahead to deal with the movers, get everything settled. It's not really the kind of homecoming I was hoping for."

"You moved out west after they caught your brother." She sensed he wanted to talk, maybe needed to, and it was probably one of the reasons he'd bothered letting her in the door tonight.

"Me and Janet, yeah. I got a transfer to the San Francisco office and it seemed like a good idea, just to get clear of it all. But we always knew we'd come back. Her family's here, and it still feels like home to me, too. When we bought the place we thought ... that all this was finally over. Then yesterday, I get a call from the Marshal's office, telling me he's escaped, and to call them if he tries to contact me. Jesus. The guy wouldn't even tell me what happened." He nodded at the television set up on a stack of boxes. "I learned more from that, but ..."

He finished off his drink and looked at her, quietly expectant.

"Maybe you could tell me, if it's not too painful."

Laura nodded. It was the least she could do for him. She told him all she could remember about her encounter with his brother. Rick never interrupted her, just looked down at the floor as she spoke.

"I never went to see him," he said when she'd finished, and she was startled by the raw regret in his voice. With a jolt she realized Rick still loved his brother: a serial killer of doctors, the man who'd brutally killed two security guards before her eyes and then taken her hostage. It seemed impossible to her.

"I just couldn't do it," Rick said. "What could I say to him? And he can't have wanted to see me."

Laura shifted on the sofa, uncomfortable with this sudden intimacy. Too much time studying impersonal things, she supposed. Cells, viruses, not the creatures who served as hosts. Sandra would know what to say, she was good at this sort of thing.

"I tipped off the FBI," Rick was saying, "testified against him in court. To him I'm just another money-loving sinner. And I'd pretty much written him off after he joined the cult, I guess. He wasn't like my brother anymore, so I tried to forget about him. It didn't really work though. Moving didn't make it any easier either. I did write him a letter, about a month ago, when I was out here. Stupid letter, I guess. Just wanted to say goodbye, and tell him about my life a bit. I didn't put a return address on it. I was afraid he'd write back with all his usual stuff. But the weird thing is, if he showed up at my door, I'd still let him in." He sighed. "And after he'd gone I'd call the police, I guess. I'm going back to the coast. I can't deal with this anymore."

He seemed suddenly embarrassed.

"Anyway, I'm happy to give blood, but I think you'll be disappointed. I've had plenty of tests over the years, and no one's ever noticed anything weird."

"Well, it might not be obvious unless you had cancer. But we can simulate an immune response in the lab to see."

"Oh. Right."

"Your parents are both dead, I understand."

Rick nodded. "I was still at Northwestern. David had quit med school and was off at that cult farm. It was a car accident, coming back from Vermont. My father, he got into this thing of falling asleep at the wheel, and Mom never liked to needle him about it. He veered across the highway right into a station wagon. I wrote David about it, and got a letter back saying, 'Let the dead bury the dead.' Can you believe that? Didn't even want his share of the house."

"Do you and Janet have any children?"

"Trying." He looked uncomfortable. "She had a miscarriage last year, and we took some time off, but—" he indicated the house around him, "the idea is to fill this place up."

"Uncles, aunts? No?"

She remembered from the genealogist's report that the parents were both only children, but she just wanted to make sure.

"Well." He stood. "You want to do it here? Or the kitchen? There's a table in the kitchen."

"That's fine," she said.

*   *   *

Swathed in the shadows of the tree, David leaned back against the trunk, his legs straddling a broad, gently upsweeping branch, finding his balance. Behind his thick screen of leaves, he had an excellent view of the back of the house, and his elevation would give him a clear shot into virtually every window on the first and second floors.

Carefully he started unpacking the pieces of rifle from his knapsack, and his hands remembered the motions of assembly, each component locking precisely with its mate. It was a Harrington & Richardson single-shot, not a particularly good gun, but he didn't care about that. It was cheap and accurate, and he could take it down in about fifteen seconds. Also, it didn't shuck its shells all over the place and make a mess. Nothing for the police.

Gail had done well. She'd picked up the gun at Wal-Mart, then gone to an army surplus store to buy the ammo, .308 caliber metal-jacketed. Then he'd had her go to an auto-supply store and buy a twenty-dollar muffler for a lawn mower. Carefully he'd duct-taped it onto the end of the barrel. It was a crude silencer, and would only last him a couple rounds, but that was all he'd need. He opened the breech and loaded in the first shell, then put two more in the pocket of his jeans. He waited.

He'd taken his time getting here, making several passes of the house to discern the best approach, the best chance of concealment. He knew how careful he'd have to be. He'd seen his own face on the covers of newspapers, flashed on television. But he realized the best invisibility was acting normally, not hurrying, not looking away from people. With his baseball cap, the stubble of his beard growing in, and the nondescript clothes Gail had bought him at the mall, he looked like everyone else. Most people, even if they'd seen his face on TV ten minutes ago, would look away without any spark of recognition.

Twilight gathering, he'd left Gail's car on a quiet residential street on the far side of the park and walked through it. Birds were just finishing off their dusk chorus, and he'd hesitated for a moment to listen to them. He'd caught a glimpse of a red cardinal and smiled.

His sense of direction was, as always, unwavering, and his instinctive course brought him almost directly to the portion of the high fence that bordered Rick's backyard. He wondered at Rick's having such a large place now, then remembered he'd married; he'd said as much in his cowardly letter. Children, he mused, would there be children? Rick hadn't mentioned any.

It was ideal, really, the way the trees grew tall and leafy against the fence. He'd scaled it without much trouble, after picking a tree on the other side to make his hiding place, a generous oak with low branches and a thick canopy of leaves. It was almost too easy, and that made him nervous in itself. He'd had much harder jobs than this, finding cover in backyards and side alleys, but back then, he'd been invisible to the world, the faceless Doctor-Killer, without even one of those laughable FBI composites to betray him. It had occurred to him that the authorities might stake out Rick's place, but that was a chance he had to take, and the sooner he did it, the better.

Through the scope he scanned the house, trying to get a sense of the floor plan. The only light emanated dimly from a set of patio doors on the first floor, which he knew must be the kitchen. A raised wooden deck had been built out, with eight or nine steps leading down to the sloping grass. Through the patio doors, he could dimly see a hallway, leading to the front of the house.

Suddenly two figures appeared, a man and, judging from the outline of the head, a woman. He shifted his weight in the crotch of the tree, checking his balance.

The kitchen lights came on, and he saw, framed in the doorway, his brother.

Rick looked the same as he had when David last saw him, testifying in court about the letters, an unrepentant Judas. In the tree, watching Rick's magnified face, he felt a sudden doomed wish to embrace his younger brother. He wished he could explain. He didn't like killing. What he did, he did out of holy obligation, because it was the right thing. When he'd shot the doctors, he'd tried to kill them instantly; he hadn't wanted them to suffer, despite their sins. What he'd done was coldly premeditated, yes, and efficient. But the killing had given him no pleasure. He was not a sadist. How could he ever make his brother believe him now?

He let the crosshairs drop to his brother's chest.

Stay still, Rick, stay very still.

Don't say his name.

To the pure all things are pure. Never forget that.

He busied himself with practicalities. He worried about the angle, maybe thirty degrees. And then there was the thickness of the glass, double, maybe even triple pane, and it was impossible to gauge the deflection he'd get off it. He'd have two, three shots max before the muffler came loose and each successive shot sounded like a godawful thunderclap.

What if Rick didn't even have the same blood? What if this weren't necessary? Was there any way he could spare his life? For a moment he let his crosshairs skid off target, and that's when he saw that the woman behind him wasn't his wife.

It was the doctor.

He hadn't imagined she'd be so quick, and he felt a sick churning in his stomach. Had she already taken his blood? But then he saw her put a black bag on the counter and start taking out a syringe, a number of stoppered vials.

He wished he'd killed her in the Gulfstream. But there'd been no time to shoot her, shift her dead or dying body out of the driver's seat; precious seconds. He'd meant to kill her when they neared the rendezvous, leave her in the mobile home with the two guards. But now he felt acutely what a mistake he'd made in waiting.

Unwanted, the dream that had polluted his sleep last night swam before him. He was back in the Gulfstream, tied to the table, and she was standing over him, taking his blood. As it left his body, one of her hands, almost carelessly, was caressing him along his exposed forearm, an indifferent, grazing sweep that lifted his hair like static electricity. Then along his upper thighs went her hand, until he felt himself stir between his legs and bloat with an evil abandonment, the very sight of his departing blood a kind of release, an ejaculation. He struggled against the straps to take possession of her, but they held tight. He bellowed, but she only turned her heavy-lidded eyes to look at him with silent disinterest.

He'd woken to find himself rubbing against the mattress, and was flooded with self-loathing. The image of the doctor had stayed with him all morning, and he'd tried to scissor it out of his mind. He remembered her arrogance in the lab, the frightening certainty of her actions. She was a tempter, speaking rationally, humanely, as Satan always did when he trod the earth, promising peace and health and compassion, and delivering damnation. Her beauty didn't surprise him. Satan always robed himself in the comeliest of disguises. Woe to those who thought he would appear as some kind of malformed fiend, horned, terrifying. He'd come in the most enticing forms imaginable, full of rational argument, shining like an angel.

And his brother had already been swayed by her.

Purge the earth of her.

He raised the scope to his eyes, the line of his vision like an invisibly blazing rod of power, an extension of God's will through his agency.

Forgive me, Rick.

* * *

"Can I get you something to drink?" Rick asked, opening the fridge door.

"Just water, thanks."

A large island counter bisected the room and left ample space for a breakfast table by the patio doors. Outside, she could dimly make out a generous wooden deck, and beyond that the darkness of the park, pricked by the occasional lights of houses at the far side, flickering through the branches.

More boxes, with "Kitchen" written hastily across them in black marker, were stacked up against the walls, some opened, revealing dishware. A few piles of plates were stacked on the oval breakfast table. She supposed Rick had been unpacking, getting his house ready for his wife, his planned family, and she felt a pang of loneliness. The entire kitchen had obviously been newly renovated, unblemished cabinets and gleaming matte white counters, pristine appliances yet to be used. The fridge looked big enough for all the food she bought for the entire year. She wondered how large a family they were planning.

"Stockbroker saves humanity," Rick said with a wan smile as he closed the fridge door, a bottle of mineral water in his hand. "I like it."

"Let's hope so," she said. Everything she needed was out on the table now. This would take no more than ten minutes. She'd have the samples back in the lab by eleven, and start working them up right then, if her energy held.

The first thing she registered—even before the unimpressive firecracker snap from outside—was the urgent gaseous hiss of coolant escaping the refrigerator. Instantly her eyes found the hole, about head level, like something bored by a precision tool. It seemed she stared at it for hours before she understood.

"Oh my G—"

She didn't even hear the second shot.

Rick's neck opened up and released a torrent of tissue and blood into the kitchen. As his knees buckled, Laura could see that the bullet had ripped a crater to the right of his Adam's apple, and severed his carotid artery. Blood pumped furiously from the wound in three jets.

She dropped to the floor as another shell bit into the fridge. Scrambling around behind the counter on all fours, she found Rick splayed in a growing slick of his own blood, hands clutching at his neck. She pushed him over onto his back, straddled his shoulders, and clamped her own hands over the wound, pushing her full weight against it. Two carotid arteries fed the brain, and if the second was intact he might have a chance—if she could stop him bleeding to death. If she had some kind of clamp, anything to pincer the artery .... but right now her hands were the only thing holding the life in him, and even so blood seeped through her fingers with terrifying quickness. Rick's hands clamped around hers reflexively, and with preternatural strength. Where the hell was the phone?

Haines. It could only be Haines, outside.

"We're going to stop this bleeding, okay, Rick?" she told him, forcing herself to make contact with his wide, unblinking eyes. His face was moist with sweat, pale, his lips starting to turn blue. Blood bubbled from his mouth—the bullet must have punctured the trachea—he was having trouble breathing, lungs filling. The wound was too big, she was losing him. She felt his grip on her hands weakening. She needed a clamp.

How long would it take the neighbors to call 911, how long for the police to come? What if they, like her, thought nothing of the sounds, as inoffensive as leftover Fourth of July firecrackers, or a motorbike backfiring on the street?

She needed to get to a phone. But she was afraid to take her hands away from Rick, afraid to stand in case Haines was still outside, his crosshairs lined up above the counter, waiting, waiting.

She saw the tool kit on the counter and quickly pulled her hands away from Rick's neck to bat it down onto the floor. Its contents spilled around her, and she snatched up a pair of needlenose pliers, their ends slightly rusted. The wound was massive, swimming with blood, and she knew now it would be impossible to locate the severed artery. She dropped the pliers and clamped again with her hands. Rick's head dropped inert to the side. Her fingers could no longer feel a pulse in his neck; she wasn't sure if he was breathing anymore.

The footsteps outside were fast, first on flagstone, then on wooden steps, flying up towards the deck, coming for her now. Her hands tightened on Rick's neck. *Sorry, Rick, sorry.* Letting go, she flung herself clear of the counter, aiming herself for the kitchen doorway, but was unable to stop herself from glancing at the patio doors. The first thing she registered was her own wild reflection in the black glass, and then above her, David Haines, the rifle butt raised over his shoulder, then smashing down at the glass beside the handle.

With the first blow the glass cracked but held; with the second, it shattered onto the kitchen floor. She was already in the hallway, running for the front door, when she heard the patio door slide open. As in her worst nightmares, her feet felt heavy, leaden, almost impossible to wrench off the floor. Every moment she expected to feel his hand take her by the shoulder and snap her around, or the numbing concussion of a bullet as it passed through her.

She had the doorknob in her hand, turned, and miraculously was out in the driveway, deliberately weaving to throw off his aim. She saw the houses across the street, lights on in the windows, people silhouetted by the blue flicker of TVs, and then headlights swung in towards her, momentarily blinding her, as a car pulled up behind her own.

You're blocking my way! she wanted to scream, before remembering she didn't even have her purse, and in her purse were her keys.

The car door swung open, and Kevin Sheldrake stepped out.

*   *   *

The terror he saw in her body and face transmitted itself to him instantly, a piercing radio shrill in his head. He was out of the car, the motor still running, his hand closed around the Glock as he hurriedly scanned the front of the house. In the rectangle of light from the wide open front door, nobody.

"What?" he shouted hoarsely, a squeeze of panic at his throat, even though he already knew the answer.

She looked back over her shoulder fearfully. Now he could see her clothes were drenched with blood, her hands black.

"He killed Rick," she choked.

"Where's Haines?"

"Inside."

Kevin's eyes hadn't left the house. Big place, Haines could be anywhere in there, behind a darkened window, lining them up in his scope right now.

"Get down," he told her swiftly, pulling open the rear door of his car and pushing her behind it.

In the quiet of the night, from behind the house, a soft, fast percussion of footsteps, first on stone, then grass, then seconds later the low, dull clang of something heavy against metal. The fence.

"Go to a neighbor's!" he shouted at her. "Call for help!"

He ran down the side of the house, hugging the wall, Glock in hand. He peered from around the corner and saw him. Crouched awkwardly at the top of the fence, amidst the arrowpoint spears, ready to jump, was David Haines, a dark knapsack slung over his shoulders. Kevin knew what was inside: a take-down rifle, the kind he favored.

"David!" he shouted, the Glock braced in both hands, but still trembling. "Don't move, David!"

David turned, his eyes reflecting the light from the kitchen like parabolic mirrors.

Later, Kevin wouldn't be able to remember if he'd had a moment, a second, in which he could have taken the shot. Maybe his hands had been trembling too hard, maybe he'd blinked, maybe he'd wanted David to surrender. But he didn't take the shot.

David jumped, flinging himself hard off the fence, and was swallowed up by the darkness of the foliage.

"Shit!" Adrenaline pumped into Kevin, and he was running for the fence. He holstered his gun and jumped, his brogues skittering against the metal before he found purchase. His arms screamed as he hauled himself up to the top, chips of rusted paint slicing into his palms. Muscles ripped across his ribs. Through the bars he could see Haines's ragged silhouette dashing deeper into the trees. He dragged his clumsy shoes to the top bar, pivoted between the spears, nearly impaling his ass on one of the points, and jumped. He hit the ground and felt the concussion drive the breath from his lungs. Glock out. He ran.

Beyond the trees that lined the fence, the park was a series of gentle undulations. Kevin steered himself away from the house, not wanting to be backlit by the kitchen lights. Ahead he could see David, weaving among the trees, nearing the point at which a greater darkness seemed to congeal in the park's center.

He could stop and take shots, but they'd miss. He'd spent his adrenaline and now his body was realizing he hadn't even had dinner, knees watery, shoulders heavy. The gun would leap right out of his godamn hands, and he'd either miss or hit him somewhere critical and kill him. He couldn't beat back his revulsion at the idea of killing him.

He had to slow down a little to pull out his cellular and look at the green glow of the keypad and screen. If they were fast enough they could encircle the park, contain him. The ground fell away unexpectedly and Kevin pitched forward, the cellular leaping from his hand and landing somewhere in the grass. Face down. Invisible.

Fuck, fuck, fuck!

He looked up and saw Haines's shadow, dipping and weaving on the uneven terrain, then sinking out of sight on the other side of a small hill. Kevin scrambled around for the phone for a few more seconds without luck, then got to his feet and kept running. He reached the hill's crest, and there was no sign of Haines.

No ... can't lose him, not now, not like this ...

Heedlessly he careened down the hill, his physical momentum overriding his reserve, even as his mind distantly quailed at the idea of plunging into this unrelieved blackness. The moon and stars were mostly blotted out by cloud, and he was trying to understand this new landscape of dark edges and textures of black. He brought himself up short, tried to breathe soundlessly, listen. Despite the heat, a cold sweat broke across his chest. He'd been swallowed up in darkness—*dark as the belly of the whale*, came an unbidden voice in his head. Then he heard the quick pant of a man running hard and thought he saw a smudge of movement by a brick utility shed, which was tall enough to reflect some light from distant lampposts.

Kevin knew how quickly David could set up his rifle. Ten seconds, twenty if he was out of practice.

If you're going to run, run now.

He pelted toward the brick building, skull afire, imagining David's sure hands snapping together the rifle, one, two, three, eye to the scope, finger curving round the trigger, Kevin's head in the cross hairs .... Chest heaving, he slammed himself against the brick, trying to choke back his breath. *Still alive. Insane to be doing this, in the dark, alone. Suicide.*

Is that what this is?

There, a soft scuffling sound, then a snap, maybe a twig breaking, maybe the sound of a bullet being loaded into the breech. David was there, just on the other side of the building.

Show yourself! he wanted to scream.

Kevin thought of Rick, dead in his house. Why hadn't he thought sooner? It was so obvious. A little sooner and he would have caught David, and saved Rick's life. He'd fucked it all up.

You can still get David. You've got to, before he outsmarts you again, and kills again and again and leaves you so far behind you'll never get this close to him, ever ...

Don't do it, Kevin. Suicide.

Silently, he edged himself closer to the corner, checked his grip on the Glock, and felt fear and anger start to warp his mind. *Whirl around that corner and you'll probably die. Right into the barrel of David's rifle. Maybe.* Maybe they'd die together. Not so bad if he could take Haines with him. He'd probably not get another chance like this ...

He took the corner, shoulder braced against the brick. Nothing, but he couldn't hold back the bellow in this throat. Yelling, he charged to the next corner and threw himself around that one, not knowing and not caring what he'd find—

There! A body!

"Jesus Christ!"

It took Kevin several seconds to unclench his finger from the trigger, drag the gun down. He felt sick, knowing he'd almost fired, that he'd wanted more than anything to send bullet after bullet into the body. It was just a kid, and there was a girl beside him, her top hiked up over her breasts. Their faces were petrified as they scrambled to cover themselves up.

"What's going on?" the kid asked, his voice still brazen through his fear.

Kevin lowered his gun but saw the glow of a cellular beside the teenager. Trust a fifteen-year-old to have a cell phone.

"Gimme that," he said.

"Yeah, but—"

"Give it to me!"

He gave his instructions to the emergency dispatcher, but even as he looked across the park, he knew he was too late. By the time they arrived, set up roadblocks, Haines would have slipped through. He'd lost him.

*　　*　　*

"Jesus Christ, Kevin, you told me there's no way this would happen. It's a goddamn revenge killing."

"This wasn't a revenge killing," he told Michener.

"Uh-huh, so what is all this?"

"He killed Rick for his blood."

Michener sighed, as if he couldn't bear to hear such childish lies anymore. "His blood."

"Haines was worried Rick might have exactly the same blood, so he shot him to take him out of the equation."

"The equation being?"

"Keep the world from getting what's in his blood."

He'd returned from the park to find Rick's house teeming with personnel from the field office and Chicago Homicide. Now, through the dining-room archway, Kevin could see Laura Donaldson sitting numbly on a chair in the living room, spattered in blood. Down the main hallway he saw the glare of the photographers' lights from the kitchen. Evidence Response was already on the scene.

"I suggested putting someone on the house," Michener said, his eyes sparking with barely suppressed anger, "and you told me it wasn't necessary. And I fucking *listened*."

Kevin had to look away from the other man's antagonistic gaze. "It didn't occur to me until tonight, about the blood." It sounded lame, and he knew it. He should have thought of it sooner—it was elementary biology—and seen its deadly corollary. He was supposed to know Haines like no one else, be able to superimpose David's thinking over his own. He'd been too late, and he felt a crushing weight of responsibility. If he'd had his thoughts together, if he hadn't been so tired, so strung out, so ball-busted by Hugh—just more excuses for himself. He'd missed the key lead, and now Rick was dead.

"As far as I'm concerned, this is a revenge killing," said Michener, "and you just cost this man his life."

Kevin was too disheartened to protest. Michener would have put a man on the house for the wrong reasons, but it might have prevented Rick's death all the same. There was no point arguing with that.

"You didn't take any shots." The look on Michener's face was one of incredulity, mixed with frank distaste.

Kevin shook his head. "Wasn't time."

Michener frowned patronizingly, as if trying to help someone remember something perfectly obvious. "You said you ran down the side of the house, and saw him on the fence, right, perched right on top, and you didn't have the shot?"

"I did not have the shot," he repeated slowly.

Mitch grunted dismissively. "Well, if we're really lucky, he's still in the park."

Kevin doubted it, though he knew Michener had cordoned off the perimeter and was waiting for daybreak to send in teams. No one relished the prospect of wading into the darkness to find an armed man.

You did, he reminded himself with a jolt, and already it seemed incredible, an act of lunacy.

Michener's cell phone rang, and he turned away. Kevin walked into the living room to Laura Donaldson, wondering if she'd heard Michener taking a strip off him. She looked like he felt, crumpled and numb. She was so far from the defiant woman he'd interviewed earlier that he felt almost protective of her.

"How'd you get Rick's address?" he asked her.

"The Internet, some research service."

He nodded. "This morning when we talked, you knew there might be a chance Rick had the same blood."

She nodded, and he winced inwardly. But his anger towards her quickly dissipated: he couldn't blame her for not volunteering something that should have occurred to him. But if she had, this wouldn't have happened.

"I wish you'd told me," he couldn't help saying.

"I'm sorry."

"Did you have a chance to talk to Rick beforehand?"

"Just a bit."

"Had he had any contact with David, called him or visited him?" He wanted to get an idea how he'd gotten hold of Rick's address.

"He said he'd written him a letter, recently, to say goodbye. But," she added, as if sensing what he was after, "he said he hadn't put a return address on it."

Out of jail less than forty-eight hours, and he'd managed to dig up an unlisted address. Such things were possible, of course. Laura Donaldson had got the same information from one of those info-thieves that were proliferating on the Web. They were fast and pretty reliable, and big corporations, credit agencies, and even law enforcement used them. It wasn't a very good lead: Haines had undoubtedly got his accomplice to make the searches for him, and probably a lot of journalists had also paid for the same information, with Haines's escape such big news.

"Did you get your samples?" he asked Laura.

She shook her head.

"Probably for the best. If you got them, and Haines was probably watching from up there in his tree, he might not have given up on you so easily. And he'd certainly come back for another try. I think it might be best if you got out of town for a while."

She nodded vaguely. Haines had chosen to stay in Chicago, and maybe it was just for Rick, but Kevin wasn't so confident anymore that Laura Donaldson wasn't a target, especially if he thought she might already have some usable blood samples.

"I'm afraid for you, Dr. Donaldson. If you stay in town."

He waited until she met his eyes, and then felt almost embarrassed—did she think he was being too personal?

"I tried to save him," she said. "Rick."

"I know."

"But there wasn't much ... I couldn't even get to the phone because I knew he was still out there ..." She trailed off, as if suddenly doubting his interest or compassion, and put a hand to her face. There was blood dried across one cheek.

"Think about getting out of town, please," he said again, gently. "I think that's best right now. You're going back to your father's apartment?"

"When I can get out of the driveway."

He looked out the uncurtained window and saw that her car was hemmed in by the bulwark of police vehicles and, Jesus, already a news van. He sighed, pain soaring across his chest from the muscles he'd pulled climbing the fence. What the hell was the media going to do with this one?

"Come on, let's get you to a washroom and you can clean up a bit."

She let him take her arm and lead her like a child across the hall to a washroom.

"Thank you," she said, as she closed the door. Kevin heard it lock. He leaned back against the wall, suddenly dizzy. He could hear Hugh's voice from the front hall. What the hell was he going to tell Hugh?

He ran through what he'd learned tonight, and it seemed far from impressive. That Haines was in Chicago. That he'd shaved his head. That he'd been supplied with a hunting rifle and ammunition, and probably fashioned himself a homemade silencer. Maybe he walked to Rick's, maybe he drove. If they were lucky, they'd find a neighbor whose memory might be triggered by their new description of Haines, someone who might have seen him getting in or out of a car, maybe they'd even remember the make. License plate, probably not. But where would David go now? For several hundred dollars, there were people who could get him new ID, a driver's license, a social security number, a passport. Within days he could be anywhere in the country, or outside it, all but invisible.

CHAPTER FIFTEEN

Gail bathed, shaved her legs, washed her hair, anointed herself with creams. She spent half an hour in front of the mirror with her make-up, and put just a touch of perfume on her wrists and throat, from that sample she'd saved from *Vogue*—the one that made her think of Hawaiian flowers and a beautiful couple lying on the sand, their legs all tangled up, even though she knew that was wicked. She wanted to be pleasing to him because, instinctively, she knew that when he came home later on, he'd need her.

Although, when the door had closed behind him earlier, that knapsack slung over his shoulders, she'd felt a terrible pang. Maybe he wasn't coming back. He'd told her he was, he just didn't know how late. But she knew there were others, other faithful followers he'd written to over the years, all hoping he'd join them too, and maybe some of them were prettier, and holier than her, which wouldn't be difficult. But she'd do anything not to lose him.

She winced as she remembered the dinner she'd made him beforehand. He'd left almost half of it on his plate. The pork chops had been all dried up and leathery, and the cream of mushroom soup she'd mixed up on top was gluey and had a slightly burny taste, too. She'd kept apologizing, and he'd just smiled at her so kindly, forgiving her. He'd said he was going to start fasting, that it helped focus him, made it easier to speak to God, but he'd probably just been trying to spare her feelings. It was true, she didn't do much cooking these days, just fixed herself little snacks when she needed to, maybe some Lipton Cup-o-Soup and crackers and pickles, or maybe just a cola and some potato chips. And then there were treat days at work, when people would bring in bagels and different cream cheeses, or danishes and big muffins loaded with chocolate. She knew she had a weakness, but she tried to make up for it by skipping meals. How could her bottom be so wide when she didn't even eat proper meals?

In her bedroom she got into her pyjamas, hating the way her lower belly swelled against the waistband. She wrapped herself up in her velour dressing gown. Ten-thirty and still he wasn't home. She knew she wouldn't be able to sleep. Last night, it had taken her forever to doze off, with David next door in the spare room. Even with the air-conditioner on, she'd been too hot, couldn't find the right position. She kept visualizing him, just on the other side of the wall, David Haines in her own house, between the sheets of her pull-out bed.

When she'd woken around four to pee, she'd had to pass his room, and the door was ajar and she'd looked in on him, and just stared for a few seconds at his shorn head, so beautiful at rest, and so pale after all those years in prison without sun. How she would have liked to sit down on his bedside and stroke that smooth head, the poor hunted thing, and maybe he'd wake up and smile at her, and pull back the covers for her to slip in.

All day at work, she'd been afraid people would know, just by looking at her.

"Hmmm, someone's preoccupied today," Nancy had said during break. "Looks like you had yourself a hot date last night ..."

And she'd blushed, unable to help herself. It was so inappropriate, but it pleased her all the same, just to savor the idea of it.

He'd asked for his brother's address, and she'd found it—it was so easy to do, but it made her feel good and clever to be helping him. It was the same when, later, she'd brought home the muffler and the duct tape from the auto shop, and he'd nodded approvingly and said it was exactly right.

The rifle, she'd already had in her basement for several months. She'd bought it at his urging, and it terrified her. She'd gone so far as to teach herself how to assemble the pieces, and load the shells, but just holding the thing in her hands, knowing what it could do, made her feel squeamish. Not because it was wrong, what she would do, but because she was weak. She would have felt the same way killing a pig or a cow to eat its meat, and there was nothing wrong with that, was there? And these doctors, they were worse than that, much worse, sinning and polluting and corrupting. But she was weak, so weak, and the rifle had stayed in her basement.

In her bedroom, she got out the guidebooks she'd bought from the mall during her lunch break: Mexico, Central America, Brazil. Last night as she'd lain awake, she'd been thinking about the kind of life they could lead together. David could stay here, maybe for years, without anyone noticing, but what kind of way was that to live, hiding and fearful every day? In the early hours of the morning, the plan had come together so quickly and simply. She would quit her job, sell the bungalow, and they could cross the border and live somewhere beautiful and warm where no one would ever find him. Wasn't that the most practical anyway? The FBI and the Chicago police and the state police were all looking for him; she'd seen the news, and it terrified her. She and David were being so careful, but what if a neighbor caught a peek at him, in the driveway, through a window?

If they could go to the coast and find someone to take them across in a boat, maybe to Cuba—people did that all the time in movies and books—then they could have their pick of where to live.

There, on the bed, looking at the glossy covers of her books, she conjured up an image of a humble little cottage set back from the beach, shielded by palm trees. They'd have to live simply, of course, but as long as she was with David, she didn't care how she lived.

After dinner he'd asked her to pray with him in the living room. For forty-five minutes they'd kneeled side by side on the floor—normally she could never have done it, but somehow she seemed to draw strength from him, his straight back, the intent look on his face (she'd sneaked a few glances when his eyes were closed). She could feel the power of prayer coursing through him like a transmitter straight to God, and she knew what a good man he was.

It was almost eleven when she heard her car pull up out front. She opened the door for him so he wouldn't need to bother knocking, and he came in quickly, his pale face blazing. He was like an angel as he stood there in the hallway, a ferocious angel, and she felt her knees weaken.

He was pulling at his shoelaces, wrenching off the sneakers and examining the soles. Gail thought she caught sight of something dark spattered there, and even though, somewhere in her mind, she knew what it was, she didn't care. He was back, he'd come back to her.

David was still breathing hard, his powerful chest rising and falling. He left his shoes on the mat and walked into the living room.

"May I have some water?" he asked.

She went to the kitchen, twisted a couple of ice cubes out of the tray, and ran the tap water until it numbed her fingers. David was sitting on the sofa, his head cupped in his hands, hiding his face. She set the water before him on the glass coffee table.

"You'll hear soon enough on the news," David said, still not looking at her. "I killed my brother."

She'd found the address for him; she'd seen him leave with the gun broken down into pieces inside the knapsack; but she hadn't let herself think any further than that, refused to do the simple arithmetic to get the answer. Even now she was only seeing little bits of it. She tightened her mouth.

"After what he did to you—" she began to say quietly.

"That's got nothing to do with it," he said, looking at her angrily. "It was his blood. He might've had the same blood as me, and the doctor was already there, ready to take it. I had to do it."

She saw his eyes fill with tears and she hesitated awkwardly before going to him, putting her hand on his shoulder. He let his head rest against her thigh, and she stroked his head, still smooth from the shave, like stroking a baby. He didn't move away and her heart swelled with joy. She'd been right: he needed her; this brave, courageous man needed her to take care of him.

It took all her courage to lean down and kiss his head, breathing in his scent. Were they sinful, the thoughts she'd harbored for him all along? She wanted him, soul and body, had guiltily imagined carnal pleasures when she brought him back to her bungalow. After all, he'd been years without a woman, wouldn't a man crave it? Even with her? And it wouldn't be sinful if they married ...

Look at him, she thought in awe, he was crying about his brother, the brother who'd betrayed him, who'd as good as executed him by putting him on death row. But he still loved him.

"You're a very good, brave man, David."

He looked at her sternly. "It doesn't horrify you, what I did?"

"Of course not," she said, her voice faltering at the fierceness of his eyes.

"It should." His voice was harsh. "God demands horrible things from us sometimes, to test our resolve. We must love the Lord our God above all things, *all* things."

"Yes, I see."

"Do you?"

She took a step back from him, as if all her desires had been laid bare for him to see. How hideous she must seem to him, inside and out, when all she could think of now were her own bodily cravings and pleasures. All that time in the bath, with her make-up.

"Leave me alone now," he said, staring at the floor.

She made it to the bathroom and turned on the taps to drown the sound of her sobs. She dashed water into her eyes to stop the swelling and watched ashamed as the mascara ran. *Vain, vain. Wash it all off.* She scrubbed her face until it stung.

"Gail."

He was outside the door.

"I'm sorry I spoke sharply to you."

"I deserved it," she said.

"No, you've been loyal and kind, and I turned my sorrow on you in anger. Are you all right?"

"Yes." She didn't look at herself in the mirror, afraid of seeing the pleasure in her eyes at this attention.

"Please come out."

She opened the door, unable to meet his gaze, but she saw the guidebooks in his hands, and felt a new pang of humiliation. All her girlish plans.

"I can't go to these places, Gail, you must know that." His voice was so gentle, so patient. "Not yet anyway." He lifted her chin so their eyes met. *Yet*, she thought, *yet*. That meant later, didn't it?

"Even harder trials await me. And I need you, Gail, to help me through them. There's somewhere I need to go. Will you help me?"

* * *

She dreamed that Sandra was healed.

Lounging at the poolside in her black one-piece, her sister was tanned by the Mexican sun, drawing admiring glances from the other hotel guests and staff. Laura felt self-conscious in her sage-green fitted suit, but she didn't want to change in case her thighs and tummy looked fat.

"How did you do it?" Laura asked. "Get better like that?"

"Pure faith," said Sandra, diving into the pool. She surfaced, skin sparkling. "Come on in."

But Laura hung back, startled and resentful at this exuberantly transformed Sandra.

"You're not supposed to be getting better."

"Oh, always so negative," said Sandra carelessly, treading water. "But I'm better anyway. You do want me to get better, don't you?"

"We'll need to do a biopsy," said Laura, as Sandra swam to the side and pulled herself up the ladder.

"Oh, Laura," said Sandra impatiently, "just look." With her hands she opened up her belly, as though her fingernails had just made a deep vertical midline incision, revealing everything inside her abdomen. And suddenly Laura was inside an operating room, gowned, gloved, panting through her mask, looking down at Sandra's liver, to see that it wasn't healed; it was studded with thousands of minuscule hepatomas.

"Well?" said Sandra, lifting her head from the gurney. "Was I right?"

Laura wrenched herself free of the dream, panting into her pillow until her heart slowed. Eyes still shut, an enveloping sorrow hung over her, and even as the dream's potency slowly dissipated, she was still locked into its ghoulish logic. Why did she have to go and do a biopsy? Why hadn't she just hugged her sister and told her how glad she was? But no, she had to open her up like a lab monkey, peer inside, a sneak preview of her imminent death.

Finally Laura opened her eyes.

Light seared through the narrow gap in the curtains. She fumbled for her watch on the night table: already ten-thirty in the morning. She didn't know which was worse, her dream horrors, or waking reality.

Even after the two long showers she'd taken the night before, the smell of Rick's blood still lingered in her nostrils. It had been years since she'd done a shift in Emergency, and she'd never seen anyone die like that before: that fast, unstoppable gush of life. Maybe she could have saved him if there'd been a phone within reach, if she'd had better instruments in her kit, if Haines hadn't been smashing in the patio doors to shoot her, too ...

You did what you could. Not your fault.

But it was her research that had stoked Haines's rage and set him on course to Rick's, and she couldn't wrench herself entirely free of the part she'd played.

That big house, and all its empty rooms waiting to be filled. And now who was going to come to take away all the boxes and furniture? Rick's wife? She winced. Maybe she'd have some firm do it for her. She'd sell the house, wouldn't she? Couldn't live there, not now.

It made her feel guilty even to be thinking this now, but she couldn't help it: all that blood she might have used, pumping uselessly through her fingers as she'd tried to stop Rick's bleeding. Now David was the only one left, and what were the chances he'd be brought in alive?

Rise and shine, everyone.

One leg over the side of the bed, now two. Good. She'd used up the last of her phenmetrizine the night before, but she had a prescription scribbled on the pad she'd swiped yesterday at the lab. She showered and dressed and went downstairs to get it filled at the drug store at the base of her father's complex. Heart racing, she bought some milk, orange juice, a cheese croissant that looked as if it had been passed over by Methuselah. At the counter, she grabbed a *Tribune*, *Sun-Times*, and *New York Times*. Her eyes darted furtively to every person who passed through the door, checking for David Haines.

Back upstairs, she took her diminished hit of speed and sat down to wait, biting absently at her croissant. She hadn't been very good about cutting back the dosage, but she felt the effects of what little withdrawal she'd achieved: a leaden pall that weighed down on her mind and body equally; sudden sweats, and swells of panicked nausea. The hit just now just might keep it all at bay so she could think. Think about what? What was there left to think about? Rick was dead. Haines was on the loose. What could she do now? From the kitchen she heard the kettle boiling and stood up.

The day passed in an unreal haze, time stretching and compressing erratically. She'd turned off the ringer on the phone but could still hear the incessant click of her dad's answering machine as it advanced to record yet another message. Her work phone was still auto-forwarding all her calls, and she wasn't about to go back to her lab and reprogram it. She'd just ignore them all. She read the newspaper, watched as much news coverage as she could bear. Apparently she was the leading lady in the breaking news story of the year.

She thought about her lab, the lights out, the machinery dormant, nothing fucking getting done, but she didn't want to go outside, not after last night, maybe not ever again. Around noon she closed her eyes for just a moment to find she'd slept for over an hour. Later, sitting in the armchair, painfully awake, her mind darted once again through the events of the night before, and when she looked at the clock, exhausted, she saw that only a couple of minutes had elapsed. Twice she got on the phone to book air tickets to Tijuana, but each time she apologized to the travel agent and hung up.

Around four o'clock the answering machine ran out of tape. Girding herself, she rewound the microcassette and pressed Play.

The first few messages were from journalists, wanting to interview her. She carefully took down their numbers, though she had no immediate plans to call them back. Still, a bit of media ammo might be useful if Vic Greene was about to launch an all-out civil rights war on her and MetaSYS. Then there was a call from Ted Wolsyk, the chairman of the AMA, and Liz Barrie from the NCI, calling to ask if they could set up a meeting to be briefed on her findings in Haines's blood—no doubt a polite way of asking her to explain why she'd decided to turn cancer research into a three-ring circus with David Haines as the prize chimp. She fast forwarded through a few hang-ups, a few terse calls from other medical colleagues.

Then came the deluge.

Her work number must have been leaked out somehow, maybe in a newspaper, probably on the Internet. Dazed, she listened to one call after another, from husbands and wives and lovers and parents, from family doctors, specialists, hospital boards, all begging her to make sure Haines was taken alive, to make the cure quickly, to call them if she needed test subjects, please, please, please ...

"Dr. Donaldson, my name's Helen Garner, and they've told my husband that he's inoperable but ..."

"Hello, this is a message for Dr. Laura Donaldson, my mother has advanced bone cancer and ..."

"Dr. Donaldson, our little boy ..."

On and on it went, a litany of hepatomas and melanomas and retinoblastomas, lesions and metastases, one call after another, she lost track there were so many, and she realized she was silently crying, as much from her own mounting frustration as from the heartbreaking desperation of her callers.

"Why are you calling *me*?" she breathed. What did they expect her to do, catch Haines single-handedly? Why weren't they calling the FBI, the Justice Department, the White House?

When the tape finally ended, she sat numbly beside the phone for several minutes, then picked it up and dialed Adrian, whose own numerous messages had punctuated the last half hour.

"Laura, why didn't you call sooner?" he asked, and she thought she could discern some aggravation in his voice.

"Sorry."

"You didn't even ... you should've called when you found out Rick Haines was in town. We would've sent security people with you ..."

"The last ones didn't help that much," she said dully.

She heard Adrian sigh and felt a bit of remorse. The strain in his voice was obvious.

"Can I come over?" he said, and for some reason her courage failed her, and she didn't ask if he'd be bringing bad news.

"Yes," she said. "Come on over."

* * *

Adrian entered the apartment like a stranger, stiff, eyes moving restlessly away from hers. She wished she'd just made him tell her over the phone.

"Would you like a drink?" she asked, needing to say something.

"No, I'm okay, thanks. I can't stay long."

She didn't want him to stay long. It was all wrong, having him here alone, reminding her of all his other visits, when they'd dined, made love, watched TV wrapped up in a blanket. It made her angry, the hypocrisy of it all: *he'd* pursued her, *he'd* made her promises, made her start imagining a life with him—not that she hadn't had serious misgivings, but maybe Adrian was her last chance at a family, children—and then he'd decided to break it off. But what angered her most was this little whine at the back of her head that she couldn't strangle silent: *Maybe if you were a better person, less prickly, he would have chosen you over his family. Maybe if you were more like Sandra ...*

She led him to the living room, sat down on the opposite sofa, took a breath. She knew he hadn't come to talk about personal matters.

"Just tell me," she said.

"The board wants to drop it."

"Wants to, or is going to?" she said doggedly, wondering why she even bothered asking.

"Going to. It's over, Laura. I'm sorry."

It's over. He could have at least chosen different words this time. She felt her anger start to swell, slow and subterranean, heart knocking in strong steady blasts at her ribs. "What are you afraid of?"

Adrian's chest filled and sank. "They don't think we can win the court case, and neither does Paul."

"Maybe not with Paul as lead counsel, but——"

"Paul may not be much in court, but he knows his law. And he knows the ACLU has pretty deep pockets and we could end up sinking hundreds of thousands, maybe millions, into a losing legal battle. The board got cold feet."

"The board. And how did *you* vote?" This was entirely unprofessional, but she couldn't stop herself.

Adrian's face was starting to show signs of angry impatience. "This is business, Laura. We're a public company and I can't ignore the wishes of my board."

"You know what I've got on my answering machine? About fifty calls, just today, from people with cancer, *begging* for Haines to be taken alive, *begging* me to continue this work. You can't just pull out now!"

"You're assuming," he said quietly, "that his blood would yield a therapy."

She looked at Adrian closely. "So this is what it's about. You've lost faith in me."

"The board has the highest opinion of you. But you've been working full throttle for the last eighteen months. You're worn down to nothing. You have everyone's sympathy and support, but you can't expect yourself to be making good decisions now."

"So Haines was a bad decision?"

"The board thinks it was, all things considered, and they're not trying to pin the blame on you. I rushed in as eagerly as you, but now we've got to pull back. We all wanted it to be some magic bullet, just like you, but it's not. I'm trying to help you out, Laura. You don't want to be associated with the Haines thing anymore. It's only going to get messier." He snapped open his briefcase and brought out a videocassette. "It's been a hell of a day. Tom Powell sent this over from ABC this morning. It's the rough cut of the 'Headline' piece they're doing on you. You want me to tell you about it, or do you want to see it yourself?"

She stared at the tape as if it were something malignant. "Show me."

For the next twenty-five minutes, she stared at the television, nauseated. She could feel Adrian's eyes on her, but she wouldn't turn to meet his gaze. She made her face a mask. Just two weeks ago, she'd imagined the "Headline" piece as a triumphant documentary heralding a new treatment for cancer—something that even her father's friends might see and call about. But after her complete failure with Gillian Shamas, she'd known the ending would be far from triumphant: a tragic and discouraging endnote.

Still, she was hardly expecting *this*, a documentary not so much about her treatment, as about *her*, the now controversial Dr. Donaldson, whose research initiatives were always, according to the doctors they'd interviewed, a bit dubious. That old shithead Kent Ovitz at Bethesda actually called her "a bit of a charlatan." And they didn't stop with the explosion of cancer she'd created in Gillian Shamas, they culled news footage from the last two days to show her latest initiative, trying to extract the blood of a condemned man against his wishes. Aerial shots of the train wreckage, the blood-spattered interior of the Gulfstream lab, and then Rick's house as seen from the backyard, festooned with yellow police tape, the patio window smashed in. By the end of it, she was right up there with Dr. Frankenstein.

"Well," she said after Adrian turned the television off, "at least they didn't show me digging up the fucking graves. We can be thankful for that."

"We've already told Powell we think the piece is entirely distorting and unfair, and that we'll consider legal action if they air it as is."

"But...?"

"Paul says really there's not much we can do about it."

"All along I was against this godamn piece, but you had to have your little publicity rush."

Adrian nodded mournfully. "It's going to look bad for you. We *will* back you. But we need you to get some R&R first, disappear for a while. A three-month leave."

"Don't bullshit me, Adrian. Is this a warmup for losing my lab?"

They were powerless to strip her of her faculty position at the university, of course, but it was well within MetaSYS's reach to withdraw funding for her lab. And without the funding she was like everyone else, scrambling for dollars, scientist and fundraiser and self-promoter all rolled into one.

"You need some rest," was all Adrian said, firmly. "I hope you take it." He stood. "I should get back to the office."

At the door, he turned to her, reached to touch her arm, then seemed to think better of it. "I'm sorry. About everything."

"Business is business," she said icily, wanting him just to leave. She closed the door behind him, leaned her head against it, and felt bloated with self-disgust.

A bad decision. Adrian's words careened maliciously through her head. Seemed she'd been making lots of them lately.

Hack. Charlatan.

Maybe Adrian and everyone else was right. She was on the medical rebound, latching onto David Haines like a coward, too afraid to go back to real work. Because maybe she just didn't have what it took. Bad science, fairy-tale science, and she'd succumbed to it, just like Sandra, clinging desperately to her miracle cures.

* * *

"Take me with you."

David looked at her, and felt a stab of pity, but he knew she mustn't accompany him.

"I need you here, Gail."

"I know I've been weak, but I can do it now," she said hurriedly. She said it with the air of someone who'd had a revelation, and was eager to convey its potency. "I can kill her. Dr. Donaldson. I can do that for you, I know I can. You've given me strength."

"No. You've done enough already." But the truth was, he didn't trust her to carry it off successfully. In these past days, he had fathomed her character fully. Left to herself, she would falter, fail, and then the authorities might be able to use her to track him down. He didn't trust her to have the discipline of Will Andrews, or the strength to martyr herself, like Bob Jarvis. He'd learned of Jarvis's death on the news just yesterday, another casualty in the name of righteousness.

"Will you come back, then?"

He saw the need in her eyes. "Yes," he lied. He needed her still.

She nodded miserably and he leaned forward and kissed her forehead.

"I love you," she said quietly.

"If you love me, you'll do my bidding."

Her car was outside, loaded, waiting for him. It was time to go.

* * *

Kevin watched the security camera footage, a grainy black and white imbued with an eerie fluorescent glow. A time line ticked over across the bottom of the screen: 04:37.12. The wide-angle lens took in the entire front of the dingy convenience store. Kevin could see a clerk slouched behind the counter, reading a magazine, and a man in a baseball cap hovering almost out of frame down one of the aisles, picking out some bottled water. As he neared the counter, the brim of the baseball cap mostly shielded his face, but as he accepted his change from the clerk, he tipped his head up slightly, and Kevin recognized David Haines instantly.

On the vast Mitsubishi Proscan monitor, the tape freeze-framed blearily. At the head of the table, Seth Michener put down the remote and looked from Hugh to Kevin, his eyes alight with barely concealed self-congratulation. It was only eight-fifteen in the morning, but the command post, on day four of the manhunt, had already achieved its own hermetic atmosphere of deodorant, sweat, and congealed coffee. Normally reserved for high-level meetings and the occasional press conference, the room suffered from the same buzzing fluorescents and pukey mauve-and-blue-fleck carpet as the rest of the field office. But it also had a few framed portraits and landscapes, blue upholstered, brass-buttoned armchairs, side tables with demure brass lamps, and a massive, lozenge-shaped table topped with glass. Hunched around it were a dozen office staff, engrossed in their telephones and radio handsets, listening to citizens phoning in with information, a rumor, a supposed sighting; and street agents calling back their leads, asking for new instructions.

"We're agreed this is our man?" Michener said, tilting his head at the monitor.

Hugh Carter nodded. "Looks good to me. Kevin?"

"It's him. Where was this?"

"Just outside St. Louis, four o'clock this morning."

Kevin took the last sip of his coffee. As he'd feared, Haines was totally mobile, and if he could be in St. Louis, he could be anywhere in the country within twenty-four hours.

"License plate?" he asked.

Michener shook his head. "We're lucky we got this at all. The kid at the counter thought he looked kind of familiar, but almost didn't want to bug the cops and the FBI." Michener laughed. "America's Most Wanted buys some bottled water from him, and he's not sure."

"All right, let's talk about this." Hugh stood and led them back to his office through an adjoining door at the far end of the conference room.

"You all right, Kevin?" Hugh asked, leaning back against his desk. "You look wiped."

"I'm fine." He shouldn't have stayed up so late the night before, reading the Bible and Haines's letters to Will Andrews until he'd felt delirious.

"All right. I've already talked to the St. Louis office," Hugh said, "and they're ready to get all over this."

"He's making the run," Michener said, clearly pleased, as he dropped, splay-legged into a chair.

Kevin remained standing, hands in pockets. He knew Mitch, from almost the very start, had been predicting that Haines would try to cross the border.

"I think we should call in the joint task force in Houston, and get the Marshals in on this if we can," Mitch suggested to Hugh. "I've already talked to Customs and the Border Patrol, plus the Coast Guard off Miami. That's second choice for me—harder to get a boat to take you across. Wherever he tries to cross, we'll pick him up."

Kevin listened with growing irritation, watching Michener yapping like some oversized lap dog on a cushion, calling the shots.

"A sighting in St. Louis doesn't necessarily mean he's heading south for the border," he pointed out.

"Is there another reason you'd want to visit St. Louis?" Michener asked with a chuckle, but Kevin refused to smile.

"Okay, sure," said Michener with schoolteacher patience. "We can waste a lot of time hemming and hawing over what he was doing there. What we know is this. He's southbound, and he was in St. Louis five hours ago. That means we've got to get our asses in gear, now."

Kevin glanced over to Hugh to see him nodding. "We're shutting down the command post up here and passing it south, under our supervision of course."

So he and Michener would be shuttled down to St. Louis and Houston to oversee the new task force. Kevin's first reaction was that it would take him away from Becky for God knows how long; his second was that it might not be the right move.

"I don't buy it," he said.

"What don't you buy?" Michener asked.

"The candid camera routine. He's not stupid."

"Everyone gets hungry, has to drink. This place is way out in hell and gone, four in the morning, kid at the counter with his nose buried in *Playboy*. Who's going to know?"

"Someone's given him a car, they can probably stock it with enough water and food for Haines to get wherever he's going. He shouldn't have to make a pit stop in St. Louis."

"You're saying he wanted to get caught?"

"I'm saying maybe he wanted us to know where he was, to sidetrack us."

"Well, he's not going north. You know Haines, right, better than anyone here? If he's smart, he knows we're going to catch him, and if he's really smart he'll know it's going to be sooner than later. So he's going to get the hell out of the country. All the blood stuff is taken care of, right? He did his brother, so we're all clear. Nothing to keep him here. Is there?"

The pointed reference to Rick wasn't lost on Kevin. He replied calmly, "He might well run for the border, but we also know he's got at least one very devoted follower, possibly more, who could harbor him pretty safely if they're careful. If I were him, I'd lie low for a while and let things die down, let the task force dwindle, wait for people to forget his pictures on the TV. That's safe."

Michener jiggled the videocassette in his hand. "But he's not being safe. He's on the road. He's making the run. And by the way, killing Rick wasn't safe either. For all he knew, we'd have the place crawling with agents. But fugitives don't usually make pro and con lists like this. They're too scared, they know their ass is wanted, they bolt. In all the time I've tracked fugitives, one thing's always the same: most criminals are idiots. That's why they're criminals. Those James Bond villains with the British accents—they don't exist. Now maybe Haines is smarter than most, but that's not saying much. I'm not going to get too exercised about any possible decoys. He's fucked up and let us see him."

Michener's nostrils flared as he sucked in air, looking around the room, and then he continued more thoughtfully. "Maybe you're right,

Kevin," he said. "Maybe it's just a mind-fuck. There's no way of knowing, and that's why you're staying up here. If he's still got accomplices up here, we need you to work on that, if that's all right with you."

It was said with such uncharacteristic respect and gravity that Kevin knew instantly its implications. He was being left behind, kicked off the task force, while Michener went down south alone to head it up and bring Haines in. He couldn't stop his eyes from flicking to Hugh, but of course this would come as no surprise to him; in fact, he'd doubtless okayed it before the meeting. Hugh met his gaze dispassionately. He could let it go, maybe bring it up with Hugh in private, but what the hell.

"I take it this is because of Rick Haines."

Hugh's expression showed some signs of discomfort at this forthrightness. For a moment, he hesitated. Then he shrugged, with an attempt at a cordial grin.

"I haven't been right since the Flood, Kevin, but I think you might be too close to this to make the right calls. It's not a reflection of your abilities, it's a question of you not being right for this job."

He wondered if Hugh was referring to the fact that he hadn't shot at Haines when he supposedly had the chance, or his decision not to post someone around Rick's house. With amazing tact Michener remained silent.

"This guy ate three years of your life," Hugh said. "He wrecked your marriage—"

"I wrecked my marriage, Hugh."

"—he wrecked your health. Be honest with yourself, Kevin. This guy makes you crazy, and it clouds your judgment. I don't want to lose you to sick leave for another six months. These weren't easy decisions, but at the end of the day, I've got to act in the best interests of the Bureau, and my people, and that includes you. The decision's made. Michener goes down to supervise the task force; you stay up here and follow up."

To argue any further now seemed undignified, and he didn't want to give Michener the pleasure of a more prolonged chastisement.

"I mind the shop then," he said evenly.

"Anyway," said Hugh, no doubt hoping to defuse the tension, "as I recall, you've got some holiday time coming up. Weren't you going up to Canada with Becky? Newfoundland or something?"

"Prince Edward Island." It was already difficult to imagine a time when such a friendly bit of intimacy would pass between them.

"You don't want to mess that up waiting on Haines out in Texas," said Michener. "Take your kid on holiday. Don't disappoint her."

CHAPTER SIXTEEN

She was packing when the phone rang, and she picked it up only because she was expecting a call back from the travel agent, confirming her evening flight to San Diego. After Adrian had left, she'd decided to get out of town and go see Sandra—something she should have done days ago. There was nothing to keep her up here right now—not Adrian, not her lab—and she didn't know how much longer she could bear the daily heartbreaking litany of phone calls on her answering machine.

"Dr. Donaldson?"

It was not the travel agent; this voice was altogether younger, with more than a hint of uncertainty in it. Laura picked up the remote and turned down CNN.

"Who's calling please?"

"Is this Dr. Donaldson? Because there's something I need to ask her. It's about David Haines. If he had children—"

"Who is this?"

The voice continued doggedly. "If he had children, would they have the same kind of blood?"

Her very first impulse was to hang up, but a raw urgency in the woman's voice made her hesitate.

"Who is this?" she demanded.

"Because I've got his son."

Laura slammed down the phone, furious, fist still clenching the receiver. Goddamn crank call, and her eyes were actually wet with tears. What kind of sick person would do something like this, call her up and goad her, after what happened to Rick Haines? Probably some rotten teenagers had her on speaker-phone and were having a good laugh in a basement rec room somewhere.

But seconds later, when the phone rang again, she snatched it up, actually hoping it was the woman, wanting to vent her rage.

"Hello?"

"Okay, I know you don't believe me," the woman said hurriedly, "but would you just listen to me, please?"

Laura's voice quavered with anger. "You're saying you had a child with David Haines?"

"And I want to know if he could have the same kind of blood."

Laura turned her face away from the mouthpiece for a second, trying to calm her breathing. Why was she doing this to herself, even listening to this? For a second time she almost hung up, but instead, she pulled the notepad closer and grabbed a pen.

"Prove it," she said.

"I was in the cult with him, the New Apostles. I was the one who recruited him."

Laura knew she didn't have much hope of catching her out. She knew little about Haines's personal history, but she was aware that countless articles and numerous biographies had been written about him. This woman could have done her research and prepared this whole story ahead of time, had notes spread out around her, for all Laura knew. But why would someone do this? Were people so bored or so demented they would indulge in this elaborate ruse just to titillate themselves?

"But you're not in the cult anymore?" No one still inside would even call it a cult, would they?

"I left when I got pregnant."

"When was that?" Laura asked. Maybe if she asked for enough dates the woman would eventually contradict herself. And she could always check in a book afterwards to make sure they jibed. She asked when she gave birth, then when she met David Haines.

"Where'd you meet him?"

"On the campus, Northwestern, he was just starting med school. We worked the campus a lot, a lot of lonely people, first time away from home, looking for companionship."

"So you brainwashed him, or whatever you call it. Indoctrinated."

"I helped."

For a second she forgot this might all be an elaborate fiction and caught herself feeling disdain for this woman who could so misguide someone (and a med student at that) with a bunch of Precambrian crap about God. Then she came back to her senses, and wondered if this caller were merely on some megalomaniacal power trip: *I was the woman who created David Haines, and I have his child to prove it.*

"So you slept with him? I didn't think such things were allowed in cults."

"You don't know much about cults, then," said the woman, with a weariness that threw Laura for a moment.

She looked back at the date of birth the woman had given her, quickly did the math, and then said, deliberately making a mistake, "So your son, he's almost five now."

"Six and a half," she said, without missing a beat.

"What's your name?"

"I went by Rachel in the cult. But that's not my real name."

"What is?"

"I'd rather not say."

Laura's eyes were shut, trying to visualize Rachel, decipher her personality. How old? Young-sounding, her intonation sometimes spiking into a question at the end of sentences; but then she'd talked to people who sounded young and were grandmothers, others who sounded like old crones who turned out to be young beauties. Rachel sounded in her late twenties, maybe not formally well educated, but fairly intelligent. In the background Laura heard the sound of a television, a muted din that sounded like cartoons.

She wished her father had call display. But her father didn't go in for the latest thing, just a plain old touch-tone. Still, she could *69 Rachel at the end, and see what came up.

"So you're not going to tell me your real name," Laura said.

"You don't need to know that."

"Have you told this to the police or the FBI?"

"No, and I'm not going to."

"Why not?" said Laura, instantly suspicious. "Didn't you see what he did to his brother?"

"He doesn't know about his son," Rachel said.

"You were lovers and he didn't know you were pregnant?" she said, pushing.

"Lovers is not the word I would use," Rachel retorted, almost testily. "Like I said, I left early on when I was pregnant, I wasn't even showing. I never told him, I never told anyone there." As Laura was trying to weigh the plausibility of this, Rachel added, "Anyway, he didn't even know my real name. How could he find me?"

Laura remained doubtful. She remembered her almost paralyzing fear the night she'd spent in the hotel, knowing that Haines might have her purse. It made her doubt Rachel's apparent indifference. If it were her, if she'd had David Haines's son, she'd gladly be put in a safehouse until Haines was locked up.

"Even so," she said to Rachel, "why not tell someone, just in case, just to play it safe? For your boy's sake."

Rachel snorted. "Tell the police or the feds and there's probably a good chance he *would* find out about us. Someone'd leak it to the papers, and then it'd be all over the place. No, we're fine where we are. We don't need the police or FBI in our lives right now."

Her dislike of them was almost pointedly obvious, and Laura wondered if this was part of a fiction, or whether she'd really had unpleasant dealings with them in the past.

"Married?" Laura asked.

Rachel gave a weary sniff. "I was with someone for a couple years, and I'm still regretting it. I haven't had much luck with men. Bad taste, I guess. I always seem to go for the ones who need rescuing from something."

In the background Laura heard a muted voice call, "Mom?"

"I'm still talking, Sean." A hand covered the mouthpiece, and Laura could hear only a low garble, then, "... make sure to put your hood up."

Laura glanced out the window at the cloudless sky. Rachel wasn't calling from around Chicago—or maybe she was, and this was just another added mind-fuck. The line was crisp, unblemished. Could be down the hall, could be Alaska.

Was the boy just part of the elaborate scam? It seemed so involved. She tried to imagine the house, the TV on, the mother stealing time to talk on the phone, and she could actually see it: a bit messy, pop cans and chip bags on the coffee table, the smell of shoes in the hall-way. She realized how much she wanted this to be true.

"No other children?" she asked. She had hoped by drawing Rachel out that she'd eventually betray herself, concoct some ridiculous fact, or start contradicting her own story; but the more she heard, the more she felt reluctantly swept up in it.

"Just Sean."

Laura wrote the name down. "Where'd you give birth, Rachel?"

"You don't need to know that."

"What about your parents, do they know?"

"No."

"They don't know you had a baby, or that the father's David Haines?"

"They don't know about David. Wasn't something I was proud of, even back then."

Convenient, Laura thought. No one to verify her story.

"Where do your parents live?"

"Sorry."

Laura sighed. "What you've told me anyone could figure out from books. How am I supposed to check you out?" She knew that with a name, and place of birth, she could at least access records to see if Rachel had in fact had a baby when she said. But that's all she'd be able to get access to—not an address, not the father's name (though she doubted that would be filled in), not even the name or sex of the child.

"Who else knows about this, you having his baby?" she asked.

"Nobody."

"Somebody must."

"Nobody I know about. Listen, Dr. Donaldson, I left the New Apostles for a reason. I'd had enough. I wanted to get out of there and leave everything behind. And it took time, a long time for some things." This admission seemed so unguardedly honest that Laura almost believed her. "When I found out what David had done, it nearly killed me. That he was the father of my son. Imagine what that's like. It's bad enough for me, but I made a promise that my son would never have to know. I've made a lot of stupid ... look, I don't want him ever to know, his life's been hard enough without that. I go to the police or whatever, and it'll get out, and his life'll be screwed up."

Laura caught herself nodding. How other people would always treat you would be one plague; the other, the worse, would be how you would treat yourself. Like father like son? Was there something in the genetic payload that would resurface disastrously later in life? Or would it just haunt you forever, this psychic shadow of your father? She could see how a mother would want to keep all that from her son.

"So why are you telling *me*, then?" she demanded impatiently, angry with herself for getting momentarily sucked in. It was a conscious effort to pull herself back from this narrative, remind herself that this could all be written down on cue cards. *Why are you doing this?* she asked herself. *Tormenting yourself. You know this is all lies.*

Just hang up.

But she couldn't.

"I know you want the blood," Rachel replied, "and I need the money." It was said boldly, but the words were hurried, as if she found something just slightly distasteful about them.

"Ah." Laura felt a stab of disappointment. So this was all it was, a pathetic scam for money; had she really expected anything different? "So you want to *sell* me your son's blood."

"I read your company buys lots of people's blood."

"Usually when we know what's in it. There might not be anything in your son's. And for all I know, you're just making this whole thing up."

"There's other people I could call."

The tone of defiance surprised Laura. "Is that right?"

"Dr. Tamsen, or maybe Dr. Corel, he works with genes and cancer too."

Laura was impressed. Whoever Rachel was, she'd done some homework. "Well, you may not find either Tamsen or Corel very eager for Haines's blood. If you've been watching TV, you'll know why. A lot of people are calling me a witch doctor."

"But you still want it." It was not a question. Was there a slyness in her voice, or was it just a kind of desperate urging? Laura could feel herself perspiring under her arms, across her neck. Of course she wanted it; she craved it.

"I want money up front, *before* you test Sean, whether he has the right blood or not."

Laura couldn't repress a startled laugh. "That's asking a bit much, isn't it?"

"Twenty-five grand." The way she audaciously blurted it out, Laura could tell it was a huge amount of money to Rachel, and she felt almost sorry for her. "Your company can afford it. And then more if it's got those enzymes in it."

Laura wasn't about to tell her that, in a matter of days, she might not have a cent in backing from MetaSYS. Likely she'd be back in a corner of the university's general lab with chipped glassware.

"I don't think they'd approve it until after I've had a look at your son's blood." But already a segment of her mind was assessing whether she could put the money together herself. Maybe seven or eight in her account, twelve in T-bills, and the rest she could suck out of her private pension plan. Or maybe, less hassle, she could just extend her personal line of credit. She forced herself to stop.

"Twenty-five thousand up front, or no blood," said Rachel stubbornly.

Just as stubbornly, Laura said nothing, waiting her out, wondering who would break first. It was Rachel.

"You think I'd be bargaining like this if I didn't need the money?" she said bluntly. "You couldn't say I've had good luck, you know? The New Apostles, they wasted a lot of my life, three years I was with them. Getting out wasn't as easy as I thought, there's a lot of ... emotional baggage." She said the last words reluctantly, as if aware how hackneyed they sounded. "I wanted to keep my kid. That was something that was going to be mine, just mine. But it was hard. I didn't have anyone helping me. My parents weren't interested. Last year I was living with someone but he turned out ... he wasn't any good in the end. I've screwed up my life, but I want Sean to get a shot at something. Whatever I make just gets eaten up, end of every week. I'll never get a good job, but he's going to be better than that. I want to have something laid aside for him. So he can go to college maybe."

Laura felt poised between sympathy and skepticism. But if it was a rehearsed sob story, it had the same frank ring of truth as the rest of the routine.

"And if you get it, your twenty-five grand up front, how do we proceed?" Laura asked, feeling even as she spoke that she was making a tactical error, just admitting the possibility of paying.

"We arrange a meeting. You give me the money, in cash. Then we can go to my place. I'll tell Sean you're the school doctor, and you're just catching him up on some vaccinations or something. You'll get your blood."

Rachel had obviously already thought ahead to this, and Laura found something sordid and ominous about all these arrangements: the meeting places, the lies, the payment in cash—behavior more appropriate to a drug deal.

"How much blood do you need?" Rachel wanted to know.

"Just a couple ccs at first."

"You don't need bone marrow?"

"Not unless he's positive. Then we'd be happy to sign some kind of contract with you about proprietary rights." *We.* She didn't know who the hell that would be. She couldn't see Adrian and MetaSYS being interested, even if she had positive blood in hand. But maybe it would be enough to win her a new home at some other well-endowed lab.

"I still think you're lying," she said, feeling she'd lost some ground.

"It's up to you," Rachel replied.

Despite how much she wanted to test the boy (if there was a boy), she had no intention of forking over twenty-five grand without proof. Birth records were useless; witnesses could be fabricated: there was only one way of finding out the truth in instances like this.

"Here's what you're going to do," she told the other woman. "Take some hair from your son. Clippings aren't any good. I need the roots, the follicles. Get me ten good hairs, put them in an envelope, label it. I'll need ten of yours too. Fed Ex it all to me."

"Why?"

"I'm going to run some paternity tests. Find out if he's really Haines's son."

"But don't you need something from David, too?" She sounded startled.

"You let me worry about that." She was already wondering how she'd get some samples from Haines. Surely, at the prison, there would be clothes, bedsheets, a comb with enough hair or dry skin for her to suck out DNA. But how to get it? She doubted the prison would volunteer her access after her role in Haines's escape. She thought of Kevin Sheldrake: he could get them. It was a risk. He might refuse to help her, or he might try to take it out of her hands altogether, so she'd never even get a chance to meet Rachel's alleged son. But it was also her only shot at proving paternity.

"That's what I need from you," she said to Rachel. "It'll take about a day to run the tests. If it's a match, you've got your twenty-five thousand up front. Deal?"

She waited out the pause, her heart blaring. This was it; this would tell her if the woman was a fake or not.

"If I send the hair, how do I know I'm not just giving you all the stuff you need? I don't know much about genetics, but I know there's DNA in hair."

"Sure, but that's not enough. I don't know which genes make the enzymes I'm looking for. I need living blood to find them and study them. The hair is just for the paternity tests."

"I don't know ..."

"Well, we don't go any further without it. It's up to you."

"Yeah, maybe I'll think about," said Rachel, and she hung up.

Phone still pressed to her ear, Laura felt all her hopes dissolving into the abrupt silence at line's end. Figured. As soon as she brought up the paternity tests, Rachel just bailed out. She must be a fake after all. Laura dialed *69, and after two rings an electronic voice answered: "We're sorry; the number cannot be reached by this method." Blocked by Rachel no doubt.

"Well, that settles that," Laura muttered, disgusted with herself. Gullible idiot. She sat for a moment, staring numbly at the numerous scraps of notepaper she'd filled. *Put your hood up, Sean.* She snatched up the newspaper and looked at the national weather map, trying to decipher its hieroglyphics. As far as she could tell, it was raining in only two areas across the country: all across the Pacific Northwest, no surprise. Summer squalls were blowing along the Gulf states, but the woman hadn't had a southern accent.

You're pathetic, she told herself. What was she supposed to do? Cancel her flight, and sit around waiting by the phone, just in case Rachel called back? And so what if she did? Say by some miracle she *did* have Haines's son. Chances were he'd have different blood anyway. And even if it *was* the same, was she smart enough to do anything with it?

Go see Sandra, that's one thing you can do right.

She turned back to her packing, and on the silent television she saw a face that rooted her in place. It was haggard but still beautiful, and she recognized Gillian Shamas instantly. Grasping for the remote, she nearly tripped. She stabbed up the volume.

"... a former patient speaks out, next."

Gillian's face faded, and Laura had an agonizing wait through a series of ads before the story came back. A reporter's voice overlaid stock footage of hospital wards, bald patients getting IV drips.

"While many medical experts have challenged the importance of David Haines's blood and the claims of Dr. Laura Donaldson, thousands of people around the world disagree. Congressmen, and the President himself, have been inundated with letters and petitions asking for Haines's safe capture, and a promise that his blood be taken for further research ..."

With amazement, Laura watched as sacks full of letters were dumped out onto mailroom floors. There were quick soundbites from a few passionate cancer patients, and then the reporter's voice again:

"But few know Dr. Donaldson as well as Gillian Shamas, a former patient and recipient of one of her controversial treatments."

Laura felt her breath snag as Gillian's face came back on. She was seated on a sofa in what looked to be her own home, and though it was clear to Laura that she was very ill, her eyes were still bright, and she looked peaceful. Staring at her, Laura saw the real price of her own failure: a young woman whose life was certain to end within months, if not weeks. *Gillian, I'm so, so sorry.* She supposed Gillian was picked to give the piece some balance, to counter the headlong enthusiasm of all those petitioners.

Laura braced herself for the worst.

"Well, yes," Gillian told an offscreen reporter, "I think Dr. Donaldson is right to want David Haines's blood for testing. I don't see how all these other doctors can be so critical of her ideas before she's even had a chance."

Backing her up? Gillian was backing her up!

"But she didn't cure you," said the unctuously gentle voice of the reporter.

"No. But she did her best, and I'd volunteer for any other treatment she came up with. I'm still very grateful I had the chance. I just hope she gets a chance to find a new cure from this blood."

How could she say that? Laura wondered, swiping at her eyes. As far as she was concerned, nothing Gillian could have said would have been too harsh. Instead, she'd gone on national television to give Laura her blessing. She couldn't remember the last time words of encouragement had moved her so deeply.

She turned off the television.

It took her only a few moments to make her decision.

She called her travel agent and canceled her flight to Mexico.

* * *

Kevin had stopped noticing the pain in his knees, and he was scarcely conscious of the trembling through his legs: like some focal vibration that was helping keep his torso balanced and upright as he knelt on his living-room floor.

What are you up to, David? Where are you going? It's not Houston is it? But where?

Forever he'd been here, in this place, and nothing was coming. Not so much as a cosmic peep from the blackness. And now his mind was becoming polluted again, replaying little snippets from Hugh's office.

Kicked off the task force in front of Michener, gently chastised like an errant schoolchild. It was humiliating, yes, but what made him even more furious was that on day four of the manhunt, he had not a single lead. Off shift, he'd come home, unable even to sleep to escape from his hunger, from David.

So come on, I'm on my knees, I've got Scripture ricocheting round my brain so bad I can barely open my mouth without some leaking out; my stomach's eating itself, I've lost eight pounds, I've been a good boy, so tell me ...

Nothing.

He was supposed to be good at this. This was how he'd caught David the first time around. Empathy, yes, but more than that: *being* like him as much as *thinking* like him. But so far what had it given him? The knowledge, too late, that David would try to kill his own brother.

Please, give me something!

Just more blackness behind his eyes. He opened them, squinting into the light, empty-handed. Like a drunk, he lurched up, blood draining from his head so that the world went to static. Staggering a few paces on senseless feet he smashed his shins on the coffee table.

"Fuck!"

Suddenly the room contracted into a tunnel of fury. He swiped up one of the file folders on the table and hurled it across the room, unleashing a maelstrom of paper.

"*Fucking* useless!"

Then another file folder, and another. Ecstatic in his rage, he took the Bible in his hand and whipped it at the television, and with one sweep of his arm he emptied a whole shelf of his bookcase, religious texts and cult tomes spraying across the room. Wanted to rip his hair out by the roots, tear his shirt from his shoulders—and his cellular was trilling on the dining-room table.

He sagged. Barely anything in his stomach to support him: his ribcage, his shoulders, his head all weighing down on this yawning space in his belly. He walked to the phone and sat down, feeling ill.

"Kevin Sheldrake." It came out as a wheeze.

"Hi, it's Laura Donaldson. I just got a call from someone who says she's the mother of Haines's son."

His weary laugh was out before he could check himself. "Well, I'm surprised you've only had one. You'll get more of them, believe me. We've had maybe eight saying they were some kind of relative, and three saying they had a baby with him."

"Oh." She sounded deflated, and he felt sorry for her immediately.

"I know, it's disappointing. There's plenty of sad people out there, desperate for attention, and there're only so many spots on Jerry Springer and Montel and all those other idiot shows. They're nuisance calls, and they waste our time. Mostly after thirty seconds their stories start falling apart like wet cardboard. But you were right to call me," he added. He wasn't just being kind; he meant it. He was desperate enough right now to entertain any possible lead, no matter how dubious. "So what was her story?"

In her father's apartment, Laura looked down at the single sheet onto which she'd neatly transcribed her scribbled notes. But now she felt embarrassed, as if she were just wasting his time. She looked out the window at the hazy sky above the lake. When she'd dialed his number, her heart had been racing with anticipation, thinking she might actually have an important lead to pass on.

"Look, I'm sorry, it's just that it sounded, *she* sounded pretty believable and ... " After what happened to Rick Haines, there was no way she was going to withhold information from Kevin Sheldrake. And if there was even a fraction of a chance it was real, she wanted to know. Anyway, she knew she'd need Sheldrake's help if she was going to run paternity tests—if it ever came to that. She tried to guess at Kevin's mood: he sounded more tired than testy, his voice interestingly hoarse.

"Go ahead," Kevin said gently. Stooping, he snatched up a ball-point and a few sheets of paper and flipped them over to their blank sides. But after only a minute he wasn't writing anymore, just listening intently, sweat starting to prickle beneath his arms.

At first he'd been prepared for nothing more than the usual melange of commonplace and lunatic assertions he got from callers: *I saw David*

Haines buying a coffee at Starbucks on Navy Pier; or, alternatively, *Satan popped by for a visit last night and told me that David was an Angel of Mercy placed here to test Mankind.* But right away it struck him that this Rachel was in a different category, and the more he heard, the more he felt his unease swell inside him.

She had her dates right; then again, anyone who'd read up on Haines could have successfully approximated them. But the name Rachel meshed with the cult's predilection for Old Testament monikers. More than likely, it *was* a girl who'd brought Haines in. Kevin knew, firsthand, about the practice of "flirty fishing," the hook used by many cults to bring in fresh blood. Still, what were the chances a well-indoctrinated devotee would go so far as to sleep with one of her charges? The Apostles, he knew, insisted on celibacy. Then again, he suspected that an exception was doubtless made by its leader, Father Abraham.

A kid? Was it possible?

Bottom line, he knew damn little about Haines's time in the New Apostles. Four years ago, he'd gone there on a hunch, seeing in their distaste for medical interventions a possible link to the as-yet-anonymous doctor-killer. He'd been greeted with intense suspicion. Hey, he was just another suit from a Satanic government agency, intent on stripping them of their religious freedoms and their firearms, leaving them defenseless when Beelzebub's marauding armies came knocking at the end time. Luckily, Father Abe was smart enough to sniff out a good public relations hit, and he'd quickly admitted that one of his flock, a Brother Ishmael, had been expelled because of his violent views.

Ishmael's real name: David Haines.

Abe had been eager to distance the Apostles from the actions of any doctor-killer. David's name, and a slice of his personal history, had been enough to lead Kevin to his brother, Rick, and start breaking the case wide open. Even so, Abe had taken some pains to tell him as little as possible about Haines's time with them, and he'd mentioned no one else by name. Certainly he hadn't mentioned a disciple called Sister Rachel.

When Laura finished, he scarcely knew what to think. He looked around the room at the mess he'd made. Quite a temper tantrum. He was losing it, getting desperate. He shut his eyes, rubbed his jackhammering temples. He needed a lead, but rationally he knew this probably wasn't it.

"You'll probably never hear from her again," he told her, forcing out the words. "You're right, it's a good story, but she's probably just after your twenty-five grand."

"Well, I thought maybe that's all it was," he heard Laura say with a sigh, "the way she backed off when I asked for hair samples. So there was never any Rachel at the cult? I guess you would've heard about her."

"Your caller isn't behaving right. If she really had Haines's son, she'd be terrified. She'd be running to the police, wanting protection, I don't care where she is, up in the mountains of Alaska, wherever."

"But she said Haines didn't even know about the baby, so why would she be scared? He doesn't know her real name, doesn't know where she lives. She's had no communication with him since leaving. Anyway, I got the feeling she didn't like the FBI much."

He gave a sharp laugh. "She doesn't like the FBI because she knows she's guilty of telephone fraud, and that's a federal offense and we'd nail her. Explains why she's not giving out her name and phone number."

There was a brief silence, but Kevin didn't expect her to give in yet, and he wasn't sure he wanted her too. He felt the need to ride through this line of questioning with her, test it. She was as stubborn as him.

"Even if he did have a son," she said, "you wouldn't tell me, would you."

It was not a question, and he could feel her need transmitted through the telephone line. He sighed. "You're right, I wouldn't volunteer that information because it wouldn't help the case. It might very well do the opposite."

"I called you because I want to make sure what happened to Rick doesn't happen again."

"I appreciate that. But be honest, Dr. Donaldson, you also called because you're after the blood, and that's nothing to do with this case."

"It is if it gives you a lead."

Kevin actually smiled. "We don't know of Haines having a child, all right? And I really doubt this woman's telling the truth. She's either a creative crackpot, or a scam artist ..."

Or ...

He was disgusted it hadn't come to him sooner.

I would've done it myself if I were David ...

He dragged a hand across his damp forehead. "Dr. Donaldson,

listen to me. There's another reason this woman might've called you."

"What?"

"Maybe she's one of Haines's acolytes, and this is a setup. You agree to meet her, she's waiting for you with a gun."

"Oh my God," Laura murmured, her breath stolen from her. It was as if the speed she'd taken this morning had suddenly been sucked from her bloodstream with the speed of a syringe's plunger. She sat down in an armchair and tucked her icy feet under her. She hadn't even thought of it. To her there had been only two options: Rachel was a fake, or she was the real thing. She wished she had a glass of water, her mouth felt stale from talking so much on the phone. It was almost impossible for her to superimpose a murderous intent on Rachel's voice—she was a scam artist, maybe, but not a killer. Women didn't do things like that, did they? Plot and kill in cold blood?

"You okay?" she heard Sheldrake ask.

Somehow, she wasn't ready to give up yet. "If it's someone who really wants to kill me, why risk scaring me off asking for money? Doesn't make sense. They'd just want to bring me in, no fuss."

"Wanting the money makes it seem more credible," said Kevin. "You were willing to pay it, weren't you?"

"Only if her hair samples were positive."

"How did she know your father's number?"

"She didn't. She called the lab, and it forwards my phone calls automatically."

"Good," he said, "that's good. Now listen, I'm not saying this woman's an acolyte, I don't know. But I'd like your permission to put a trap-and-trace on your line, in case she calls again."

"What if I say no?" she asked, surprised at herself.

"Why would you do that?" He sounded incredulous.

"You find out who she is, you're going to check her out, right?"

"We'd question her, yes. This might be someone who wants to kill you!"

"But she might also be the mother of Haines's kid. Maybe it's not likely, but there's a chance."

"All right. In that case, we'd make sure she's in a safe location."

Safe from me, Laura thought. "You'd put her up in a hotel, you mean, like you did for me."

"Possibly."

"And you wouldn't tell me where she was, would you?"

"Dr. Donaldson, if this woman's intent on selling you her son's blood, she knows how to contact you."

"That means no?" Even if Rachel could get a hold of her, maybe she'd be too angry at Laura for telling the FBI to grant her the blood. She remembered the vehemence in her voice when she'd said she didn't want her son to know who his father was. Maybe Rachel would decide to sell the blood to someone else, or maybe not at all.

"I'm not sure I want to give permission." Laura knew she sounded unreasonable but she wasn't willing to risk losing Rachel. "I'm sorry, but I get the feeling you really don't want me to get this blood."

Infuriatingly he said, "As a special agent I have no professional opinion on the matter. The Bureau has no interest in whether you get the blood or not."

"Personally, then," she insisted.

Pacing his living room, Kevin sighed, tired of his own evasions. "Dr. Donaldson, if this woman really is the mother of Haines's son, and she wants to sell you some of her son's blood, then I have no problem with that. I sincerely doubt she's telling the truth, though."

"Let me prove it for you, one way or another," came her reply. "If she sends the hair samples I asked for, let me run paternity tests."

"How? You don't have any blood from Haines."

"Blood's the best way to rule paternity *out*. But DNA's the only way to rule it *in*. I don't have blood, but if we can get some skin or hair from his prison clothes, I can do an RFLP, a Restriction Fragment Length Polymorphism."

"A DNA fingerprint."

"Right."

"And that proves paternity, beyond reasonable doubt?"

"Absolutely. Even works on dead people, like President Jefferson. They tested his paternity of black slaves, remember? All I need is hair from all three people: Haines, Rachel, and her son."

He wanted the trap-and-trace; she wanted Haines's clothing. Fair enough.

"All right, listen. I can get you Haines's clothing. But I need your permission for a trap-and-trace." He could apply for a court order, but it would take too long, and he doubted he could request one on an emergency basis—there simply wasn't enough evidence yet, and he doubted Hugh would be in any mood to back him on this. "Is it a deal?" he asked.

"And if Rachel calls to say she's sending the samples, will you let me run the tests before you go out and investigate her?"

Unbelievable, she was still bargaining with him!

"How long would the tests take?" he asked.

"A day, tops."

"Fine. Do we have a deal?"

"We have a deal."

"I'm calling Ameritech now and arranging the tap. If Rachel calls, talk to her, and write down the exact time the call starts and ends, and then phone me right away. All right?"

"All right," he heard her say. "Thank you."

A thank-you. Somehow he hadn't expected that.

He hoped he was doing the right thing.

*   *   *

The turn of the millennium had gone badly for the New Apostles.

As Kevin pulled up in front of the Old Town mansion that housed their city mission, he thought it looked a little more dilapidated than he recalled: with a faint, inexplicable disappointment, he noted the paint peeling, a busted eavestrough, the front lawn in need of mowing, and the garden plots untended. It was a bad sign, since this was, after all, the Apostles' Chicago flagship, the place they brought their prospective converts, for concerts and barbecues in the capacious back gardens, for Bible study and inspirational orations in the airy wood-paneled rooms.

The iron gate was open, and Kevin walked through towards the front door. Despite humanity's best efforts, the end of the millennium had come and gone without cataclysm—just some minor Y2K computer glitches, a few power outages and drunken scuffles—and it looked as though everything was going to grind on pretty much as normal. As he lifted the heavy knocker, he wondered if the Apostles had lost some of their faithful, bitterly disappointed that they were still alive and still compelled to listen to Father Abe's increasingly strained rantings about the end time. He actually doubted it. People needed to believe things, and sacred teachings and texts were eternally malleable. Though the world wasn't consumed on December 31, 1999, they could still look forward to a fiery ascendence to Heaven within the next decade or so.

Still, his cynicism in no way quenched the powerful pang of familiarity he felt as the door was opened to him and he was welcomed into the front hall. The age of the home and its fixtures lent an air of respectability to the cult, which many, he knew, lacked. The high ceiling, the chandelier, the sweep of the central staircase. Doubtless the mansion had been a bequest from a rich convert who'd giddily sold everything for God, or at least for Father Abe. Kevin knew little about him, but he did know that he'd been a real estate developer before finding God; obviously his talent for promotion and fundraising had not been dulled by his conversion.

"How can we help you?" the young man asked. He looked reasonably well fed, and Kevin assumed he'd already served his time on the cult's communal farm up north, and was now on city duty, recruiting and fundraising on the streets and university campuses.

He'd done it himself, under the thirty-watt sky of a long Seattle winter, selling flowers, pamphlets, and prayer books, promising people the money was helping send needy kids to summer camps, or whatever seemed to work best. He'd got through the long days by singing hymns internally and *thank you Jesus, praise you Jesus* and never straying far from his partner in case Satan came tempting. Twice he'd been beaten up at night, but it had only made him more convinced of the righteousness of his cause. If the world hates you, you must be on the right track.

"I'd like to speak to Father Abraham." He knew his real name but thought it best not to antagonize anyone just yet.

"Father Abraham is at prayer."

"I can wait. Tell him it's Kevin Sheldrake. We've talked before."

"Would you like a meal?"

Kevin almost smiled, wondering if he really looked so hungry—or maybe it was just his crumpled Sears suit.

"Thank you, no," he said, and almost added, "I'm fasting." He could smell, from the back kitchen, something good, and his stomach gave a muted spasm, like some small starved animal with only a little life left in it. If the Apostles were anything like God's Children, the food here would be better than what was served at their farm. Rice and potatoes and very occasionally chicken would be the staples up there. The Old Town mansion was the face the cult presented to the world at large: unobtrusive, inoffensive, wholesome. The fire would be downplayed here. This was the place where the indoctrination would begin, where the brothers and sisters would make their first incursions with the unconverted, not pushing too hard, just offering companion-ship and the teachings of Scripture.

All Kevin wanted right now was to find out if Sister Rachel was real. And if she was, whether it was even possible she had slept with David, and carried his child.

He stepped slowly around the hallway, looking at the two display racks of hand-stapled pamphlets. It was easier now to see the signs of decrepitude about the house. The furniture and carpets were showing their age. Still, the overall effect was pleasing. The mansion didn't have central air-conditioning, but it was cool enough with the windows open, and he liked the quiet mustiness of the place. He doubted Abe would keep him waiting too long.

A dozen young men and women came down the hallway from the back of the mansion, from lunch he guessed, talking and laughing excitedly. A woman in a colorful tube-top smiled at him, and he felt an uncomfortable jolt of arousal.

"Has someone taken care of you?" she asked.

"Yes."

"We're talking about the Scriptures. First Samuel. Would you like to join us? "

Yes, he said to himself with a hunger that should have been reserved for food. *Yes*. He could see the pages opening before his mind's eye and before he knew it, he was quoting aloud.

"'The word of the Lord was rare in those days; visions were not widespread.' First Samuel, 3:1."

His voice startled him—had he really said that? Now that he was fasting, things had a habit of slipping out—memories, thoughts into words; passages from the Bible would suddenly materialize in his head with the surreal clarity of a desert mirage.

The girl was smiling and nodding. "Very good. And so," she said, "how blessed was Samuel when the Lord called upon him. 'And Samuel said, Speak for your servant is listening.'"

First Samuel 3:10, Kevin thought. Samuel had it easy, or maybe he just needed a good dose of antipsychotics. But this time he said nothing.

"We can all be Samuel here," the girl told him. "Join us."

Kevin smiled and shook his head, and he watched the girl and the others withdraw, with a sensation of something stretching and ripping inside him. In the large front room to the right, they sat down in a close circle and began their discussion. The girl was leading, smiling, eyes wide open, frequently reaching out to touch someone's arm, everyone held within her tight gravitational pull. It all seemed so pleasant, these young earnest kids, bent to each other's voices. He remembered it all.

He remembered the circle he'd sometimes sat in with seven or eight others, both hands closed around the electrical cord, the insulation sliced away so everyone's fingers were on bare wire. Then Elder James would plug it into the socket and they would ride out the 120-volt spirit of the Lord. One by one Elder James would tell someone to let go, and the others would have to bear the added load. Kevin was good at it; he'd made it down to just three people, holding the wire, singing aloud, transported by God's energy. Once they'd had to pull the cord on him: he wouldn't let go, hadn't wanted to be without that divine spark coursing through him.

Kevin turned and the young man who'd opened the door was suddenly at his side like an apparition, like an angel before Abraham in the heat of the desert. *Be careful*, Kevin told himself, feeling himself start to slip.

"Would you like to come up now?" the young man asked.

One flight of stairs and he was out of breath, heart purring. He paused on the landing, touching the cool banister for support. He heard music coming from somewhere, something sweet and ethereal, and for a moment wondered if he were hallucinating. He was led down a hallway with threadbare carpets towards an open door. Inside was a bright, simply furnished room, and Father Abe walking towards him with a smile.

At first glance, everything about Abe seemed thoroughly suburban. He was dressed in new blue jeans and a short-sleeved plaid shirt. His hairline was high, and he had a visible bald spot atop his square, powerful skull. Kevin guessed he must be pushing into his fifties now. All the energy was in his eyes, amazingly kind eyes that held your gaze in such a way that you didn't feel the need to look away; the same gaze a child can fix on you, pure, nonjudgmental, and you sense the best is invited of you, and assumed.

"Kevin, it's a pleasure to see you again. Please. Have a seat. Can I offer you anything to eat or drink?" His manner was informal, almost intimate, but Kevin knew Abe's feelings towards him must be far from agreeable. *What must you think of me, Abe? Still a veritable Saul of Tarsus, a demolition man among poor, struggling Christians?* Before Haines, he'd shut down half a dozen cults, nailing them on charges of kidnapping, cross-border money-laundering, sexual misdemeanors, stockpiling of automatic weapons. But part of him wanted Abe to know that his persecuting zeal had become dulled in the past couple of years. *With those eyes of yours, can you see into me like that, Abe?*

Too late he realized that Abe had seated himself directly in front of a bright window, and now Kevin had to squint as he looked at him. Stupid to let that happen—an elementary interview technique, and he'd fucked it up.

"Thank you for seeing me," he said.

"I take it," said Abe, "that the suited gentlemen we've seen skulking around our properties here and in the country are your doing?"

Kevin was well aware that Michener had posted street agents to keep an eye on the city mission, as well as their farm up north, just in case David Haines was seeking refuge at either location. Kevin was certain he wouldn't: David's antipathy towards the New Apostles had been abundantly clear in the letters he'd written to Rick after he'd left. And he would have known the role Abe played in exposing him.

"It's a precaution only," Kevin said diplomatically, "as much for your own safety as anything."

"They've been harassing my congregation, questioning them as they come and go. At the farm they're making people nervous. One might conclude that we should prepare ourselves for a siege."

His choice of words was no doubt a veiled threat, meant to conjure up the carnage of Waco, Texas, and other fatal confrontations between the government and cults.

Kevin smiled amiably and shook his head. "We're just trying to catch David Haines."

"I find the suspicion we're harboring him repugnant."

He was doing a damn good job projecting moral outrage, Kevin gave him full points on that one. His voice was smooth and authoritative—a man used to speaking without doubt or fear—and Kevin had to brace himself against the inevitable response of the supplicant.

"Between you and me," Kevin told him, hoping to put him at ease, "I'm not leading this task force. If I were, you wouldn't have agents bothering you. But I can get them to lay off." It wouldn't be hard to follow through on that; now that the task force had moved south, it had already happened.

Haloed in the light from the window, Abe looked at him, unblinking, and Kevin forced himself to hold his gaze. "I appreciated your help four years ago, and I was hoping you might lend us a hand again."

"I can't imagine having any information that would be of use to you, Kevin."

You know what I want, Kevin thought.

"Those who left the Apostles," he began, "around the same time as David, or later, people who knew him, who might've been sympathetic to him."

"Well, you asked me the same thing when we last spoke. David Haines had no close companions. His mind was distorted. Others sensed that; they stayed away. When he left, he took no one from us. You discovered as much when you caught him. He acted alone. He had no circle of sympathizers here. My only regret was that I didn't see sooner that he came to God out of hate."

It was smart of Abe to claim to be appalled by Haines when really, Kevin suspected, he probably had more than a little sympathy for his actions. Haines had probably been expelled less for his views than for the force of his own personality, a fervor that Abe might have feared would dwarf his own.

"Still, any names would be helpful."

"Kevin, even if I could remember, I'm not at liberty to disclose the names of my members, past or present, to you. That's private information, you know that."

"I know, and I'm asking you as a favor. The Bureau would appreciate it. You were so cooperative before."

"That was different. David Haines was engaged in heinous crimes. You seem to be suggesting that other members of my church might have been in collusion with him, which, as I've said before, I find very distasteful, Kevin."

Fuck off with the "Kevin." He knew the constant use of his Christian name was supposed to evoke intimacy, but it only jarred him now. He decided to try another direction.

"I never asked how David came to you."

Abe's head tilted slightly, as if he were trying to remember. "I believe he attended some of our Bible study sessions here and became interested."

Who hooked him? he almost asked, but caught himself in time. "Who introduced him?"

"That I can't recall."

"Who was she?" he asked pleasantly. He thought of the attractive young woman downstairs. *Follow me and I shall make you fishers of men.* He knew how the recruiters worked. They were your escorts, you became attached to them, even in a quasi-romantic way, and they didn't discourage that exactly. They were so attentive, so generous, so fascinated by you, you, you, it was like being shot up with Demerol. Then you met other people, you were surrounded by friends, and your recruiter gradually drew away, ready to devote herself to someone new. Kevin himself had been mildly heartbroken when he'd discovered his recruiter wasn't in love with him. But by then, he was part of it, this big thriving thing, and it didn't matter very much, not at first anyway.

"Kevin," Abe was saying patiently, "we don't keep track of such things. Every one who comes here is a blessing to us, but we don't keep accounts. There is no tally sheet."

Bullshit. The light around Abe's head was starting to give him a headache, and he had to look away more often than he liked.

"Maybe a Sister Rachel?"

He watched Abe's face carefully, waiting for a flicker of recognition or discomfort, but none came. Abe shook his head.

He'd come expecting to be stonewalled but hoping for better. He had one last tool at his disposal.

"Well, I appreciate your time," he told Abe. "As I said, I'll do my best to get our people out of your hair. There might be a problem, though."

Abe looked at him, waiting.

"Some of your neighbors up north have been telling our agents they've heard a lot of gunfire coming from your place."

"We have an outdoor rifle range, yes."

"Well, they said it sounded more like automatics."

"They're mistaken, then. We only have legally owned firearms. With permits."

"I'm sure. But we both know there are ways around that." With the help of a totally illegal little clip called a "hellfire," which fastened around the trigger, you could turn a semi into a fully automatic weapon.

"I don't know what you mean," said Abe.

"I'm glad," said Kevin, "because I don't think anyone really wants to bother you folks with search warrants. But we certainly don't want you starting a little Armageddon stockpile out there."

Abe's reciprocal smile stretched his mouth, but no other part of his face. This was the best Kevin could do, threaten. You couldn't force someone to talk; you couldn't charge him with obstruction of justice. All you could do was squeeze him, and right now, Kevin didn't have much to squeeze with.

Talk, he urged Abe with his eyes.

"You're welcome to come and view our permits and our farm any time, Kevin," said Abe. "Any time."

CHAPTER SEVENTEEN

The strip plazas were a gaudy smear in his peripheral vision. *How ugly we've made things*, he thought. Mile after mile of asphalt and power pylons, gas stations and car lots, Speedy Mufflers and Mr Lubes and Donut Times and Taco Bells and shopping malls and all the rest of humanity's excrescences, glittering in the dark. He tried not to look. He wished it could all be wiped away, torched from the earth.

He guessed he was about half an hour away from the rendezvous. He lifted a hand from the steering wheel and scratched at the bristles of his beard, still unused to its feel. He was glad it was coming in full and thick; it changed the look of him altogether. So too had the fasting, costing him some fifteen pounds now, sharpening his nose and cheeks. But he could not change what was inside him.

He'd looked.

Before he'd left, he'd asked Gail to buy a microscope kit at a toy store. He'd lanced his finger, made a smear, peered through the lens. The manual white count was indeed freakishly high. Within the quivering membranes of his T-cells was what the doctor, and the world, wanted. He'd been praying fervently for his condition to be taken from him, sometimes with a feeling approaching panic. If they caught him, they would leech it from him, and he didn't know how long he could go without being caught. *Long enough for you to finish your work*, he admonished himself.

In his most anxious moments, he'd even thought of purging himself. A seven-day protocol of oral Busulfan and Cyclophosphamide and he could effectively wipe out his immune system, all the way down to the stem cells that were producing his deviant T-cells. All he had to do was break into a hospital pharmacy somewhere, steal the drugs, and begin the treatment, with the help of some anti-nausea meds and antibiotics to ward off infection. It was the same process used to prepare a leukemia patient prior to bone marrow transplants. Of course, they would have perfectly matching donors waiting for them with new marrow, ready to repopulate their immune systems with normal cells. He had no donor, and without one, he would become a walking dead man, struck down by even the mildest of infections, or he'd bleed to death because he had no platelets and was unable to clot or make new blood. It was nothing more than a form of self-murder, a kind of despair. To even consider such a thing was sinful, he knew that. To use the doctors' blasphemous techniques even to eradicate their blasphemous cure was wrong, and he did not believe for a second it was what God expected of him. If God wanted to purge him, he would purge him. But his path was to be different, and all he could do was try his best to submit to it.

He hurtled through the night, navigating the swirling choreography of headlights and taillights and highway lamps, and then, mesmerized, he caught himself beginning to drift. He'd been driving for eight hours solid now. He sat up straighter, turned up the air-conditioning, hoping the chill would keep him awake at the wheel. He clicked on the radio and suddenly a song from his college days flooded the hatchback's interior.

Just for a moment, the heady, driving rhythm snaked its way into his head, carrying with it all the greedy, lustful vanities and appetites he'd renounced. The music gleefully tore at the careful order of his mind and faith, erasing and superimposing and blurring until nothing mattered except the pulse of the music, and he felt as if his very chest would rip apart and release some kind of dark, ecstatic bellow.

He was sweating, his fingers tight around the wheel. He unlocked one hand and quickly fumbled with the radio, turning it off. He'd forgotten how potent a siren call the music was. His breathing calmed, but it was as if a portal had been opened to his past, and he couldn't resist peeking back, as he sometimes did from the safe vantage point of his salvation. It was not self-congratulatory—look how far I've come, look at the lofty height I've achieved—it was amazement at what he'd once been. Always, he found it profoundly humbling.

What he once was was a hive of sin. He'd believed in nothing but his own intellect and satisfying his own hollow, lustful appetites. He'd believed in nothing, and he *was* nothing.

They'd laughed at him when he'd first talked to her.

She'd stopped him on his way back from the med-sci building, saying she was with some kind of campus Bible study group, and would he be interested in coming to one of their meetings? It was a crystalline autumn day, he'd just finished his last lab of the week, and the girl, he realized, was good-looking. He wouldn't even have hesitated otherwise, just shaken his head and walked on with Steven and Karl. But he'd never had a girl approach him like this, with such a wide-open smile; she was pale but with a nice lipsticked mouth and big dark eyes, and an enticing swell of breasts beneath her cable-knit sweater. He caught a trace of her perfume, and felt his cock harden.

Lust, always lust, gnawing away at you like an ulcerous stomach.

It was a game, of course, a malevolent game, and it amused him and his friends—they'd put money on it, Steve and Karl betting he wouldn't be able to screw her by the end of October: these born-again Christians could be tough. David took the bet. He was surprised at how easy it was to pretend he was interested in these little biweekly meetings, filled with earnest, outgoing young men and women. Within a week she had invited him to a barbecue at a mansion in Old Town, and then, a few days later, to a weekend retreat up in Dalton County. A retreat, like camp! He imagined cabins, paddling canoes, forest hikes, plenty of opportunities to get in her pants. So far the most he'd managed was some heavy petting in his residence room—he'd lured her back after one of the Bible meetings—which had seemed to both sadden and arouse her. It wouldn't be hard to take her the rest of the way.

He was keeping her separate from his real life at Northwestern, his weekly studies framed by pub crawls and floor parties, which he hurtled through, dancing and drinking and crowing as if he could never get enough, and in the early hours of morning, more often than not, pairing off with someone he'd met, just for that night.

Fill me up, his soul had screamed, but he hadn't been listening, hadn't heard it above the blare of his sinner's heart. *Fill me up, fill me up*. But he was never full.

He regretted his decision to come to the retreat as soon as he arrived. It wasn't even a proper camp, just a shitty old farm with a big house and remodeled barn and a bunch of ugly, drafty outbuildings lined with bunks. They spent the first day in the barn, and it was like one marathon Bible session, and people were singing and there were lectures and people giving testimonials. She sat beside him the whole time. Her hand would squeeze his reassuringly, and sometimes she'd let it slide down along his upper thigh, not too close, but close enough to set his mind wandering, and she'd beam that smile on him.

It wasn't until late afternoon that they got to leave the barn and have free time before dinner. It was late October, and it was already starting to get dark when he convinced her to walk with him down behind the outbuildings where tall grass grew alongside the fields. His head felt strange, fuzzy, with all the Bible stuff echoing. Over the past couple of weeks it had been resurfacing in his brain, like subliminal advertising, in the middle of a meal, or during an epidemiology lecture; it was like some computer virus that had been fused into his brain. He looked back towards the outbuildings to make sure no one was watching. He hadn't forgotten the reason he came to this dump.

She didn't want to at first. He'd anticipated some resistance, but he thought she'd come around, the way they mostly did. Over the past couple of weeks he'd started to doubt she was even a virgin at all, the way she kissed, her coy little tongue just grazing his with the tip, as if it were all an accident; the way she shifted into just the right place whenever he pushed his hips up against her. They were down on his jacket in the grass and she kept saying, "We shouldn't." She kept saying, "We should stop, it's not pure, it's not right," and he just wanted to fuck all that holiness out of her. Who did she think she was, talking like that, Mother Teresa? All this crap about holiness and purity, and he wanted to get laid, and win his bet, and get out of this shithole camp.

"If it's what you need," she finally said, "if it's really what you want," and he said yes, and she let him come into her, her skirt hiked up over her thighs, and he knew she enjoyed it as much as he did. But afterwards, when he pulled out, she was crying, really weeping without making much noise, and her face looked all caved in. He'd never seen anything like it. He wanted to get angry, but he couldn't for some reason. He felt sick. He peeled off his condom, his fingers unpleasantly sticky. He retrieved her underwear from the grass and laid it beside her. He'd never seen such grief in a face, and almost for the first time it struck him that she really believed all this Bible stuff. That she'd been impure, that she'd sinned. Look at her, heartbroken.

And what's ever meant anything to you? What have you ever believed in?

What do you love? he'd wondered. His own pleasures: money, status, always sex, a twenty-four-hour-a-day marathon of covetousness. *And*

224

does it make you happy? And suddenly he saw the tyranny of it, always wanting it, always lusting for it, seeing this parade of flesh all around him and wanting more than it could ever give him, even if he could couple with it temporarily. It was like being shackled day in day out, and he wanted to be free of it.

"You see, don't you," she said. "Anything my body can give you is just enough to remind you of something else. The ecstasy you can never have on this earth."

By screwing her he'd wanted to extinguish her, but all he felt was a suffocating mass inside himself. He hadn't even touched her. Look, whatever it was inside her, it hadn't left her, it was still there, aflame— it was he who had been extinguished, and always had been, stone cold.

He'd won his bet, and he felt nauseated with regret. He'd won, and he felt utterly diminished; he had nothing. She dressed. He told her he wanted to go. She nodded and found a ride for him, someone going back to the city that night. The rest of the weekend he tried to study. He lied and told Steven and Karl he'd lost the bet, and paid up. His thoughts echoed like the words of God spoken in that big barn.

When she called two days later, he'd never felt so happy.

She was just the beacon, she was unimportant, except that she showed you the way.

As Christmas break neared, he spent more and more time with her; he grudgingly agreed to read the Bible with her; he went to more meetings. It was happening. His med school friends seemed so loud and braying; his textbooks seemed alien. What did it matter, this minutia, these chemicals and molecules and equations? What did it have to do with the spirit?

Everything that had gone before now started to show itself for what it was—like a photograph developing slowly and sharply in the chemical bath until it was painfully clear. How he'd led his life, his studies; the thought of all the women he'd slept with, all the scientific knowledge he gloatingly hoarded in his head, a rat's rotting detritus, it sickened him and he wanted to flee from it. The easy comfort of his upbringing, divorced from any kind of spirituality. Not so much as a Gideon Bible in their house. His parents disgusted him, as did his brother, a little money-grubbing weevil. The complacency of it all, the frightening complacency. It was this, of all things, he started to find most chilling. How could you never even *think* about God, yet all around him were people who trafficked in nothing but the world.

She showed him how profoundly unhappy he'd been, only he hadn't known it. Then the other elders and Father Abe helped him. They brought everything into focus for him. Five days before Christmas he quit med school and moved onto the farm ...

His headlights plowed away the darkness before him. He was on the outskirts of the city's sprawl now, and mercifully the shopping centers were starting to give way to fields. He passed under a railway bridge and, half a mile on, pulled off onto a side road and into a lumber yard's empty lot.

Empty, except for a pickup. David killed the headlights. He didn't have to wait long. The door of the truck opened and a man stepped down and walked towards him. In the wash of the distant highway lamps, David was pleased with what he saw: a big man, the same kind of build as him; and even though he must have been nervous, his gait was confident and unhurried.

David opened his door and stepped out to greet him.

"Thank you, Henry." His handshake was firm.

"It's an honor. I'm honored you called on me."

"A lesser man wouldn't have come."

They spoke for only ten minutes, but for David it was enough. After his long correspondence with Henry, he'd needed to meet him face to face, to test for any faultlines in his character and resolve. He was not disappointed, though he knew it was necessary to give Henry extra support for what he was about to undertake.

"God bless you, Henry. We'll speak again."

Henry handed him the keys to his truck; in return, David offered him Gail's.

His trust of Gail, during his stay, had deteriorated rapidly. It was so obvious she'd allowed herself to think she was in love with him, and this false love had clouded what should have been her real fervor. He'd left as soon as he could. Out of sloppiness, or even out of malice, she was capable of making a serious misstep, and he didn't want to be linked to her by her car. When they found it, if they did, he would be far away.

He started walking to Henry's truck.

"David?"

He turned, wondering if there was uncertainty in the man's voice.

"Yes, Henry?"

"I never had any doubts, you know. Not even when you asked me to kill. I just wanted you to know that."

"It's not the doubts that are wrong," he said gently. "The world fills our heads with doubts, like smog. The only sin is letting them paralyze you, stop you from doing what's right. But I can see your resolve, Henry."

He lifted his hand in farewell and got into the truck. At the highway junction, he turned back north, the way he had come. The road stretched ahead of him in an arrowhead of light, leading him to his purpose.

* * *

Kevin had the phone in his hand before he was even fully awake, croaking his hello through a throat hoarse with exhaustion and hunger.

"Brother Jonah?"

The last wisps of sleep evaporated from his mind. He glanced at the fluorescent hands of his alarm clock: four-sixteen. Elbowing himself into sitting, his pulse picked up speed.

"How'd you get my number, David?"

He wasn't particularly interested. He knew such things were cheap these days, any info-thief could spit out an unlisted number for a hundred bucks. Still, it was the first question that came to him, and he didn't want to appear flustered. Goddamnit, he had David Haines on the line, and no proper way of tracing him.

"You never answered my letter," David chided him.

Reflexively, Kevin's eyes rose to the bookshelf beside his bed. Even in the darkness, he knew the exact spot, top shelf, behind his George Eliot novels. From whom was he hiding it? Two sheets of onionskin paper, both sides covered, still folded within the envelope. He had only to blink to see the shape of the words filling the page, knew every one by memory. Their little secret.

"You really expected a reply?" he said.

David's letter had come shortly after his incarceration, when Kevin had still been with Diane and Becky, fighting through a depression so paralyzing he'd been unable most days to even get out of bed. He'd kept the letter, hadn't ripped it up, hadn't told anyone at the Bureau, and especially not Diane.

Dear Brother Jonah, it began, its tone so familiar it implied a relation-ship, a shared world-view which, though imagined, nonetheless made him feel uncomfortable and guiltily secretive. David had read up on him after his arrest, that was obvious: he knew about Kevin's long-ago involvement in God's Children.

I forgive you, but you *must ask forgiveness for what you have done. I pray for you every day, that you will find your way out of the whale's belly, just as Jonah did, that you will stop denying God and have the courage to once again take up the glorious yoke of the convictions you held before.*

He'd never written back, though God knows he'd caught himself on and off over the years forming replies in his head. At the height of his depression, before the tricyclics began to pull him back, he'd even considered visiting David at Illinois Correctional.

"I won't say I was surprised you never wrote back," David said. "But I know you miss it."

"Miss what?" Kevin lied.

"I'd expected more honesty from you."

Kevin detected a note of rising anger in David's voice, and was worried he might hang up. More placatingly, he said: "Well, I couldn't keep the faith, David, but neither could you. You parted company with the Apostles."

"Only because they were cowards who wouldn't act on their convictions."

"Killing doctors?

"I agree, what I do is in itself abhorrent, but it was always a prophet's way to say the unspeakable, demand the unthinkable, and act on both."

Many false prophets will arise and lead many, Kevin thought, but instead he said, "You've made your point, don't you think? And no one's listening."

He was aware of his face burning. He hadn't felt so utterly engaged in anything for a long time. He didn't want it to stop.

"Our tendency has always been to race after what nourishes us least," David said. "Things, bodies, status. This obsession with our earthly life, keeping it at all costs. Our bodies are false idols. This is *nothing*, the here and now. What do you have here, Brother Jonah? Nothing."

Involuntarily, Kevin looked around his room, how little there was in it. Like a prison cell. He felt that freefall temptation to plunge back into the past, the enticing certainties of God's Children. So simple. Who could deny the world was a wicked place; he only had to look at the files stacked on his desk. The evil of this empty world. The good of God and his paradise.

"Is this why you called, David, to preach to me? Save it for your faithful. I've been in the belly of the whale a bit too long. By the way, I hope you've made some nice arrangements for Bob Jarvis in heaven. Maybe a private room with en suite plumbing."

He was surprised at the venom that had seeped into him; he wanted to insult David now; he wanted to blaspheme.

"You see, there is still feeling there," he heard David say over the pounding in his ears. "You can't pretend to hide it. If you truly didn't believe, why would you get so angry about it?"

"We know about the others, too, David."

"If you did, you wouldn't be telling me."

"We got the post office box from Andrews. He kept all your letters under his toilet, actually. Nice and neat in a Ziploc bag, with his gun."

"It doesn't matter. We're as many as the grains of sand in the desert," said David, and Kevin felt the hairs on his forearms lift.

"That's a lot of mouths to feed, David."

"And you're one of the hungry."

Kevin forced a chuckle. "Not just to preach to me, but *convert* me over the phone!"

"You could come with me, with us."

"Come where? Where're we going, David?" He tried to sound jocular, but he was listening very carefully.

"Paradise."

"Mexico? Maybe a little island somewhere in the Gulf? Start your own church?"

"It's your decision, Brother Jonah."

In his darkened room he forced open his eyes in self-defense, locked onto the bookcase, the clock, the chest of drawers, anchors to reality. *Weaker than I thought.*

He said quickly, "Why are you really calling?"

He heard David sigh. "You know I was willing to die before they tried to take my blood."

"Yes."

"I might surrender if I was sure they'd never get it."

The statement shimmered in his mind, suspended between truth and mirage. He knew this was probably bullshit, but he played along. "That's what your lawyer's fighting for right now, David. Greene's got the ACLU on your side, he's filed a motion to counteract any further court orders to take your blood. MetaSYS just filed a press release saying they're not contesting."

"There'll be others. They'll try to find some way."

He thought of Laura, her passionate intensity, and then said something that surprised him. "You turn yourself in to me, and I'll do my best to make sure they never get your blood. But there's a lot of anger out there, David, after the two guards, after Rick."

"You understand why I had to do it."

Within the logic of Haines's custom-built faith, he understood. What he said was, "I can respect your beliefs, David, but never how you enacted them. We'll catch you, and you'll still face execution. But I can try to help make sure no one gets your blood. If you turn yourself in."

He knew they were probably only engaging in an elaborate masquerade.

"I don't fear death," David said wearily. Maybe he was tired of running. "You come to me, and I'll turn myself in. Only to you. You're the only one I trust."

"How can I do that, David, if I don't know where you are?"

"You'll know."

"David, I'm giving you my mobile number. Call me if you want to talk again." He recited the digits into the phone, hoping they were being copied down.

Then, without a word, David hung up.

Kevin turned on his bedside lamp and dragged the pen and notepad closer. Feverishly he punched *69, not even daring to hope. All Haines would have had to do was hit *67 before he'd called. And if he hadn't, it was obvious he wanted Kevin to know where he was: the whole purpose of his call. He only had to wait for a second before an electronic voice came on.

"The last number to call your line was ..."

Breathlessly, Kevin scribbled it down. It was from the 713 area code. Houston. Why would Haines want him to know where he was? Maybe he didn't particularly care. He'd know it was information of limited usefulness, considering that he was mobile, so near the border, able to be hundreds of miles away in a few hours. But it was hard to shake his words—"Come to me, and I'll turn myself in"—this powerful sense of being summoned. Haines could be long gone within hours, but if he was serious about turning himself in ... it wasn't hard to believe he'd only be willing to do so with Kevin. Kevin, who hadn't taken a shot at him in the cemetery; Kevin, who'd once been a brother at a cult so similar to his own ...

No, he couldn't force himself to believe it. If Haines wanted him down in Houston, it was just a mind game, a distraction ...

Another thought occurred to him. This was a check-up call. David must have assumed he'd be heading up the task force, and if he was still in Chicago, holed up in his apartment having a snooze, it must mean they were still looking for him up here. Maybe he wanted to know if the time was right to cross the border. Was that why he called? Or did he actually *want* them looking down in Houston?

For several long minutes, he sat on the edge of the bed, naked, shivering in the air-conditioned chill, not knowing what to do.

CHAPTER EIGHTEEN

She wanted to smash the phone.

All yesterday afternoon and evening, Laura had hovered around the living room, picking up every call, but it was never Rachel. Now it was almost eleven in the morning, and the last time she'd answered, ever hopeful, it had been the O'Connors, her dad's friends, who'd kept her on the line for fifteen minutes, asking after Sandra.

Face it: Rachel was not calling. It was all bullshit, a scam, just as Kevin had predicted. There was no Rachel. She sat in one of her father's voluminous wing-back armchairs, her legs folded up beneath her, just the way she had when she was little. Staring at the phone, hating it. She wanted to leave the apartment, be free of its tyrannical hold. There'd been no shortage of calls, which only made it worse. More journalists, curious colleagues, pleading patients.

She wanted to get out. But she couldn't force herself out of the chair. A panicky swirl was starting in her chest, like some malignant internal weather front. She was going to lose her lab. Adrian would take it away, and with it, the patents and rights to all the processes she'd developed while under his funding. She'd lose her lab, her staff, and, temporarily at least, her ability to do research. Who would want her after this, after the "Headline" profile painted her as a mad scientist, lurching from one crazed failure to the next? She'd been counting on Haines's blood—in one form or another: his brother's, his son's—to use as leverage to get new backing. If she had that, someone might give her a chance. And always, at the back of her mind, she hoped that if she worked quickly enough, she would develop a prototype therapy that might help Sandra.

The phone rang and she stared at it with loathing. But she had it in her hand before it had even finished its second ring.

"May I speak to Dr. Donaldson, please?" A man's voice, formal and ancient-sounding.

"Speaking."

"I'm calling from the mail room." It sounded as if his words were being sucked back into his mouth, and at the end of every sentence was a papery exhalation.

Her mind was addled. "I'm sorry, what mail room?"

"University of Chicago's. The general mail room." There was a tone of slight exasperation in his voice. "There's an envelope here for you. It came earlier this morning."

She felt her heart stutter beneath her breastbone. "A courier?"

"Yes, Fed Ex. Do you want to come pick it up, or should I just forward it through campus mail?"

"No, no, I'll come pick it up." Campus mail might get something to you the same day, or two weeks later. "Could you tell me who it's from, please?"

She heard his breathing for a moment, and shuffling noises. She imagined someone bone thin, peering myopically through glasses, the envelope held at arm's length. "It just says Rachel."

She closed her eyes, nodding to herself. *Thank you, thank you.*

"I'll be right there," she said.

*   *   *

"I want to go down," Kevin said.

"I just don't buy it, his offering to surrender," said Hugh impatiently, tilting back in his chair. "He's got nothing to gain. He knows he's dead once he's caught. He's just yanking your chain."

"Probably. But do we really want to rule it out? Maybe he's already made an abortive attempt to cross the border, seen how hard it's going to be. Maybe his plans are falling apart—he's scared, worried about getting shot. Me going down might make the difference between this ending badly or well."

Last night, after talking to David, Kevin had waited, counting his fast heartbeats, trying to decide what to do. In those few long moments he'd even briefly flirted with the idea of telling no one, going down himself, tracking the location of the telephone number, and waiting there ... for what? For David to call him again, arrange a meeting, come walking towards him with his forearms lifted, ready to be shackled?

In the end—the decision had taken him all of sixty seconds—Kevin had done it by the book. He'd called Mitch, and told him. To his surprise, Mitch was already down in Houston, coordinating efforts with the border patrol, Customs, the Coast Guard, and the U.S. Marshals. Reluctantly, he'd given Mitch the number David had called from, knowing that he'd have it traced within seconds and surrounded within minutes.

After that, he'd been unable to get back to sleep. As the first light painted his bedroom gray, he'd wondered if David had already been caught, maybe killed.

At eight o'clock Kevin was at the field office, stomach queasy, to check in with Hugh. No surprise: David had called from a pay phone in the suburbs of Houston, but he'd been gone by the time Mitch had arrived. The cashier at the gas station across the street had seen a tall, bald man driving a red Honda Civic, but hadn't thought to look at the plate. Kevin was actually relieved: now maybe he had another shot at bringing David in himself.

"Put me back on the task force, Hugh," he said. "Send me down there."

He was surprised by Hugh's silence. He'd expected a hearty "I haven't been right since the Flood" and a quick turndown. Instead, Hugh was frowning, shifting restlessly in his chair.

"This isn't even official yet," he said, "so don't go repeating it. You've seen the news, thousands of people petitioning the White House, wanting Haines's blood?"

"Yeah."

"Well, it looks like the President's starting to cave in. He's in discussions with the Attorney-General about a possible deal."

"If Haines turns himself in?"

"And gives blood. He does that, the President's thinking of commuting his death sentence to consecutive life terms without parole. Nothing's been finalized yet, but that's the general idea. One thing's for sure, though. They definitely want him alive."

It was all Kevin could do not to smile. If Justice wanted David alive, that meant Mitch was probably not the best person in the world to be leading the manhunt. And Hugh knew it.

Reading his thoughts, Hugh said, "I've had a talk with Mitch, you don't need to worry about that. He's proceeding with the utmost caution."

"I'm sure."

Hugh sighed. "Kevin, what's wrong with you? You look like a ghost. When's the last time you ate?"

"I'm fine, Hugh."

"You're fasting or something, aren't you? Like last time."

"I'm fasting," he admitted.

"That's great. Maybe I should get the whole field office to do it. We can all fast, lose some weight, go staggering around Illinois like geriatrics. Cut it out, all right?"

"Send me down there, Hugh."

"I'm thinking about it. Right now, you stay. I still want his accomplice. What's happening with this woman who said she has his kid?"

"The trap-and-trace is set up, but so far she hasn't called. Just a half-baked scam probably, but I could tell Dr. Donaldson wanted to go for it." It felt strange using her professional title when, in his mind, he'd been calling her Laura for days. He wondered if she'd ever invite him to call her by her first name.

He didn't think they'd hear from Rachel ever again. For all he knew, David's accomplice might be traveling with him, fronting for him, smoothing his path. All he had now was David's admittedly suspicious offer to turn himself in, and Kevin was clinging to it against all better judgment—and hoping that Hugh changed his mind, fast.

* * *

The envelope was incredibly light and seemed no thicker than its own packaging. It might be totally empty, or it might contain nothing more than a few strands of hair. Laura thanked the mail room manager— who, as she'd suspected given his voice, was old and cadaverous—and breathlessly carried the envelope back up the basement steps and across the hot asphalt loading bay where she'd illegally parked.

Inside her car, she sat with the envelope on her lap and looked at the label. Rachel was indeed the only name given, and she'd left her address blank. Obviously, she'd prepaid at an outlet somewhere and put it into a drop box. There was a multitude of codes on the envelope and her eyes soon caught the word Seattle. She remembered the weather forecast: rain across Washington State. *Put your hood up, Sean.*

She grabbed hold of the tear strip and then faltered. There was a chance she was an acolyte, Kevin had said. Vague memories of the Unabomber came to her. But those had been pipe bombs in bigger packages. Surely no one could fit an explosive in something this thin. Gingerly she lifted it from her lap, shaking it gently. She felt nothing, and heard nothing but a faint hiss of air when she delicately squeezed the envelope. If there was anything inside at all, it had to be paper. No bombs. Still, a single piece of paper saturated in a microbial cocktail might be enough to give her an infection no antibiotic could touch ... but Haines wouldn't have access to such things. Would he? Maybe she should call Kevin right now, and wait for him. But she knew what he'd do. He'd bring in the bomb squad, and they'd X-ray it and hem and haw over it and it would take hours. And she still wasn't sure she trusted him yet—for all she knew, he would seize the samples, and never give her Haines's clothing, as promised. The FBI was quite capable of running its own RFLP paternity tests without her.

She dragged the tear strip across the length of the envelope and let out her breath. She was still in one piece. Parting the two sides of the envelope she looked inside. At the bottom rested two small, sealed envelopes and a piece of folded notepaper. She pulled out one of the envelopes, held it up against the windshield, and through the thin paper she could see the fine strands of hair, feel its raspy crinkle between her fingers. On the outside was written "Sean." The second envelope held more hair, and Rachel's name was on the outside. The piece of notepaper had a handwritten message on it: "Stay at the Sea-Tac Airport Hilton, I'll call you there tomorrow. Remember the money please."

Seattle, tomorrow, with twenty-five grand. The presumption of it might have irritated her, except that it could only mean one thing: that the hairs would test positive, that her trip would be justified. Tomorrow didn't give her much time. She could start the tests now, run them overnight, and have the answers tomorrow morning, but she'd need Haines's samples too. Fast.

She drove down to the medical center, nodded at the security guard posted in the entrance hallway, and took the elevator up to her floor. At the door to her lab, she was halfway through punching her security code when she faltered.

What if Adrian had changed the locks on her?

It was such a terrible thought that she forgot the rest of her number. The security panel buzzed impatiently. *Just calm down*, she told herself, but her finger was shaking. She punched in her security number again, closed her eyes as she gripped the doorknob. It turned easily. Quickly she slipped inside.

She forced herself to sit down for a moment and take a few deep breaths. In her office she called Kevin's mobile number and got his voice-mail. She left a message. Then she unhooked her lab coat from the back of the door, washed her hands thoroughly, and started clearing space around her workbench.

* * *

There wasn't much to sign out: a couple of pairs of underwear, a few T-shirts. He made sure to get the comb, the toothbrush, the disposable razor, anything that might have come in contact with his body. It was all neatly sealed in swaths of cellophane and Ziploc bags. He hesitated when he saw his Bible, an ugly, dog-eared Gideon, and yet he felt an almost totemic power in it. The Bible of David Haines. He touched it through the plastic, imagining how often it must have been read. When they were packing up the contents of his cell he'd had a chance to look through it: no underlinings or turned-down pages, no illuminating marginalia. And why would there be? David's mind contained the whole Bible and his own personal gloss. With some reluctance, Kevin left it on the metal shelf. Then he shoved the rest into a padded mailing envelope, logged it out of the evidence room and carried it through the office, hoping he wouldn't run into Hugh.

Strictly, what he was doing was against regulations—but there were rules, and there was getting the job done. In the past he'd assiduously played by the rules. But if he told Hugh, he would stall it by insisting they run the paternity tests themselves. He'd want to subpoena Laura's hair samples and Fed Ex it all down to the Crime Lab in Washington. Not only would it take longer, it would piss Laura off, and right now, she was his only solid connection with Rachel. Rachel wanted to deal with her, not the FBI, and he was reluctant to jeopardize the link. Let her run the tests herself. She'd do it fast, he knew, and she probably had better equipment in her lab. And there was something else: he wanted to help her.

As he stepped aboard the elevator on the eighth floor and dropped down to parking, he felt an excited stirring in his stomach, a sensation he hadn't known for years. He wasn't entirely convinced Rachel's samples were the real thing—it could be anybody's hair in those envelopes—but then why send them? A malicious practical joke, maybe. She'd been foolish to open the envelope without him: you could plant an explosive in practically anything now. Though the package was safe, he still couldn't completely quell the fear that this was part of some setup by Haines or one of his acolytes. If Rachel knew the samples would send Laura to her lab, someone could be waiting there for her ...

He unlocked his car, slung Haines's clothes onto the passenger seat. He'd told her to stay in the lab, keep the doors locked, stay away from the windows, and let no one in until he got there. He gunned the car up the ramp onto Adams, turned right, and headed down to Lakeshore. Through the windshield, the sky was the bruised color of pewter.

*　*　*

Both samples were good.

Rachel had done exactly as she'd asked and taken the hairs with the follicles still intact. Laura deposited them into separate labeled test tubes and added the lysis buffer, beginning the process that would break down the cellular constituents of the hair. After an hour she'd be able to spin it all down in the centrifuge, lyse again, and then extract the DNA.

It felt like a long time since she'd worked at a lab bench, and she recognized the familiar channeled energy and serenity that came with absorbing work—over the past year pretty much the closest synonym for happiness she'd found. Thank God she'd been able to get inside the lab.

She had some time while the cells broke down, so she started preparations for the next stages, defrosting the vials of the primer DNA she'd need and mixing up a batch of electrophoresis gel, like a big dish of Jell-O, in a low rectangular tray. Then she paced.

All this would be pointless if she didn't get a sample from Haines. Would Kevin come through for her? Or would he simply swoop down on her lab with a team of gloved agents and take her samples? She remembered the last time she'd seen him, kneeling before her at Rick

Haines's house, talking to her with such gentleness, as if ... no, it was stupid, but she'd almost thought he seemed genuinely concerned for her, not as a citizen or a witness, but just for her. Of course, she'd been completely stupefied at the time. Still, it was this image of him that had given her the courage to call him yesterday, to tell him about Rachel, and ask for his help.

She'd just finished her first centrifuge when he called from outside the building. She gave him directions to the lab. Waiting by the door, her fingers reflexively gathered back her stray wisps of hair into the elastic, then made sure the collar of her lab coat was folded flat.

Opening the door to him, she wondered if he'd lost weight. His dark eyes seemed even larger, his mouth fuller; it made him look younger, and more vulnerable. For the first time, she felt a pang of concern for him. God, imagine the strain he was under, trying to hunt down a serial killer while the whole world watched, your success or failure naked for everyone to see. She knew what that was like. Her eyes dropped to the big padded envelope in his hands.

"You got it?" she asked as he closed the door behind him.

He held it out to her, and she took it gratefully.

"Thank you."

She watched as his eyes swept across the lab. She was glad she'd thought to make sure all the blinds were lowered, the slats angled to create a solid shield.

"This place is totally sealed?" he asked.

"There's a back exit, but it has an identi-lock too."

"How're the tests coming?"

"I've just started really. I'm back here."

She led him down the central aisle to her workbench and gestured to the rack that held her samples. "I'm just breaking down the follicles so I can extract the DNA. Shouldn't take much longer."

"Where's the envelope they came in?" he wanted to know.

"The hairs came in these." She pointed at the two small envelopes still on the lab bench. "And the Fed Ex envelope's in my office. I'll get it for you."

When she returned, he was depositing the smaller envelopes into Ziploc bags.

"Fingerprints?" she asked.

"Would've been better without yours all over them," he told her, but without any real reproof in his voice. "But I'm assuming yours won't trigger a match in our system. Rachel's probably won't either." He took the Fed Ex envelope and looked at the labels. "There was nothing else inside, no note?"

"Nothing," she said, forcing herself to meet his eye. Rachel's note was jammed into a file in her desk. She didn't like lying to him, but she'd thought it through. If she gave him the note, he'd have people all over the hotel out in Seattle, maybe even have a female FBI agent check in under her name, take Rachel's call, trace it, get to her before she did. And then who knew what would happen? But she felt a simmering of doubt now; he'd brought her Haines's clothes, as he'd promised. But she didn't want to risk losing Rachel and her boy. Wouldn't.

Kevin nodded, wondering if she was lying—why else would she be making such a concerted effort not to drop her gaze? He decided not to press it right now.

"How long will the tests take?"

"For Rachel and Sean," she nodded at the test tubes before her, "about eight to ten hours more. A bit longer for Haines since I'll be starting him now. Assuming I can get hairs or skin." He saw her look impatiently at the envelope he'd brought.

Kevin glanced at his watch. It was almost two o'clock.

"How long do they keep the security guard downstairs?"

"Six."

He'd checked out the terrain as he'd approached. There were plenty of hiding places for a sniper to insert himself. The windows of the medical science buildings, a stacked parkade off Maryland that might give a good shot. Still, the blinds were down, the room was sealed, and there was a guard outside. He knew the University of Chicago campus police were one of the largest and most vigilant forces in North America, but all the same, he didn't feel right leaving her to work alone. He didn't mind playing bodyguard for the rest of the afternoon.

"You should clear out by six, then," he told her. If he left at six, he would still have time to take the envelopes into the office for finger-print analysis ... and make it over to Diane's dad's place to see Becky. "And if you don't mind," he added, "I'll stay."

He hoped the look on her face was merely one of surprise and not irritation.

"Sure. Pretty boring for you, though. Don't you have, I don't know, important leads to follow up?"

She half smiled, as if aware how hackneyed that sounded, and he chuckled. "Believe it or not, right now, you're about my only lead." He wondered why he'd told her that; probably just the fasting again, short-circuiting the route between brain and mouth. "Is there somewhere I can make a call?"

"My office. It's down here."

Alone in her office, he dialed up the Fed Ex security office and asked them to run a trace on the bar code on Rachel's envelope. As he feared, it brought up only the address of the Seattle depot where she'd dropped it.

He put a call in to Ameritech and asked them to check Laura's incoming calls for Washington State area codes. None yet. She wasn't hiding anything there at least. He felt the pressure of impatience building under his breastbone. He could wait here in Chicago for the results of Laura's test, and then for Rachel to contact her, or he could go down to Houston on his own and try to find out if Haines was serious about surrendering. Both options were far from certain. Even if the paternity tests were positive, it wouldn't lead them to David.

He looked around Laura's office briefly. He didn't even have an office. The Bureau's press officer had an office, a nice one on the ninth floor, with a TV (on slow Friday afternoons often tuned to the Cubs game) and his own computer terminal, fax machine, VCR. Kevin got a desk with a phone. Laura's office didn't do much to inspire envy; it was unremarkable, though it could have been more attractive if she'd tidied up the files on her floor and put up some pictures. But he could see this was not a place to meet people; it was a space whose occupant was interested only in work.

On her desk, a few photographs were stuck under her plastic blotter. An older man, patrician, standing between Laura and another woman he assumed was Laura's sister. She was beautiful, but in an altogether less interesting way than Laura. Even posed for a photograph he could see the subterranean energy and discontent of Laura in her brow and mouth; her sister was too perfect, all her features in line, and she exuded sunshine. The father had an arm around both their waists.

Framed diplomas and certificates on the wall: Johns Hopkins,

Stanford, Latin calligraphy, blazing gold seals. He wondered how many years she'd been in school.

He looked at her photograph once more, and felt ugly. This morning, he'd had to cinch his belt one notch tighter, and, always slim, he'd felt even more insubstantial, his clothes ballooning ridiculously around him. Now he ran his fingers through his hair (at least it was still there) and walked back into the lab.

For the first time he realized he envied her. She had faith: he supposed that was it. Faith in all the test tubes and beakers and glassware stacked up around her lab, the inscrutable chemical names on the sides of boxes and charts—all the instruments of rituals more elaborate and arcane than any religious rite he could think of. This was her place of worship, he could see that now, and he could see the appeal of the certainty of chemical reactions and computer readouts, providing, if not the answers, at least the certainty of some cause and effect. There was a dialogue between man and the scientific world that had been sorely lacking between him and his hoped-for God.

He tried not to stare at her as she worked. He found he was staring at a lot of things lately; everyday objects were starting to take on a hyperreal aura. The toaster. The shadow of a chair in the living room. His own face in the mirror. Had they always looked like that?

He caught himself gazing at the backs of her knees, that creamy fold of flesh above her calf, and had a startling image of the tip of his tongue grazing her there, dipping into a shadowy pool. He forced his eyes away, reminded himself why he was here.

It wasn't just for her own protection. First of all, he didn't altogether trust her; she might get her results and take off without sharing them—he could see her doing it. But he also *wanted* to be with her. He hoped his breath wasn't stale.

Laura glanced over at him, wondering if he'd been staring at her. It needled her that she felt his presence so intensely; normally nothing distracted her when she was at work, but he was making her nervous. She'd just finished her first centrifuge of Rachel and Sean's samples and was now adding a second series of microdrops to the test tubes, breaking down the cells even more.

With gloved hands she carefully unpacked Kevin's envelope and laid out the specimens on a clear stretch of workbench. She felt distinctly creepy handling the underwear, and decided to start with his comb.

Pulling the flex lamp down, she examined its teeth under the magnified lens. It was a cheap black pocket comb, the teeth fine and close together; Haines's hair was a dark brown she remembered, hard to see. After a few minutes she found one and pulled it off with the tweezers, depositing it in a tube. Two more hairs, one without a follicle, one with a partial. Not a huge sample. At least it seemed unlikely that it would be anyone else's hair. She assumed death row convicts didn't share their toiletries or clothes with the other inmates. With her microvac she stroked the surface of the comb to get any sloughed-off skin cells from the scalp.

She glanced up to see Kevin seated at a workbench across the aisle, head lowered, squinting into the binocular eyepieces of a microscope.

"You need to turn it on first," she said.

He looked up quickly, almost sheepishly, and she couldn't help smiling.

"Sorry," he said. "I shouldn't be touching anything. I have no idea what I'm doing."

"It's all right." She stood and walked over to the microscope and powered it up for him. From the shelf she took down a case of slides. "Have a look if you like."

"What are they?"

"Stains of malignancies mostly. The little bastards I fight every day. Here, you put them in like this." She inserted a slide on the tray. "And focus is here." She bent her head to check, and her cheek brushed his ear. He smelled good, and she pulled back quickly, irritated by the quick arousal that pulsed through her. What the hell was she doing, getting out slides for him like some high school show-and-tell? Waste of time. If he wanted to stick around, why couldn't he amuse himself without bothering her?

"There you go."

"Thanks," he said.

Back at her own workstation, she tried to clear her mind, and started on Haines's clothing. Peering through the illuminated magnifying glass she scanned the fabric: a pubic hair in a pair of shorts, with a partial follicle. Nothing much on the T-shirts. She stroked them all with the microvac, just to make sure.

The toothbrush was tricky. There might be a good sample of mucosal cells within the bristles, but it would be hard to get at them.

Possibly she could cut off the bristles at the base, and soak the whole thing in lysis enzymes. She started another tube for that, not wanting to taint the other samples.

With care she opened the microvac canister and emptied the contents into a tube, an almost invisible mist of dead skin and dust and lint. She rinsed the canister out with saline to make sure she'd got everything and put that in the tube too. She hoped she had enough.

With her dropper she added the lysis buffer and started to break it all down.

"Why d'you want to cure cancer so much?" Kevin asked suddenly.

The answer already forming in her head seemed self-evident, but when she opened her mouth, she didn't know what to say for a moment.

"Well, I guess I believe this is the only life we have and we may as well make it as long and enjoyable as we can—or at least bearable," she added. After saying it, she felt false, like a grade-eight student regurgitating a lesson. Masquerading as an outraged humanitarian.

"Did anyone close to you die of it?"

"My mother, when I was twenty," she said, "and my younger sister has advanced breast cancer." That seemed to have heft to it, this litany of family tragedy, but again, she felt deceitful, knowing how inadequate it was as a way of explaining herself.

"That must be really hard," Kevin said. It was a simple thing to say, but he seemed to mean it, and it touched her.

"Yeah, she's down in some crackpot clinic in Mexico getting shark cartilage and voodoo cocktails pumped into her. *That's* hard. Knowing she could've done better up here. She's dying, and she decides to check her brain and hope for the best with some quack. And a God who, statistically, isn't any more likely to heal believers than atheists. If she'd agree to real treatment, I could probably give her longer."

She said it with some fervor, but Kevin wondered if her own faith was really so perfect. A beautiful, unmarried overachiever who had a speed habit, restless eyes riddled with doubt—and he found these things the most alluring of all about her. *Misery loves company, you selfish prick.*

"Well, it's admirable, what you're doing," he said.

She looked at him dubiously, then laughed. "I didn't have you pegged as a fan of medical science."

"I think a cure for cancer would be amazing. But there's always going to be something killing us. Anyway, good health, the length of your life, they're pretty coarse measures of happiness and fulfilment."

"A pretty good foundation, though."

"Okay, but they won't get you answers to the big questions. What's right, wrong. What's true."

"I don't expect my work to explain everything in the universe."

He walked with her as she carried the test tubes to another work bench and inserted them into a centrifuge. She closed the lid, hit buttons and the machine began a high-pitched whir.

"You're religious, aren't you?" she asked.

He hesitated, wondering if there was antagonism in her voice. "Well, I'm very interested in religion, but if you're asking if I'm a believer, the answer's no."

"But you want to be."

"Yes."

This talk, Kevin knew, was a professional misstep, an irrelevance to the case. And yet he couldn't rein himself in, inexplicably wanting to reveal a vista of himself he mostly kept cloaked.

"Well, I'll stick with science any day," Laura said. "I'm not saying religion doesn't have some nice, comforting ideas. But it's just wish-fulfilment, a distraction from what's real. In the end it might even do more harm than good. Look at my sister. Look at David Haines— killing doctors for God."

"People have never been short of reasons for killing each other," he said. "If not God, something else. A hunk of land, ethnicity, political ideology. Everyone gets through their lives with an irrational faith in something. Maybe it's science."

"I'd hardly call a belief in science irrational," she said, bristling. "That's about as rational as it gets."

"Maybe. We all have our holy causes, is all I'm saying."

She gave a noncommittal grunt, extracted her samples from the centrifuge, and carried them back to the lab bench.

"What's that do?" Kevin asked, nodding at the machine she now slid the tubes into. He'd said too much, probably offended her, and he was glad now to focus their conversation on the work at hand.

"It's a PCR machine. Polymerase Chain Reaction. I add a whole bunch of primer DNA to Rachel and Sean's samples, plus some heat-activated enzymes. It all goes into a bath inside, and the machine goes through a series of cycles, heating and cooling. The enzymes are heat-activated, and they start replicating the subject's DNA over and over again so we have a big enough sample to test."

"And that takes how long?"

"Three, four hours. That just gives us a good sample batch. Then we've got to do the RFLP." She checked her watch. "If I set it going at six, we'll probably have results by eleven."

"All right," said Kevin. "I'll pick you up at your place and we'll come back together."

She didn't like the idea of leaving the lab, but she had no intention of staying there alone.

"You're still waiting for Rachel to call?" Kevin asked her.

She nodded; at least this part wasn't a lie. What she hadn't told Kevin was that she'd already booked a noon flight out to Seattle tomorrow. If the samples matched, she'd be on it, and after she'd taken Sean's blood, she'd call Kevin and tell him where they were.

Outside, a long roll of thunder spanned the sky, and rain abruptly pelted the windows. Looked like the beginnings of one of Chicago's biblical summer deluges. There was little for her to do now but wait. She and Kevin spoke little, but her mind kept circling back to their conversation. *Holy cause.* Was that the way he saw her work? It irritated her, but what surprised her was that she didn't dislike him for it. She was used to defending her work to the likes of Sandra's husband, but Kevin's intelligence was so obviously of a higher caliber.

It was close to six by the time the PCR machine had finished with all three samples: Rachel, Sean, and Haines. Laura had a vial of restriction enzymes ready from the freezer.

"These cut the strands of DNA at specific loci," she explained as she bent over the test tube rack, counting microdrops. "The idea is that everyone's DNA cuts at different locations. It's distinctive. You compare the lengths of mother's piece, and father's, and the kid should have exactly half of each to make a complementary set. That's how we'll know one way or another."

Earlier she'd prepared the brick of gel into which the DNA samples would be placed for the electrophoresis. It had the consistency of Jell-O, a four-inch by six-inch plate, about half an inch deep. She cut three quarter-inch wells parallel to one another along the gel's surface, and now she carefully poured each DNA sample into its separate well, and placed the plate in the RFLP machine.

"What happens in there?" Kevin asked.

"You apply an electric current, and the DNA migrates through the gel at different distances, depending on their length. Then we compare."

A roll of thunder shook the windows.

"Ready to go?" Kevin asked.

She looked anxiously at the RFLP machine; she hated to leave it. "I guess," she said.

"Give me your car keys."

"Why?" she asked, alarmed.

"I'm going to get your car and drive it to the emergency pickup for you. If there's anyone outside waiting for you, I don't want to give them any opportunities."

"Haines is still in town then?"

"Probably not. But one of his acolytes might be."

She handed him her keys. "It's down Drexler. A green Volvo convertible."

Outside, Kevin ran through the rain and was immediately drenched, the street now a river flowing almost at the same level as the sidewalk. He found her car, opened the door, and slung himself inside. Damn nice car; leather seats, too. He pulled up in front of Emergency on East 58th and she stepped out from the doorway. He quickly got out and let her in.

"Thanks," she said.

"You should've called me as soon as you got the package," he told her. "And you shouldn't have come out here alone."

She just nodded.

"I wish you'd stop putting yourself at risk." *Listen to me and let me keep you safe*, he thought. "I'll pick you up at your father's place at 10:30, all right?" He felt an unaccountable pulse of embarrassment, as if he were taking her on a date.

"Okay," she said.

He nodded and watched her drive off before running for his own car.

*   *   *

The rain was still coming down hard when he pulled up in front of Peter and Isabel's. The suburban solidity of the house felt like a reproof to him, an edifice that kept him on the outside of his own family. During his marriage he'd spent so many evenings here with Diane and Becky. He opened the car door, popped up his umbrella, and ran. Even though he hadn't been here for years, as he bolted through the rain everything had the feeling of familiarity: the slam of the car door, the smell of the grass, the stone path, two steps up, the loop of brass rapping the wood.

Rebecca had left a message for him that morning on his voice-mail: "Hey, d'you want to take me out to dinner tonight? I checked with Mom and she's fine with it." He'd missed last weekend and was anxious to see her.

Peter answered the door, a tall, angular man with a prominent nose, and only a little hair left around the rim of his head. His quick movements gave him the look of a gaunt, dour bird.

"Jesus, Kevin, come on in," he said, peering out at the downpour.

He stepped into the hallway, carefully collapsing his umbrella so it didn't spray the carpet.

He'd always liked Peter, and often regretted how impossible it was to continue their friendship after the divorce. They'd tried initially, had a few stiff lunches together, but those had quickly become too awkward. Amazing how fast a part of your life can drop away, atrophied. Divorce was like that: you signed the papers, took your friends back, took your stuff back, and retreated to your own withered little life. He looked around the living room: this place that was, at one time, like a home to him. His own parents had never figured very prominently in his married life; he'd always liked Diane's family, and they were good grandparents—better parents to Rebecca than he'd been when he was working the Haines case.

"How's Isabel?" he asked.

"Oh, fine, fine, very busy at the moment with the alumni association."

He wasn't surprised that she didn't make an appearance. Unlike her husband, Isabel harbored considerable animosity towards him—the man who'd abandoned her daughter and granddaughter, the man who couldn't keep it all together. Peter, with his slightly dyspeptic air, seemed to have a much more dispassionate view of the divorce, and married life in general.

"Hi, Kevin."

He stood up as Diane came into the room—a strangely formal gesture, he supposed, but it seemed appropriate.

"Thanks for being so flexible about things," he said, meaning the unscheduled dinner with Becky.

"Oh, she really misses you. I'm glad you could make it."

Hard to say whether this was meant as a reproof or genuine pleasure. He found something painful about being in her presence; he still found her attractive, but in her face and body he detected a hardness, a surface he could no longer get past, and that was hard to take. *She was once mine, no more.* He thought of her boyfriend, their shared smiles, shared bed.

"How're things going?"

"Well, they're hoping they'll have him soon," he said. He realized he'd used *they*, not *we*, and wondered if Diane had noticed this flag of his demotion.

"Is it safe for us to go back home?"

"What's the hurry?" Peter said. "Stay here as long as you want. Until they catch him."

"Dad, it's no fun having houseguests for this long, come on."

"It's no trouble."

"I never thought there was much risk," Kevin said hurriedly. Oh God, the last thing he wanted to do was stir up tension among Diane's family. "Honestly, it's just for your peace of mind, and mine."

For the first months of the divorce he'd held on lazily to the notion that they could always get back together, but with each passing week, each conversation of suppressed accusation and anger, it had seemed more and more of an impossibility. Talking to Diane now, he was sweating, heat blooming beneath his arms and down his neck. Being in this house made him acutely uncomfortable—all that he'd lost, and he was never getting it back.

"This is confidential," he said, wanting to regain his sense of authority, "but we think he might be down in Texas, trying to cross the border. I'll let you know just as soon as there's any news."

"Thanks," said Diane.

"Hey, Dad."

For the first time since arriving his smile was unforced.

Becky was looking more and more like her mother, he thought. The blond hair, round green eyes, the high forehead that gave her a somewhat solemn countenance. At twelve, she was starting to become a woman—a transformation that filled him with amazement and pride.

But as always the sight of her triggered an intense protectiveness. Even though he was apart from her most of the week, he still worried about her daily, a sudden anxiety welling up in his mind unbidden, usually when reading the paper, or going over a new file, watching the news. Worried about trench-coated kids coming into the school with shotguns, worried about sickos cruising the playgrounds, worried about her not looking when she crossed the road.

"Hey, sweetie," he said. "Ready to go?"

* * *

They ended up at a Chinese place in a nearby plaza, nearly deserted because of the rain, sharing out their dishes of lemon chicken, egg rolls, and fried vegetables.

"I don't understand David Haines," she told him gravely, after fumbling a piece of chicken into her mouth with her chopsticks. She said it with the air of someone who'd given it a lot of thought.

"In what way?"

"It's like he's concentrating on all the wrong things. I mean, Jesus says, 'Love thy neighbor as thyself.' Nothing about killing people—even if they do you harm, even if you think they're against you. There's that part about just dusting the sand off your feet and moving on."

"Well, the Crusaders in the twelfth century killed lots of infidels in the name of God. I guess David Haines sees himself like that: that's his way of honoring God above all else. I don't agree with it either."

"Jesus wouldn't've wanted it," she said, watching him carefully.

He breathed in, let it out silently. "I don't think so. I hope not. It's hard to know what Jesus wanted sometimes."

She had a few more bites and then sipped at her Diet Coke pensively. "I'm glad you're here. There's something I wanted to tell you." She said it with the sort of gravity a parent is supposed to invoke when disciplining a child, or at least imparting great wisdom. At the same time, there was an excitement playing across her cheeks.

"Oh?"

"I want to be a Catholic."

Any impulse he might have had to laugh it off as a joke was vanquished by the seriousness and delight in her eyes.

"When did you decide this?" he said, putting down his chopsticks.

"Last week."

"You've thought about this a lot?"

"I think so. I liked those times we went to mass together, and I've been going with Kira and her parents sometimes. We talk about it a lot, and I finished reading the New Testament again."

She said it with some pride, and he remembered how, some months ago, she'd shared with him her resolution to read all of it. He imagined her under the covers with a flashlight, concealing it behind a magazine so Diane wouldn't find out. Diane. She was going to kill him when she heard about this. It would all be his fault. And maybe it was. What had he expected out of all their weekend field trips to churches? Had he really meant it solely as an educational and aesthetic exercise? No, if he was honest, he must have hoped that something would lodge itself in her heart and mind. His mind skittered back to Diane's threat—to try to bar his visits if Becky got involved with anything weird. He was pretty sure that not even Diane could construe the Catholic Church as something weird, though she might give it a damn good try.

"Why Catholicism?" he asked her, curious. He didn't know if he would ever have chosen the Catholic Church, but he could see its attractions: a long history, a reputation for theological rigor, a strictness in upholding its doctrines and tenets. And for a child, the drama of the mass, the sumptuousness of the iconography.

"Well, I started with a pro and con list first," she said, and at this he couldn't help smiling, his methodical daughter totting up the benefits and demerits of world religions on a lined notepad.

"And Catholicism won out?"

"Not really. I mean, it was impossible. Some things were more important than others, and it got so there was no way to compare them. In the end I guess it was the praying."

"You've been praying?"

"I fall asleep sometimes in the middle."

"Yeah, me too."

"Kira says I should kneel at the side of the bed. Keeps her awake."

"Good idea."

"I just kept praying to know which was the right one. And more and more it just seemed like I could believe in Catholicism. It makes me feel good. It feels right." She dropped her eyes. "Anyway, so that's how I decided."

He nodded, and for a moment didn't know what to say. He tried to imagine the expression on his face, and could only assume it was stupefaction. She was twelve. On what level could a twelve-year-old make such a decision? And yet, didn't the Catholic Church confirm its members at eleven, making them full communicants? Becky was brighter than most her age, brighter than a lot of people he worked with, and more level-headed, but still ... he could see all the obvious influences. Her best friend was a Catholic. And despite his own attempts at impartiality, he gravitated towards the Judeo-Christian tradition. Was this just a hangover from God's Children, though, or because it contained the most divine truth?

He laughed at himself, thinking of all his dabbling with religions, all his reading and clinical observances. He'd treated it like some all-you-can-eat buffet and pecked and sampled until he felt bloated but never satisfied. He'd been playing at faith, analyzing it like an anthropologist, but he felt so little in his heart, unable—or maybe simply unwilling, he didn't know—to commit. Was it some gloomy certainty in his heart, or just his fear of being wrong, a naive, blinkered fool? Waiting for a sign, a big special effect that would split the heavens. Maybe holding back was the easy thing to do, and all the work lay in commitment.

He envied his daughter. Maybe it was an immature decision, but so what? If it was, it wouldn't hold. It would crack under examination, under the duress of life, and she'd have to make new choices. He didn't wish those on her yet. He could see the purity of her feelings, the simplicity of them.

"I'm really happy for you," he told her. "And proud of you. You've thought a lot about this."

She nodded. "I've already talked to the priest."

He coughed into his water glass. "Already?"

"He says I just need my parents' permission and he'll start me on catechism lessons after school."

"Well, you've got mine," he said. "But I don't know about your mom, Becky. She's going to flip."

"I was wondering if you could talk to her about it."

"Probably best if you do it first, so it doesn't seem like it was my idea. Oh God, she'll think I've been brainwashing you."

Becky nodded. "If I tell her how important it is to me, don't you think she'll be okay with it?"

252

"I hope so."

"She knows I go to mass with Kira, and she's seen the Bible I was reading, and she doesn't mind."

"Good," he said, surprised he hadn't gotten an accusing phone call about this, too. He looked at her, smiling across the table, and felt a surge of happiness. It was what he'd wanted for her, what he'd hoped for, and in some way, her faith went some way towards erasing the emptiness of his own faithlessness. *A fisher of men*: maybe there was some kind of divine tally sheet he'd gain some marks on.

"Child of light," he said to her.

"What's that?"

"The term the priest uses when you're baptized."

"I like that," she said.

The rain was still coming down as he drove her home, and when he kissed her goodbye on the doorstep he felt as if something cold had touched him. It was hardly the first time he'd had an unpleasant premonition that he might never see her again; they were like rogue electrical impulses, and they never came to anything. But it wasn't a nice way to leave his daughter.

"That's great news," he said. "Break it to your mom gently."

"I will. Thanks for dinner."

"I'll see you soon, I hope."

"Okay. Be careful." He smiled, remembering how, as a little child, she'd learned to echo these words of Diane's as he left for work. "I pray for you, too, you know," she told him. "Every night."

"That's good. I need a lot of work."

She chuckled, having no way of knowing how touching a child's benediction was. Kevin saw her indoors and turned back to his car, wishing he could believe in the power of prayer.

CHAPTER NINETEEN

Looking south down Michigan from her father's balcony, she saw the skyline decapitated by the low cloud, the Hancock's twin antennae glimmering dully through the mist before being extinguished. Even standing back against the sliding door, she was getting soaked by the hammering rain, but she didn't want to go back inside just yet. She needed air, an open window to quell the swelling anxiety she felt inside; she needed the rain and noise to distract her from that little bottle of phenmetrizine in her purse. No more until tomorrow morning, or she'd screw up her whole withdrawal regimen.

Lightning backlit the fog over the dark lake and then, like splitting wood, came the thunder's reply. From a construction site down Burton came some resonant, cataclysmic gonging noise that she could only guess was a winch swinging against the side of its crane. The rain itself created an ambient roar, beating at windows and metal balconies, punching leaves, cratering the swift shallows of North Michigan and Lakeshore Boulevard.

At last she went back in, slamming the door shut against the storm's din. In the bathroom she took a towel and dried her hair, pacing absently, unable to get rid of her nagging guilt about Rachel's note. Maybe she should have shared it with Kevin. She didn't have to, did she? It wasn't *illegal.* Could they put her in jail for concealing something? But it was sent to her, it was private property.

The only thing she was worried about was Rachel's safety—but this was still conjecture, she reminded herself. She still had to prove paternity. *Wait until you know.*

Wait. That was about it. She still had over two hours before she could get back to her lab.

She sat down in front of the TV and surfed without seeing anything, the speed of the images unsettling her enough that she soon switched it off. From her briefcase she extracted the fat folder she'd brought back from the lab. It was the file her researcher had put together on David Haines over a week ago, when they'd been hopeful of getting his blood or tracking down other family members. Mostly it was photocopied articles from magazines and papers, but there were a couple of paperbacks, too, the kind with hot-stamped covers sold in supermarkets. Idly she picked one up, noted the appropriately lurid cover and title (*Dark Angel*) and the long list of *Newsweek* writers who'd doubtless churned it out mere weeks after Haines was captured. She hadn't the slightest interest in the case, really, or in David Haines.

She wanted to find out about Kevin.

She started at the beginning, skimming through the paragraphs of tedious investigative procedure, stopping only when she spotted his name. She was hoping for personal details, but there weren't many. Served with the Chicago field office for fifteen years ... a specialist in cult psychology ... in the past he'd been instrumental in blah blah blah. "Tall and rangy." That was about it in the way of description. Jesus. She flipped to the front of the book and looked at the list of writers' names again. Figured. What was it with male writers? Didn't they notice his eyes, that lupine balefulness? Nothing on the way he spoke, or dressed, or whether he was married. Or single. Or whether his fourth finger had ever held a wedding band. She supposed the readers of these books didn't really care about that kind of thing.

She was getting ready to skim again when the chapter hit a portentous end note: "No one knew it yet, but Sheldrake would turn out to be the task force's most valuable asset. In the early days of the DOCKIL file (the Bureau's abbreviation of Doctor Killer), no one had yet surmised that the murders were religiously motivated. But it was ultimately Sheldrake who identified the killer's modus operandi, Sheldrake who anticipated Haines's next fatal moves—a man who, twenty years earlier, had been a member of a religious cult not unlike the one that forged David Haines."

She felt almost angry, as if someone should have told her. But here it was, public knowledge. Maybe if she'd been in the country instead of working up in Toronto when Haines was killing, maybe if she were the type of person who scrupulously followed such things and read shitty little books like this one, she would have known. She was surprised at herself. A month ago, if any man had confided in her that he used to be a member of a cult, she would have instantly classified him as a loony: a weak mind and spirit.

But right now she couldn't help finding it bizarrely, maddeningly perplexing. A man who'd been in a cult, and spent the rest of his professional life debunking them, while at the same time craving religious belief. It was a bit twisted. Was this how he could want to imprison David Haines but at the same time be so infuriatingly sympathetic towards his precious civil liberties?

Well, Kevin had *left*, that was the important thing; he'd seen through it all, and was smart enough to shake it off.

In the middle of the book were a few pages of black-and-white photos. Haines's victims. A few crime scenes, which made her wince: windows shattered by high-powered rifles, yellow police tape, cruisers. There was only one picture of Kevin Sheldrake. It wasn't a particularly good shot. He was standing against a map, pointing at some location, probably for a press conference. His posture could use some work, his shoulders starting to round. He had nice hands. And his eyes ... she still couldn't decide if she liked them or was simply mesmerized by their intensity. She couldn't say as much for his style of dress. In the photo it even looked as though he was wearing the same banal suit she'd first seen him in. He looked younger. It wasn't his hair; he still had pretty good hair. In most men his age, it was the first to go: hair, gone or receded into a monk's tonsure; face, squared out with jowls; expression, smug with a fat income, in the case of most of the men she met.

Kevin's age showed in his face. He was gaunter now, more weary. She wondered what had happened to him in the last three years. Maybe just life. She looked at his hands again. There we go: a wedding band on the fourth finger. So he'd once had a wife, maybe kids, and was now on his own. Interesting.

Staring at the photo, she wondered what it would be like to hold him. After Adrian's broad shoulders and barrel chest, Kevin would be hard and edgy as a lightning rod. Be like wrapping yourself around a current of electricity. She felt a pleasant flush through her upper thighs.

Thunder vibrated through the floor, and the lights flickered. She checked her watch. Nine-thirty. The RFLP would probably be done within the hour. Again the lights dimmed, more deeply this time. Shit. She closed her eyes, tried to remember if the RFLP machine was plugged in through a surge-detector. Yes, probably. But now all she could visualize was a blinding snake of electricity coiling from the outlet into her machine, an exuberant shower of sparks, and inside, a smoking puck of electrophoresis gel, her DNA samples fossilized.

In less than five minutes she was in her car, windshield wipers on full, brushing a strand of wet hair away from her face. She pulled onto Lakeshore, feeling the water through the wheels. There weren't many cars on the road, and the beaches were deserted as she swung around behind Streeterville. She'd called Kevin before she left, got voice-mail, and told him she'd gone in early to make sure the samples were okay: she'd meet him there.

A bony finger of lightning stabbed down over the dark glass plateau of McCormick Place. She moved into the center lane, away from the deep slicks of water to the side, and gunned it, her thoughts surfing ahead to her work.

Check the samples. They'd be fine. When they were done, she could move the gel to the storage vault that doubled as the darkroom, and do the photographs. The gel contained a small amount of radioactive material, which, over the last four hours, would bind to the DNA. The gel and photographic paper were put together for a quick exposure, and voilà, you got pictures of the DNA in a ladder configuration, Mom, Dad, and baby. Or so she hoped.

The rain was letting up as she pulled off Lakeshore onto Ellis. In the small lot off Drexler she found her usual spot and parked. Hunched under her umbrella, she crossed the lot, looking up at her lab windows, relieved to see no sign of flames or smoke. She felt a jittering in her stomach, that familiar swirl of apprehension whenever she awaited test results.

A strange pop sounded behind her, a jubilant champagne cork liberated from the bottle, and at virtually the same instant, she felt two savage bites below her shoulder blades, twin barbed tugs at her flesh. Crying out, back arching, one hand flew instinctively to the place; she started to turn—

Cheek against asphalt. Whole world tipped onto its side. The smell of damp grit, oil, and gasoline in her nostrils, and something else, the subtle ozonated promise of lightning. How did she get here? *Where* was here? Slowly, some memories come back, like something laboriously dredged from a murky lake. Rain, driving through rain, the campus, a parking lot. Good. Getting out of her car: she saw that. And then?

And then she was on the pavement, collapsed. She tried to move.

Nothing worked. Not even her eyes. They wouldn't obey her, just kept taking frantic, skewed snapshots of the night. *Keep still, goddamnit.*

She seemed to be on her right side, right arm pinned beneath her chest, her left splayed out before her. She caught a glimpse of her hand, jerking spastically, but felt nothing, no connection between that hand and herself. Then her busy eyes were darting away again without her consent. Her umbrella, still open and rocking slightly. Her purse. The tread of a car wheel. A rainbow smear of gasoline in a puddle, glittering in the streetlight's wash. A patch of clearing sky and in the far distance the lights of a passing jet. All those people safe inside.

A pair of legs, not hers.

Standing over her.

Then her eyes skittered off again, rolling helplessly in their sockets. The legs again.

Help me.

But her mouth wouldn't speak.

She wanted to move her head, tilt it back so she could see who was above the legs.

Help me.

Again and again, her mind shrieked the words she tried in vain to utter.

But no one was helping.

* * *

Gail bent down and clipped the two wires before shoving the Taser back into her purse. It had made a louder pop than she'd remembered, practising in her house, but maybe that was just her imagination. There'd been sparks, too, and the smell of matches. A quick look around—good, still no one in sight, no cars turning into the lot. She knew the rain would keep people inside. She walked closer to Laura, looking down at her.

David had told her not to, but that was because he thought she couldn't do it, she was too weak. And that's why he'd left, he was disgusted with her. But if she could do this for him, she could tell him next time he called, and he would be proud of her. She would bring him back. She felt sure of it. After all, he'd taken her car and promised to return it, and he would never break a promise.

She couldn't believe her luck—could it be God, helping her, showing her the way after all? She'd never liked to think good things happened to her because God wanted them to; it seemed so vain. She'd never felt she deserved special attention from God, not like some of those TV preachers who were always going on about their talks with Him, and how He did this and that for them.

But the doctor had come; on only the second night of waiting, she'd come. Gail had hardly thought it possible—after all that had happened, she was almost sure the doctor would be off hiding somewhere.

Gail had recognized her car right away; she had it down pat, all those times she'd spent watching her before David escaped, watching, planning, but never doing what she was supposed to. Now here she was, parking her car in the same old spot, walking towards the hospital, late at night, and no one around. She knew she'd never get a chance like this again, and her stomach felt all watery, like she was going to have diarrhea.

She'd made little black curtains for the license plates of her rental car, front and back, attached with picture wire, so she could keep them tied back out of way as she was driving here. Then, in the parking lot, she'd flipped the cloth down over the plates, covering them.

The back one had given her some trouble—the wire was all worn and it snapped on one side. Fumbling she tried to splice the two pieces together, poking them through the cloth. There, it would hold, it just had to hold long enough. Just in case anyone saw.

Then the doctor had arrived.

Gail had made her footsteps silent as she crept up behind her. The doctor wasn't paying attention, looking up at the hospital, umbrella held low over her head.

It was easy to hate her. She was slender and beautiful and she knew what clothes to wear to make her breasts look big and her waist all slim. She looked rich, and she was famous. Just another beautiful bitch. She'd tried to rape David, take his holy blood out, his soul. Her hatred made her knees feel weak, but she felt good, too, like she was about to say something smart and powerful and important and everyone would look at her and listen and not see a fat, plain cow of a woman, but see her for all the things she wanted to be.

She wanted to make the doctor ugly, like her.

Almost there. Her hand slid into her purse, closing around the

Taser. Amazing, the doctor didn't even turn. Maybe she'd even seen her, out of the corner of her eye, and just ignored her. Nothing but an ugly fat woman to tune out.

Well, don't ignore me.

She pointed the stun-gun and squeezed the trigger and heard the pop and saw those two little barbed probes go flying and snag her blouse. Then the doctor just dropped like a big boneless slab of meat. Her head made a terrible clunk on the concrete, like something hollow, like a melon or something; she couldn't help wincing.

And now she had to do the next part.

Do it for David.

* * *

Coronary infarction? No pain, doesn't explain numbness of limbs. Migraine? Maybe. Grand mal seizure? Could be. Stroke? Maybe. Cranial aneurism? She was still breathing. Didn't know how long she'd been out.

Laura couldn't move, just shudder uselessly, though her eyes were starting to behave a bit better.

Another snapshot: a face, sculpted by the harsh shadow of the street-lamp. A woman's face.

A cry caught in her numb throat, eyes filling with tears of relief, unable to blink them clear. Underwater. She was so lucky. A woman would help another woman.

You'll help me.

She realized she was being moved, not as gently as she might have liked, dragged away from her car by her arms. Her head, she was dully aware, was scraping along the asphalt, though she felt no pain. She tried to lift it, but couldn't.

Careful, she thought, a five-year-old cautioning a rambunctious friend. *Careful.* At least she didn't feel anything.

She wasn't moving anymore.

Where was the woman?

She tried to lift her head, but that just sent her cheek down against the pavement, where she saw nothing but a woman's sandals, surprisingly tacky things with little bursts of plastic coral around the strap. Now they were moving away.

Leaving her.

Hey!

Laura tried to follow, all the images cut up as her eyes danced erratically. There she was, and where the hell was she going? Getting into a car. Good idea. Bring the car over so you can get me to the hospital.

The door slammed closed. The engine turned over.

She was slowly feeling out the truth, like a child with eyes closed, trying to discern the shape of a familiar object with her hands.

Not helping me. Could do anything she wanted to me. Only now did she remember the pop, the twin sharp nips in her back. Shot? Shot in the spine, paralyzed? She felt no wetness around her, but then she felt little of anything at all. Panic was starting to thrash around her inert body, threatening to burst out.

Oh, Jesus.

The car was just sitting there, not moving, engine growling. She could feel its vibration through the asphalt. She tried to move her right hand, and sent it flailing up into the air, numb, like a limb that you've slept on all night.

Move.

Her right hand came smashing down against the pavement, trying to push her over onto her side. A spider's web of sharp pain through her knuckles. Good. Pain meant something, something coming back.

Push. No good. Push.

She dug the fingernails of her right hand into the asphalt, trying to drag herself over. One foot kicked.

The car squealed towards her.

*   *   *

Gail lined up the wheels so that the left ones would go right over the doctor's neck. She stamped down on the gas pedal until it hit the floor, unable to repress a whimper. Wheel held tight, she looked straight ahead. A horrible dread swelled inside her.

Do it for David. This is what's right, don't be afraid. To the pure all things are pure. Don't look. Don't look.

*   *   *

With sudden neural synchrony, her limbs did what she wanted and her body jackknifed, her cheek and ear scraping asphalt. She could hear the car's approach, and tried to drag her anesthetized legs out of its path, writhing for the concrete island that divided the parking lot. No way she'd make it. She imagined the wheels catching her across the base of the spine, snapping her vertebrae.

Like claws, her fingers sank around the rim of the concrete island and pulled. Chin up and over, fingernails scrabbling for purchase, *come on, kick!* Blood thundered in her ears, or was it the roar of the car? She was sure she could feel its urgent heat washing over her, and her body clenched in anticipation—

The car was past. She could tell by the sound of its engine.

Sluggishly she turned her head, looked back at her legs, expecting to see them buckled and pulpy. But they seemed all right, and she dragged them up onto the concrete divider with a feeling approaching elation. As if being there, all of two inches above the road, would save her. The car had stopped, about fifty feet up the lot, idling.

In the red flare of the brake lights she could see the license plate. The numbers and letters seemed to sear themselves into her brain so, even as she tried to stand, she was reciting them in her head, trying to say them through her Novocain lips. Where was her Volvo? There, over there. She looked back at the other car, expecting the door to swing open, the woman to come running towards her—no way she could get away.

The car's engine roared again, but it kept heading out of the lot, took the corner fast, and raced down East 58th.

She had no idea how long it took her to reach her car, half crawling, half walking, shedding bits of memory as she went. She fell often, took time to rest, marshal her strength for another spastic few feet. Her purse and umbrella were still by the door, and she spent a tearful few minutes fumbling for her keys. Pain was starting to sing through her now, the back of her head, her arms and hand, her whole right side down to the hip where she must have first hit the pavement.

Inside the car she locked the door and sat with her forehead against the wheel. What did it feel like to have someone try to kill you? Nothing, that's what. Absolutely nothing. No, that wasn't quite right. Sleepy. She wanted to sleep. That was about it. No earth-shattering revelations about the sanctity of life, no immense gratitude to be alive. Just sleepy.

She slouched back against the seat and shouted in pain. There were still things in her back. Patting gingerly with her fingers, she felt two rounded knobs protruding from the ripped fabric of her blouse, each trailing about a foot of thin wire. She jiggled them gently, but that only sent more agonizing splinters through her upper back. Like two goddamn fishhooks. The thought made her suddenly queasy, the image of her flesh impaled.

Stun-gun. One of those Air Tasers probably; they were legal in Illinois. She'd briefly considered getting one herself when a female acquaintance was attacked. With a compressed-air cartridge they shot out twin probes that latched onto your skin and clothing and jolted you with a pulsed electric current, turning your muscles to Jell-O and wiping your head clean for a minute or two.

Vaguely she was aware that she should get inside to safety, hobble up the road to Emergency, but instead she flipped down the lighted vanity mirror. The right side of her face looked as if it had been sand-papered, pulpy and red, and it was peppered with bits of asphalt. Starting up in her temple, a dull jackhammer pain. She touched it, felt the lump through her hair, and brought her fingertips away brown with clotted blood.

Index finger to jawbone, she checked her pulse—a little fast but there didn't seem to be any arrhythmia. Breathing sounded okay: there was a stethoscope up in her lab. Focus still wasn't great, but coming back.

The license plate. Amazingly, she could still see its image, though when she opened her mouth and tried to recite it, she still couldn't form the sounds, either because her lips and tongue were still numb, or because she couldn't verbally remember them. Inside her purse she scrounged for a pen and didn't find one. She took her lipstick, the back of an old bank receipt, and laboriously drew each character. She stared at it hard. My God, it looked like something a preschooler had done. She shut her eyes, conjuring up the image of the license plate, and then opened her eyes quickly at what she'd written, and the two seemed to superimpose perfectly. Kevin would be pleased with her. The thought somehow cheered her up. Absently she dropped her lipstick and slip of paper back into her purse, already forgetting.

Now the woman. Against her closed eyelids, she had her, but only in split-second frames. She was unable to isolate her individual features. Nose, eyes, hair color—she couldn't do it, partly because of the deep shadow cast from overhead, partly because her eyes had been dancing around. She seemed tall, but that might've been the angle. She seemed fat.

She might have slept, she couldn't remember. Now, across the street, she saw a car pull up outside her lab, and Kevin Sheldrake got out, stepping back so he could look up at the darkened windows. Gratitude and relief surged through her, and she had to bite down hard to stop her tears. She honked her horn and he turned and came walking quickly towards her.

*   *   *

"You're sure about this?" he asked gently, looking up from the crumpled piece of paper she'd fished from her purse.

Under the fluorescents of the Emergency Room, her skin looked blanched and taut, the fiery laceration across her right cheek a lurid contrast.

"Yeah," she said, "I wrote it down as soon as I got into the car."

He stared again at the lipstick scrawl, the numbers and letters drawn like hieroglyphs, strange foreign scratchings copied out with no recognition of their meaning. Jesus, it looked awfully shaky. Still, it was a plausible combination of numbers and letters. A charge of excitement swept through him.

"But the car itself? You get a make?" He felt lousy about grilling her right now, but he had to know.

"I've never been good at that. Under the streetlamp it looked maybe greeny blue, something dark, black, I couldn't tell."

"And you didn't get a very good look at the woman."

"Big. Overweight. That's about it."

He wondered if she'd be able to ID her in a lineup. She could remember the license plate but nothing else; that didn't seem right. He knew the effects of stun-guns; it wasn't that unusual for the victims to suffer short-term memory loss, especially if they'd lost consciousness, which she certainly had. The fact that she'd even *seen* the license number was miraculous, but he wondered if she could be trusted. She might have suffered a concussion on top of everything else.

"It's right," she said, looking at him angrily.

"You were just hit with a Taser, is why I'm asking."

He needed to be sure. If it was right, he could get a name, an address,

Social Security; he could get this person's life within minutes. A woman ... must be the person who sheltered Haines in Chicago. He wanted to get back to the field office right now and access the DMV database. This was concrete, what he had in his hands. If he could get to this woman, he could get to Haines. Haines calling him from Houston, a woman in Seattle saying she had his son—he didn't know what to do with these. But the license number would lead him somewhere.

But if Laura was off, even one digit or letter, it could scupper the whole search, or at least slow him down by days or weeks.

An impossibly young-looking resident appeared before them. As far as Kevin was concerned, she didn't look that much older than Becky, shoulder-length hair permed into a loose wave, bright blue eyes and rosy cheeks undiminished by the long hours of her shift. She smelled like gum.

"Okay, Dr. Donaldson, my name's Dr. Kirby. We're just going to take you down to the minor treatment room and have a look."

"I'll be right down," Kevin told Laura.

"Are you family?" the resident asked.

"I'm better. I'm FBI." He walked down the hallway to a quiet spot and called the field office. He got Shaughnessy, a young recruit who'd just come up from Quantico.

"I need a DMV check," he told him, and read out the number. "I want as much information as you can get. Address, phone, background. I'll be coming in in about half an hour." He left his cellular number and went down the hallway to the treatment room.

"You're certainly not our typical stun-gun victim," Dr. Kirby was saying to Laura a touch nervously. "Usually they're whacked out on PCP and have to be held down by the cops."

Laura lay quietly on her stomach, head resting on folded arms, her attitude not so much one of despondency as of impatience. Kevin winced at the site of the two barbs protruding from her blouse, wires trailing like bizarre insect antennae. With surgical scissors, Dr. Kirby carefully snipped the wires flush with the shafts, then cut a generous square of cloth around both electrodes.

"Sorry about the shirt, but it's the only way."

Beneath Laura's bra strap, her skin had risen into two angry welts around the Taser contacts. Kevin watched as the resident gave her a shot of something. Then almost right away she made a small incision at the base of the first shaft, deftly twisted out the hook—a single barb but a mean little son of a bitch—and repeated the procedure for the second. Laura made not a sound.

"I don't think you'll need suturing," Dr. Kirby said. She cleaned the wounds with disinfectant and applied a dressing.

Laura sat up, and the resident took a look at the deep abrasion on her face. "Okay, I'm going to put some xylocaine on there and then do a scrub." With the flats of her fingers she gently smeared some jelly across the wound. "I'll be back in five minutes to clean it out."

"How you feeling?" Kevin asked her.

"I've got to check my samples."

"Laura." It was the first time he'd called her that, but she showed no surprise. "Forget the samples, that's all bullshit. You were set up. The woman who tried to kill you just now, that's your Rachel. All right? She made the calls. She knew you'd be working at the lab. She was waiting for you."

For a moment Laura's face was motionless, her eyes on his but not seeing him, as if too busy testing his hypothesis.

"Don't you get it?" he said.

"The envelope came from Seattle. You're saying she went all the way out to Seattle to send it to me and flew back here to zap me?"

"Could've. Or Haines might have another acolyte out there, helping. They coordinated all this. They want you dead. I need to get to work on this." He shook the piece of paper with the license plate. "But I also need to know you'll be safe. I want to check you into a hotel."

"I'm staying here to finish the paternity tests."

"They'll be negative!"

"Let's see."

"You're not thinking clearly." It came out sounding sharper than he wanted, when what he felt was concern for her. Look at her, she'd just been whacked with a stun-gun, almost run over, and she wanted to stick around and check out hair samples that had probably been picked off a hairdresser's floor. Her eyes, always flicking away from his; he remembered the speed in her purse. Depending on her dose, he knew it could completely distort her thinking, make her feel confident, grandiose, immortal. It could get her killed.

"Are you still taking phenmetrizine?" he asked with an apologetic sigh.

Her face flinched with surprise, and then hardened. "Isn't that against the rules, looking in my purse?" But he detected a halfheartedness in her rebuke.

"I didn't have to look in your purse. I saw the inventory list from forensics. They're sometimes more thorough than they need to be."

"They're diet pills."

"You look great to me. You don't need to be on a diet."

"That's really none of your business."

"It is if I think it's affecting your judgment, and you're putting yourself at risk. Which you've done a lot lately. You opened that Fed Ex envelope without me. Stupid. You come here late at night without me. You want to stay here alone in your lab when you know there's people out there who want you dead, and know *exactly* where you work. I know you're not stupid, so I'm thinking it must be the speed."

"I take the speed to keep going," she said quietly through a taut mouth. "My work is demanding, and I don't want to fall behind. I'm not addicted, if that's what you're getting at. I only ever took it sparingly. In fact, I'm getting off it altogether."

He could only nod, hoping she was telling the truth. He wanted to gather her up in his arms and hold her until she started making sense.

"They want you dead, Laura," he said. "I've got to go track this car down, and I'll feel a whole lot better if you're somewhere safe."

They fell silent as Dr. Kirby came back into the room and ripped open the packaging of a surgical sponge. It looked like one of those stiff brushes you use to get under your fingernails. She touched it to Laura's face. "Okay? Don't feel anything?"

Kevin clenched his teeth in sympathy.

"Fine," said Laura tonelessly.

He saw her shoulders twitch upwards with pain, but her face was composed. Somehow it reminded him of Becky, of how brave she'd always been when she fell and cut her knee and he'd clean it out with hydrogen peroxide.

"I'll give you a tetanus shot in a minute." After taping a series of gauze and cotton pads to her face, Dr. Kirby put the stethoscope to Laura's chest. "Heart's still beating a little hard. You don't have a history of cardiac disease? Mitral valve prolapse, or arrhythmia?"

"No."

"Are you taking any medication?"

"No."

Kevin wondered if the doctor had registered her split-second hesitation. He looked at Laura, but she didn't meet his gaze.

"I'd like to get an EKG anyway, just to be sure everything's okay with your heart."

"It's really not necessary," Laura said, turning her professional gaze on the poor resident. "Trust me."

"I know," said Kirby apologetically. "It's virtually unheard of to get any cardiac disturbances with a stun-gun, but if there's toxicity or underlying heart disease, it can be significant. There have been cases of cardiac arrest—"

"Why're you talking about toxicity? I already told you I'm not on any meds."

Dr. Kirby nodded vigorously but said, "I'd still like to take a reading."

"For God's sake, let her take the reading," Kevin said. "What's it matter?" He was genuinely worried now. If she'd had speed pumping through her heart when she was zapped, it was lucky she hadn't bought it right there in the parking lot.

"Thank you for cleaning me up," Laura told the resident. "You did a good job. And you're very thorough. I'm going to call the head of Emerg and say so." She hopped off the bed.

"Well, I think you should stick around for a few hours anyway," said the resident, "with that bump on your head. Just to make sure there's no concussion."

Kevin had to hand it to Dr. Kirby, she was tenacious.

"I'll keep an eye on it," said Laura, walking out of the room.

For a moment, Kevin and the young resident just stared after her in mutual hopelessness. Kevin smiled apologetically. "Thanks, Dr. Kirby," he said, and hurried after Laura.

Out in the hall, he touched her arm to slow her down.

"Are you okay, really?"

"Yes." Through clenched teeth.

"Go home, Laura. What do I have to do, put you under lock and key?"

"Can you put me under lock and key?"

"Well, no."

"You going to arrest me?"

"Can't arrest you either." There was no way he could make her do anything she didn't want to, and it was making him angry now. "But I don't think you know what you're doing. You were set up."

For a moment, she seemed to flag, her eyes fixed on the floor, and he felt another pang of tenderness for her.

"I'm going to check the samples," she said. "They'll be negative, and then I'll go home. I don't think anyone's going to try to kill even me twice in one night. Okay?"

His cell phone rang. "Just wait a second, all right. Hello?"

It was Shaughnessy.

"I ran the plate. It's a rental car. Hertz."

"Shit." It was going to slow him down. "Okay, look, I'm coming right in. Let's start waking people up." To Laura he said, "I've got to go."

"It's right," she said, nodding at the slip of paper on which she'd written the license plate.

"Please be careful," he told her.

She nodded.

He watched her walk stiffly away from him down the hall, her bandage showing through the gash cut into the back of her shirt, and wanted to hurry after her, stop her, lean his forehead against hers, kiss her mouth, tell her she was an idiot. Instead he turned and ran for his car.

*　　*　　*

Couldn't sleep.

She hadn't even bothered to change out of her clothes, just sat on her bed without pulling back the covers, lights off, curtains drawn.

Should've held the trigger longer, given the doctor a bigger jolt; but she'd dropped so quickly, like a marionette with its strings cut. She'd thought it would be enough. She'd pushed the gas all the way down, but even then the doctor was already starting to move, clawing herself across the lot towards the divider. She was really fast.

You turned the wheel.

No, she moved.

You turned the wheel. You did. At the last moment you went all weak, and you turned the wheel a bit, just a bit, but enough.

How long had she sat there, looking back in her rearview mirror, seeing the doctor reach the divider and sit up? Even then she could have done something. The doctor was still dazed, too dopey to run. Put the car in reverse and try again. Pop in the extra canister for her Taser, and run back and zap her a second time. But she was frozen there in her car, watching her, knowing she'd failed, knowing she was too weak to do it properly. She'd driven off, stopping after several blocks to unveil her license plates just in case she happened to pass any police cars.

The rear license plate was already exposed, the little black curtain limping down on a single twist of wire. Oh sweet Jesus, how long had it been like that? Maybe only after she'd taken that quick corner out of the parking lot.

The doctor couldn't have read. She was too far away, and there wouldn't have been enough light, enough time. She was half unconscious, wasn't she? She'd seen the way her eyes were when she'd dragged her away from her car: flick flick flick, staring at her a few times, glazed over, terrible, like the eyes of a suffocating fish or something. No, she wouldn't have seen the license, even if it was uncovered.

Clumsily, Gail twisted herself off the bed and onto the floor, and tried to pray, the way she'd seen David do it. She could feel her heart blasting away against the carpet, her big whale's heart, and all she could manage was a moronic, *Please, oh please.*

She was so weak, so weak.

She needed to talk. But who was there? Since David had come into her life, she'd let practically everyone else go. She went to work and came home and that was that. She was a little slimy fat snail in her shell. Her mother she hardly called anymore, and the idea of talking to her now was simply exhausting. She knew nothing. Nobody knew anything at all about the most important thing in her life. That, she'd kept secret, and now she was alone with it.

Please call, David.

If he'd given her a number, she'd have called right away. After his last call, she had no idea where he'd gone. He wouldn't tell her. All he'd said was that he'd call soon. She'd wanted to make sure he came back. But now that she'd failed yet again, what would happen to her? *Please call.*

On her knees she looked over at the phone on her night table, willing it to ring, inventing games. *It'll ring in the next ten minutes if I pray. It'll ring in the next ten minutes if I hold my breath and make it to sixty.* And she prayed, reciting the words without even touching on their meaning, round and round in her head.

In the darkness the room contracted and swelled. David's painted face looked down at her. He hadn't liked her paintings. Just the way he'd looked at them, she could tell. Without him, what did she have? Before he'd come to her, every day had been spent composing letters to him, hoping for letters. Her job was just marking time between waking and coming home to check the mail, to paint his picture, over and over in one form or another.

She had the phone up on the first ring, heart pulsing so fast her vision blacked out for a moment.

"Hello?"

"Gail, what's wrong?"

As if he knew, as if he'd been watching over her. Just his voice brought her to tears, unleashed a torrent of words. "Oh, David, I tried, I tried to do it with a stun-gun, and run her over, but she got away."

"Who, Gail? Calmly."

"The doctor. I tried but I missed. And my license plate, I'm worried she might've seen it. I'm scared. When are you coming back?"

There was a short pause. "I love you, Gail. Do what you must."

"David?"

He was gone, and all that she heard was telephone emptiness, as big and terrifying as those shots of outer space. Very carefully she replaced the phone in the cradle. Maybe he'd call back. Maybe he'd just been cut off. *Count to fifty. Something bigger, then, just to give him more time.*

If they caught her, would she talk? How did she know she wouldn't give anything away? What would they do to her? Look what they'd done to David, trying to suck the blood right out of his veins. They'd have tricks to make her talk and she wouldn't be strong enough or smart enough to hold back.

Do what you must, he'd said.

David, if you call back, I'll do whatever you want.

The phone sat sullenly on the night table.

She gingerly lifted the receiver, just to make sure she'd put it back correctly, and there was a dial tone, and David wasn't trying and trying to call and only getting a busy signal. The dial tone droned out from the speaker.

She put the handset down gently, then snatched it up and smashed it against the table, and that wasn't enough, so she picked up the whole thing and yanked and yanked until the cord whipped out of the wall. She smashed the handset into the phone until the plastic cracked and components started rattling out onto the carpet. David was watching her, seeing everything, and she hated him seeing her like this. She lumbered onto the bed and gouged at his face with her fingernails, wanting to hurt him, wishing they were his real eyes, gouging and tearing at the canvas, paint crumbling beneath her nails. Not enough. She snatched up the nail file from her dresser and plunged it through the taut canvas. *See! See what I can do!* Again, that sharp pop of the point piercing the canvas, and then the quick tear as she dragged it through.

She stopped, her heart beating with slow, deliberate thuds, and looked at his portrait, his face lacerated, hanging down in strips, the nothingness behind it.

As if she'd hit him herself.

What have I done, what have I done?

Her remorse and self-loathing took her in a huge, numbing squeeze. Like a winter sea inside her. She imagined blue fingernails, blue lips, all the blood leaving her. And then a terrible calmness unraveling something inside her, something that wouldn't reveal its name, not yet.

Slowly she walked to the kitchen.

* * *

It was a house like all the others on the street, an ugly suburban bungalow set back behind a square of lawn, without trees to soften the concrete driveways and aluminum siding and jaundiced brick. The car was out front.

Kevin circled the block and parked across the road, several houses back. No lights on that he could see. Three-fifteen now. On the passenger seat was a fax of the Hertz rental agreement, forwarded to him from their regional office. The rental agreement gave him her name, her Mastercard number, her driver's license. The rest was easy: Gail Newton, 1462 Clarke St., out in Cicero. Unless he was mistaken, this would be the woman who'd picked David up after his escape and harbored him. That it was a woman encouraged him: at least it matched the sex of Laura's assailant. But a woman meting out premeditated death? Statistically, it was practically a zero chance.

And why murder in a rental car? Surely she wasn't so naive as to think it would somehow shield her identity. Shaughnessy had plugged her name into the DMV system and found the plate of her own car, a red Honda Civic hatchback. Kevin hadn't seen it on the street during his passes, and it certainly wasn't in her small driveway.

She'd given it to David. That would explain his mobility. He looked at the date on the agreement: two days ago. Which was when David had been caught on the security camera outside St. Louis. And last night, from Houston, that gas station attendant had seen a man with a red Honda Civic hatchback making a call from a pay phone. It fit.

Or it didn't. Kevin sighed with frustration. Always shimmering in his mind was the possibility that Laura had got the plate wrong—maybe just a number or letter, or maybe the whole damn thing. Her testimony was not likely to impress a judge when it came time to get the retroactive court order he'd promised the Hertz people. And it was also unlikely that he'd be able to get a wire tap or search warrant. What was he supposed to do, start knocking on doors and talking to neighbors? Screw that.

Softly closing the car door behind him, he crossed the deserted street towards the woman's house. A dog barked from someone's backyard. He touched the hood of the car but couldn't feel any warmth through the metal. *Please, Laura, be right.* As he walked down the side of the house to the backyard, he could see a dull spill of light onto the grass from a window. Crouched low, he rounded the corner. The window was high enough so that he needed to move back a bit to see through it. The top of a refrigerator, cupboards. He ducked down briefly when a woman came into view, but she was not looking his way.

Gail, isn't it a bit unusual for someone to be fully dressed at three-thirty in the morning?

She came up to the counter and her gaze fell below it, to drawers, he guessed, and she seemed to be picking something out, though he couldn't see what.

She was a big, unfortunate-looking woman, heavily overweight, and if someone had asked him if she might be capable of murder, he would have laughed. But Laura had described her as a big woman, big enough to drag a smaller one with ease across the parking lot. Something eerily still about her face as her hands fumbled around the drawer. Skin blotchy and swollen around her eyes, as if she'd been sobbing. Then she turned, but too quickly for Kevin to see what was in her hands. Out went the lights, and then, a few moments later, a dim glow came from somewhere else in the house, washing back into the kitchen.

Kevin looked back along the side of the bungalow. A small square of frosted bathroom glass was lit up now, one of the panes slid open just a notch. He stepped closer, paused to one side, his staccato heartbeat churning up his empty stomach.

He could hear a little. Water running in a sink. The squeak of the faucet being stopped. Then something hard hit the floor. A curdled silence, then a low, inarticulate sobbing that sounded as though it was being muffled through a handtowel. Even so, it was increasing in pitch, and Kevin recognized the sound of terror. His damp hand closed around the grip of his Glock.

He ran back to the front of the house and threw his weight against the door. Three brain-jarring slams with his shoulder and he still wasn't getting anywhere. He fired a shot into the lock, stepped back, and kicked like hell. The door splintered open and he was inside, his whole body ablaze with electricity.

"This is the FBI! If you need assistance call out now!"

The only light was the spill from the streetlamp through the open door, and, down the main hallway, a vertical slash coming from a door ajar. Bathroom. He moved quickly, pure reflex, eyes trying to take everything in, knowing how easy it would be for him to be shot, some pedantic part of his mind running down the Quantico checklist on securing the room before entering. No fucking time.

Outside the bathroom hallway he kicked the door fully open with his foot and fell back against the wall, gun pointing its accusing finger. A sink bright with blood snapped his eyes to it, and red splotches on the pink fluffy carpet. But no one in the room. Jesus.

He turned his face almost directly into the knife's path, but instinctively jerked his head back. Not quickly enough. No pain, only a seeping wetness across his left cheekbone, eye suddenly awash. But he could still see her, blood shimmying down her own slashed forearms as she came at him again with the carving knife.

Left hand clamped instinctively to his wound, he staggered back and swung the gun up to Gail's chest.

She stumbled, landing on one knee, the knife jumping from her slick fingers. She patted one puffy hand towards it along the carpet, but Kevin stepped forward, caught the knife behind his heel, and kicked it down the hallway.

"You get out," she said weakly. "Get out of here."

She was trying to push herself back into a sitting position, and succeeded in slumping against the wall. Shivering violently, she stared perplexed at her own wrists. In the shadow of the hallway, through the blood in his eye, it was hard for Kevin to tell how deep her wounds were, or whether she'd cut across the veins or parallel. Across, she'd be fine; parallel, there was a chance she might bleed to death.

He took several steps back and pulled out his cell phone and called 911.

"Get some towels and wrap up your wrists!" he told her, but she just sat there. He wanted to check his own face but didn't want to step past her to get to the bathroom. Even weakened, she was big enough to topple him if she threw her whole weight against him. He looked at his left hand, awash with blood, and put it back over his cheekbone, pressing hard.

"Shit," he muttered. "Gail! Get up!"

She seemed to be asleep. He snapped the handcuffs off his belt, planted his feet wide so she couldn't pull him off balance, and started to manacle her. Stirring sluggishly, she made a halfhearted attempt to push him away. Both loops snapped into place. With relief he saw the slashes were across her veins, slowly pulsing blood. He backed up, blinking to clear his vision.

Behind him, a darkened doorway. He put his hand around the corner and flipped on the light switch. Took a peek. A bedroom. Bed near enough the door that he could dip into the room and snatch a couple of pillows. He'd started pulling off the pillowcases for bandages when his attention was pulled up above the bed.

A large painting hung there, and even though much of the face dropped down grotesquely like ribbons of flayed skin, it was obvious it was a portrait of David Haines.

* * *

On the photographic paper: three parallel columns of DNA fragments, arranged by length into ladders.

Rachel.

David Haines.

Sean.

Laura sat hunched at her workbench, staring.

A child got exactly one half of each parent's DNA. Every fragment of DNA Sean had should be traceable back to one of the parents. There shouldn't be a single piece unaccounted for.

She scanned it into the computer, and then did it herself by eye, twice, just to make sure.

Then she turned off the lights of the lab and went home to sleep.

CHAPTER TWENTY

He sat down beside her bed on the only chair.

"I want a lawyer."

"You'll get a lawyer, Gail, that's no problem. As soon as we get you into the lockup, there'll be one waiting for you. You don't have to say anything until then. But there are a few things I want to tell you."

The hospital staff had bound her wounds and tethered her forearms to the siderails. Outside the door stood a security guard. In the corridor, a nurse had told him that Gail had contemptuously refused a unit of blood, as well as painkillers and antibiotics. Seeing her there on the hospital bed, her skin sickly pale but livid and swollen around the eyes, withered blue lips, Kevin pitied her, even though she'd tried to slash his face just a few hours ago. He'd been lucky: all he'd needed was twelve stitches and a tetanus shot. Less than an inch higher, the doctor said, and he'd have lost his eye.

Gail wouldn't look at him.

"It's not going to go well for you, Gail. We've got Dr. Donaldson's eyewitness testimony. She *saw* you, she *saw* your license plate. That's how we found you. We've got the stun-gun, too. Our team's going through your house. I talked to them just a few minutes ago. Know what they've found? Your scrapbook, Gail. The one you started when David was first caught, all the photos and news clippings, and then, on the last page, that little bit of David's hair, taped down and dated two days after his escape. So we know you were harboring him. Attempted murder, harboring a known fugitive. That's really serious, Gail."

He was hardly expecting her to collapse into a tearful confession, but he figured it wasn't a bad idea to start off scaring the shit out of her. He wasn't particularly interested in a confession; he wanted more than that. He wanted to know where David was, and to get that, he would have to convince her to betray him—virtually impossible in the short space of time he had.

Looking at Gail, it wasn't difficult to imagine a life raw with disappointments and loneliness. He felt another pang of sympathy for her. He could see how it must have started. She would have sent him a letter, and David would have seen something, some kind of hunger he could shape. And before Gail even knew it, she'd have sensed her chance to finally be special, to believe in something that would haul her clear of the neglect and derision she'd suffered, and make her part of something rare and glorious and holy. But it was David who held it all in place for her. Remove him, and it would all come down. She didn't slash her wrists because she'd failed God; she did it because she'd failed David. And feared he was never coming back.

He imagined her own sense of loss—like the aftertaste of the medication he'd taken during his long depression, wondering how many pills he'd have to choke back to escape the terror of his waking hours, forever. If it hadn't been for his daughter, maybe he would have entertained the whispers in his head, turned whimsy into action. Again he looked at the bandages binding Gail's wrists, and felt a visceral shudder.

"I know you didn't want to kill her," he began. "David's a very charismatic man, a very smart man, and he gave you something to believe in. I think I know why you wanted it. I can relate, I really can. I've spent a lot of my life wanting to believe in something good. When I was younger I joined a group out west, and a big part of the attraction was the chief elder, Elder James. Amazing man, smart, devout. I thought, if a man like that believes there's something to it ... He *made* me believe, just through who he was. I believed everything. Putting kids in the cellar all night for punishment, okay by me. Beating his five wives, okay too. Jews and Muslims Satan's ambassadors, fine by me. The plans to take over the whole damn island and kill everyone else just before the end time so we'd be safe—seemed good sense. There was a family there, with two small kids, and one of them, Jacob, got sick, very sick. Elder James wouldn't let them take him to a doctor, said if they did, they weren't welcome back. And he died, that little boy, and I thought that was okay, too. Just part of God's plan. It's amazing what you can make yourself believe, isn't it?"

He forced himself to pause, to catch his breath, surprised at the bitterness that had crept into his voice. But he was talking now, unable to stop the hot rush of words.

"I never saw it on my own," he said. "Know when it finally happened for me? I was driving a van back to the farm one night, the roads were wet, I was tired, and I flipped the van. Broke both my legs. At the hospital, I told them to call Elder James. You know who came to pick me up? My mother. Elder James couldn't be bothered with me, now that I was laid up. The time I'd take to heal, I'd just be a drain to them, so he wrote me off."

It was not an admission he made often, even to himself. It seemed to him to indicate a huge weakness of character, but here he was telling it to Gail Newton because ... she was a fellow sufferer, a victim like him, and he hoped it might help bring her away from David.

"I trusted him, Elder James, I certainly loved him, and he betrayed me. He wasn't worthy of all my love and trust, just like David isn't worthy of yours. 'By their fruits ye shall know them.' David's are rotten, Gail. He kills people. He asked you to kill, and you didn't want to, not in your heart. I can tell just by looking at you now. And I bet you think you failed him, don't you. But he's the one who failed you. He tricked you, used you. And I don't think it's fair for you to go to jail while he takes off in your car to Mexico. It doesn't have to be that way."

She closed her eyes.

He uncrossed his legs, stood and walked to the foot of her bed, his vision constricting momentarily with fatigue and hunger. "As soon as the doctors say you're ready to go, we'll be taking you down to the field office. We'll take your picture, do prints, and then you'll be formally charged. You'll be in a cell in the courthouse until your arraignment hearing. You won't get bail. After that it could be months before your trial."

Nothing. Maybe she was smarter than he thought. A lawyer could claim she'd never set eyes on David Haines, that the stun-gun was a weapon of self-defense, that Laura Donaldson was an unreliable witness. That he, Kevin Sheldrake, had trespassed in her home, and she'd slashed him thinking he was a thief.

He looked at her bandages. "You're right about one thing. He's not coming back. He's washed his hands of you. You couldn't kill for him. You couldn't even kill yourself. You even screwed that up."

Her eyes flickered open, filled with hatred. Good.

Kevin forced a laugh from his throat. "Come on, Gail, those weren't serious cuts. You could've gotten take-out and driven yourself to the hospital before you bled to death. You weren't going to kill yourself. You just wanted him to feel sorry for you. But he doesn't. He doesn't think of you *at all*. He's not coming back, and why would he? You sheltered him when things were hot, you bought him his rifle, clothes, food. He's got your car, Gail. He's set. That's all he wanted from you."

He sighed, compressed his mouth into a mask of regret. "I'm sorry, Gail, but you're going to have to get used to hearing the truth now. He couldn't've cared less about you."

He felt grimy doing it: for all he knew, David had treated her well, never lied to her, never made her promises. But he had to bet there was at least some deception on his part, and a huge amount of self-delusion on hers.

"You actually thought he'd love you? What were you thinking, wedding bells, a nice honeymoon in South America? A little beach house made of palm leaves?"

"I don't want to talk to you!" she said.

"You don't have to talk to me, Gail. I'm doing all the talking. I'm just trying to think of what he'd tell you. Oh, let me guess, that you were beautiful on the inside, and that's all that mattered, that you had a good soul, that serving God was all you had to worry about, and shouldering your cross as best you could. You fooled yourself into thinking he *cared* about you, but Jesus, Gail, let's be honest here. Look at yourself! What would induce him to fall *in love* with you?"

"You go to hell! Get out!"

Her mouth clamped shut like a cage, chest heaving, face splotched with anger. Kevin made himself count to ten, tried to look contrite, wanting to slam the wedge in all the way, to drive Gail to the point where she'd think: *If I can't have him, no one will.*

More quietly he said, "It's nothing to do with the way you look, Gail, honestly. That's got nothing to do with it. Being beautiful wouldn't've made a difference. All he wants is to get back to Rachel and his son."

Her quick wince seemed less pained than genuinely confused, and for a moment, Kevin wondered if he'd misstepped. At once his mind started leapfrogging back, testing the circuitry of his logic. Gail *had* to be the one who'd impersonated Rachel over the phone. But he doubted Gail had come up with this elaborate fiction by herself: it had to have been fed to her by David, to lure Laura back to the lab. And David would have assured Gail that it was nothing but a story. Now Kevin wanted to make her think it was real. But there was something wrong. Had he fucked up, said too much?

"Come on, Gail," he continued, as calmly as he could, "he told you about them, but you thought it was just a story, right?"

"I don't know what you're talking about," she said.

Oh, Jesus, he thought, *I think she's telling the truth.* But maybe he was only tripping himself up, misreading her. Because if *she* didn't make the calls, who did? He tried to shove it away, not wanting to lose momentum.

He said, "I didn't know for the longest time either, Gail. Big surprise for both of us, huh? Having a kid with the woman who brought him into the New Apostles."

Words shoved through her teeth: "You're a liar."

"It makes sense, really. They had so much in common, the shared purpose, they were both young, good-looking, fervent. Pretty hard to compete with all that, isn't it? I guess Sean would be about six now."

"There's no son!"

Kevin snorted and shook his head sadly. "There's more to David's story than what you clipped out for your scrapbook, Gail."

"I would know!"

"Think we spill everything to the media? I've spent years chasing David Haines. And even I don't know everything about him. Know what I don't know? Where Rachel and Sean live. 'Cause I know that's where David's headed. That's only natural, isn't it, to get back to the woman you love, your own son you haven't seen in years? First place I'd go, no matter what, just as soon as I could. Back to the people you love."

Even as he spoke, he felt his lies taking on an uncomfortable but undeniable plausibility. Gail had fallen silent again, but the last of her restraint had seeped away, and her eyes traveled the walls restlessly.

"Gail, you know you're going to jail, don't you? You help us find out where he's going, and we can help you, make sure you get into a good facility, shorten your sentence, make sure you're up for parole faster. We can do that for you, Gail, if you give us just a little help."

She was crying. Good, that was good. A breakthrough. Kevin felt a sympathetic moistening of his own eyes. He pulled a Kleenex and tried to dab her eyes, but she jerked her face away from him.

"I'm gonna be sick."

He took the kidney-shaped bowl from the table and held it under her mouth with one hand, gathering her hair out of the way with the other. When she was finished, he lifted over her plastic cup of water and slipped the straw into her mouth so she could rinse. He was encouraged by the throwing up. It showed anxiety and dismay at the very least, possibly regret.

"All right?" he asked.

She said nothing, but tears continued to stream down her puffy cheeks. She looked like a heartbroken child.

"Your cat's fine, by the way," he told her. "We gave it to one of your neighbors to look after for the time being."

"She liked him," Gail said miserably. "David." And her eyes suddenly screwed tight and she was sobbing.

Kevin sat back and waited, wondering if he should have brought up the goddamn cat. Her nose streamed, and this time, she allowed him to wipe it with a tissue.

"I didn't want to do it," she sniffed. "I did it because ..."

"You wanted to please him, I know."

"But I couldn't. I turned the wheel. At the last moment I closed my eyes and turned away, and when I looked back and saw her moving, I was ... relieved."

"You did the right thing."

Looking him face on for the first time, she said: "He never told me."

"Where he was going?"

"About her, and his son."

And again, he believed her. But if Gail hadn't made those calls to Laura, then who? The possibilities scrolled out quickly. Another of Haines's accomplices in Seattle? A bloody-minded prankster? Rachel—the *real* Rachel?

"I know, Gail, being betrayed is ... it's very upsetting. And if you know anything about—"

"He wouldn't tell me. He never told me anything."

"When did he leave?"

"Three days ago."

"Have you talked to him since he left?"

"Yes."

"When was that?"

"Same time he talked to you." She sniffed, as if pleased to surprise him. Kevin felt an unpleasant sandpaper stroke of electricity across the back of his neck.

"I don't understand."

"That time he called you early in the morning. Don't you remember? You talked long enough with him."

"I remember. He was in Houston."

She shook her head, almost eager now, maybe finally realizing that she had nothing to lose. Or maybe just glad that she'd done something deserving of attention, of a man's full and undistracted gaze. "Nope, Lincoln, Nebraska. That was me. I made it so it looked like he was calling from Houston."

"How'd you do that, Gail?" He tried to keep his voice conversational, admiring, even as he felt a fist closing around his guts.

"From work. At Ameritech."

"You're an operator?"

"International directory assistance. I can get pretty much anyone's number. I gave David lots. His brother's. Yours."

There was something almost brazen about her divulgences now, the same kind of loathsome, barely concealed glee he saw on television talk shows when the guests aired their misdemeanors for the nation. *I slept with my daughter's lesbian lover! I slept with my pets! Look at me. Look at me up here. I transmit therefore I am.*

"And you could make it look like David was calling from Houston when he was really in Nebraska." Jesus Christ.

"Well, I needed someone in Houston to place the call first."

"Who's in Houston?"

She shrugged. "He never told me names, so there's no point your asking."

Nebraska, why the hell Nebraska? He projected a map against the blank hospital wall. From Nebraska, where else could you go? Well, pretty much fucking anywhere, north, south, east, west. But assume he's not going to backtrack, he's on a straight trajectory from St. Louis, the last place he was seen. Wyoming, Montana, north across the Canadian border—wasn't the smartest thing to do, but maybe he had someone waiting for him on the other side. He got mail from Canada, one of the correspondence officers had remembered that much. And if not Canada, then he could always go farther west to Washington State. Seattle.

Traveling to Seattle to find Rachel and Sean. No, that was bullshit, had to be. But why was he going to all this trouble to misdirect everyone: somewhere he had to get, something he had to do?

"Gail, do you have any idea why he'd be in Nebraska? Were there any other of his followers around there? People who could've helped him?"

"He's going to them, isn't he," she said, and her face crumpled again. "He's going to them and he's never coming back, never, ever, ever." Like a child reciting a mantra of heartbreak, thrashing her head from side to side on her pillow, wrenching her tethered arms against the metal rails. He wanted to ask her more, but her weeping seemed unstoppable, and all he could do was pat her arm and lie and tell her it was going to be all right, until the nurse came with a sedative.

* * *

"I think he's heading for Seattle."

Racing along the JFK, cellular to his ear, Kevin shoulder-checked, pulled into the left lane one-handed, and shuddered alongside the eighteen-wheeler.

Hugh's voice stuttered over the line, and Kevin squinted to hear him. "Kevin, he's in Houston."

"Look, I grilled Gail Newton. She's an operator for Ameritech. That time Haines called me from Houston, she just made it look that way. He was in *Nebraska*."

He passed the truck, and the line cleared so that he could actually hear Luna panting in Hugh's office.

"Kevin, he killed a doctor three hours ago. In Houston. I just talked to Mitch."

"You've got him?"

"No, but we have an eyewitness who saw him fleeing. Mitch thinks we'll have him in twenty-four, tops."

"No. He has an acolyte in Houston."

"Says who?"

"Gail. The acolyte made the call from Houston, and Gail just patched it through to Haines in Nebraska. He's the killer."

284

"How d'you know Gail's not lying to you? Come on, Kevin, we have a *body* down there. We have a witness who described Haines perfectly, down to the bald head. I'm going to go with that over Gail's story any day. And incidentally, her attorney's pissed as hell, said you interrogated her in her hospital bed while she was still recovering—"

"I told her she didn't have to talk to me."

"He said you harassed her. The guard at the door heard you talking for a long time. It's all inadmissible, Kevin."

"It doesn't matter." He heard Luna barking in the background.

"Luna, come here, boy! Lie down, lie down! Sees another dog out the window or something ... Look, Kevin, Gail was just feeding you a line, covering for Haines."

He thought of her tears, the collapsed anguish of her face. He'd known, of course, that she might be lying, but he didn't think she could do it so convincingly. He hadn't thought she was so smart. Was it all a show to get him to divert the whole task force to Seattle?

"I don't know, Hugh. The convenience store in St. Louis, that call from Houston—there was no reason for either of them, except to throw us off."

"It's Gail throwing you off. You're a good interrogator, Kevin, but this woman doesn't have much to lose lying to you."

"She's buying him time to get to Seattle."

"Why Seattle?"

"The kid's real," he said. "That woman, Rachel, from Seattle, she sent hair samples from her and her kid. Donaldson ran paternity tests. I got her a few pieces of Haines's clothing from the evidence room—"

Kevin almost felt he should pause to wait for Hugh's indignation, and he wasn't disappointed.

"You gave her evidence?"

"It was the fastest way, Hugh. She had the samples in hand, she had the equipment, I knew we'd have the results faster than if we sent them down to Crime Lab."

"You're saying they're positive?"

"I'm assuming."

The first thing he'd done when he'd finished with Gail was call Laura. Again and again he'd tried the lab, her father's, her own apartment, and got voice-mail each time. She either wasn't there, wasn't answering, or wasn't able to. Through his anger at her, he felt fear,

but couldn't quite believe she'd come to harm. For a moment he'd
wondered if the tests were negative, and she'd been plunged into a
depression dark enough to hurt herself. It had taken him twenty-five
minutes to get to the lab and get security to open it up. Not there.
He'd driven back to Gold Coast, to her father's apartment, and got
the superintendent to let him inside. Not there either, and neither were
any women's clothes. She'd packed up.

"I talked to the doorman at her father's building, and he said an
airport limo arrived for her around ten-thirty. If she's heading for
Seattle, it means the tests were positive. The kid's real."

"If there are test results, we'll need our people to look at them first,
Kevin. We can't just take her word for it."

"I trust her."

"Yeah, and she didn't even call to tell you the results. Look, if it
makes you feel better, I'll put a call in to Fred Werner out there. We
can try to get her picked up at the airport."

"I've already got Shaughnessy calling airlines, trying to find her
reservation. I'm almost at O'Hare."

"Kevin, I'm sending you down to Houston."

"What?" He braked suddenly, almost rear-ending a minivan.

"I just talked to the Attorney-General. The President's going ahead
with this amnesty deal. They want Haines alive. And I want you down
in Houston, heading up the task force."

A smile soared across Kevin's face—nothing sweeter than finally
being vindicated, finally being fucking appreciated—and just as quickly
contracted. He didn't know what to say. Twenty-four hours ago, this
would have been the best news imaginable, and he would have gladly
flown down to Houston. But now ....

"Kevin, you hear me? You're back on the task force. I've already
talked to Mitch. Haines is all yours. Just bring him in without bullet
holes, all right?"

"Hugh, I can bring him in, but I don't think he's in Houston."

"Just get yourself on the next flight down, okay?"

Through the windshield, he could see a wide-bodied jet angle
steeply into the sky. Shit. This was not a decision he wanted to make.
A chance to head up the task force, take back the position he should
have had from the start ...

He said, "I'm going to Seattle."

"This is not a request——"

"The kid's real, and if David knows where he is, he's going to kill him, just like he did Rick."

Hugh sounded openly exasperated now. "But he's not *there*, Kevin. He's in Houston, he's killed a doctor, he's been sighted twice, and he's not getting out. That's why you're going."

Kevin winced. "If I go, I'll lose David, and I'm not going to do that. I'm sorry."

"I hope you know there are going to be serious consequences from this——"

"I know, and ... sorry, Hugh."

He hung up, hoping he hadn't just made the worst decision of his career.

*　　*　　*

At her departure gate, Laura called the Tijuana clinic, but Sandra wasn't picking up her phone. She was just having some routine tests, the nurse at reception told Laura. Call back later, please.

Routine tests. Laura didn't even want to imagine what the resident alchemists down there considered routine. A little bleeding with leeches maybe, or the application of dead pigeons. For a few more moments anger coursed through her, then spent itself, leaving only a sickening worry for Sandra. She'd have to call from Seattle—she didn't feel like having a conversation on the plane, wedged between other passengers.

In the lounge she took a seat and stared blankly at one of the many television monitors. Shifting restlessly, unable to get comfortable. Who the hell designed these chairs, the Marquis de Sade? She crossed and recrossed her legs, foot pumping. She felt jittery, like some infernal wind-up toy, and didn't know if it was the spiteful withdrawal of the speed or some aftereffect from the Taser. Her fingers reached up to the gauze pad on her right cheek. When it healed a bit she could lose the pad and at least mask it with foundation. She wondered if it would leave a scar. She must look a sight. Self-consciously, she scanned the lounge, but everybody's attention was fixed on the televisions. She looked.

Swirling lights, yellow police tape, a shattered dining-room window. Houston. Another doctor ... oh my God, it was Vikram Chaudhuri, a hematologist she'd worked with briefly back in grad school. She stood, moving closer, face rigid with disbelief. He was shot through his window, early this morning, having breakfast with his wife and daughter. Right there, in front of them. Laura shut her eyes, afraid they might show his family, not wanting her imagination to start recreating the horror of that moment. It was David Haines, she heard the television reporter say. A paper delivery boy saw him fleeing the scene.

She sat back down, mouth parched. Well, she knew one thing at least. Haines was in Houston. Nowhere near Seattle, nowhere near Rachel. She was safe.

But how long did it take to drive from Houston to Seattle? Two days? Much less if you drove without sleep. The fact was, Haines didn't know anything about Rachel, or her child, or where they lived. So what was the risk?

But she remembered Rick Haines, his throat opening up from that single rifle shell.

She remembered the weariness of Kevin's face, asking if there was a note from Rachel inside the envelope. He'd made good on his promise. He'd got her Haines's clothing, didn't stop her from finishing the paternity tests. But if she told him about her rendezvous with Rachel now, how did she know he wouldn't shunt her away from it, swoop down with some paramilitary team and make Rachel vanish? The only thing stopping the FBI was that they didn't know Rachel's real name or address or phone number.

And neither did she, yet. And the only way anyone was going to get it would be if she checked into the Sea-Tac Airport Hilton and waited for Rachel to call.

What if Rachel's wrong? What if Haines does *know about the boy?*

She looked at the clock. Her flight would start boarding in a few minutes. If she called ... could he simply notify the airport and have security come and detain her? Maybe she should wait and call him from the plane, or even better, once she was in Seattle.

She took out his business card, flexed it between two fingers, then slid it back into the Filofax, clamping it shut with both hands. *Don't think about it. Just get on the plane and do what you need to do.*

Shit. She couldn't. It wasn't right. It wasn't fair to Kevin. Worst of all, if she didn't tell him, she might be putting Rachel at risk.

At the pay phone she dialed and heard the crackle of his mobile as he picked up.

"It's Laura."

"It was positive, wasn't it?"

She sniffed, surprised. "How'd you know?"

"I'm thinking there was probably a note in that envelope, with her address in Seattle."

She was already sorry she'd called. "There *was* a note," she confessed hurriedly. "But she didn't give an address or phone number. She just told me to check into a certain hotel and wait for her to call."

"Okay, listen to me. There's a chance Haines is heading for Seattle. I caught the woman who tried to kill you. Now, she might be lying to me, but I doubt it. Haines was in Nebraska about twenty-four hours ago. That's plenty of time to get to Seattle."

"But Rachel said there was no way——"

"He had an Ameritech operator as an accomplice. If he knew Rachel's real name ... he could have found anyone on the goddamn continent with a phone."

She looked helplessly at the television. "But what about the news? They're saying he's in Houston."

"I know, and maybe they're right, but it's not a chance I'm taking."

Over the PA system, she heard her flight called for boarding, and the announcement seemed to reverberate bizarrely over the phone.

"I'm going out there," she said.

"I was counting on it," he replied. "I'm going to need you in that hotel to take her call, and then I'm going to go get her."

"With me."

He said nothing.

"You need me," Laura reminded him, "you need me to take that call. She's only going to talk to me. Anyone else answers and she'll hang up."

"It won't matter once we get a trap-and-trace. She calls, we know where she lives."

"Not if she calls from a pay phone. Also, I haven't told you what hotel she wanted me to check into."

A weary chuckle was not what she'd expected. She was braced to withstand a flare of anger and a stern rebuke, even a promise of criminal charges.

"Laura, I'm trying to protect you." She felt herself soften. He sounded so worn-out. "We don't know if Haines is on his way. Maybe he's already there, and killed his son. Maybe Rachel's his devotee, and they've cooked this thing up together to kill you."

"I believe her."

"You believe her because you want to."

"Fine."

"You've got to help me protect you."

"I don't want protection. I want you to help me meet her so I can take her son's blood. You promise me that, and I'll tell you the name of the hotel."

"How do you know I won't break my promise?"

"You didn't last time. Look, I've got to board now."

"Look to your left."

She turned and saw him walking towards her, one hand holding the cell phone to his cheek, the other holding a boarding pass.

"We're on the same flight," he said.

*   *   *

He'd be in Seattle in twenty minutes.

After he'd joined the New Apostles, he'd seen less and less of Rachel. Day by day his fervor had grown. *Why have you been so unhappy?* they asked him. *Why doesn't your life have any meaning?* As if they could see inside him some vast tundra of despair, and they were right.

Rachel seemed to spend most of her time in the city, recruiting and fundraising, while he stayed up at the farm, learning: the Bible flooded him, a baptismal deluge. They made him a Shepherd within a year. Soon enough he saw Rachel for what she was. The church used her as a fisher of men, and she was good at it, connecting with people, showing them all that they could have if they only left the world behind.

Yes, he'd been jealous at first, had seen, at the weekend retreats, how she spent time with these wary young men, and he could guess what they did in their stolen time together. But already he felt a distance from it all. She was the channel that had brought him onto the path of glory; the means seemed not very important.

He'd been there a little over a year when he started having misgivings about Father Abraham's doctrines. The megalomania of his claims grew and grew until they were so transparently idolatrous that David was amazed the others could respect him. Abe preached that he was the Holy Spirit enfleshed, come to prepare them for the New Jerusalem. He preached that the New Jerusalem was located not on this planet, but another, and at the end time the souls of the faithful would be shuttled there. He preached that he must father the children of a new and final tribe of Israel.

Rachel was one of the women chosen for this task. David remembered how, during dinner up at the farm, Abe would come and summon her openly to his bedroom, and she would bow her head in humble consent, finish her meal in silence, and go to him. Each time, he tried not to watch as she left the room, tried not to imagine what was to follow.

Was it a desire to attack Abe's authority, or merely a reawakening of his old, violent lust that made him do it? It was fall, and one night, he waited outside the farmhouse until she emerged and began walking back to the women's quarters. Up until that moment he hadn't known what he would do.

But seeing her, he'd been seized with a terrible, rapacious hunger.

She submitted to him in the grass, her arms loosely twined around his neck, but without any signs of either pleasure or indignation. How quickly she'd become a whore. As soon as he was spent, a glacial shame filled him. He'd worked so hard to free himself of these hideous appetites, and he'd fallen. He started to sob, and she touched his cheek with a kind of detachment that maddened him all the more, and told him it was all right. Sounding so tired. She'd been turned into a whore, and she hadn't protested, just submitted to it from Abe. From him. He slapped her hard, turned, walked away.

Two months later, she was gone, disappeared one night while working in the city. Back at the farm, Abe told everyone during a gathering that her soul had blackened, she had fallen away from them, given in to her carnal appetites. David wasn't surprised, and yet he still remembered that night—a frosty November evening, the trees naked, fields barren, stars hard in the sky—and felt a moment of utter abandonment.

Overnight, it seemed, dozens of rumors had incubated concerning Rachel's departure. She'd run off to become a prostitute. She'd been seized by her parents, who wanted to brainwash her. She was pregnant.

This one he overheard in the kitchen after dinner. Sister Mary had shared a room with Rachel, and claimed that in the last two weeks before she'd left, the first thing Rachel did on waking was hurry to the bathroom to throw up. She'd left with one of Abe's children in her womb. She'd *stolen* one of Israel's own children from them, and Abe was heartbroken. Who was to know she wouldn't have it aborted?

Listening, David didn't know what to think. He told himself it didn't matter, and yet, he couldn't help wondering whether the child she carried, if she carried one at all, was his.

Abe expelled him early in the new year. David had been unable to hide his disapproval of the new teachings. He saw the faith, which had at first so impressed him, being diminished and sullied. This was not what he had changed his life for. He'd left deceit and egomanical vanity behind, and he was not prepared to embrace it in a new form from Abe.

They were straying from the true path, he told Abe. They should stop fantasizing about the end time. There was so much work to be done here on earth, now.

Abe had preached against medical science; he forbade all medicines, held the blood sacred. Yet they were doing nothing to stop the seeping of sin through the world by doctors who, day by day, constructed their own god out of medicine. David thought of his colleagues in medical school, and his professors, and remembered their chilling arrogance, their unholy project to build a towering Babel that would replace God altogether. They'd used words like *sinful* and *moral* to their own blasphemous ends. Denying God's sovereignty, God's existence, day after day, milligram after milligram.

How to make the world hear his cry? A world already so filled with noise and talk and greed? Preaching was pointless. The only way was to give his beliefs substance through action.

Through extinguishing life.

His expulsion from the Apostles, he knew, was only partially because of this new ministry he was advocating. Abe was a coward, and he didn't like David's disapproval, was afraid it would infect others. He was sent away. None came with him.

Only rarely did he think of Rachel as he began his work. He had little doubt of her wickedness, that she had simply used her calling as a fisher of men to indulge her own appetites. Sometimes, in a moment of weakness, he considered trying to find her, but he never put it into action. He would not tempt himself that way. She had disappeared from his mind almost altogether, until last year.

A wrackingly hot day in his cell, supine on his cot, awash in sweat. Too hot even to think or read or pray. It was one of the few times he'd ever turned on his television. He was watching some travel show about the Pacific Northwest and stared hungrily at the sea vistas, the grass, which, even in the grainy black and white of his set, he could imagine as lush green. The locale moved to Seattle, and there were images of the skyline and then a park somewhere, children happily at play.

Perhaps it was the heat's stupefying effect, but when he saw her he felt no surprise, as if it were the most ordinary thing in the world. He recognized her instantly, perched on the edge of a large sand-box, still an attractive young woman, a shovel in her hand, helping a little boy fill up his plastic bucket. The little boy looked up at her and smiled and it was *him* there in the sand. His own face and eyes, his smile, suddenly conjured up before him from long-forgotten family photos.

His son.

The shot couldn't have been longer than five seconds, but so acute was his sense of timeless immersion that when it cut away he grunted in dismay, snapping upright on the cot, as if a better vantage point would bring them back. He was shaking, unprepared for the involuntary rush of love he'd felt, and something else too: pride.

From that moment, there wasn't a single day he didn't think about the two of them, Rachel and his son. She was still Rachel to him, even though he knew her real name. In his early days at the New Apostles, Abe had entrusted him with some office duties, and he'd stumbled across some kind of file, an archive maybe, of old documents from the faithful. He himself, during his baptismal celebration, had symbolically given up his driver's license and Social Security Number—all the things that tied him to the world. He saw Rachel's driver's license, and her real name: Deirdre Mason.

From prison, he couldn't resist asking Gail if she could find Deirdre's address in Seattle, including her name among a list of doctors he wanted to locate. Gail sent back all the listed and unlisted D. Masons in the Seattle area. There were three.

It was for the best, he'd realized quickly. If he had a definite address, he might be tempted to write to her. How he craved it. Rationally, though, he recognized how unlikely it was she'd be sympathetic. She would rip up his letter without reading it, or worse, turn it over to the authorities; all his acolytes would be at risk, and his ministry would be put to a quick end.

Up ahead he saw a gas station with a restaurant complex and pulled into the exit lane. The map he'd bought before crossing the state line had only a cursory diagram of the city; he needed a more detailed one.

Since they'd tried to take his blood, he'd consumed himself with prayers, wondering why God was testing him in such a way. But he understood now. His pride in the child, an earthly thing, a false idol.

He was Abraham, being asked to sacrifice Isaac, only this time he knew there would be no last-minute reprieve.

CHAPTER TWENTY-ONE

They got adjoining rooms on the top floor of the Airport Hilton. Walking through the connecting doorway, Kevin checked the view from Laura's windows (he'd requested rooms without balconies, just as a precaution) and noisily dragged the curtains shut, plunging the room into twilight. When he turned, Laura was standing at the foot of her bed, watching him curiously, as if about to ask what he was doing.

"There's a couple other buildings within shooting distance," he explained. "Rachel sent you here, and I'm not ruling out the chance she's one of David's acolytes. This whole thing could be a setup."

She just nodded quickly and clicked on one of the table lamps. Kevin wondered if she was experiencing the same discomfort he was. Probably it was just him. But the closed curtains, the darkened intimacy of the hotel room, their sudden silence as they'd checked in together and ridden up in the elevator—all of this distracted him like the infuriating persistence of some leering onlooker. As much as he tried to block it all out, he couldn't. Jesus, this was what happened when you stopped dating, when proximity with a woman became a novelty. Granted, he found her a particularly appealing woman. Even the bandage across her right cheek couldn't obscure that.

Now, having explained the curtains, he was at a loss for words, witless as a teenage boy. Boarding the plane at O'Hare, he'd felt some disappointment that their seats weren't together; now he was grateful. Four hours of polite, awkward conversation and even more awkward silence; it would have been too much. He was out of practice.

"Now we wait," he said.

On the flight he'd had plenty of time to writhe internally about disobeying Hugh. It was a career first, and it made him sick—even if he *was* sure David wasn't down in Houston. He'd committed a serious breach of discpline, and he knew it was unlikely Hugh would let it go with just a warning. Rogue agent. Probably there'd be a suspension out of this—another permanent blight on his file, maybe the *end* of his file. It mattered, but not as much as getting David.

On their way in from the airport, he'd called up the Seattle field office and talked to one of the weekend duty agents, Lee Garrity. Kevin had been half afraid Hugh might have called ahead and told them to refuse assistance, but Garrity had readily agreed to set up a trap-and-trace on the hotel's main line. Kevin figured the Hilton probably got hundreds of calls every hour, but if he timed the length of Rachel's call accurately enough, he hoped they wouldn't have much trouble distinguishing it from the others.

"You hungry?" he asked Laura.

"Actually, yes. Thanks," she added, then felt the gratitude was somehow out of place: she was with an FBI agent, not a dinner date. She wasn't even clear who was paying for these adjoining rooms and room service, her or the FBI. Bottom line: she needed something to eat. She'd been offered something deplorable on the flight, some kind of roll oozing mayonnaise and pickles in a plastic flip-top container, with a little tub of cole slaw that smelled as if it had been used as a petri dish for a bacterial culture.

"What do you feel like?"

"Um, is there a menu?" She looked around and spotted it neatly laid out on the side table in a thick, padded brown folder. She felt almost foolish, scanning the all-day entrées, and suppressed a giddy laugh. Stress, she told herself. When Kevin had pulled the curtains, she'd actually *flinched* at the noise, and then, when he'd turned to her, she'd have sworn to God he looked like a hopeful lover, awkward in the sudden privacy. It was ridiculous, of course. She'd thought of it herself, closing the curtains as a safety measure. Just doing his job. She wondered how long they'd be together like this; if they'd actually spend the night here, with that adjoining door wide open like that. Through it, she could see the corner of his bed. She looked away. It all depended, she supposed, on when Rachel called.

She chose a salad Niçoise and Kevin made the call from the phone in his room, just to keep hers free. She'd brought only two carry-on bags: a couple of changes of clothes, and the equipment and compact cooler she would need to take and store Sean's blood for the return trip. She stood looking at her luggage, wondering if there was any point in unpacking. To pass the time, she hung up her two summer suits in the closet and checked on her medical kit and storage flasks.

"You've really got twenty-five grand in there?"

Kevin was standing in the doorway and nodded at her shoulder bag.

"In my purse, actually." She smiled. "It takes up surprisingly little space. I got it in five-hundreds."

"All your own money, huh?"

She shrugged, and said lightly, "What else am I going to do with it?" For some reason, she started thinking about what, given a different life, she might have spent the money on. A down payment on a house, a holiday, things for kids she didn't have—and maybe never would. Not for the first time she thought of Adrian, and knew how foolish she'd been even to flirt with the idea that they might have made a family. Absurdly, she felt her face warm, as if she'd divulged these thoughts to Kevin.

"What're the chances the boy's got the same blood?" he asked.

She sat down on the edge of the bed. "Pretty small, probably."

"And that you can get a cure from it?"

"Well, not a cure," she said diligently. People were always talking about outright cures. "I'm hoping for a *therapy*, which might work for some but not all cancers. And for that I figure I've got as good a shot as anything else." Immediately her thoughts snapped back to Sandra. "I've got to call my sister. Which phone should I use?"

"Mine. Go ahead."

She walked through into Kevin's room, dialed using her calling card, and, to her relief, Sandra picked up after the third ring.

"Hi, I called earlier. They said you were having tests?"

"Hey. Good to hear from you." Sandra sounded sleepy.

"Were you having a nap?"

"It's okay, I'd much rather talk to you." Her words, still thick. Laura wondered if she was doped up. "Are you coming down?"

"Well, I'm actually in Seattle right now, but I was thinking of flying straight down when I'm finished."

"What're you doing?"

"First tell me about these tests you had."

"Oh, just more blood work and a CAT scan and an ultrasound blah blah blah. Half the time I think it's just to keep the technicians busy. Frieda said it's all routine, nothing to worry about."

Laura wondered if Sandra was being straight with her, or if the valor she had to show in front of her kids had simply become habitual.

"How're you feeling? Honestly."

"Okay. I mean, it varies, you know, day to day. Some days I can't even face getting out of bed, other days, I'm out in the gardens most of the afternoon. When it's not scorching. I'm glad you called." There was an almost imperceptible faltering in her voice that put Laura on alert. She could imagine Sandra's face, taut, fighting tears.

"You okay?"

"The bad days are hard." A distinct quaver. "I get scared sometimes, think that I'll always feel like this."

"Today's a bad day?"

"Pretty bad."

She felt a complicated spasm of pity and frustration and impotence. Her sister was down there, probably getting sicker, if she'd only admit it to herself, and there was nothing Laura could do about it—not yet, anyway.

"Is it nausea, or pain?" she asked, fighting hard against her inclination to tell her to leave the clinic, come home, let her set her up with some real treatment.

"Both, but I think the nausea's the worst, and even the things they give me for the pain make me feel sick sometimes."

In her sister's voice, Laura discerned the bewildered helplessness of a child, and she caught herself pushing the phone harder against her ear, as if to force some part of herself over the line to Sandra for comfort.

"How is it right this minute?"

"All right. They gave me something a while ago, and it helps."

"Where is everybody?"

"Daddy and Mike took the kids to the beach for the morning. You *are* coming down, right?"

She couldn't restrain herself any longer. "I've found someone who might have the same blood as David Haines, and I'll get a chance to take some samples soon, maybe even today ..." She faltered, fearing it was futile. "It might be a while, months maybe, but I'm going to ask you again, Sandra: if I could offer you something, would you try it?" She was unable to endure even her sister's brief silence. "Say yes, please."

"You know, Laura, sometimes I'd just like you to be my sister. Not my doctor. My *sister*."

Laura frowned impatiently. "I don't—"

Sandra's good-natured laughter surprised her. "You're really not very good at this, are you? It goes something like this. When I say I feel lousy, you say, oh, I don't know: 'Poor you!' Or maybe: 'You'll feel better soon, there's good days and bad and this is just one of the bad ones. You'll push through it.' Like that, see?"

"Okay, fine," Laura said. "I could *say* those things, but what's the point? I want to *really* make you better!"

"I know, but I feel like for the past two years all I've been is your patient. A patient of the great Dr. Donaldson! A little sideshow in your fabulous career."

Laura leaned forward on the bed, eyes squinting in disbelief. "You are *not* a sideshow in my career!"

"Look, it's just not easy being your sister, Laura."

She was dumbfounded, her mouth agape, trying to shape various words in reply. "Not easy being *my* sister?" she finally spluttered. "And what about me? You think it's easy living alongside your beauty and easy temperament and happiness, and Oscar-winning compassion? Everyone sees you as some big, lush, tropical flower. And I'm a cactus."

She fell silent, ashamed at her childish outburst, and hoped to God Kevin hadn't heard in the other room. "I'm sorry," she said more quietly, but her sister was laughing.

"When we were kids," Sandra said, "I wanted to be just like you, you know. But I figured out pretty quickly I couldn't be."

"Yeah, you must've been grief-stricken. You ended up happy with a perfect family."

"I'm not saying I haven't been mostly happy with my life, but it's hard work. I get the feeling you think it all just fell into my lap, that it's so easy. It's not. Anyway, I have doubts all the time. Surprised?"

Laura said nothing, but she was. The idea of Sandra being jealous of her still seemed absurd. For so long Laura had assumed that her sister was blissfully content with her own life, and quietly pitying, and even faintly dismissive, of hers.

"Maybe I should've done more," Sandra went on, "not been a full-time mom. Done more for myself. And with you it seemed like every few months there was some new degree or Albert Einstein genius fellowship or scientific breakthrough or *something*, and it got so I just didn't want to hear about them. And I made excuses for myself, thinking, well, she doesn't have a husband and kids or a house to keep up, all she has to worry about is herself and her career. But they were just excuses for who I was, and what I'd chosen. And I knew how impressed Daddy was with you."

"Dad? *Our* Dad? The one who fathered us?"

"Sure. He loves you, just differently. And he never expected as much of me, really. It was enough that I was pretty and cheerful, gave him grandchildren, made him good meals."

"Come on, Sandra—"

"With you it's your accomplishments, and he won't be satisfied until you get the Nobel Prize."

"Doesn't seem too likely right about now. If you were back here, you'd see what my so-called colleagues have done to my reputation."

"Probably just jealous."

"I wish."

"Know what I'd like right now?" Sandra said. "You to comb my hair. Remember how you used to do that when we were kids?"

Laura nodded. "Yeah. I even remember that thick pink comb you liked, with the yellow tulips on the handle."

"Yes! It felt so good. Mike does it for a bit sometimes, when I beg, but he gets bored, and he was never as good as you anyway."

"Well, when I get down there, I'll comb your hair as long as you like." Oh God, she was going to start crying if she wasn't careful. "Listen, I'm going to have to play doctor again for just a second. You never answered my question. Would you take it?"

She heard her sister exhale tiredly. "I don't know. I don't know if I want any more experiments done on me. My body's all used up, and I'm used up, too. Right now, I feel I should just keep going with this as long as I can and see what happens. I've already lived longer than everyone said; maybe if I stop it, I'll die. I know you don't agree with it, and you think it's stupid and naive and wrong, but in the end it comes down to faith, really. You have faith in what you do; I'm trying to have faith in this. You'll just have to accept that."

"It's not easy for me, Sandra. But you'll keep thinking about it at least?"

"Yes. As long as you remember we're sisters. Go take your blood, do what you need to do."

"Sandra, you think I can do it?"

"Come on, you hardly need me to tell you."

Laura shook her head in frustration. All those degrees she'd mounted on her office walls: was she trying to convince herself? The scientific articles she'd penned, the citations she'd won, why couldn't any of it dam up the unceasing current of her doubt? That she wasn't good enough, that she wasn't trying hard enough ...

"Tell me I can do it, Sandra."

"Oh, Laura. If anyone's going to cure cancer, it'll be you. I've never thought any different."

"Thank you."

"You come and see me like you promised!"

"I will."

"You've tired me out," Sandra said. "I love you."

"Love you, too."

* * *

"You didn't order anything for yourself?" she asked, after their room service trolley was wheeled in.

"I'm not hungry," Kevin said, pouring himself a glass of mineral water.

He *looked* hungry. He'd definitely lost weight since she'd first met him. Was he ill? He didn't look unwell exactly, though his cheeks did have a feverish flush. Still, there was something superb about the angularity of his face, the prominent ridges of his cheekbones and brow, which accentuated the deep set of his eyes. Maybe the stress of the case had simply wiped out his appetite. He didn't seem nervous; on the contrary, since their arrival in Seattle she'd noticed an almost preternatural calm about his movements, as if every unnecesary gesture had been eliminated and those that were essential had been foreseen and economically planned. But far from making him seem listless, it just heightened the sense of energy fiercely contained and focused, and you could only catch its blaze through his eyes. She wondered if *her* eyes ever got that obsessive nuclear meltdown look when she was working late at the lab. Probably—especially on speed.

Somewhat self-consciously, she started in on her salad. When she was three-quarters through it, the phone rang. Momentarily paralyzed, she looked at Kevin, who had stood calmly and was nodding her towards the phone, where he'd laid out a notepad and a pen.

"Let's do it," he said.

Intentionally, they hadn't rehearsed, and she was glad, not wanting to sound stilted. She sat down by the phone, forced air into her lungs, exhaled, and picked up.

"Hello."

"You made it."

"I'm here. Thanks for sending out the samples. So when's a good time for us to meet?"

She wondered if she was sounding too breezy, overcompensating for the leaden weight she felt on her tongue. Rachel didn't seem to notice.

"You've got the money?"

"Of course."

"I guess it's simplest to do it out here. It's not a lot of blood, right? He's pretty brave, but he wasn't crazy about his last shots."

"It'll just take a couple minutes."

"I don't have a shift tonight, so you could come by around six. I'll give you directions."

Carefully Laura wrote them down. It was, Rachel said, about an hour north of the city, halfway to Everett.

"You haven't told anyone, have you?"

"No," said Laura, looking at Kevin. "But are you sure you're safe out there? You don't think it would be better if you stayed somewhere else until they caught him?"

"They spotted him in Houston, I saw it on TV."

"Yeah, I saw that too."

"I'm not worried about him. More worried about my ex-boyfriend coming out to hassle me." Rachel gave a small hard laugh, and then, as if worried she'd revealed too much, hurried on. "So I'll see you around six, okay?"

Laura said goodbye and put the phone down, holding it firmly in place for a moment. Kevin was looking up from his watch, jotting down the time span of the call.

"Good work," he said to her, and picked up the phone, in his haste brushing her arm and breast. The contact startled her, and she moved back quickly, and then felt foolish, girlish, hoping he hadn't noticed.

"Sorry," he said. Lifting the phone to his face, he smelled her perfume, still felt the nudge of her breast against his arm. He had to stare at the keypad hard for a split second to remember the number of the Seattle field office.

"Lee, it's Kevin, we just got the call. Here's the times. And the address is ..." He looked down at the piece of paper and read it out.

He hoped Rachel was calling from where she said she was, and not a pay phone. Without a matching home address, they wouldn't be able to run a check on her.

"I'll call Ma Bell and see what they've got for us," said Lee. "I'll be talking to you."

Kevin hung up and spread out his map. It didn't take him long to find the address. He remembered that stretch of road. On the map, it was a whisker-thin secondary route that clung to the shoreline, heading north. He'd driven it plenty of times in his youth, and it was a bit too remote for comfort. He wondered if Rachel had given them her real address, or just a stretch of deserted road where a gunman waiting in the trees might get a clear shot at a passing car. For all he knew, the whole strip might have been developed into a monstrous beachfront subdivision. He doubted it, though. There was a big pulp mill further along the shore, so the air was often tinged with the sepia haze of sulphur. And it was probably still too remote to attract a lot of people from Seattle or Bellingham.

His eyes slid west across the map, across the countless bays carved from the shore, to Cordova Island. He'd always thought it was shaped like a miniature, elongated Britain, with that broad base tapering upward to a point.

Where you found God.

The proximity of Rachel's address to the island would have alarmed him more if he hadn't known God's Children had disbanded several years ago. According to his sources, the compound was deserted, the land sold to a patient developer. Still, it troubled him, that ribbon of water between Rachel and Cordova.

Coincidence. He couldn't quite believe that Rachel would be an acolyte. If all this was just an elaborate plot to lure Laura to her death, it was a hell of a risky one for David. He was giving too much away: the fact that he had a son, and where he could be found. Surely he would have assumed Laura would tell the authorities, and that they might get to Rachel and the child first.

Five minutes later, Lee called back.

"It's a match. The address she gave you goes with the phone number. The account holder's listed as Deirdre Mason."

Thank you Jesus, praise you Jesus—the old words of gratitude from God's Children slid unexpectedly into Kevin's head. He glanced up at Laura, but clearly he hadn't spoken aloud. "Can you get me everything on her, Lee?" he asked. "And do an NCIC, please."

"Sure thing."

He felt encouraged: Deirdre was calling from her home. If you were inviting someone out to be executed you wouldn't give them your home address. You'd send them someplace else, and wait.

"Deirdre Mason," he told Laura. "The address is real. When did she want you?"

"Six."

It was three-thirty now. He knew one thing: he was going to show up as early as possible. If it was a setup, he wanted at least to have the advantage of surprise. *If the goodman of the house had known in what watch the thief would come, he would have watched, and would not have suffered his house to be broken up* ... He blinked away the words of Scripture scrolling through his head. As soon as he got Deirdre's profile, he'd go. If David was looking for them, Kevin had little doubt of his purpose. He would kill that boy, his own son, just as surely as he'd killed Rick.

Fifteen minutes later, Lee called back. "Okay, here's what we've got." He ran through her Social Security Number, her driver's license. "She traded in her Illinois one four years back." Kevin nodded; it seemed to fit. "She's renting, the utilities are under the landlord's name. Works at a restaurant in Everett, Iron Jim's. Two years she's been doing that. Now, there's this. She popped up on the NCIC. Nothing too hardcore, a couple minor drug-related charges from two and three years ago, mostly possession, but she's linked here with a dealer, who turned out to be her boyfriend at the time, says here. Maybe he still is, I don't know. She's got nothing on her for two years. The boyfriend comes up with lots of flashing lights, though. I've heard of him, actually. He's wanted right now, cross-border. And that's about it. You're going out to see her?"

"Yep."

"Need some help?"

"How much you got?"

"Well, me. Sunday and all. Everyone's off."

"I've heard this about the west coast."

Lee chuckled. "Yeah, just let me know if you want some backup. I'm here until eight."

"Thanks, Lee. I'll let you know."

He hung up and turned to Laura. "Looks like our Deirdre has a bit of a troubled past." He told her about the drug charges. "It fits, too. Coming out of a cult isn't easy. You have regrets, doubts about whether you did the right thing. You miss the highs. Drugs get back that euphoria."

"Maybe that's why she didn't want to talk to the police or FBI. Protecting her ex-boyfriend."

"Maybe. Anyway, it's good news. Makes it harder for me to believe she's an acolyte. Drugs sure don't fit into David's theology."

"I'd like to go alone," Laura said.

He'd been waiting for this. He shook his head.

"Just for as long as it takes me to meet her and take the blood. Then you can go talk to her yourself."

"Forget it. You go with me, or not at all."

"But if I turn up with an FBI agent, she'll—"

"What? Tell you to get lost? I doubt it. She wants her twenty-five grand. Sorry, but there's no way I'm letting you go out there by yourself."

His cell phone trilled and he flipped it open.

"Kevin, it's Hugh."

Kevin felt himself tighten, almost wanting to hang up before Hugh told him he was being stripped of his authority, that he was to return to Chicago immediately to face disciplinary action.

But Hugh's voice was calm, even good-tempered. "They just found Gail Newton's red Honda down in Houston. Parked out in the suburbs. He's definitely down here."

"Seems so," said Kevin. One of the first pieces of information he'd got on Gail was the license plate of her own car, and he'd passed that on to Mitch right away, assuming that this was the vehicle David was using. Relief and anxiety pulled equally at his mind.

If David was down there, it meant Deirdre was safe up here.

If David really was down there, Kevin's disobeying orders seemed all the more heinous and, worst of all, futile.

"News gets better," said Hugh. "Once they found the car, they staked out sixteen square blocks, and they think they've got him penned up in a big low-rent apartment complex. Mitch says we'll have him tucked back in at Illinois Correctional by tonight."

"Good, that's good news, Hugh," he said numbly.

"You get hold of Donaldson?"

"I'm with her now in Seattle. The tests were positive."

"So this Rachel's really the mother of his kid?"

"We've already talked to her, and we're going out to see her."

"Well, doesn't look like there's any urgency with her. I mean, you can advise her to find other accommodation if it makes her feel safer, but I wouldn't push it. He's not going to be a problem for her."

"All right."

He knew there had to be more to come, and when Hugh next spoke his voice had an icy formality.

"Kevin, I'm allowing you to finish this because I don't think it's desirable to create any embarassment for our Seattle office. I've put in a call and advised them of the situation, and they've agreed to assist you in this one instance. You talk to the woman, and then hand it over to Seattle. I'll expect you back in twenty-four hours."

"I understand."

He hung up, and saw Laura watching him curiously. He wondered if he looked like a whipped dog.

"They think they've got Haines surrounded down in Houston," he said. "Doesn't look like we'll be needing any backup. You ready to go?"

"It's not even four."

"I know." Despite Hugh's news, he still wanted to go early. He didn't want to take any chances. *Therefore be ye also ready, for in such an hour as ye think not the son of Man cometh.* "Listen," he told her, "they could be wrong about Houston. Even if they're not, this still could be dangerous."

"Now you're trying to talk me out of going altogether?"

"I just want you to be sure." He knew this was all pointless, could tell by her face. Seeing how much she wanted it, how great her faith was in her work, he wasn't about to stand in her way.

"Let's go then," Laura said. As she stood, a breathless constriction seized her chest: her feet suddenly felt incredibly cold, and a tingling began in her toes that seemed calibrated to the hazy whine in her skull. She touched the back of a chair and sat down heavily, panting.

"You okay?" Kevin asked, looking over at her with concern.

"I'm fine. I'm just ... I didn't get much sleep last night."

"You're sure you don't want to stay?"

"No!" She looked up at him, her nausea blotted out for a moment. "I'm coming, just give me a second."

She sucked in air, pushed it out—*again, do it again*—slumped forward, elbows on knees. She could feel the panic, like a pall, hovering on the horizon of her consciousness. Staring furiously at the floor, as through a long tunnel, she was still aware of Kevin standing near her. Simultaneously she wished that he would go away and that he would touch her, touch every part of her, roughly, with both hands, ploughing away all the panic in her flesh.

Kevin looked down at her, her bowed head, and at first was worried that this was some delayed side effect from the stun-gun. But as he looked at her, the rigid hunch of her shoulders, the silent glare at the floor, he could tell it wasn't a heart attack she was fighting. It was pure terror. He saw himself, his legs swung over the side of the bed first thing in the morning, depression vised against his temples, wondering what the point was of planting his feet on the carpet, taking one step, then another, each one exponentially more pointless, and why not just give up?

He touched her, not with companionable concern on the shoulder, as he'd intended, but just above her ear, the tips of his fingers following the sweep of her hair down towards the nape. When he'd touched her skin there, he pulled back his hand, surprised and appalled at what he'd just done.

She was looking up at him.

"I'm sorry," he said.

"No, no, it's okay."

"You all right now?"

She nodded, stood up, and walked to the bathroom.

Door locked behind her, she changed her bandage in the mirror, then hesitantly touched the place Kevin had. What a hag, with her own personal oozing sores. But he'd touched her. The sheer surprise of it seemed to have evaporated her panic, though she still felt its aftergrip in her chest and head. She wanted to clear it away, bleach it clean. In her purse was the vial of phenmetrizine, two 10 milligram pills rattling around at the bottom. She tipped them out onto the counter, ran a glass of water, and popped them onto her tongue.

Look at you. It's pathetic.

But I need it. To get where I want to be. And without it, am I good enough?

She tried to pool all the good things together. Gillian Shamas telling her across the television screen to keep going. Sandra saying, "If anyone's going to cure cancer, it'll be you." Kevin touching her on the back of the neck. Trying desperately to convert these things into some kind of balm, felt it failing, but ...

Fast, before she could change her mind, she spat the pills into the toilet and flushed.

CHAPTER TWENTY-TWO

The Old Samish Road snaked northwards, an ancient two-laner crumbling away into gravel shoulders, flanked by ditches overgrown with high grass and wildflowers. To his left, through the trees, Kevin caught the occasional glimpse of water and the low, bristled humps of the islands. Cresting a rise, he made out Cordova, still hazy in the distance, Mount Morrisey crouching above the steep pine edifice of its south coastline.

He drove with the window rolled down—a novelty after the asphyxiating humidity of Chicago—and a fresh breeze slapped at his arm and cheek. The tang of the trees, the promise of the ocean: he was startled how much memory was packed into these smells. From Sea-Tac he'd taken the I-5 up through Seattle, and was amazed how little he'd forgotten. Despite some highway work, and a lot of new construction, the vistas were the same, stamped into his memory forever, and his hands on the steering wheel seemed to remember the very curves of the road, his eyes anticipating the next view.

At O'Hare he'd walked onto the plane with nothing but the clothes on his back, his wallet, his Glock and two magazines clipped to his belt, and he'd felt strangely exhilarated—despite, or hell, maybe even *because of*, his argument with Hugh. Now, driving alongside the ocean, this sense of release was twinned with an electric anticipation. It wasn't just the thought of meeting Deirdre Mason. It was something else, something more. His eyes swept the trees, hoping for another glimpse of Cordova.

"You grew up out here, didn't you?"

Surprised, he glanced over at Laura, wondering when he'd mentioned it. "Yeah."

"It was in one of those books about the case. *Dark Angel*, I think." As if anxious to explain, she suddenly added, "When we were trying to get Haines's blood, we had our researcher put together a big pile of material on the case."

Did this mean she'd been reading up on him? Vain to think so: probably she was just being exhaustive in her research. That was the kind of person she was.

"It's not the greatest book," he said. "A lot of the information is wrong."

Still, he was pleased. At the close of the case, he'd become a minor celebrity, but his own enjoyment of it had been eclipsed by his black dog depression. Had she read about that, too? It wasn't in the *Dark Angel* book, but a few months after Haines was caught, a feature writer at the *Tribune* had done a follow-up story and found some prick at the Bureau or the police who'd fed him stuff about his depression and failing marriage. Kevin was still convinced it was Seth Michener.

"I guess Haines pretty much made your career," she said.

"The opposite, more like it," he replied with a rough laugh. She looked surprised. She didn't know, then, but he felt a powerful urge to tell her. Out here on the road, under the sun, away from Chicago and work, he wanted to talk. He wanted her to see who he was, for better or worse. "It burned me out. I had to take six months off, terrified of getting out of bed."

She was silent for a moment, face turned away from him, and he wondered if he'd confided too much, embarrassed her, or maybe even repelled her. Just because she was a driven overachiever who'd let herself get hooked on speed didn't mean she liked weakness in others.

"You worked on the case for over two years, right? There was bound to be some kind of anticlimax—depression, too. It's not uncommon."

Laura stopped herself, afraid she sounded too clinical, too politely distant, and that's not what she felt at all. His admission had surprised her, stirred in her a sense of kinship, and a powerful urge to reveal a frailty in return.

"I know that feeling," she went on hesitantly. "Afraid to get up."

"Afraid of screwing up?"

She gave a quick laugh of surprise, and also pleasure. How many people knew that about her? Not her team at the lab, not her family, not Adrian. She'd made it her business never to convey uncertainty. And this man beside her, whom she hardly knew, saw it. Saw *her*.

"Yeah. Afraid I'd never find the cure, that my sister wouldn't take it anyway." And something else she wasn't willing to divulge yet. Afraid that even if she was successful, could heal her sister, it *still* wouldn't be enough to free her from the cold purgatory of inadequacy she'd felt all her life.

"So the speed covers it up?" Kevin asked.

"Probably wasn't speed I needed. More like antidepressants."

"Sounds like both of us are having trouble getting what we want," Kevin said.

"At least you caught Haines. You did it."

"Yeah, but he still had something I wanted, locked up with him, and no court was going to get me that."

"You don't mean his faith."

"Oh yeah."

"That cult you were ..." She wavered over the right word. A member of? Affiliated with? It sounded too much like a union membership. "... *involved* with," she decided. "It was the same kind Haines was in?"

"Similar. The views on medicine and prayer matched, hatred of worldly authority. I like to think mine was a little more temperate when it came to fire and brimstone. And firearms." He looked at her with a grin, then sighed. "Let me guess what you're thinking. Should a person like me be doing what I do? Working with cults, tracking down David Haines? Maybe I'll crack up, get sucked back in."

"It did occur to me," she said. "But I figure you've been immunized. It was twenty years ago, anyway."

"Youthful mistake," he said, not without some sarcasm.

She shrugged. "You left. They were out here, right?" She remembered that from the book, though it hadn't given many details.

He nodded. "They recruited me at the University of Washington. I was a freshman, I didn't know anyone. I was homesick for a home I hadn't had since my parents split up. You've heard about 'flirty fishing'? They get a good-looking woman to glue herself to you. First time a woman had been that nice to me. Scripture goes down a lot more easily with a little flirtation." She laughed with him. "And then there's the whole community thing, the barbecues and weekend retreats and Bible studies. And everyone made me feel unique, special, loved, safe—all that stuff. And I hadn't felt that before really."

Sounded good, she couldn't deny it. Who wouldn't want to feel all those things? Humorously she asked, "So why'd you leave?"

"I didn't."

She looked at him sharply, and he must have seen the alarm and confusion in her eyes, because he laughed apologetically. "I didn't leave. They left me. I wish I could say I saw through it all by myself, denounced the leaders, took half their members with me. But that's not how I got out. Changed your mind about me yet?"

She didn't know what to say. Right now, her curiosity won out. "So how *did* it happen?"

"It was on this road actually."

It was a risky thing to be telling her, and he knew it, but the conversation had achieved a certain momentum, and he didn't want to put the brakes on it.

So he started telling her about how he'd just dropped a bunch of people off in Seattle to fundraise, and was coming back north to the ferry terminal in Anacortes. It was February, night, and it had been raining. He was anxious to make the last boat, anxious to get back to the farm on Cordova. Since joining God's Children, the city disgusted him, its Godlessness, its filth. He was looking forward to pulling down the farm's long gravel driveway and seeing the lights of the big house—*praise you Jesus, thank you Jesus*—and he took a corner too fast. He could feel that moment still, that instant when he knew the wheels had lost their grip on the road. Vehicle horribly light, he was slewing out across the road and crumpling over in the ditch, the side of the door punching in low and gripping his left leg.

And they never came for him.

"Not the most glorious exit," he admitted, "getting picked up by Mom at the hospital. I sure as hell wasn't glad to see her. She'd brought a deprogrammer with her. Not really a deprogrammer, some psychologist she'd looked up at the university who knew about cults, and he just talked and talked at me for about two days until ..." He looked through the trees, caught a glimpse of water. "Until it was just all gone. Until it made no more sense. He was a good guy. I liked him. He helped me get back into school. It's because of him I studied cults."

"But you still want to believe, even after all that?" Laura wasn't sure whether his persistence was admirable or simply perverse.

"I'm not talking about their doctrine, or anyone else's right now. At this stage, I'm still working on the *existence* of God."

God. She didn't even really know how to talk about it, it came with a vocabulary so foreign to her, and so irrational. But she felt the same exhilaration that comes from a really good first date where everything's clicking, wanting it never to stop.

"What would it take?"

He chuckled. "I ask myself that all the time."

"No, really."

"For me, to believe?"

"Uh-huh."

"A sign, I suppose." He looked slightly embarrassed, as if making a childish admission.

"What kind of sign?"

"Oh, something pretty damn big."

"Parting of the Red Sea?"

"Ah, you did go to Sunday school. Sure, that would be good, but they can do so much these days with special effects. There'd be the problem of authenticity. Isn't there some Vegas magician who levitates helicopters?"

"Exactly," she said. "And if you saw bright lights or the heavens part, or heard the voice of God, wouldn't you worry you were having some kind of manic episode, or schizophrenia?"

"Signs are tricky little bastards, I'll admit it. How do you prove things in science?"

"Replication. If I can do an experiment under identical conditions, and get the same result every time, or even ninety-nine times out of a hundred, that's good enough for me."

"Seems fair."

"Sandra thinks she can pray and make herself better. Did you believe that, too?"

"Once."

"So could David Haines be a sign for you? Someone with cancer who can self-heal?"

"It's a teaser, I can't deny it. But he might just be a genetic fluke, as you say. Then again, why is *he* in particular a genetic fluke?"

"What about if *I* cure cancer? Cure it from the blood of a man like David Haines. Is that a sign?"

"I've thought about that one too. Maybe."

"Well, I'll try and do my best for you."

"Thanks," he said with a laugh.

Through the open window, a smell like burning garbage reached his nostrils, and above the trees he could see the yellowish pall of the mill. They were getting close to Deirdre's. The trees were sparser here, and to the left, power lines slouched down off the road to sad-looking little places on unkempt lots. Littered amongst the unmown grass Kevin saw broken toys, stacks of car tires, a toilet, an atrophied Camaro up on blocks, which he thought may have been there on his last visit.

He slowed down, trying to read the numbers on the houses, and then the mailboxes as the trees crowded up more thickly to the road. He missed it the first time, did a U-turn, and came back to the peeling green mailbox. The wheels dropped into the ruts, biting gravel, and they shuddered down the gentle slope of the driveway, weeds and wildflowers swatting the sides of the car. He checked the clock on the dash. It was three-forty.

*　*　*

At the bottom of the hill was a crooked wood-frame bungalow encircled by a mangy lawn that needed mowing. At the fringes of the property, tall grass and weeds took over and melded with the woods on either side, the tall conifers growing thickly all the way down to the water. The drop was steep enough that he couldn't quite see the actual beach, but guessed there must be a path that cut down to it.

From his vantage point among the trees, David checked his watch. It was just past three o'clock.

He'd had bad luck, wasting most of the day checking the other two addresses on his list, both in Seattle. The first, in an upscale suburb, had been the home of an Indian couple with three children, but it was the second that had eaten up most of his time, an apartment in a small building downtown. The buzzboard listed the occupant as D. Mason, but in the end he'd found that it was a Donald.

The Old Samish Road address was his last chance.

After finding the right mailbox, he'd driven on about half a mile until he'd found a salvage yard, and parked in the lot amongst the gutted cars and piles of tires and twisted metal. It was a Sunday, and there was no one around. His knapsack slung over his shoulders, he'd walked back along the road to the green mailbox and slipped down through the woods flanking the driveway.

Now, crouched behind a thick cedar, he watched the bungalow. Out front was parked an old pockmarked Chevy Cavalier, which seemed to fit in with the surroundings, and behind it, a gleaming new Jeep Cherokee, which did not.

The aching hunger in his belly had, over the days, contracted into something as precise and hard as his resolve. The less of the world he took into him, the less he needed, and the less it could exert its pull on him. His limbs felt momentarily light, hollow-boned like a bird's, but he knew he would be given the strength for what was to come. In the past days he had avoided naming it, watching it from the corner of his mind's eye like some silent, hooded stranger he would ultimately have to unmask. *Blessed be God ... the Father of mercies, and the God of all comfort; who comforteth us in all our tribulation ...*

After ten minutes he heard the low drone of a motorboat and turned to see it swinging in towards the shoreline of the property. He stood and took a few more paces through the trees, and saw the tip of a weather-beaten dock jutting out from the beach. At the wheel was a spectacularly overweight man in his fifties, and judging from the gear strewn across the deck of the boat, he'd just been fishing.

He felt his stomach start a slow swirl. He had trouble believing this man and Rachel were connected in any way. And he was too fat to be a cop, an FBI agent, or even a private security guard. Dear God, had he really thought he could find her this way? Seeing her on television like a desert mirage, like a hallucination? She might only have been *visiting* Seattle when the footage was shot. If she'd ever lived here, maybe she'd moved. It was over a year ago. He watched as the man slowly tied up the boat and began hefting his gear out onto the dock.

The sound of a child's voice wafted up to him from the bungalow and his pulse quickened. He slipped back through the trees, closer to the house. A woman came out carrying a basket of laundry and set it down near the clothesline that ran off one side of the bungalow. From his knapsack he extracted his rifle's telescopic site and held it to his eye.

Rachel.

With a twinge of sadness, he saw she'd lost the bloom to her face; there was less flesh on her bones now, wrinkles etched around her eyes, and something hard and bitter about the set of her mouth. She'd cut her lovely red hair short, in an almost mannish cut, as if disavowing part of herself. But he could still see her as he'd known her, as if she were all still there subcutaneously, that eager face turned up to him when he'd first seen her on campus.

He lowered the scope and watched as she started pegging the laundry onto the line: a sheet, small pairs of jeans, T-shirts.

At that moment the screen door flew open and two boys burst out, armed with water pistols.

Two boys.

David stared, confused. Never had it occurred to him that she might have had a second child, or even married. Not the man on the dock, surely. The two children were both browned by the sun, dark hair bleached lighter by the summer. They looked about the same size, surely too close in age to be siblings.

Unless they were twins.

Dear God, please, not two.

"What about your movie?" Rachel called out, her words seeming to float lazily up to him in the trees.

One of the boys said something he couldn't make out, and Rachel cocked her head and said, "Sure, that's fine, but remember, Tyler, your mom's picking you up at five-thirty, so maybe you should finish the movie first, then play outside."

A friend. The boy was just a friend.

Rachel was saying, "Stay away from the dock until I can come down with you, all right? Just around the yard." And the two boys plunged through the grass with their water pistols.

Despite the day's warmth, his fingers felt cold as he assembled the rifle. The pieces didn't seem to fit as easily as he remembered. He pressed the first shell into the breech, laid out six more beside him on the earth, and put his eye to the scope. The boys were moving so much, and the scope pulled everything in so tight, it was difficult to get a good long look.

There you are.

Yes, this was the boy he'd seen in the sandbox on television, and for the second time, an incredible yearning coursed through him. *My son, flesh of my flesh, blood of my blood.* His finger crooked round the trigger.

God of all comfort; who comforteth us in our ...

Look at his face. The radiance of pure, unblemished skin, and the eyes, not just reflecting the light, but seeming almost to project it. How did they do that, look so bright, so unsullied? Abraham did not ask God for any further explanation; he was obedient, even in an act he found so repugnant.

Unbidden, he had a sudden image of himself putting down his gun and walking out from the trees, walking down towards them, and they would see him, Rachel's face slowly transfigured with a smile, the boy running to him excitedly, being enfolded in arms, welcomed home.

He lifted his face from the scope, wiped his slick hand against his shirt. Up in the trees, the cicadas' high-voltage drone made him feel feverishly hot, his throat parched. The man in the boat had not yet emerged from the dock. Maybe the fancy new Jeep was his.

Down on the lawn, his son was playing with the other boy. Just the way he and Rick had once played.

You did what you had to with Rick, and he was your brother. You knew *him, you grew up with him. This boy you don't know, will never know. He is* nothing *to you.*

He'd seen Rick.

When he'd smashed through the sliding glass door to see if he'd hit the doctor, he'd seen his brother, sprawled behind the counter, and his eyes ... He'd blinked, made a sound, he'd still been alive. And he, David, had looked away, intent on the figure of Laura Donaldson hurtling down the corridor to escape. When he'd turned to run outside, he hadn't looked back at Rick. But the image of him lying there, the shape his blood had made beside him on the floor, was still with him.

Now he saw his small son superimposed on the blood, and he clutched at the grunt that threatened to rise through his throat. He squeezed his eyes shut so tightly that coronas of light exploded across the insides of his eyelids, blotting out his own memories. *Don't let this sinful narcissism hinder you. Stop looking. Stop distracting yourself.*

He forced himself to go through the plan once more. Tim Drent had driven down from Alberta in his RV and was waiting for him in Blaine, due north, just south of the Canadian border. He was a handyman; he'd carved out some kind of secret crawlspace beneath the floor where he could hide as they went through customs. Then he'd be safe, for a while anyway. Long enough for Drent to help him arrange a new identity, get fake documents. He knew someone who could do that, he said. Drent would be waiting there for him now, no more than an hour's drive. *Shoot the boy, and your work here is done.*

Scope back to his face.

Be still.

There, there. The crosshairs searing into his son's bright yellow T-shirt. A clearer shot he couldn't have hoped for. The gun dipped off target and he turned his face away and dry-heaved silently against the tree trunk, retched again, as though a fist had closed round his stomach. A terrible wave of weakness swept through him.

He could not do it.

You must do it.

I can't.

Drone of the cicadas, a crow, the distant sound of a motorboat out on the bay, the shush of the wind through the trees.

God help me.

Then another sound: the bite of tires on gravel. He looked over and saw a car wobbling down the rutted driveway towards the house. He pulled the gun back to his cheek and through the site saw Kevin Sheldrake at the wheel, and beside him, the doctor.

Kill them all.

Start with Sheldrake, then the doctor, then Rachel, the man in the boat, and then ...

He had Kevin jittering wildly in his crosshairs. His hands were shaking; he was out of practice. He'd have one chance, and if he missed, he'd just announced his presence, and lost all the advantage of surprise. Without that, someone might get away. His son might get away.

And now he knew what he must do.

He could not kill the boy.

But he could take him with him.

* * *

Laura stepped out of the car.

"Rachel?" She didn't want to use her real name, felt guilty about how much she knew. Deirdre Mason looked to be in her late twenties, a redhead in jeans and a tube-top that revealed sunburnt, freckled shoulders. On her feet she wore platform sandals. She had a nice body, though her upper thighs and hips seemed a bit too squashed inside the tight denim. The setting, her clothes, all screamed trailer trash, but there was something in her bearing as she approached, an intelligence in her eyes, that made Laura think she didn't fit here. Though her skin had a coarseness to it now, Laura could imagine how pretty she must have been more than seven years ago when she'd met David Haines. Judging from the ramshackle house, money was indeed tight. Immediately she understood her demand for the twenty-five grand. She wanted out—to be liberated.

"You're early," Deirdre said, her mouth compressed in displeasure. Her eyes flicked. "You didn't say you were bringing anyone."

"I insisted on coming," Kevin said, "it wasn't Dr. Donaldson's idea."

"You're a cop!"

"FBI."

She gave an incredulous pant, shaking her head. "Jesus, this is exactly what I said I *didn't* want. You promised not to tell anyone." She turned and looked back at the two boys, as if anxious they might overhear. But they'd already lost interest in the newcomers and were charging off behind the house.

"She was worried about your safety, and so was I," Kevin told her. There was a breeze off the water, snapping the laundry on the line, blocking his view of the waterfront. His eyes quickly roved across the darkened windows of the house. He didn't like how wide-open things were. And that Jeep worried him.

"Are both these vehicles yours?"

Stiffly she replied, "The Jeep belongs to my landlord. He's down at the dock, checking out his boat. He keeps it moored here. It's about the only reason he ever shows up. As you can see, he doesn't put much time in on the house. He's just down there. Take a look if you want."

A few steps, and Kevin could see down the slope to the tip of a decrepit wooden dock. A small motorboat was tied up there, and on board was an obese man in his early fifties, absorbed in cleaning the vinyl seat covers.

As Kevin walked back to Laura and Deirdre, the two boys ran past him. They both looked to be about six.

"Hi, Sean," he said to them.

One of the boys looked up immediately, slowing down, and Kevin was taken aback by his face. It was uncanny: the slant of the bones, the mouth, the eyes. He was his father's son, no question. The boy muttered "Hi," and sped up again.

"Are they both yours?" he asked Deirdre when he came back.

"Just Sean. I babysit for a woman up the road on weekends. If you'd come at six, it would've just been me and Sean."

"And it's just you two living here?"

"Yep."

"What about Tom Florczak?"

She snorted, just staring at the ground, shaking her head. "I knew it. My whole life's going to get dug up now, right?"

"I'm not interested in investigating you or Florczak."

"He's gone. I don't know where he is, okay, and I couldn't care less. I haven't had anything to do with him in a couple years. He was a big mistake. One of many in my life."

"Deirdre, look, my only concern right now is that David Haines might find you and your son."

"I told you," she said, turning back to Laura, "he doesn't know about the baby, and he never knew my real name. Anyway, one of the first things I did when I left the Apostles was go unlisted. I didn't want any of those creeps trying to get back in touch with me. Especially Abe."

"He said he couldn't remember you," Kevin said.

She sniffed derisively. "Not surprised. Last thing he'd want is me talking to the Feds. Remember that case a few years back, I read about it in the papers, about that family that said he'd molested their daughter? It was true." Again, she looked back over her shoulder to make sure the boys were out of earshot. "And it wasn't just her. He had this thing about siring the new tribe of Israel, and he picked out a whole bunch of us as his holy wives. There was me, and a bunch of younger girls, fourteen, thirteen, I think one who hadn't even started her period. The parents just let it happen, they thought Abe was one of God's chosen. But it's hard to believe someone's divinely chosen when he snorts cocaine to try and get it up. I didn't tell anyone he was impotent—maybe it was just me—he told me I was unclean, and I didn't have any trouble believing that. But I'd stopped caring. I just wanted out of there. If anyone knew I was pregnant when I left, they must've thought it was Abe's. David included."

She didn't seem to want to talk about her relationship with David at the cult, and Laura was hardly going to press her.

"You didn't want to report him?" Kevin asked.

"See, this is the thing. I just wanted to leave all this behind, this whole sorry part of my life. I want things to change now. That's the only reason I called you. I need the money to give us a boost." She looked fiercely at Laura. "But I didn't want people poking round in my life, and it all getting out in the papers."

"This doesn't need to get out," Kevin told her.

"Near the house, guys!" Deirdre shouted to the two boys, and Laura saw them obediently veer away from the shore. Deirdre watched them for a moment longer. "This is not what I wanted to happen," she said. "I want my son to have a shot at a decent life. And that means not being branded the son of a psycho. Imagine what'd happen to him at school. You know what kids are like. And the teachers, and after that there'll be girlfriends and bosses. Worst thing is what it'd do to *him*. I don't want him worrying he's crazy or no good and start obsessing about it. Because I do enough of that myself already. Every day."

Laura felt a pang of sympathy for her. During their telephone conversations, she'd thought her main interest was the money; now she could see it must have been hard for her to risk her son's anonymity for the money. She was a good mother. Laura hoped the twenty-five grand would be as useful as Deirdre hoped; hoped too that the boy's blood was positive, so Deirdre and Sean stood to earn even more in royalties.

"Are you absolutely sure David doesn't know where you might be?" Kevin asked.

She exhaled tiredly. "Not absolutely sure, no."

"When you left the Apostles, was he attached enough to you to want to follow you?"

"No way. He was puritanical. We ..." Her face flinched in distaste. "There were only two times we had sex, once at the beginning, to bring him in, and then about a year later, it was more like a rape. But he didn't love me or anything. Once he was in, he became more fanatical than anyone. I don't know which was worse, the before or after. When I met him he was a real prick."

Laura couldn't help smiling.

"But he had no interest in me romantically." She seemed saddened. "No one did, really. I was just useful at bringing men in, like a whore. David always hated women, I think. It was a relief for him to do without them. So why would he follow me? Anyway, he's in Houston, right?"

"Yes," said Kevin. "But he has followers. We've caught three so far, but there may be more."

For the first time, Laura saw fear in her eyes. She looked anxiously across the yard at her son.

"You're sure you never communicated with him after he left?"

"No."

"Never saw him, wrote to him, spoke to him on the telephone?"

"No." She looked aghast. "You're saying he'd tell someone *else* to find us and ..."

"If he knows about you and Sean, maybe. I'm not trying to scare you, you just need to know it's a possibility. We may have caught all his accomplices. We just don't know yet."

"Sean, Tyler!" she called out. "Why don't you guys watch that video now. Go on in, and I'll get you some popsicles in a second, all right? Go on, now."

When she turned back to them, her eyes were angry. "So what am I supposed to do about this? You're saying, maybe, some freak might find us one day. How are we supposed to live like that?"

"If you want a new start, I can help you."

"What, like the witness protection thing?"

"If we think there's still a risk for you, we can give you new names, relocate you."

For the first time her face seemed to relax a bit. "You could do that for us?"

"Yes."

Laura looked at him, liking him for the kind tone in his voice.

"So what do we do now?" Deirdre asked.

"That's up to you. If you want, I can put you both up somewhere for the next few days, and by then, we might have a better idea if he has any more acolytes. If we think there are, we can start the whole process of relocating you."

"What about the blood tests?"

"Strictly between you and Dr. Donaldson."

"I think I'd like to go to the hotel. Maybe I was stupid not to go somewhere, but I can't exactly afford a hotel. Can't just disappear from my job, either." She turned to Laura. "Do you mind if we do the blood later at the hotel, when we're settled in?"

"That's fine."

Kevin's cell phone chirruped and he walked a few steps off to answer it.

"It's Hugh. Where are you?"

Give me a break, Kevin thought. "With Deirdre Mason. She's just agreed to let us put her up in a hotel."

"Look, ah, Kevin ..."

The slight constriction in Hugh's voice started the machinery of panic whirring in Kevin's chest.

"... Mitch just called from Houston. It wasn't him."

There was no explicit logic in Hugh's statement, but instantly Kevin knew what he meant. *Oh, Christ.*

"Not Haines? The shooter *wasn't* Haines?"

"He was holed up in an apartment, and Mitch smoked him out. Damn well looked like Haines. Bastard even shaved his head ..." Hugh's voice was soundingly increasingly distant, or maybe it was just him, Kevin, all his attention sucked away from the phone and into the trees surrounding the house, the shoreline, the beach he couldn't see.

"Okay, Hugh. We're going to get Deirdre and her son out of here."

"Um, right, probably best to ... put them into a hotel for a couple nights until we figure out what's going on."

Kevin clicked off. He didn't need to figure out what was going on. The dreadful certainty of it was already swelling within him. He walked back to Deirdre and Laura, and his expression must have been stricken, because when Laura looked at him, her own face instantly mirrored his alarm.

"What's wrong?" she said.

"Get the boys and let's go. David's not in Houston. They just caught the killer down there and it was one of his acolytes. A decoy."

"Oh my God," whispered Deirdre.

From the beachfront came a distant shout, a man's startled "Hey!" and then nothing. In that split second of silence, Kevin felt an asphyxiating pressure in his chest, his vision clouding, all sound obliterated— and then the world came back to him with blinding, deafening clarity, and he was running.

"Check the boys," he barked over his shoulder, pulling his Glock. "Keep them inside with you!"

Blood pounding in his ears, he skirted the side of the bungalow, taking a wide arc to the shoreline so he had the shelter of the trees. He heard Deirdre's cry of dismay from the house at the same moment he saw the two boys down at the dock, one of them being dragged towards the boat by a man with a rifle. The overweight landlord stood at the dock's end, one outstretched hand offering keys to David Haines.

"Sean!" It was Deirdre, with Laura at her side, running for the path that led down to the shoreline. Kevin ran too. Nothing in his stomach for four days, but it didn't matter, he was as light as vapor and just as quick.

"Stay back!" he shouted at them.

Too late. He saw David swivel, the shotgun nestled against his waist. Before Kevin could even shout at the women to get down, he heard the gun's great coughing whack and ducked reflexively. Not hit, no one was hit, and he knew it would take David at least a couple of seconds to shuck out the shell and reload. He ran the rest of the way to Deirdre and Laura, intercepting them at the top of the path. Bordered by high bush, it offered cover if they stayed low.

He grabbed Deirdre by both arms, tight, and braced himself against her hysterical rage, trying to keep her down. She was gagging on air, terror knotting the tendons of her neck.

"Get him back!" she choked. Then, raising her voice to a piercing wail: "David, don't you hurt him! David, you fucker, you let him go!"

"Stay here!" Kevin hissed at her. "Laura, hold onto her, for Christ's sake."

Hunched over, he scrambled frantically down the path towards the dock, shielded by brambles. Halfway down he stood, gun out, sweeping the dock. David had picked up Sean and was stepping onto the boat with him, his back to Kevin. *Good, good, stay like that, just let me get a little closer for the shot* ... Eyes fixed on David, he made it to the foot of the dock.

"Untie it!" David was shouting at the landlord, swinging the gun towards him. The landlord crouched, fingers fumbling with the knot. David had to put the boy down to turn the key in the ignition and take the wheel.

Kevin had a shot and, arms braced, he lined it up. *Shit, if I take it this high I'll get him in the upper back or head—any lower I might hit the kid—just take it for Christ's sake!* He squeezed, and felt the hard, controlled kick of the discharge. He heard a pop of glass and saw the shattered windshield pane of the boat and knew he'd missed.

David whirled, dropping low, pushing the boy out of the way of the long barrel. *God help*—Kevin heard the thunderclap as he hit the wood planks, cracking a tooth, and scrambled up, knowing he had just a few seconds for his own shot. But David was staying low, and had dragged Sean right in front of him for cover. He turned the key in the ignition. The motor turned over.

No, no! Kevin ran, ran even as the boat was tearing away from the dock, not daring to take another shot for fear of hitting the boy. Jump? Should he jump? Too far, he'd hit the water, no good, no fucking good.

"He came into the house!" Tyler was gasping at him. "And he grabbed us."

"Said he'd kill me," the landlord said desperately, his hand still tight on Tyler's shoulder. "If I didn't give him the keys. Oh, God!"

Kevin turned at the sound of Deirdre's and Laura's footsteps hammering along the dock.

"What do we do?" Deirdre sobbed, and he felt her clawed fingers sinking into his arms as she grasped him and shook him with unnatural force. "He's going to kill him, isn't he?"

"We're going to get your boy back," Kevin told her, with all the force he could muster. Then he turned to the landlord. "How much gas in the engine?"

"Not more than a third. Less, 'cause the needle sticks."

"How far can he go on it?"

The landlord was shaking his head. "Maybe up into Admiralty Point, Port Townsend if he's lucky, doubt he'd make it across to the other side. Depends on the current and winds ..."

Kevin was already looking along the shoreline, and a few hundred yards to the north he saw a motorboat tied up at someone else's dock. "What's the quickest way over there?" he asked the landlord.

"Cut through the trees, across the lots. It's the Walshes'."

He looked at the landlord's gear on the dock. "You got a pair of binoculars?"

"Yeah."

"I'll need them. And the make and serial number of your boat." He snapped out his pad and pen and wrote it down, never letting his eyes stray too long from the water, where he could still see the boat, quickly getting smaller as it headed deeper into the bay and the mosaic of islands. Another ten minutes and he'd lose sight of it altogether. The sun was starting its afternoon descent, firing the water's surface into a searing web.

He took the binoculars from the landlord and started running back up the path.

"I'm coming!" Deirdre said.

"You're staying! Call the police and tell them what's happened, the make of the boat, where it's headed. I need you to do that, Deirdre. I'll get your boy back." And looking at her stricken face, he knew he was going to stop at nothing to make good on that promise. *The God of all comfort; who comforteth us in our tribulation ...*

"You need me," said Laura, running alongside.

"No." He'd been an idiot to bring her with him, a civilian in a breaking field investigation—it shattered every rule in the book. He certainly wasn't letting her get into that boat and within striking distance of David's rifle.

"You promised me."

"Different now."

"Look, if someone gets hurt, you'll need me."

He said nothing, thinking of the boy, thinking too, surprisingly, of David.

"You'll want me over there," she said again, insistent. "I can help."

He made no reply but gave a quick nod, and together they ran through the trees, towards the boat.

CHAPTER
TWENTY-THREE

He looked over his shoulder, saw the shoreline receding swiftly, Sheldrake and the doctor and Rachel, motionless as statues. He felt a surge of jubilation, to see them shrinking away, hear the roar of the engine and the slap of water against the boat's sides. He hadn't driven a boat since the summer before med school, up at the cottage his family always rented, but it had all come back to him.

Now he looked down at his son, hunched on the seat beside him, stricken face turned back to the shoreline. He saw that the front of his shorts was dark with his own urine. David looked away in distress, wanting to say something kind, something to assuage his fear. How did you explain to a child that what happened here, right now in this world, didn't matter at all? What was important was the world that awaited them. The boy looked so small.

"Put that on," he told him, nodding to the lifejacket.

As David watched, the boy stretched his thin arms through the holes, fingers trembling as he tried to insert the plastic clips. His eyes drifted once towards David's face, then darted away as if scorched. He looked back to shore, then down at his feet. His body seemed to shudder slightly, as if from the effort of keeping every limb absolutely still.

"What's your name?" David asked.

"Sean," he replied after a moment.

"Do you know who I am?"

Sean said nothing.

"I won't hurt you," said David. "I'm your father."

Sean glanced at him, his eyes, for just a moment, surprised; but then his face seemed to close up again and he quickly looked back to his feet. He seemed about to say something, then changed his mind.

"Your mother probably never told you, but it's true," David said gently.

David scanned the bay. He was lucky. It was dotted with white sails and motor cruisers, making the most of a Sunday afternoon. The glare on the water became more intense with every minute, and he was glad; it made it all the more difficult to spot and identify other boats in its fiery haze. He was less happy about the fuel gauge. The needle trembled around the one-third mark. He didn't know the size of the tank, the power of the engine, but he hoped it would be enough.

He'd committed the map to memory, and he figured he could find his way to Blaine by boat. He was halfway to the southern base of the big island almost directly across the bay. He'd swing around the west side, putting it between himself and the mainland, and then cut northeast, up and back through the San Juans. Third of a tank should be enough. There were so many islands here, so many boats, and how long would it take the local police to mobilize? He could be in Blaine in a couple of hours. He and his son. Surely his small body would fit in the crawlspace Drent had prepared. He hardly took up any room at all ...

For a moment his thoughts sailed, untethered, and he saw a place for the both of them, in some remote northern wilderness, a place they would carve out of the forest, and he could school his son in the true faith, and there they could live unmolested. The boy would be reluctant at first, but he would be patient and firm, and in time the boy would understand.

"Who was that man on the dock?" he asked, wondering if he was indeed the boy's stepfather.

"Mr. Barnes. We rent from him."

David nodded, pleased. Just the landlord, no attachment to Rachel at all.

"You're not my dad," Sean said in a small, fractured voice. "Mom showed me pictures. He's dead."

A twitch of anger surprised him. Rachel, inventing a new past for the boy, lying to him. Denying him.

"Look at me and you'll see we look the same," he told the boy, but Sean didn't turn. He was crying. David placed his hand on the back of his head, felt the heat of his hair in the sun. But the boy's neck went rigid under his touch, and David reluctantly drew away.

"Where we going?" Sean choked out through his tears.

"I'm not going to hurt you," David said again, but his promise, and the boy's sorrow, threw a dark scrim across his thoughts. Only a third of a tank of fuel. What if he missed Blaine? What made him think he'd recognize it from the water? And the boy might be difficult. He might struggle.

He'd had his plan. Shoot Sean, and escape. But he'd abandoned it, he'd sinned, and he knew everything was up for grabs now. He'd sinned, and things would get harder. That was what happened.

He could still do it. Idle the engine, shoot, and topple him into the water afterwards. But he looked at the boy's small head, imagined the fair hair lifting from his forehead as he sank through the water and was quickly enveloped in darkness—and a quick contraction of horror seized at David's insides.

They were nearing the steep southern base of the island, an impressive, unbroken forest of conifers running down to a rocky beachline, where the trees draped themselves over the rocks.

"Look, an eagle," David said suddenly, pointing.

He'd been unable to contain his delight, but he was also glad of the chance to distract the boy. Sean lifted his eyes to the bird's silhouette and said nothing. Maybe it was commonplace to him, living out here. David watched the bird wheel, and for just a moment, wished he could project some part of himself onto its winged body and get lifted away somewhere, anywhere. How easy it would be.

He thought of Gail's paintings. He'd sneered at them, her abstracted angels, the sheer sentimentality of it. In his own portrait he'd almost seemed to have wings cresting his shoulders, or maybe it was just the aura of light she'd put around him. But now, he felt an unabashed yearning.

The bird disappeared against the dark summit of the mountain, and the engine gave a sudden cough, ran clear, then sputtered again. He checked the fuel. The needle still pointed to a third—in fact it was in exactly the same position as before. Sharply he tapped the glass and in dull horror watched as the needle gave a jolt and leaned way back, grazing empty.

"Where do I get gas?" he snapped, before he could check his panic. But Sean just shook his head. It was the landlord's boat, after all. Why would he know anything about it?

David looked around, wondering if he could hail a passing boat for a tow, or better yet some gasoline. He doubted the boy would say anything, but his face radiated fear, there was nothing he could do to conceal it, and anyone taking a good look at him might see he'd wet his pants.

The light danced diamonds on the water and he felt his concentration splinter. Just an hour ago, his plan had been mapped out in his mind, clear as a quicksilver highway to the horizon. Now it was fractured. He'd left the narrow path, the righteous path. His mistake, his pride, his vanity. Oh, God, forgive me for what I've done and what I may have to do.

At least he'd almost made it around the southern curve of the island, away from binoculars, or observers from the mainland. He studied the looming profile of the coast. It seemed totally uninhabited.

"Are there people on this island?"

Sean nodded.

Water washed against high rocks, but here and there David picked out small pockets with a shallow curve of pebbly beach, shrouded by trees. He aimed the boat and hoped he had enough fuel to make it. If he could, he would get some gas from someone, siphon it from a boat at night, and then continue on. If necessary he could take someone hostage and get them to take him and Sean off the island to Blaine.

The boat lurched across the waves, engine hacking.

"What's this island called?" he asked the boy.

"Cordova," he said.

* * *

He'd lost him.

By the time Kevin pulled away from the dock in the Walshes' seventeen-foot Vanguard, David's boat had evaporated in the band of searing light to the west. Through the binoculars, the last hazy image he had was of David heading for the southern coast of Cordova. From there he could swing south, maybe make Port Townsend, and certainly Whidbey Island. If David pulled around the far side of Cordova, his options were wide open. He could try to cross the Strait of Juan de Fuca and head for Vancouver Island, or else come around to the northeast and through the San Juans. With even a third of a tank of fuel he could be anywhere within two thousand square miles in just an hour. And there were so many islands, so many bays and inlets ...

"Can you take the wheel?" he asked Laura.

"Sure."

"Just keep us pointed at the southeast point of Cordova."

He stepped back and lifted the binoculars to his face. With the magnification he needed, the image jounced and veered with the Vanguard's humping. Shit. There were boats out there, plenty of them, and that was about all he could make out.

Before he'd pulled away from the dock, he'd called Garrity at the field office and told him everything. He had no doubt Garrity would mobilize every agency he could muster. County police, state troopers, and most important the Coast Guard. But they had only a handful of ships at their disposal, and the potential area of search was huge, and getting bigger by the minute.

In frustration he lowered the binoculars. If only he'd taken Deirdre and Sean out of there right away, not stood gabbing idiotically on the front lawn. His fault. If only he hadn't faltered for even a split second when he'd had the shot, just bitten back his horror at the idea of killing David. If only he weren't such a *lousy* shot ...

"He'll kill the boy, won't he?" Laura asked, snapping him from his reverie.

"He could've shot him," Kevin replied. "He had plenty of time." It gave him some cause for hope. If David had faltered, if he'd found himself unable to execute his son, then he might falter again, start making mistakes. He couldn't believe this was part of David's plan. Too haphazard, too accidental. The boat as getaway, the third of a tank. Still, the boy made everything worse: he was a hostage, and he'd make it a hell of a lot harder to take David down.

They were nearing the southeastern point of Cordova, and again he tried to scan the shoreline to the north, and then down south to open water. Which way?

He made his decision: he'd take the boat around the south shore of Cordova, then swing up north along its western side. Port Townsend was too far; when David realized how low he was on fuel, he'd want to hug the island's shore.

He handed Laura the binoculars and took the wheel again. "See if you can spot them. Keep it close to the island."

She quickly perched on the back of her seat, one leg out and braced against the dash, and squeezed the eyepieces tight against her face, arms taut. At the dock when she'd seen the boat veering away from them, she'd tried to take a mental snapshot of its profile in the water. That was gone now, and all she had was a vague sense of its size, and the fact that it had a red stripe along its hull.

So many boats out today. She tried to disqualify them all as quickly as possible. Pulling a water-skier. Three people in that one. Too big. *Please let me find them.* Deirdre's face was seared into her memory; she'd felt the grief and panic radiating from her like heat. Laura had to get her son back. It was just like Rick, just like Rick, she was some harbinger of disaster, leading David to his prey ...

If it hadn't been for the flash of sunlight off the chrome trim, she would have missed it. Nestled in a cove, half-hidden by drooping foliage, was a small motorboat. No one seemed to be on board.

"Wait, wait!" she said, "back there!"

"Where?"

Impulsively she handed Kevin the binoculars and took hold of the wheel, throttling back and turning the boat in a wide arc. She remembered enough about motorboats from her childhood vacations in New England.

She pointed to the shoreline. "See it? Is that it?"

"Jesus, I think it is. I can't make out the number ... but I'm pretty sure. Stop for a second."

She throttled way back, pointing the boat into the swells. Kevin pulled out his cellular and dialed.

"Shit." He dialed again, held the phone to his ear.

"What?"

"No goddamn dial tone. Must be in a dead spot, maybe the mountain." He jerked his head up at the high bluffs back from the island's shore.

"Must've run out of gas," said Laura, "just ditched it there. Will he go for fuel?"

"He's got a walk ahead of him."

Kevin knew this island, knew that this shore led right up to Mount Morrisey. It was all parkland, just a few dirt roads. Maybe since his time there'd been a lot of development, but he guessed an hour's walk minimum before David stumbled across someplace he could get fuel.

"I've got to call this in," he said. "We need to get to a real phone."

"Does anyone live around this part?"

"Up the west coast. Take us about twenty minutes maybe. But ..." He hesitated. "I don't want to leave the boat. In case he gets back before us." Unlikely, he knew, but he had David landlocked now, and he couldn't risk letting him slip away.

"I want that boat," he muttered.

If he could disable it, or tow it out from shore, David's escape route would be well and truly severed. He let his eyes move up the densely forested slope: a sniper's dream. But it wouldn't make sense for David to hunker down there, on the off chance that someone might find his boat and come in close. His first priority would be fuel, or stealing another boat, and getting the hell off the island.

"You want to take the boat?" Laura asked. "You mean, go ashore and bring it out?"

"I think so." He didn't like the idea of going in close, but there was no other way. Sure, he could try to shoot the engine to pieces, but to get close enough even to attempt a decent shot, he'd be within range of David's rifle. Anyway, from a rocking boat, at a small target tucked into the foliage, it would probably be impossible—especially for a pathetic shot like himself.

"Take it in, okay?" he said to her, moving off to the side.

As she brought them in towards the shore, he watched through the binoculars. Impossible to be sure there was no one on board. Could David and the boy be lying flat? Or maybe just the boy's lifeless body ... He stood up on the seat for a better angle and was relieved to see nothing but bare deck. The boat was clear.

"A little closer," he said, looking over the side until he could see the bottom, stones wavering. "That's good. You stay down, all right? Nice and low."

Crouching against the dash, Laura said, "You sure about this?"

"Yeah."

Eyes still sweeping the trees, he stripped off his jacket, pulled off his shoes and socks. He took the gun from its holster and placed it on the deck beside Laura.

"I don't know how to use that," she said.

"If it gets wet, it's not much good to anyone."

Carefully he vaulted over the boat's side. Right up to his armpits, sucking back air as the cold seized his legs and torso like a vise. His toes touched the slick rock and he bounced clumsily towards the shore.

A trap? Keep moving, keep moving. He swam, head up, eyes stabbing up into the trees, searching for movement, the flash of an optical sight catching the sunlight. He hit the shallows, and came lurching and stumbling towards the small motorboat, streaming water. It was definitely the right boat. David had the sense to tilt up the motor. A taut painter was tied to a low branch. It took him a while to unknot it. He walked the boat out into the deeper water and half pushed, half swam it out.

"Laura."

It drifted back lazily towards their motorboat, and she caught the bow before it nudged. Kevin heaved himself back in, shivering himself warm. Laura had already cleated the smaller boat's painter to their stern.

"Thanks," he said, and put the boat in gear and pulled gratefully away from the shore. "Now let's find someplace with a phone."

* * *

The slope up from the water was steep, and David had to scramble through the almost impenetrable weave of undergrowth, stooped for balance, clawing at branches, while clumsily herding the boy ahead of him. He'd broken the rifle down and stuffed it into his knapsack, and in his left hand he gripped the red plastic canister from the boat. Mosquitoes droned around his head.

All he had to do was get gas. Who would deny him? A father and son out for an afternoon on the water, and he'd been foolish enough to forget the fuel tank, and here they were, stranded. If anyone got suspicious, he could assemble his rifle in twenty seconds.

He headed for a spot where the tangle of the woods seemed thinnest, hoping to break out onto a road or path or campsite before long.

"I thought about you every day," he said to the boy. "Your mother took you away before you were born but I thought about you. I wanted to come see you, get to know you. I'm sorry it's taken so long."

Maybe if he could get the boy to talk, he'd lose some of his fear of him.

"Where we going?"

"To get some gas."

"After that?"

"Does your mother ever read the Bible to you?"

334

"I don't know."

David watched the back of his head as he struggled up the rise, through the whippy branches, and felt a rush of love. He wanted to take his hand, help him along.

"Are you all right? Do you need a rest?"

"I'm okay." He wouldn't turn to look at him. "You'll take me home, right?"

"If you want," he lied. An urge to talk, to tell his son of his plans for him, swelled within him. But he knew it was only likely to horrify the boy, the idea of being separated from his mother. He needed time to adjust, to accept his father. If only he could get him to understand that he wanted the best for him, what was right.

The hollow caught his foot and he fell hard, landing on top of the canister, its spout catching him in the breastbone and punching all the air out of him. Gasping on the ground, he saw Sean turn, look, and then start running.

It took him several seconds to lurch to his feet.

"Sean!"

The boy was fast, propeled by fear and adrenaline, and he had the advantage of being small, dodging more easily through the lush under-growth, skipping over the roots and tangled detritus of the forest. David lurched after him, branches spearing him in the side, in the face. In the distance, the boy's yellow T-shirt flashed through the trees.

"Sean, slow down! You're going to get lost!"

For a moment, the paternal tone seemed to confuse the boy, and David saw him falter, turn round to look. But then he was off again, and then—he was gone. David charged ahead in panic. The ground was starting to level off, and roll, and who knew when they would finally come out at a campground, a road, a town.

He knew now that the boy would never love him, never come to know him. It was fantasy to think otherwise. He'd been poisoned by the world, by his mother. This is what all earthly lust and pride came to. He'd lied to himself and said no to God, and he'd put everything at risk, all he'd worked for over the years.

He ran harder, but the knapsack and the canister were slowing him down, and the boy was running on unencumbered, putting more distance between them. David saw the pieces of his rifle in his knap-sack, put them together in his mind's eye in a split second. No, there was no time, he'd never catch the boy. Catch him first, before he makes it out from the trees, before he reaches a campsite or a house.

Then: do what he should have done back at the house.

* * *

After ten minutes, Laura saw a narrow bay cut into the shoreline, with a single rickety cottage perched over the steep slope. At the base of a precipitous path down to the water was a slip with a small motorboat. Kevin swung alongside and tied up, and together they started up the path.

Halfway to the top, Laura heard raucous marching band music wafting down on the wind, getting louder by the second; by the time they reached the door it sounded like the Oktoberfest parade. As they skirted along the side of the cottage, looking for the door, she realized that more than just music was emanating from the cottage's open windows: she flinched as she caught a pungent whiff of the most diabolical fish smell she'd ever encountered. She saw now that some of the windowpanes were steamed up, with little wisps floating out and up into the open air. They rounded the corner, and parked out in front of the cottage was a VW Bug. A narrow dirt track curved up through the woods.

The screen door was ajar, and Kevin knocked hard on the doorframe. "Hello?"

He waited only a few seconds before walking in. Laura followed. It was an appalling place, raw floorboards all but invisible under fishing gear and tackle, piles of yellowing newspaper, cardboard boxes overflowing with tin cans and plastic containers, and all manner of junk. It looked like a scrapyard. After the sunlight, it seemed particularly dismal. Inside the smell was almost unbearable; she doubted it could be any more intense were she actually *inside* a fish. She held a hand cupped over her nose.

"Hello!" Kevin shouted.

They walked straight back, past a couple of rooms, similarly cluttered. At the end of the hallway, to the right, was the kitchen, more of a narrow galley. There didn't seem to be a refrigerator, but there was a disproportionately large gas stove, with flames raging under four huge, steaming soup pots. Tending to them was a tall man with a head of white hair and a long, briny beard that extended down to his sternum.

He was wearing only a pair of olive drab army surplus shorts, cinched around his emaciated hips by a cloth belt. The thin arms and legs were all bony protuberances and razor-wire tendons and ligaments; his feet for some reason reminded her of nothing quite so much as dinosaur feet, all hamstring and joint.

He jolted when he caught sight of them and reached up and turned down the volume on his portable radio, set on a shelf among various tins and bottles of spices.

"Didn't hear you come in," he said, without sounding the slightest bit annoyed. His head wobbled slightly from side to side, some kind of tremor, Laura supposed. Looking at his face she saw that he probably wasn't past his mid-fifties, but all that white hair made him look much older. Out of politeness, she'd removed her hand from her nose, and she was trying to breathe only through her mouth to avoid smelling whatever was in those pots.

Kevin showed him his badge. "There's a fugitive on the island, David Haines."

The man showed no sign of recognizing the name.

"He's got a boy hostage and he abandoned his boat on the south shore about half an hour ago. He'll be looking for gas, or another boat. Do you have a phone?"

The man pointed. Laura saw, mounted to the wall by the sink, an old black rotary phone. She couldn't remember the last time she'd seen one.

"You might want to think of heading into town for the time being," he told the man as he dialed. To Laura he said, "I've got to call the field office, then the local police. They're going to need to set up a cordon and start warning people who live nearby. Lee, it's Kevin ..."

The man just stared at Kevin in amazement as he talked into the phone, as though he'd never seen anyone use such a device in quite that fashion before. The smell was starting to make Laura feel ill. She smiled at the man and started backing out of the kitchen; she needed air. She made her way to the door and stuck her nose out, inhaling greedily.

The boy came out of the woods so quickly, so quietly, that for a split second, Laura thought he was some kind of woodland animal, a faun motionless by the roadside, taking a timid glimpse at the world of man. She half expected him to turn and bound back into the trees.

Sean.

Rooted in place, fifty yards up the dirt path, just before it curved out of sight into the trees, he stared down at the house. It was as if, after making it this far, he was suddenly transfixed by the sight of sanctuary. Why didn't he run? Didn't he see her? Maybe he did, and the sight of a grown-up was enough in his mind to make him feel safe. Or else he was simply in a state of stupefied exhaustion.

She stepped out the door, lifted her hand, waved in a high arc, beckoning.

"Sean!"

Still not moving. The boy needed help. And obeying a primal instinct she started running towards him up the dirt path, her eyes darting into the trees, wondering where Haines was. At first Sean just stared at her, almost in alarm, and then, when she was less than ten feet from him, he suddenly broke into a run, and flung himself against her. Laura closed her arms around him, holding him tight. He was trembling.

"You were at our house," he rasped, as if to reassure himself.

"Yeah. Where is he, the man?"

"He fell, and I ran. Back in the woods. He was chasing me."

"Let's get inside, Sean, right now."

She turned and with a start realized how far she'd run to meet him. The house seemed impossibly far, shrouded by trees. A horrible premonition electrified her, a sense they'd never make it back, and at that moment, David Haines stepped out from the woods, halfway down the path, blocking their return.

He was panting, already unslinging his knapsack from his shoulder, unzipping, and extracting pieces of metal. Snapping them into place with frightening speed.

"Kevin!" she screamed, and then again, "Kevin!" his name raw against her throat. In Haines's hands, it was as if the gun was assembling itself. Grabbing Sean's wrist, she ran, pulling him off the path and into the woods. She had no idea if Kevin had heard her inside the house, on the phone, those pots boiling furiously, the *Biergarten* music, goddamnit.

Through the trees, not knowing where she was going, branches whipping at her face, her sandals skidding on buckled roots and stones, tangles of dead bush and twigs tearing at her bare ankles like barbed wire. Impossible to even see the ground sometimes it was so overgrown with enormous ferns and low-lying shrubs. Over her pulse's roar, she thought she heard a gunshot. Sean slipped his damp hand from her grip and pulled ahead of her, as if he knew where he was going. She risked a glance over her shoulder and couldn't see Haines, but she wished the trees were thicker here.

After a few minutes, her chest and throat burned, and she put her hand on Sean's shoulder to slow him down. "Wait, wait," she whispered, and she crouched low behind a huge trunk, panting, listening. She knew she couldn't just keep running headlong forever. She needed to find a road, a house, somewhere safe. Where was safe when a man had a rifle? She needed a plan, and right now it was all she could do to gag back the acidic wash in her throat and catch her breath.

She heard a distant crackling, a rustle of leaves, then nothing. Cheek pressed against the bark, she edged one eye around the tree trunk. He was standing so still, her eyes almost passed over him, there in the distance, the rifle held with both hands diagonally across his body. Like a hunter, listening.

Move or stay, move or stay? Maybe he'd walk right past if they were quiet enough. She looked at Sean, and he looked right at her, a gaze so penetrating, so expectant, she almost couldn't bear it. *You'll take care of me*, the eyes said. Christ, when had she been able to take care of anyone? He was twisting his hands together, less frightened when he was running. She was worried he would make a sound, whimper, give them away. Where was Kevin, why wasn't he coming?

Move.

She couldn't stand it any longer. The impulse to get away was undeniable; she had to get farther away from Haines. She put a finger to her lips and gestured Sean to go forward. Crouched over, she followed, steering him with her hand, trying to keep the big tree between them and Haines.

Impossible to walk quietly. Every time she took a step it seemed something crackled or rustled, or maybe it just sounded monstrously loud to her own ears. Could he see them? Was he lining them up in his crosshairs even now? She turned, scanned the trees, saw nothing. She hoped to God they were far enough away now. Taking Sean's hand again, she broke into a run.

Up ahead the trees thinned, and there was a sudden metallic flash of light through them. A car. A road. She ran faster still, bursting out from the woods, leaping the ditch, running to the edge of the two-lane asphalt road. The car she'd seen had already disappeared out of sight. She crossed the road with Sean, dipped into the trees on the other side, and kept moving; she wanted some cover as they watched the road and waited for another car.

They walked for several minutes. Then, with almost no warning, a hatchback was flashing through the trees.

"Stay here," she told Sean. The car was already fifty feet down the road when she reached the asphalt; she shouted, running into the middle of the road and waving her arms. At first she thought it wouldn't stop, but then, with huge relief, she saw the brake lights flare and the car crunch over onto the gravel shoulder.

"Sean, c'mon!" she called. She hurried to meet the boy, scooping him up into her arms, barely feeling his weight as she ran for the hatchback.

"What's wrong?" said the driver, a young man, stepping out. "Is he hurt?"

She was choking for air. "There's a man. With a gun. Chasing us." She sucked more air into her lungs. "Get back in! Just drive us out of here!"

He was looking at something past her, down the road. She knew what she'd see, even before she turned. Haines was stepping out onto the road, rifle leveled.

"Shit," breathed the man.

Laura threw open the back door and heaved Sean inside on top of the camping gear strewn across the seats. She squeezed in beside him as the driver slung himself behind the wheel. A young woman was in the passenger seat, face stricken.

"Keep down," Laura cried, pressing Sean down behind the front seat. The driver turned the key, hit the gas, and the car lurched and stalled.

"Shit!"

"You're in third!" Laura shouted at him, seeing the gearshift. He slammed the stick up into first, started again, and this time the car lunged forward with a roar. The driver rammed the car into second, picking up speed now. *Thank you, thank you, thank you—*

Laura heard the crack of the rifle, and the driver's companion shrieked. Third gear, and a second crack sounded, and suddenly the car pulled hard to the right.

"I think he hit my tire!" the man said, braking and turning the wheel wildly to the left as the car went into a skid. Laura grabbed hold of Sean as the car left the road, spun on the gravel, and tipped over into the ditch.

The doors on the right were blocked. Laura kicked open the opposite door and struggled out, holding it with one arm so it wouldn't swing back on top of her.

"Sean!" She reached back and pulled him out.

They were all out on the grass now. She turned and saw Haines sprinting towards them.

"Just run!" Laura said.

Back into the woods, and she was aware of the driver and his companion running alongside them for a while, but then suddenly they peeled off, maybe thinking they were safer on their own, away from the gunman's quarry.

Sean was beginning to flag, and so was she. A cramp sent a jittery spiderweb of pain through her left side. Suddenly through the trees she saw a dirt drive, flanked by tall trees, and almost ran straight into a low fence, three parallel strands of barbed wire marking off a property line. She lifted Sean into her arms and hopped over, running closer to the drive. There, at the end, was a big farmhouse; behind, a barn and all sorts of other buildings bathed in the red light of the coming dusk.

"Okay, Sean, we're gonna be okay now."

With Sean straddling her hips, she ran for the big farmhouse. They could call the police, maybe they had guns there, maybe they had a big truck or van they could all drive off in—and run over Haines while they were at it.

It wasn't until she was almost at the generous veranda that she realized the screen door slouched on broken hinges, the central pane of the front bay window was smashed, everywhere the paint was peeling and, oh my God, it was like some movie ghost town. To her left, all the fields were overgrown with high grass: why hadn't she noticed *that* sooner? Not a vehicle in sight, a car, truck, a goddamn tractor. No signs of life at all. She vaulted up the steps, threw open the screen, and hammered on the front door, then gave up and peered in the smashed bay window: the room was dark and emptied of all its furniture.

"Hello!" she called into the empty room, and her voice rang dully through the house. Glancing back down the long dirt drive, into the trees, across the wild fields, she saw no sign of Haines. She looked down at Sean, who was watching her worriedly.

She faltered. Head on into the woods some more, now that the light was failing, or get inside? Maybe it was a pathetic notion of a safe haven, the house, *inside*, that made her want to stay. She could run some more, but not for long, and if she had to carry Sean ... They needed to rest.

With a fractured piece of wood from the porch railing, she quickly knocked away the jagged remnants of the windowpane.

"Okay, Sean, let's get inside."

She lifted him up and through, and then squeezed herself in after him. She had no idea if she was making the right choice.

CHAPTER TWENTY-FOUR

He dropped the phone the moment he heard Laura shout his name, and he was at the front door just in time to see her and the boy rushing off the dirt drive into the woods. David was already turning to him, the rifle to his cheek. Kevin jerked back inside the house, heard the gun's clap, and saw the mesh of the screen door pucker as the bullet went through and took an oblique strip out of the wall.

"Stay back!" he shouted to the man in the kitchen.

He moved over to a small window and peered out. David was running up the path, disappearing into the trees after Laura and Sean. Shit. Fingers tightened around the Glock, he burst out the screen door and into the trees on the opposite side of the drive, deep enough for some cover, watching for Haines across the way. Would he take time to lie in wait for him? Risk letting Laura and the boy get away? He'd want the boy, but why hadn't he killed him yet? God knows he'd had plenty of time.

Kevin paused for a moment, listening, hearing nothing. He grimaced, sucked in air, and charged out into the open, across the drive and into the trees on the other side, welding himself to a broad trunk. He forced his eyes to make a slow, careful sweep, deep into the woods.

In the distance, David disappeared over a rise. Kevin ran. But by the time he'd got there, and carefully cleared the top of the slope, he couldn't see David anywhere. His impulse was to keep running, but he knew it was probably futile. He could run around for days in here and not find them, keep missing them by a hundred yards, circling endlessly.

He forced his mind back to his days here on the island. This part he'd known well, and he tried to conjure up an aerial view, superimposing roads. Laura would know that there must be a main road somewhere; she'd head for that—if David didn't force her away from it, if she wasn't too terrified to think. She'd head for a road and try to flag someone down.

He turned and ran back the way he'd come, and within five minutes he'd reached a two-lane road. Laura would turn to the north; she'd seen the mountainous south shore from the water, she knew it was pretty much uninhabited. She'd head north.

The two gunshots, within seconds of one another, seemed to reach him from all directions at once in the still air. Eyes closed, he strained to trace the last remnants of sound, and then ran.

By the time he was halfway round the slow bend to the north, he could see the hatchback tipped over into the ditch. *Please, God, no.* Laura and the boy must have been inside. He ran towards it on the far side of the road, screened by trees. Alongside the car now, panting, he couldn't see anyone inside, but the angle was bad, and he was still too far away. If they were dead, they'd be slumped out of sight down on the ditch side of the car. He crossed the road, eyes never straying from the trees.

When he saw inside, he grunted with relief: no bodies, not even any blood that he could see. The rear right tire was blown down to the rims. They must have got out in time; Haines wouldn't have bothered taking them hostage. He would have shot them and left them inside the car. So where did they all go?

He looked down the deserted road, looking for mailboxes, driveways notched into the shoulder—any place where Laura might have reasonably fled. With a jolt he realized that he knew this stretch of road. But he almost never came this far south when he used to drive it: he would have turned off before this point, down the long drive to the farm. Yes, it wasn't far, just about half a mile to the north. He broke into a jog.

The gate was just as he remembered it, and the trees flanking the long drive. The "For Sale" sign must have been there for a while, too, judging from the height the grass had reached around the posts. If she was heading north, Laura would have seen this place, and wouldn't she have turned down the drive in the hopes of finding refuge somewhere? If she'd left the road, traveled through the woods, she wouldn't even have seen the sign. If she was alive, moving northwards, she'd almost certainly have come here.

He turned down the drive.

Twenty years later, he was coming back.

*   *   *

On the main floor, she moved through the big gloomy rooms, splintered floorboards creaking horribly. Sean held on tight. She kept trying the light switches, hoping that a bulb would flare, hoping she could have light blazing from every window so that Haines would think the house was inhabited. If he came this way, she wanted this place lit up like Times Square. Maybe if he didn't come too close, he wouldn't notice the signs of dereliction. Another switch, nothing. Electricity must have been cut, probably for years. But by the time night fell, he'd see how unnaturally dark the place was. The sun was already hovering above the high treeline to the west. She didn't want to be alone here in the dark.

The house was huge. She forced herself to take stock. Three doors on the main floor, front, back, and side, all of them still locked with deadbolts. What use was that when the front window was smashed open? At least it meant there was only one way Haines could get in. Unless he blasted a door open with his rifle, or smashed another window ...

Two staircases, the main one opposite the front door, and a small servants' staircase leading up to the second floor from the kitchen. Good, that was good. There was a third floor, but she wasn't going up there. Even if there was an attic she and Sean could get into, there was no way she was cutting herself off.

She faltered for a moment. Was it crazy to stay here? They could still go out the back, back into the woods, and try to find another hiding place. But the thought of being out there in the utter darkness filled her with dread. She couldn't do it. Her hand was on Sean's shoulder, the bony ridge and summit of his clavicle under his T-shirt. She knelt down before him.

"You're a good runner," she said. "You're doing great. I think we've lost him."

She wondered if he believed her, if he knew this was just a grown-up lie to jolly him along. It made her feel better to say it anyway. "There's an FBI agent looking for us, and the police, too."

"Yeah?"

"Yep. They'll be all over the place in a few minutes, and then we can get you home to your mom."

"Yeah," he said vaguely.

345

She had no idea what was going on in his head, how he could possibly process all that had happened to him in the last few hours.

"Let's go upstairs," she said.

Every step up was like hitting notes on an arthritic accordion. On the landing she paused. A skinnier set of stairs continued up to the third floor. Down the long hallway, with rooms off it on both sides, she could see the back staircase that led to the kitchen. Good. Their escape route. Quickly she went down it into the big kitchen. Only a few feet to the back door. She pulled back the bolt, opened it, closed and locked it again. She didn't want any last-minute surprises. Then she went back upstairs, leaving the stairwell door just slightly ajar.

In the dying light, she made a tour of the rooms, looking out each window with a mounting sense of childhood nightmare. Soon it would be dark, maybe totally dark. The front bedroom gave a straight-on view of the dirt drive and the deserted farmyard, the overgrown fields. From the sides and back she saw sagging outbuildings and more woods bordering the property. She supposed she could keep making a circuit past the windows all night, and hope there was enough moon to see by. Hoped that she'd get some advance warning if anyone approached. She made sure all the windows were open, too, so she could hear. The birds were finishing their dusk chorus now, and after that, she knew how quiet it would get.

A weapon. She didn't even have her can of pepper spray. It was in her purse back in the car. Nagging at the fringes of her mind was the thought that she should be hatching some ingenious plan, digging a spiked pit beneath the front window, rigging something to drop on Haines's head when he came through. She wondered if she could try to wrestle the gun away from him—movie thinking, dream thinking. She'd be too terrified.

"Do you need some sleep?" she asked Sean.

He shook his head fervently. "I'll stay with you."

Together they did sentry duty. With every circuit, Laura realized how increasingly pointless it was. It was too dark to see any distance now; and she was beginning to realize how dark it would soon be inside the house, too.

They were making their way back to the front room when she heard footsteps outside. Involuntarily, her hand tightened around Sean's, her breath caught in her throat. She felt her whole body weaken down through her torso, down through her legs, and fought an almost uncontrollable urge to empty her bladder. Her toes tingled. She went back to the window, looked. Nothing. Silently, Sean hurrying after her, she tried the next room. The footsteps had stopped. Impossible to tell where they'd come from; he must be close, so close maybe she wouldn't even be able to see him against the sides of the house.

She heard the back door rattle. Sean whimpered. Footsteps around to the side. Another doorknob turning, shaking. She drew Sean against her, knowing that soon he would probably start to cry.

She had no idea how long she waited in the silence, imagining Haines ghoulishly slipping in through the window without a noise, his feet not even touching the creaking floors, skimming over the stairs as he swept, wraithlike, up towards them.

Footsteps again. And this time she placed them instantly.

He was coming up the steps of the veranda.

* * *

There was enough of a moon that Kevin could make out the farm-house at the end of the drive, and behind it the high roofline of the barn, and one of the chicken coops that they'd long ago converted into a bunkhouse for the men. It was drafty as hell, and he remembered how cold he'd been the winter he'd spent here, the damp from the sea bottled in his bones.

Seeing it all, dark and derelict, he almost faltered. During his time here he'd come back at night plenty of times, but then the windows had always been lit up; the sight had never failed to fill him with joy, a homecoming, people waiting for him. Was this, then, the sign he'd been waiting for, to be brought back here, summoned, no less, to see this? The decay of the place where he thought he'd found God?

Screened by the trees to the right of the drive, he moved swiftly towards the house, feeling himself drawn as if by the gravitational force of a black hole, the tight focus of his mind unraveling.

You fuckers, if it weren't for you, I might've been here still.

He'd never left; they'd left him. Broken-legged, broken-hearted, they'd forsaken him, and he'd spent the rest of his life trying to crush them, all of them. That was the truth. Out of envy, malice, and vengeance, trying to strip them of the faith they'd denied him.

Palm slick with sweat, he loosened his fingers on the grip of his

Glock, clenched them again. If she'd seen the driveway, she would have come down, he still believed that. But would she have holed up in the house? Or one of the outbuildings? He scanned the windows of the big house, rectangles of greater darkness against the sky. And David, what would he do?

You could've gone back, nothing stopping you.

But it was him, it wasn't them. It was him. After his leg had healed, after he'd been talked down by the psychologist, after a few weeks of good sleep and good food, he didn't have it in him anymore. And whose fault was that? Was he supposed to feel guilty and penitent that he couldn't believe? If there was a God, why hadn't he been given the capacity to believe?

But you had it, once.

That was all bullshit, all group hysteria and sleep deprivation and craving for belonging. It was blindness, there was nothing rational about it.

So what? What's it matter how you have it, only that you have it.

You know better.

It all defies belief, it's all unscientific, so what's it matter how crazy it is? As long as it's there.

Bullshit. The faith to kill? Your own brother, your own son? No, you can't just shut your mind off like that. That's not what you want, that kind of faith.

Behind the window on the second floor, he thought he saw a smudge of movement. Blinking he looked again, and saw nothing. Look into blackness and everything starts moving on you; everything's up for grabs. He pushed himself deeper into the trees, in case it was David, waiting with his rifle.

But if it was anyone at all, it wasn't David.

Kevin saw him come round from the side of the farmhouse, walking purposefully towards the veranda. Footsteps on gravel.

Kevin judged the distance, knew it was too great for him to take a shot, and ran, willing his footfalls to be silent in the grass. Closer, closer. David was stepping up on the veranda, pulling at the door. Almost in range, Kevin burst from the cover of the trees across the yard. Now looking into the bay window, David heard him running and whirled.

Kevin lifted the Glock high, felt its kick as he took the shot, then twice more. Awkwardly, David threw himself at the bay window. No sound of breaking glass, but Kevin heard the thud as he landed inside. Shit, he had no idea whether he'd hit him. He cleared away from the window, running to one side of the house.

From above, he heard a boy's keening cry, obviously muffled, but in the silence of the night, it carried across the entire farmyard.

Laura and Sean were inside with David.

*   *   *

She held Sean against her, trying to muffle his cries against her blouse, but he was too far gone. The sound of the gunshots had blasted away the last of his control. It was all she could to choke back her own cry of horror. What the hell was David doing? Firing into the room first to make sure no one was there in wait? She'd heard the thud as he'd landed, then a quick, efficient, scrambling sound, and then, worst of all, a horrible sentient silence. He knew they were here.

Sean had stopped crying, but he was panting, and to Laura it sounded too loud.

They were in the hallway, poised halfway between the main staircase and the kitchen stairs. One hand grasped Sean's. From below, a floorboard creaked—or was it one of the stairs? Oh, Jesus, how was she supposed to tell?

Then, from outside, she heard the sound of Kevin's voice.

*   *   *

"David! There's police and state troopers on the way. They're going to flush you out of there, David, and they're not going to be careful, I can promise you that. Now you throw out your gun, throw it out over the veranda where I can see it, and we can end this right now."

Pressed tight against the wall, he could feel the words flowing out of him like some desperate mantra, even as he knew how futile they were. What did David have to lose? Still, he wanted to make noise, to distract David, to give Laura and Sean a chance to get out of the house before he found them.

"David, you come out right now. You remember my promise. I'll do my best to make sure you never have to give your blood. I'll testify at any hearing in your defense, I swear to God."

Get out, Laura, get out!

He tried to remember the layout of the farmhouse. Doors ... one around back, definitely, maybe even one at the side, too. And upstairs? Two staircases, he absolutely remembered that.

Carefully he started down the side towards the back.

He'd never left properly, never of his own free will.

This time he would.

*   *   *

His left shoulder felt as if it had been kicked by a steel-toed boot, and the core of swelling numbness where the bullet hit was now starting to send out swift tendrils of pain, down his left arm to his fingertips, across the top of his chest. He could still move his arm, and that's what was important.

He'd heard the boy's cry from upstairs, and knew he wouldn't have much time. Outside, Kevin Sheldrake was ranting like a prophet in the wilderness.

At least he'd be able to make amends, finish his work. As quietly as he could, he moved into the hallway to the bottom of the staircase, floorboards creaking underfoot, and waited. No sound came from above. Arm afire with pain, he knew he had to act quickly. He forced himself to walk down towards the back of the house, taking note of the side door, the kitchen, the rear door ... and one other. At first, he thought it was just a door to a pantry, but it had been left slightly ajar and through the gap he could see the outline of a first step. Maid's staircase, wasn't that what they were called? Slowly he walked back to the front of the house. He silently pulled back the bolt on the front door, counted to twenty. He would take the boy, the doctor, and Sheldrake.

He vaulted onto the second step of the staircase and hammered his feet on it as though he were running up the entire flight. Then he swiveled, and ran out the front door to the outside.

*   *   *

Laura tripped halfway down the kitchen stairs, yanking Sean off the steps as she fell, landing hard on her shoulder. She lurched up, dragging Sean along with her into the kitchen. Jesus, it was almost pitch black. She slammed her hand at the door, found the deadbolt, and had to let go of Sean for just a second to grapple with the doorknob. Open. A spill of moonlight from outside. She grabbed for Sean again, caught him by the shoulder, kicked the screen door wide, and shoved him out.

Down the three crooked wooden steps and they were on the grass.

"Come with me!"

It was Kevin running to meet them from the corner.

"He's coming!" Laura wheezed.

"This way."

They were racing along the back of the house, and as they cleared the corner, David Haines was not twenty feet in front of them, rifle nestled in his arms.

It seemed simultaneous, the crack of the gun and Kevin snapping over backwards as if smacked by some invisible paw. She saw the singed fabric in the center of his chest, and then the quick seep of blood. By his twitching fingers, his gun glinted darkly on the grass, inches from her foot. She fell to her knees and snatched it up, aiming at Haines.

In the moonlight, he stood before her, face sallow and greasy, not even looking at her as his hands opened the breech and fingers extracted the spent shell and, just as quickly, made to slip in a new one.

"Don't," she barked, throat clenched. He looked at her now and saw the gun aimed at him.

She was aware of Kevin beside her, bleeding to death, maybe already dead, but she could do nothing for him now, nothing. Behind her, Sean stood paralyzed.

She'd never fired a gun before, Haines must know that, must know by the way she was shaking, her arms straight out like a TV cop, one hand grasping her wrist for support. Her eyes were fixed on Haines's hands, the shell she knew he had in his fingers, just inches away, one swift motion away, from the breech of his rifle.

"You drop that," she said, "that bullet, drop it!"

He stared at her balefully, doing nothing. She adjusted her grip on the gun. Was there a safety thing on this? Would Kevin have it on or off? She didn't have time now to examine all the ridges and protuberances. How hard would she have to squeeze the trigger? How many bullets were left inside? She could see now that Haines was wounded, a dark stain around his left shoulder.

"Put it down, or I'll shoot you!"

"You can't," he said. "You might kill me, and then you'd lose all your precious blood."

351

Shoot, she told herself, *just shoot now*. But she couldn't. Aim for the leg and she might miss altogether. Hit his femoral artery and he might bleed to death. Aim higher and she might perforate a major organ, slice an artery, and he would surely die before they could get him to a hospital.

She saw his eyes stray to Sean for a moment, and was surprised to see something approaching pain in his face. Then he turned back to her, spread his arms invitingly.

"Go ahead," he said. "Shoot."

"Put down your gun!"

Instead, he turned his back on her and started walking slowly away.

"Stop!" she shouted.

One step, two steps, three, and she couldn't see his hands now, maybe putting the shell into the rifle, ready to whirl and shoot her, and with every step getting farther and farther away so she was bound to miss.

"Stop, goddamnit!" she shouted again, following after him.

She didn't know how many times she fired, four or five, low across his buttocks, but the impact pitched him forward onto his face. She stood watching from a distance, shaking so badly through the shoulders that she lowered her gun. She hadn't wanted to shoot, but she'd had to, no way was she letting him walk away from her into the woods, where he could just reload and shoot them from a distance.

"Haines?"

It was hard to tell how badly hurt he was, but she wasn't going any closer. He might simply be waiting for her to get near, just faking, ready to grab her. She wanted him unconscious first; then she could take the rifle away, at least.

Where was it? She thought she could see part of the butt sticking out past his stomach. He was lying on top of it, one arm splayed out to his right, the other still tucked under him to the left.

"Can you hear me?"

No answer. Gun aimed at him again, she moved in a wide arc to try to see his face. His eyes were closed.

Shit. She needed to get back to Kevin right away, see if she could treat him. But what if Haines was just faking? What if he could drag himself away, what if he could still walk, or at least sit up and pick up that rifle and shoot her in the back?

She wanted to scream. She wanted to kick his body.

Walking backwards she returned to Kevin and Sean, without taking her eyes off Haines. She knelt down.

"I need you to help me keep an eye on him," she told Sean, nodding at Haines. "You watch him, make sure he's staying still."

"He's making funny noises," said Sean, looking fearfully at Kevin.

"Yeah, I hear it."

Unconscious, Kevin was taking small, rattling breaths, and his pulse was racing and incredibly weak. There was surprisingly little blood around the entry hole in his chest, but its location made her shudder, despairing. In all likelihood it had severed the aorta, and passed right through the chambers of his heart. But why so little blood? She snaked her hand beneath his back and found an exit wound, and she expected to encounter a huge mass of clotting blood in the grass and dirt, but her fingers came away remarkably clean.

"Kevin," she said, with a surge of hope.

She didn't know much about gunshot wounds, but she'd heard her share of stories. Bullets were unpredictable things. One of her colleagues had seen a young girl who'd died after being shot in the hand with a low-caliber handgun. Upon impact the bullet had bizarrely changed course, with enough energy to veer up her radial artery straight back to the heart. And then there were the stories of someone shot point-blank, center of the chest, and walking away.

Kevin wasn't walking anywhere. But he might be lucky: it looked as though the bullet had passed through cleanly, without causing any catastrophic damage. But when she ripped his shirt open down the middle she saw instantly that his chest was hyperinflated on the left side, and the veins of his neck were horribly distended. Hand spread flat against the wall of his chest, she tapped the end of her third finger, and with dread, heard the kind of hollow report you get when you rap an empty milk carton. Dear God, even the skin of his neck and chest were starting to crackle like parchment under her touch, inflating from the buildup of air seeping into the tissue.

It was an acute tension pneumothorax, and right away she knew that Haines's bullet must have punctured his left lung, and it had collapsed, imploded by the pressure building between the lung wall and chest cavity. Surviving on one lung wasn't the problem, but the intense inner pressure could easily stop his blood from returning to the heart. That would kill him without question, and soon.

She could scarcely hear Kevin's breathing anymore. Her only hope was stabilizing the pressure on either side of the lung, fast, and for that she'd need to make an incision right through the chest wall.

"Do you have a jackknife?" she asked Sean. He shook his head, eyes wide.

Shit. What else could she use? A pen. Hurriedly she patted Kevin's jacket and felt his pen, buried inside the breast pocket. She snatched it out. Good, a cheap one in a transparent plastic shell, with a blue-pegged bottom. It was a fine point, but she still wondered if it was sharp enough. She knew she didn't have much time.

* * *

He kept his eyes shut.

The slightest movement, even the inhalation of his breath, sent pain through his body. His legs burned with cold. He took his breath in quick, shallow sucks, holding on tight, afraid that he might whirl apart if he relaxed his muscles.

He'd failed. God had released him from prison, given him a chance to finish his work, to make amends for his earthly pride in the child, and he'd failed.

You knew this was coming.

The moment he'd let the crosshairs drift off the boy's chest, he'd known he couldn't do it. And that everything he did from that point on would be worthless and in vain. What did he have now? Nothing. *We come into the world with nothing, we leave it with nothing. Ashes to ashes, dust to dust*—he'd taken such comfort from those verses, the notion that he would finally shed his earthly body, leave it behind to feed worms, while his soul vaulted up to heaven; it was a promise of final arrival.

But. He wanted.

He wanted release from the pain that had capsized his body, he wanted a blanket for his legs, that song he'd heard on the radio. He wanted to touch Rachel's shoulders again, he wanted to touch the back of his son's head again, feel the feverish warmth of his hair.

He could not walk. His lower half felt numb and shattered. But the gun was still beneath him, its barrel hard against his ribs, the scope digging into his sternum. In his left hand, the shell.

One last thing.

With a jerk he dragged his hand beneath his body and with his fingers felt the familiar outlines of the breech. He moaned to cover up the sound of the shell sliding in, the bolt closing. Where was she? He couldn't see her to the side. Was she still behind him, the gun leveled at him? If he tried to sit up and turn, would he have enough time?

He wouldn't let her take his blood, he could do that at least. The boy might have it, he acknowledged that, but it was out of his hands now. *Take this cup from me, Lord.* It would be up to Him now. But he could take care of the other. He would finish this part properly.

He felt the end of the barrel nudging the soft flesh on the underside of his jaw, and he smiled. He pushed his face flat into the gravel, in line with the gun barrel, and poised his finger around the trigger.

Verily I say unto you, today will you sit with me in paradise.

* * *

Laura jumped at the muffled shot. She stood, saw Haines's body twitching, and ran towards him. His shattered jaw and face spilled black blood onto the gravel, the dry earth sucking it back hungrily. She stared in mute horror. No ... all that blood, leaving his body, dying.

Stop it.

Do something to save him.

He must have hoped to blast his brains out, but his shot had misfired, and he'd ripped apart his mandibular artery. With pressure, she might be able to stop him bleeding to death, but she'd have to stay at his side the whole time until help came ...

Kevin.

If she didn't make that incision, stabilize the pressure inside and outside his chest, he'd die soon.

She couldn't treat them both.

She stared at the blood pumping doggedly from Haines's face. In despair she thought of all her medical gear locked in the trunk of the car on the mainland. There was nothing here she could store Haines's blood in. She needed her test tubes, the heparin, and the EDTA inside, which kept the blood from clotting uselessly. No, if she wanted Haines's blood, she needed to keep him alive.

Kevin would die.

But if she could save Haines, with his blood she might save countless lives ... Sandra's life.

355

Don't make me do this. Please don't make me decide. What about the boy? The boy might have the same blood.

You can't know that. Haines might be the only one, ever.

Might be.

She turned away from Haines, wrenching her gaze from the blood still flowing into the dust, and hurried back to Kevin. His breathing wasn't even audible anymore. The pen might not work, it might not even be sharp enough to cut through the tissue and muscle around the chest wall—and the nib would block the air flow, and how the hell was she supposed to pull it out backwards?

"Stay with him, Sean, talk to him, please, I'll be right back."

"Where you going?" he asked worriedly.

"Inside to get something. I'll be right back."

She went through the kitchen door into the pitch-black house, slapping at the walls for doors, flinging them open, hoping for a closet. She finally found one in the front hall. She flailed into it, touched the cool metal rail, and whisked her hand from end to end, hoping for a coat hanger. *Please, please.* Nothing, not a single goddamn one. Who the hell took those shitty metal coat hangers with them when they moved? Swearing, she knelt down and scrabbled around on the floor of the closet, hands mired in years of dust and God knows what else and—

A single coat hanger, all bent out of shape, but it didn't matter. She careened back through the house, out the kitchen door, and knelt down beside Kevin, her thighs shaking under her, hands trembling.

Get a grip. Should've taken the speed. Then I'd be up for this.

You don't need the speed.

We'll see about that.

She uncurled the hook of the coat hanger, felt its sharp point. Jesus, it was probably rusty; she wished she had something to sterilize it with. No matches, no booze, nothing, and she didn't have time. It was straightened out now. With her fingernails she dug out the blue peg from the bottom of the pen, then clawed out the nib and skinny shaft of ink. She slid the straightened length of coat hanger through the hollow shell. Good, it protruded slightly from the tip. She experimented with her grip, slipping her hand around the inside of the hanger, her palm flush against its coiled neck, her fingers closed around the pen shell. Good enough.

"Sean, come over here, sweetheart. Can you hold onto him tight, just hold him tight around his shoulders, and try to keep him still for me, all right?"

She picked a spot three inches beneath Kevin's right armpit and plunged the coat hanger and pen between his ribs, shoving hard, harder, through the muscle.

Got it.

There was an explosive blast of air through the pen shell as the pressure stabilized on either side of the lung. Holding tight to the shell with one hand, she pulled out the coat hanger. The plastic shell seemed to be holding up. She tapped Kevin's chest, checked his pulse, listened to his breathing, and hoped it would be enough until help came.

Then, hunched over his unconscious body, she sobbed.

* * *

Wow, look at that, look how bright they are.

Kevin couldn't remember the last time he'd seen the stars like this, so many of them, and so bright they seemed to draw you right up into them so you couldn't even remember the ground anymore. Was he still *on* the ground? Hard to tell. There was someone nearby, the woman, Laura, and a boy he didn't know, and he felt a tremendous rush of love for them both, but ... the stars really were something up there.

Distantly, he was aware that he should be looking for something else. *Come on, game's over now, show yourself.* Expecting the stars to coalesce into a face maybe, or to hear a voice. Stars, stars, nothing but the stars so far. *Where are you? Don't you think I've waited long enough? Come on. Don't you think I've earned a peek after all that's happened to me?*

What happened?

For the first time, he felt a vertiginous lurch of panic, wished he could slow down his rapid ascent, because he truly was rising now. It had all happened so suddenly, and he wanted to remember things.

Hold on, just give me a second here ... not frightened really, but if I can have just a little time. Just a little more time to gather my thoughts ...

CHAPTER TWENTY-FIVE

Shadows moved about through dense fog.

He remembered stars, a giddy sense of weightlessness and expectation, and then a heavy shroud of pain that sank him back to the ground, back inside his airless body. He remembered a voice, and it was her voice, close to his ear, saying things he couldn't understand but which reassured him immensely. Then a long smear of time, dipping in and out of sleep, and a sense of panic as Laura's voice was usurped by many. Swirling light, shouts, his body being moved, and a godawful roar, the Four Horsemen of the Apocalypse traded up to Harleys.

Now the shadows were slowly resolving themselves into featureless human silhouettes. He assumed he was dreaming. Annoyingly, someone was saying a name, over and over again, and eventually he realized it was his. Looking up hopefully, he tried to focus through the fog. Laura?

"You need to wake up now, Mr. Sheldrake," a strange woman was telling him. "You've just come out of surgery." She seemed to be talking very quickly, and he was having trouble following what she was saying.

A gunshot wound to the chest, perforated lung. Infection from the wound, intravenous antibiotics. Lucky to be alive. All this rattled out from her mouth as she took his blood pressure, checked monitors, hooked sacs of fluids on a stand beside him.

"Laura Donaldson," he said, wincing at the deep sweep of pain through his tightly bandaged chest. "Sean Mason."

She seemed to understand what he was asking. "We haven't admitted anyone by those names," she said. "I'm sorry, but that's all I know."

* * *

When he next woke, Seth Michener and Hugh Carter were standing at the foot of his bed. He was less surprised by their sudden appearance than by the huge bouquet of pink and yellow tulips Mitch clutched in his hand. It was the most incongruous sight Kevin could have imagined.

"Mitch, I'm touched," he managed to rasp.

"There's never enough vases," he said with a frown. "I'm just gonna see if there's something back at the nurse's station." He put the flowers down on Kevin's tray and disappeared.

It was Hugh who filled him in, told him about how Laura had shot David, and how he'd finished himself off. How Laura had performed emergency surgery on him before the Medevac flew him over to Seattle. She was fine, and so was the boy. Back with his mother in a hotel.

"It's a miracle it turned out this way," Hugh said. "You did good work, Kevin. Great work."

"Where is she?"

"Donaldson? I saw her outside. I told her we needed to debrief you first."

Hugh didn't have much more to say, but he said it as many times as possible, padding it out with a few "I haven't been right since the Floods," and finishing off with a resounding "At the end of the day ..." Mitch returned with a pink plastic vase that was too short, and busied himself trying to arrange the flowers and prop the vase somewhere so they wouldn't tip over. He didn't say much; Kevin was amazed he'd put in an appearance at all.

"We'll let you get some rest," Hugh said. "Should I tell Donaldson to come back later?"

"No. She can come in."

He couldn't remember the last time he'd been so glad to see someone. She was wearing a fresh set of clothes; she was smiling; and she looked tired and utterly desirable. She had luggage with her, and she set it down inside the doorway. As she came round the side of the bed and sat down, he was suddenly self-conscious. He felt vile, and he most probably looked vile, or significantly unappetizing at the very least. But he wanted her close; he hoped he'd be able to smell her perfume.

"You're the talk of the hospital," Laura told him. "I've heard the word miracle about a dozen times. Even I'm tempted to use it."

He chuckled hoarsely. It hurt to speak, even softly. "Miracle you were there, from what I hear."

"You're saying this doesn't qualify as a sign?" She said it humorously, but he saw there was a genuine, and respectful, curiosity in her eyes.

A sign. His own personal sign, what he'd been craving for years. But wasn't there something arrogant and self-congratulatory about it in the end? *Hey, look what I got. Check this out, bullets go right through me, and for my next act, walking on water.* He was grateful, no doubt about it, for whatever combination of events, earthly or supernatural, had guided the bullet through his chest, clear of arteries and the chambers of his heart. He tried to imagine it, this cauterized corridor in the center of his body, and through the painkillers, thought he could feel the ache of his muscle and tissue healing around it. A miracle? By Laura's scientific standards he'd have to get shot point-blank a hundred times and survive each time to prove it. He wanted to laugh at himself. *You'll never be satisfied; you'll never know.*

"I think I was hoping to see God," he said. "But He was a no-show. Even if He wasn't, I'd have told myself it was just a hallucination. I'm through with signs."

He was smiling, but serious. It seemed a shirking of responsibility anyway, expecting someone else to do all the work for you. Maybe he'd never make the leap, but he knew he'd always care about it, grapple with it, curse it, and that might be as much faith as he was ever going to have.

"Thank you," he said, "for what you did."

"Well, I'm just sorry about the conditions."

"I heard something about a rusty coat hanger."

She winced apologetically. "You're still grateful though, right?"

"Extremely. You did all the work. I just got shot."

"I didn't want to shoot him."

He nodded. "You did the right thing. He would've killed you. And Sean."

He saw her eyes become distant, and look away, remembering something unpleasant.

"Outside the farmhouse," she said, "when you were calling out to Haines, saying if he gave himself up, you'd try to make sure he'd never have to give blood: you meant that, didn't you."

He nodded. "But I never expected you to share that opinion."

Laura doubted she'd ever be able to understand it, but then again, she doubted she'd ever be able to fathom Sandra's decision to carry on with her so-called therapy. She didn't like it, but in the end, she'd have to live with it, even if she couldn't accept it.

"He bled to death?" Kevin asked her.

"Yes."

"You didn't get any of his blood, then."

"No."

She was hardly going to tell him about the choice she'd made—it could only come out like some self-promoting aria of compassion and self-sacrifice, when, really, she felt what she'd done, in some ways, was the exact opposite. She'd done the selfish thing, she figured, saving one life when many might have been saved. Might, might, might—she'd bent her whole life to this conjecture. Instead, she'd saved just one man, a man she was *attracted to* into the bargain. She could easily believe she'd even done it out of cowardice, because saving Kevin was something she *could* do, whereas the other choice presented a tortuous road of work, like a mirror's view of infinity. If she'd been acting rationally she would have tried to save Haines, let Kevin's heart stop. The choice she'd made might have been the wrong one, but she didn't regret it.

"I'm sorry," Kevin said, and she could tell he meant it. "There's still the boy."

She smiled tiredly. "Yeah. If Deirdre ever lets me near him again."

"If we hadn't been there, she would've lost him. She'll be in touch with you. If not, I'll help you get a message to her."

"Thanks. I'm going to Tijuana first," she said. If the boy's blood was positive, it would be positive when she got back. It could wait. But not Sandra. She'd put her sister off long enough. "There's a flight to San Diego in a couple hours I'm going to try for."

"That's good." Kevin nodded, feeling a strange pang of abandonment. He looked at her luggage by the door. He didn't want her to go, and now he was suddenly awkward in their silence. Was this the end? She'd saved his life and, like any good doctor, had come to see her patient for a final follow-up visit. He saw her look towards the door as if distracted by something, and he wondered if she was impatient to leave, restless as ever. The moment of her departure loomed, and he dreaded it. He didn't want to lose everything again, not like last time, the close of the Haines case creating a kind of vacuum that would suck away his entire life. There, beside his bed, she was so beautiful he could barely look at her.

But what had he expected? All they'd ever really had in common was David Haines, and that hardly seemed an auspicious premise for a relationship. Maybe the sense of intimacy between them was just illusory, an invention of his own hopeful mind, or a kind of chemical byproduct of their common purpose. And now that their official business together was over, it had diffused like vapor.

"Well, congratulations," she said with a note of finality, and inwardly he winced. "You'll probably get a few more books written about you. Make sure you get a promotion this time." She forced a laugh. "Next time I visit, I want you to have your own office."

"When'll that be?" he asked. "Your next visit."

His heart was beating hard in his bruised chest, each pulse like an unpleasant memory of even greater pain. She must have heard the blunt urgency in his voice, because he saw her polite smile falter. She frowned, and he let his eyes drop away, knowing he'd only succeeded in embarrassing both of them now.

"As soon as you like," she said, with a melting sense of relief. He wanted to see her again.

When they'd flown him out in the helicopter, she'd insisted on accompanying him. He'd been doing badly, conscious for only brief moments before sinking down again, his body beginning to shudder with fever—probably from the rusty coat hanger she'd had to use. But she'd felt a happiness she thought must be hallucinatory, a kind of post-traumatic mania. In Seattle, she'd briefed the surgeon as they were prepping Kevin, wishing more than anything that she could perform the operation herself.

But just now, as the awkward silence had stretched on, she'd felt a despairing paralysis. She'd deluded herself. Two people with less in common she couldn't imagine. His interest in her had been strictly professional, even exploitive. He'd needed her to get to Deirdre and her son. The only moment that had given her any hope was when he'd touched her, so unexpectedly, in the hotel room during that panic attack. The sensation was still imprinted on her flesh, and she'd summoned it up many times, the fingers cool on her skin, the exact path his palm took across her neck.

Impulsively, she leaned forward and touched Kevin in the same place, watching his eyes. They said yes. Before the tyrannical machinery of her mind could kick in, make her falter, she bent her mouth to his. His lips felt chapped and he tasted tired, but it aroused a delicious heat through her body.

"That beats the hell out of Demerol," Kevin said when she pulled back.

She smiled. "They'll probably let you out in a few days. I'll call as soon as I get to Tijuana. Check up on you."

"Good."

"You're going to be fine."

"You are too."

She kissed him once more, and they said their goodbyes.

Walking down the hospital corridor, she felt a powerful urge to go back to him, talk more, but she also wanted to be alone with her happiness, this moment of pure potential. She would go to Tijuana to be with Sandra, and then return to Seattle to see if she could take Sean Mason's blood. And no matter what she ended up bringing back to Chicago with her, she knew she would keep working.

Outside the hospital, she hailed a cab to the airport.

"Great day for flying," the driver said as he pulled away from the curb.

Absently Laura tilted her head to look up through the window, and smiled, feeling as if she'd caught a glimpse of a favorable future in the translucent sky.

"Yeah," she said, "you're right."

Acknowledgements

For their willingness to share their expertise, and endure my many questions, I would like to thank Dr. Andrew Moore, Dr. Lloyd Oppel, Assistant Crown Attorney, Arun Maini, Jake MacDonald, and Special Agent Ross Rice at the Chicago field office of the Federal Bureau of Investigation. I am also indebted to the friends who read and commented on early drafts of this book: Danielle Bochove, Chris Torbay, Carol Toller, Elke Maini, and Cristina Campbell. Richard Shepherd helped me shape the idea from its very beginning, and Al Zuckerman spent two patient years generously tutoring me as I turned it into a novel. Thank you also to my editor Iris Tupholme, who trusted me enough to take the book on while it was still very much in progress. Finally, my greatest debt of thanks is to my wife, Philippa Sheppard, who listened tirelessly to my rantings, read countless drafts of the story, and made brilliant suggestions throughout.